PRAISE FOR
THE SEAN McPHERSON SERIES:

PRAISE FOR *INIQUITY*
BOOK FOUR

"Never less than heart-pounding, Buchanan knows how to keep the pages turning."
— **ONLINE BOOKCLUB**

"A first-rate storyteller who creates believable characters as familiar as your neighbors."
— **MIDWEST BOOK REVIEW**

"It's one of those rare, stay-up-all-night-reading novels. Loved it!"
— **J.A. WRIGHT**, author of *How to Grow an Addict* and *Eat and Get Gas*

"A perfect continuation to a riveting series!"
— **LINDA ULLESEIT**, author of *The River Remembers*

PRAISE FOR *IMPERVIOUS*
BOOK THREE

"A propulsive plot with engaging characters . . . "
— **KIRKUS REVIEWS**

"Don't miss this engaging story filled with an intricate plot, realistic characters, and mesmerizing suspense!"
— **DEBBIE HERBERT**, *USA Today* bestselling author

"Readers beware—the immediacy of the violent act just as Mick and Emma's wedding ends is jolting—but signals the dangers ahead. The contrast of the cozy writer's retreat with it's mouth-watering meals to comfort all who abide there with the reality of a revenge plot against Mick and others yet to be thwarted kept me glued to the book. Now that the characters are as familiar as family to me, the stakes are high; can't wait to see what's in the next book!"
—MAREN COOPER, author of *Finding Grace*

"Buchanan is an up-and-coming star of crime/thriller series. And book three is the best yet. As I read the ongoing adventures of Sean McPherson and his family, friends, and foes, I think to myself this really would be excellent for a television series. Wouldn't be surprised if it's not on Netflix's radar!"
—SHERRY BRISCOE, author of *The Man in Number 7*

"Buchanan has a fresh, very different and fast-paced style. And somehow makes a chef's meal integral to the thrilling suspense. I go from salivating to shocked, chapter by chapter."
—CHRISTINE DESMET, novelist and screenwriter

"Another winner from Laurie Buchanan. The focus of this story is less on the guest authors who are staying at Pines & Quill than it was in the first two books. It's more on the bad guys working for Gambino, including current police officers who are doing his bidding and trying to permanently silence Mick, Emma, and anyone else who gets in Gambino's way. Buchanan uses lush prose to describe the setting, the food, and the relationships. She takes us deep into the thoughts of all the major characters by frequently switching POVs. Consequently, you know who the bad guys are and what they are trying to do, but you're still riveted to the plot and committed to discovering what happens because Buchanan keeps you turning pages until the end."
—CHRIS NORBURY, author of the Matt Lanier mystery-thriller series

"At Pines & Quill, the deadliest writers retreat in the Northwest, Buchanan delivers one knockout punch after another, leaving the reader reeling."

— SHEILA LOWE, author of the Beyond the Veil paranormal suspense series

"*Impervious* is my favorite of the three-book series so far. I love the combination of a type of 'cozy' mystery with the incredible writer's retreat — Pines & Quill; the romance between different couples, all who live individually with some damage, physical or emotional; and the goofy large and lovable dog. But that's the background to not-cozy murders and evil underpinnings that threaten the safety of the characters, and the sanctity of love and living. Death enters, and it's not pretty. Readers are glued to each page that offers suspense interwoven with cozy; page-turning action; and thrills and chills and of course, lots of 'hooks.' I'm hooked on Buchanan's Sean McPherson novels!"

— PAMELA WIGHT, author of *The Right Wrong Man*

"*Impervious* delivers. From the first tragic explosion during a wedding to the last flying bullets in the woods, I was riveted to book three in the Sean McPherson series. Hitchcockian suspense and tension reign in this page turner. I found myself worrying about 'the good guys' throughout the story, given the author's ability to create likable, strong, yet vulnerable characters. The successful overlay of terror and joy jerked me around to provide a heart-pounding, satisfying read."

— SHERRILL JOSEPH, author of The Botanic Hill Detectives Mysteries

"Definitely the high-octane offering of the Sean McPherson series! Readers will hold their breath until the last page, hoping that the hero makes it. For fans of suspense and action, this is the perfect tale!"

— IND'TALE MAGAZINE

PRAISE FOR *ICONOCLAST*
BOOK TWO

"An involving thriller with compelling characters. This propulsive novel ably expands Buchanan's entertaining series, which is built primarily on engaging characterization."
—*KIRKUS REVIEWS*

"Buchanan shows a sure hand as an action writer. . . . A smooth, ultra-professional read."
—*BOOKLIST*

"An absolute page-turner . . . Not the one to be missed. With its atmospheric setting, page-turning suspense, and luminous insights into trauma, resilience, recovery, and friendship, this thriller will hook readers and keep them hooked."
—*THE PRAIRIES BOOK REVIEW*

"I devoured every page of *Iconoclast*, turning the pages viciously because I couldn't wait to find out what would happen next."
—*ONLINE BOOK CLUB*

"Another deftly crafted and riveting crime novel by Laurie Buchanan, *Iconoclast* is a compulsive page turner of a read from beginning to end."
—*MIDWEST BOOK REVIEW*

"Buchanan has knocked it out of the park with this one. The descriptions pull the reader right into the middle of the action. Plan to stay up late!"
—*InD'TALE MAGAZINE*

PRAISE FOR *INDELIBLE*
BOOK ONE

"Buchanan's narrative is well-paced, flying right along. . . . the author has delivered an exciting beginning to an intriguing series."
—*KIRKUS REVIEWS*

"The author of this impressive novel has poured elements from radically different genres into the blender and set it on high spin . . . The last page promises further surprises in a sequel, which Buchanan better deliver soon."
—*BOOKLIST*

"Hard to put down, this page-turner is worthy of praise!"
—IND'TALE MAGAZINE

ILLUSIONIST

ILLUSIONIST

A SEAN McPHERSON NOVEL

BOOK FIVE

LAURIE BUCHANAN

This book is dedicated to authors,
their creative muses, and the craft of writing.

Published by SparkPress, a BookSparks imprint,
A division of SparkPoint Studio, LLC
Phoenix, Arizona, USA, 85007
www.gosparkpress.com

Published 2025
Printed in the United States of America
Print ISBN: 978-1-68463-300-5
E-ISBN: 978-1-68463-301-2
Library of Congress Control Number: 2024924100

Interior design by Tabitha Lahr

PREVIOUS WORKS
BY THE AUTHOR

Indelible: A Sean McPherson Novel, Book 1. An ex-cop haunted by survivor's guilt. A killer who won't let him forget.

Iconoclast: A Sean McPherson Novel, Book 2. A whale-watching cruise goes terribly wrong. Two lovers on deck, one sniper on shore, and no way out.

Impervious: A Sean McPherson Novel, Book 3. The bride, the groom, the toast, the explosion . . . What should be a joyous occasion turns lethal.

Iniquity: A Sean McPherson Novel, Book 4. When a human trafficking ring kidnaps PI Sean McPherson's pregnant wife, McPherson learns the lines he'll cross. Because a person who has it all has *everything* to lose.

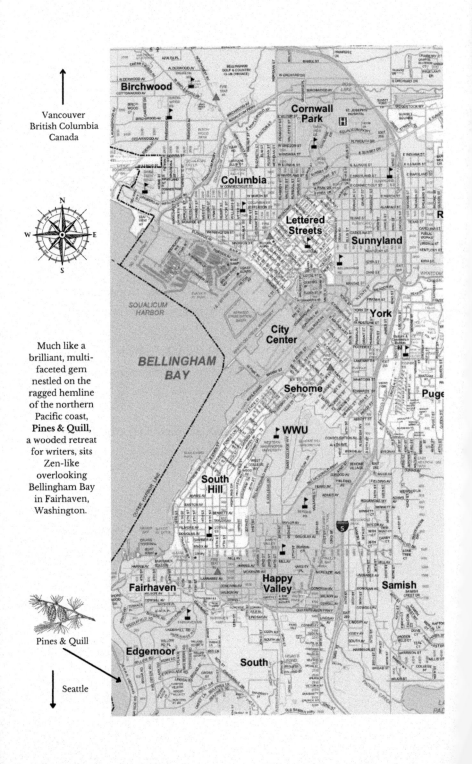

Vancouver
British Columbia
Canada

Much like a
brilliant, multi-
faceted gem
nestled on the
ragged hemline
of the northern
Pacific coast,
Pines & Quill,
a wooded retreat
for writers, sits
Zen-like
overlooking
Bellingham Bay
in Fairhaven,
Washington.

Pines & Quill

Seattle

Bluff, Cliffs, &
Bellingham Bay

Dickens Cottage

Bellingham &
Fairhaven Historic District

Garage & Workshop

Austen Cottage

Back View of Main House
& Mudroom Door

Entrance Gate

PINES & QUILL

Niall's Garden

Brontë Cottage

Tai Chi Pavilion
& Event Center

McPherson Cabin

Bellingham Bay
National Park & Reserve

Thoreau Cottage

AUTHOR'S NOTE

While historic Fairhaven Village and Bellingham
are actual locations in Washington State,
I've added fictitious touches to further the story.

*"The greater the illusion
the more captivating it becomes.
But . . . it's still an illusion."*
—DAN O'CONNOR

PROLOGUE

*"Being a writer all boils down to this: It's you, in
a chair, staring at a page. And you're either going
to stay in that chair until words are written, or
you're going to give up and walk away."*
—ALESSANDRA TORRE

The sunshine on the lake's surface glistens just like the
tears that had pooled in the eyes of Gambino's most
recent conquest before he extinguished her life. *My favorite
part is when I see the realization that it's not a sex game dawn
on their faces.*

He's aware of the statistics: women subjected to non-fatal
strangulation are eight times more likely to be murdered. He
scoffs at the idea. *If they're with me, it's one hundred percent
guaranteed.*

Georgio "The Bull" Gambino is a man who thrives on
research, precision, and covering his tracks. He knows many
women of his most recent victim's generation—those ages

forty and under—have grown accustomed to the idea that plain, vanilla sex is for prudes. Women have been trained to believe it's empowering to ask a man to choke them. Some women's magazines even normalize it as "breath play." To suggest there might be anything wrong with this potentially lethal practice is dismissed as kink-shaming.

Gambino glides the tips of his manicured fingers over his white mustache as he stares out the massive plate glass window in his opulent home. It overlooks Lake Whatcom—from the Lumi word for "loud water"—and is the drinking water source for the county's residents.

He picks up his cell phone from the antique table next to his leather wingback chair and initiates a video call.

Carmine, his right-hand man, comes into view.

"Are you in position?"

"Yes."

"Show me."

Carmine reverses the camera on his cell phone, then scans the student-filled room from his seat in the upper left quadrant of a university lecture hall. Unlike a traditional classroom that accommodates between one and fifty pupils, the enormous room's pitched floor and tiered seating allow for a capacity in the hundreds. After zooming in on a single student to Gambino's satisfaction, the men consider the difference in their time zones and synchronize their watches.

"Make the call on time, Carmine. Not a moment sooner or later." Gambino disconnects and returns his gaze out the window.

Not nearly as massive as his high-rise in Seattle, this well-hidden luxury residence is nestled in the woods. He bought it through a shell corporation a few years back when he realized Bellingham Bay is part of a much larger waterway system, thus ideal for his purposes—trafficking guns, drugs, and humans. Optimal for rapid movement and concealment, Bellingham

Bay is a bay of the Salish Sea—the encompassing term for the near-shore Pacific Ocean, Strait of Georgia, Johnstone Strait in Canada, Strait of Juan de Fuca, and Puget Sound.

My hate for Sean McPherson is no longer just about the missing $10 million of heroin I had stolen from the SFPD lockup. That's a pittance. Because of him, a half dozen of my foot soldiers are dead, and he rescued twelve women I'd contracted to sell, making me look foolish.

He bristles at the embarrassment he felt when facing a kingpin in the Russian mafia to tell him their deal was off. They were on one of his container ships in the Bering Strait. He'd had to make it up to him, which included everything on the bill of lading. *It cost me dearly, and McPherson's going to pay.*

Gambino picks up his cell phone and makes another call. His heart races with anticipation. When the recipient answers, he says, "If you hang up, I'll kill your child. Do you understand?"

"Is this some kind of sick joke?"

"I assure you this is no joke. When I disconnect, you'll receive a video call from my associate. He's visiting your child's class—Market Power in the New Economy. If you don't do what I say, it will cost the life of the person you love most."

"Who is this? What do you want from me?"

"I'm the person who's going to kill your child if you don't do what I say. In two days, you're heading to Pines & Quill writing retreat. While there, you will frame Sean McPherson for murder."

"Frame someone for murder? What do you mean?"

"No, not just someone. You're going to frame Sean McPherson. You're going to kill one of the other writers in residence. I don't care which one, nor do I care how you do it. You're a crime writer. Figure it out. You arrive at Pines & Quill on October first and leave on the twenty-first. You have three weeks to accomplish the task."

"But—"

"Do *not* interrupt me again. The murder will be real. You're the one who's going to do it. But you'll act as an illusionist, making it *appear* as if Sean McPherson did it— framing him for the death. It's your job to ensure that he has a motive, opportunity, and means. And that there's enough of his DNA at the scene to arrest and convict him. Everyone, especially the police, must believe that he's guilty. If you fail, your child dies."

"Wait! I have money. I can pay you."

"It's not a matter of money. It's a matter of service. You do this service for me, and I'll do you the service of not killing your child." Gambino glances at his watch. "When I hang up, you'll receive a video call proving that my associate is within arm's reach of your child ready to do my bidding."

"But how do I contact you?"

"You don't. And understand this. You're under surveillance, and all of your technology is being monitored. If you so much as even *consider* contacting the police, your child will die."

Gambino disconnects the call and sets the phone down. *With McPherson convicted of murder, it's a trifecta win: he goes to prison, he won't see his child grow up, and it'll destroy the reputation of Pines & Quill.*

Picking up a pair of binoculars, he continues to track a bald eagle he'd been admiring through the massive window while on the phone. Gambino uses the center focus knob to bring clarity to the bird of prey.

The raptor swoops down, catches its mark, then soars skyward.

Gambino's face breaks into a reptilian smile.

CHAPTER 1

*"There is, in fact, only one rule in writing fiction:
Whatever works, works."*
—Tom Robbins

B rent Gooding, a former NASCAR driver, lived through
a paralyzing accident that sent him from the driver's seat
of a race car to a motorized wheelchair. Coming out of the
dreaded "Tunnel Turn" at Pocono, Gooding's car lost a tire,
sending him up the track where he kissed the wall. Several
drivers barely managed to maneuver by him. Then, unfortunately, through the cloud of smoke, another driver hit
Gooding flush on the driver's side door, shredding the vehicle.
Now, from his new set of wheels, Brent writes white-knuckle
thrillers that take place on the racing circuit.

If he could stand, Brent would be five-feet-ten inches
tall. *I'm in good shape.* He runs his hand over the top of his
head. His salt-and-pepper hair is beginning to thin. *Even with*

my constraints, I work out every day with everything I can. So, I'm especially looking forward to the tai chi sessions I read about on the Pines & Quill website.

He moves his wheelchair into the bathroom to finish packing his Dopp kit. The accident left him the use of his natural right hand and arm, but his left hand and arm are "bionic." And though Brent has no feeling from the waist down, his back is usually in excruciating pain. Hence, his prescription medications: Prozac for depression and Tramadol, an opioid for the pain. In his thoughts, he hears his doctor say, "They are *never* to be ingested simultaneously because the combination can be lethal."

An ideal way to kill someone.

Brent moves his wheelchair back and forth between his closet, chest of drawers, and the open suitcase on the bed. *I can't believe my publisher changed the release date of my next book*—Checkered Flag. *Even with three weeks of protected time for writing at Pines & Quill, I don't see how I can hit the new target.*

Ellen, his wife, steps into the room. "Need any help?"

"I've got it, thanks. I'll be ready to leave when we agreed. I'm supposed to be at the Daytona Beach International Airport two hours before my flight takes off. And even though I'm pre-checked with TSA, there's always a hassle with my wheelchair."

"Okay then," Ellen says. "You've got plenty of time. I'm going to make a quick trip to the grocery store. With Bradley back at home, we're suffering from 'Old Mother Hubbard Syndrome'—the cupboards are bare. He's eaten everything that's not nailed down."

Brent watches his wife retreat. *After twenty years of employing Ellen, her company decided to "right-size"—their term for cutting staff to the bone—and, in doing so, let go dozens of longtime employees, including her, because they had the largest paychecks.*

That, along with all of the other pressures, financial and otherwise, is more likely what'll kill me rather than the permanent aftereffects of my wreck.

While packing, Brent refers to an article on his laptop screen advising him of the seasonal temperatures in Fairhaven, Washington, where he'll be a writer in residence at Pines & Quill from October first through the twenty-first. "Snow isn't unheard of in Bellingham, but it's also not the norm. Just south of the Canadian border, the city is built around Bellingham Bay. The Olympic Mountains to the southwest, and the Cascades to the east offer protection from severe storms. Most months produce more moderate temperatures and less rainfall than Seattle."

Brent checks the weather app. *Right now, it's eighty-three degrees in Daytona Beach and only fifty-nine in Bellingham.* He shivers. *That's a friggin' twenty-four-degree difference!*

Jennifer Pruett finishes packing a small carry-on with autumn-weight clothing. And though she's heading to a three-week writing retreat at Pines & Quill, one of the two husband and wife owners, Libby MacCullough, asked if she'd perform a magic show one evening.

"I'd be happy to," she said.

A resident of Las Vegas, Nevada, Jennifer is the only woman listed among the top seven illusionists: David Copperfield, Penn and Teller, David Blaine, Criss Angel, and David Gatti. *It used to be a man's world, but no longer.*

Jennifer places a stack of business cards in her tote. The fronts are embossed with her favorite quote: "MAGIC IS THE ONLY HONEST PROFESSION. A MAGICIAN PROMISES TO DECEIVE YOU AND HE DOES." —KARL GERMAIN

That Libby used the term "magic"—implying that I'm a "magician"—would have bothered me in the past, but not

anymore. Magicians and illusionists often work in the same profession, but their approaches to the art of deception are quite different. I realize that people outside the industry don't know any better and use the terms interchangeably. So that's not the reason I'm angry and sick to my stomach.

Jennifer rummages through the bathroom medicine cabinet until she finds antacid tablets and pops a few. *What's eating at my gut is that I'm in the middle of a divorce from Steven. The man I've been married to for over twenty-five years—a successful business partner in a lavish hotel on "The Strip" who can't keep his hands off young showgirls.*

She closes the medicine cabinet, leans in, and examines herself in the mirror. *I never thought I'd have to compete against other women for my husband's attention. At five-foot-eight inches tall and one hundred and thirty-five pounds, I'm tall and slender.* She touches one of her high cheekbones. *And with my olive complexion and dark curly hair, Dad always said I was a "Grecian beauty."*

She opens the cabinet and pops two more antacid tablets. *The other thing that's making me sick to my stomach is that Elaine, our only daughter, called from the University of Michigan, Ann Arbor, where she's studying actuarial mathematics, informing me that she's pregnant. And though she only has one more year to go until she gets her degree, she's thinking about dropping out.*

"Who's the father?" Jennifer asked.

"One of my professors," Elaine said.

Another lecher who can't keep his dick in his pants. I'd like to disappear Steven and him!

Jennifer gives herself permission to "let it go," as her therapist suggested, and instead focus on the tasks at hand.

She packs her laptop that contains the manuscript she's working on—*Now You See It.* Her popular mystery novels include magic, illusion, and sleight of hand.

On second thought, she removes it, opens the lid, and clears her search history. *If push comes to shove, this could be incriminating.*

The last bag Jennifer packs contains a scaled-down version of the props she needs to do magic tricks. And though all illusionists are magicians, not all magicians are illusionists.

Magicians perform close-up sleight-of-hand tricks in smaller venues: card, ball, doves, and cup stunts. They tend to perform without an assistant or enormous props.

An illusionist manipulates physical reality to make a person think they see, or don't see, what the illusionist wants. Some of the most popular illusions include barstool levitation, sawing a body in half, and the dove-in-a-cage to a woman-in-a-cage illusion.

Jennifer thinks of David Copperfield. *Damn, he's good! He was awarded for the largest illusion ever staged when he vanished the Statue of Liberty on a CBS television special.*

Like me, illusionists usually work in large venues and often have multiple assistants, a stage crew, lighting, and sound. Both magicians and illusionists use misdirection tactics, making us excellent at hiding things and creating an atmosphere of mystery in front of an audience.

Jennifer picks up a length of silk rope. An audience favorite is where a magician cuts it in half and then restores it. She wraps each end around her fists and pulls it taut several times, testing its strength. Then she remembers what she read on the internet. She unwinds the rope and ties a strangle knot in the center.

There, that ought to do the trick. Jennifer smiles at her play on words as she adds it to her kit.

Adam Richmond tells his wife, Helen, that he wants to leave for George Bush Intercontinental Airport Houston in plenty of time to swing by their latest acquisition—an apartment building with eight units, four up and four down.

"I'll want to make sure that none of our crew is being hassled." *I really want to get my drafting compass; I left it on the blueprints.* Made of metal, it consists of two "legs" connected by an adjustable hinge that allows changing the radius of a circle. One leg has a sharp spike at its end for anchoring; the other holds a drawing tool. *It's perfect for killing someone.*

Adam met Helen decades ago at Rice University in Houston when they got their bachelor of arts degrees in architecture. Since then, there's been a lot of water under that bridge. After graduation, it didn't take long to realize they were miserable working for others in large firms. So that's when they set out on their own and became real estate investors and professional house flippers—buying a property at as low a price as possible, then renovating it to sell or "flip" to a new buyer at a profit.

Adam and Helen aren't the kind of house flippers who cut corners and use minimal effort on a home or building as many do. They're knowledgeable about construction, permits, and quality materials. They understand the local market and ordinances. They've made a lot of contacts in the industry: other real estate agents, attorneys, contractors, building inspectors, and insurance brokers. They take personal pride in creating value and the ability to achieve financial returns.

They hire skilled undocumented migrants and pay them the same wage they pay everyone else. The problem is that "everyone else" doesn't show up. And on the rare occasion when they do, the work isn't skilled.

Adam and Helen haven't found that to be true with illegal immigrants. They learned a long time ago that this population segment is eager to work hard and do a good job. Nor do they play the entitlement card. And though this husband and wife duo end up paying a lot of fines for this practice, it's something they believe in and feel good about it. The part that feels bad is the number of people who'd like to put them out of business for hiring those type of workers. They've dealt with threats of violence, even with arson on one of their properties under construction.

That prompted them to get a License to Carry a Handgun, formerly called concealed handgun license or CHL, in Houston. It requires the completion of a four-hour classroom course. The Texas Safety Academy at Texas Gun Club offers comprehensive CHL training in Houston that satisfies the education requirement and helps people become more proficient with a firearm.

They're teaching their children (Sandi, a high school senior, and Brittany, who's getting her bachelor of arts degree with a major in architecture at Rice University) about doing the best job you can and hiring the best people for the job—those who show up and apply themselves.

His daughters are much more excited about their dad being a crime fiction novelist. His books involve real estate scams, and there's either a murder in a vacant rental or a body found in the structure during renovation. Adam's current work in progress is titled *Good Bones*. That's what he's working on during his writing residency at Pines & Quill.

Adam walks through the gutted apartment complex smiling, nodding, and shaking hands with his crew. He sees his reflection in a window. At six feet and one-hundred-and-eighty pounds, with reddish-brown hair, beard, and mustache, he's been told by his wife, "You look like a giant gnome."

When he reaches the makeshift table of sawhorses and plywood with bricks holding down each corner of his unrolled blueprints, he lets his gaze take in the surroundings.

When no one's looking, Adam slips his drafting compass into his briefcase.

Lucy Fleming and her husband, Rick, co-own Spoke Easy, a high-end road and triathlon bicycle shop in Chicago that caters to professional cyclists. They live in a large apartment over the store; the two are connected by an enclosed stairwell. Lucy smiles. *The best part is that our commute's damn short.*

Although she's a former professional triathlete—swim, cycle, run—and a World Triathlon champion, a five-time Olympian, and a two-time medalist (gold in London, silver in Rio), Lucy is an active Ironman competitor and champion. That's why she's packing her wetsuit and Dahon Speed Pro TT folding bicycle to take along to Pines & Quill. In addition to writing, she plans to train. *New terrain, new pain.*

An Ironman Triathlon consists of a 2.4-mile swim, a 112-mile bicycle ride, and a marathon 26.2-mile run, raced in that order. It's globally considered one of the most grueling one-day sporting events.

Lucy gazes at her reflection in the full-length mirror. She has short, dishwater-blond hair. And at five-feet-eleven inches tall and one hundred and fifty pounds, she's solid muscle.

Her thriller novels take the reader into the secret world of Olympic training, professional coaching, international travel, sponsor funding, antidoping, athlete nutrition, sports medicine—and murder. Her current work in progress is titled, *All That Glitters.*

Lucy flexes the inner tube between her fists, twists it, then pulls it taut. *This ought to do it.* She adds it to her bicycle repair kit.

"Rick!" she calls down the stairs, frustrated. "Where did you put my suitcase?"

"What suitcase?"

Lucy blows out a sigh. "The suitcase for my folding bike. It's not in the closet where I left it."

"Oh, *that* suitcase. Sorry, it's down here in the shop. I showed it to a customer because *you* took the last one, and a customer wanted to test it with their folding bike."

What? Now the missing suitcase is my fault? Way to deflect blame, Rick.

Their sons (Doug, a high school senior, and Greg, who still lives at home while earning his MBA at the University of Chicago) work there part time.

"Hang on, Mom. I'll bring it to you," Greg calls up the stairs as his footsteps pound in the enclosed space.

"Thanks, son," she says as he lays the case on her bed and opens it.

"No problem. I'm starving," Greg says over his shoulder, heading toward the kitchen. "I was coming up to eat anyway."

Lucy's bike can fold down in less than fifteen seconds, and with a little hex-wrench work on the handlebars, it's completely collapsed to thirty-by-fifteen-by-twenty inches in less than a minute. She separates the wheels from the frame, packs the bike inside the Dahon's Airporter mini suitcase, and smiles. *No extra baggage fees.*

After consideration, Lucy reaches back into her bicycle repair kit, removes an inner tube, and imagines herself using it to strangle someone.

CHAPTER 2

"The idea is to write it so that people hear it and it slides through the brain and goes straight to the heart."
—MAYA ANGELOU

Sean "Mick" McPherson drives the Pines & Quill van to Bellingham International Airport. *The last time I went to the airport was to drop off the September writers in residence who barely lived to tell about their stay.*

His thoughts home in on Gambino, head of a trifecta-based crime family—Seattle, San Francisco, and New Orleans. Mick tightens his grip on the steering wheel. He told himself, *You learned the hard way that Gambino's reach is long and elusive. That his minions infiltrate even the most inaccessible places to do his bidding, so stay on your A game.*

Last month, over the Labor Day weekend, Emma (Mick's pregnant wife) and Carly and Brianna (the daughters of one of his best friends, Joe Bingham) were abducted and held hostage in a secluded cabin on Mount Baker by Gambino's thugs. Joe, a Bellingham homicide detective, took a bullet in his right shoulder, saving his daughters.

After the incident, local police chief Bruce Simms referred to him, Joe, and Rafferty, Mick's other best friend, as "The Three Musketeers" at a press conference. He went on to say, "Though nontraditional—an ex-cop turned PI, a homicide detective, and an FBI special agent—they accomplish what no others do; they solve crimes and put bad guys behind bars. *Consistently.*"

Mick smiles at what Simms *didn't* say to the press—*They let me assist in criminal investigations because, unlike Rafferty and Joe, I have fewer restrictions, protocols, and no red tape as a PI.*

Mick takes backroads to the airport because he hates driving under freeway overpasses. They open old wounds and cut fresh ones, triggering a grim reminder of what happened. It doesn't matter that five years have passed. When Mick closes his eyes, the memory is as fresh as if it had happened today.

A bullet explodes between his partner's eyes. The amount of blood that hits Mick is small compared to what covers the back of the cruiser.

Sam slumps forward; the shoulder belt prevents his weight from hitting the steering wheel, but not from gunning the accelerator. The cruiser surges onto the right shoulder, and Mick braces himself for the inevitable impact of metal against the concrete abutment.

The snap of shattering glass mixed with the high-pitched scrape of steel fills his ears. He chokes on the scream lodged in his throat as the cruiser collides with the bridge's unforgiving underpinning.

It hurts to open his eyes. Mick's aware that the underpass is lit by flickering red and blue lights shimmering on cement. He hears people shouting. "This one's alive, the other one's dead. We're going to have to cut him out. Get the Jaws of Life," one of them yells. "Hurry—I smell fuel!"

Suspended by the seatbelt system, Mick hovers over Sam. He sees his eyes wide open and vacant, his mouth parted. And though Mick witnessed death many times in his career, nausea clenches his stomach. Sam isn't only his partner; he's Mick's best friend.

Mick shakes the all-too-clear vision from his mind.

Months after the accident, Mick's sister, Libby, and brother-in-law, Niall, picked him up at the hospital and took him to Pines & Quill, their writing retreat in Fairhaven, Washington, to finish recovering in one of their four writers-in-residence cottages—Austen, the wheelchair-friendly one.

Swallowed by the unending tasks of groundskeeper and all-around handyman, Mick soon discovered that the zen-like energy of the wooded acres breathed life back into his weary soul.

He taps his fingers on the steering wheel in time to the tune playing softly on the radio. *Before Emma came into my life, my daily mantra was, "Just make it through today." But now, my toes are on the edge of fatherhood. I'll do well if I'm only half as good as Dad was. I'm excited at the prospect but scared out of my wits!*

Mick pulls into a parking space at the airport—a single building with a stone and wood exterior. *Man, is this different from the airport in San Francisco, where I grew up. Emma calls it a "gentle" airport. It reminds me of the airport in Missoula, Montana, where Dad and I used to fly to go fishing.*

He turns off the ignition, removes his hands from the steering wheel, and balls them into fists. His fingernails bite into the flesh of his palms. *I miss him so much. Anything good about me came from my parents, but Gambino had one of his thugs kill Dad.*

Removing the nameboards from the passenger seat, Mick steps out of the van, takes a deep breath of crisp October air, and fobs it locked before heading into the structure. His limp is more pronounced after this morning's run—he ran five miles instead of three.

Inside the terminal, he removes his sunglasses and slips one of the temples through a buttonhole on his shirt. The arrivals and departures board indicates that the plane for the first guest, Brent Gooding, will arrive soon from Daytona Beach. The flights for the other three guests are staggered for arrival over the next hour.

Mick enjoys getting to know the guests who carve out three weeks from their schedules to write in near seclusion. Each has a unique process for transferring ideas from their head to the page. January through October, four different writers arrive on the first day of each month and depart on the twenty-first. Three weeks offers them significant time to work on their manuscripts.

The fourth week of each month is guest-free, giving Niall, Libby, Mick, and Emma time to relax and prepare for the next group of writers.

November and December at Pines & Quill are reserved for family and friends to enjoy the holidays. They arrive from near and far and stay in the cabins and four large guest rooms—a new addition this year—over the workshop.

Mick taps the nameboards against his thigh. Each month when Libby hands them to him for meeting their guests at the airport, she shares a brief commentary of what she imagines their personalities are like. She bases it on the phone conversation or email correspondence she has with them.

Since the most recent incident with Gambino's foot soldiers breaching their property, they started running criminal background checks with their potential guests' permission. *October's the first month we've implemented that strategy. They're all clean. Let's hope it reduces the chance that one of them is on Gambino's payroll.*

Mick enjoys indulging his sister because her predictions are darned close, if not dead-on.

"Let's see now," she'd said, tapping an index finger on her chin. "Brent Gooding is a former NASCAR driver. He was paralyzed in a high-speed accident on the track, so he's our wheelchair guest this month. He's married and has two children. He mentioned that one of them recently graduated from Emory University in Atlanta. And the other one's in their third year there. Brent authors the popular Burnt Rubber suspense series that takes place on the racing circuit."

"How about the next guest?" Mick asks.

"Jennifer Pruett is a professional magician," Libby says. "You've probably seen her on television. She's up there with the likes of David Copperfield and Penn and Teller."

Mick raises his eyebrows. "You're right. I *have* seen her perform on television. She's darned good."

"I asked her if she'd do a little magic for us one evening after dinner, and she said she'd be happy to."

"Wow. How much is that going to cost?"

"Jennifer said it would be complimentary, but I'm reducing her retreat fee. She doesn't know it yet. She'll just see that it *disappeared* from her bill." Libby laughs at her joke.

Mick rolls his eyes. "Oh, brother."

"Jennifer's married, but in the midst of a divorce. Together they have a child who's currently studying at the University of Michigan, Ann Arbor."

"Okay, that's two of our guests. What about the third one?" Mick says.

"Adam Richmond is an architect turned real estate investor and professional house flipper. He strikes me as a shrewd businessman with a good sense of humor. His wife is his business partner, and together they have two children. If I remember correctly, one's a senior in high school, and the other attends Rice University in Houston, Texas. The apple didn't fall far from the tree with the college-age child because they're majoring in architecture."

"And the fourth guest?" Mick says.

"Lucy Fleming is a two-time Olympic medalist."

"I'm impressed," Mick says. "What's her sport?"

"She was a triathlete—swim, cycle, run. And though she no longer participates in the Olympics, she's an Ironman champion and still competes. Lucy said she's bringing a wetsuit with her so she can swim in the bay and a bicycle so she can ride on new-to-her terrain."

Mick raises his eyebrows. "Bellingham Bay? It's October; the water's practically snow melt!"

"At any rate," Libby continues, "she and her husband own a high-end road and triathlon bicycle shop and have two children—one's in high school, and the other attends the University of Chicago."

Amid a hubbub of travelers coming and going, Mick's thoughts return to his surroundings. *Once a cop, always a cop*—his gaze sweeps the space, taking everything in like a dry sponge soaking up water. At the onset of his police training, he learned, "It's all in the details." He notes people's hair color, facial expressions, body language, tattoos, jewelry, clothing, footwear, and baggage details.

A man with a bandana worn as a headband walks through the doorway—a popular style for music artists like Justin Bieber and Harry Styles. But with gang activity steadily increasing in Whatcom County, the royal blue color piques Mick's interest.

The Sureños gang identifies with nearly all shades of blue, but they're best known for royal blue bandanas worn around the neck, tied around the wrist, or as a headband. *As brutal as the Sureños are, they're child's play compared to Gambino. God help us if they ever start working together.*

Passengers from Daytona Beach begin to enter the building. One of the first is another man wearing a royal blue bandana as a headband.

Mick's adrenalin kicks up a beat.

The man Mick first noticed flashes a hand signal at the new arrival, juts his chin toward Mick, then leaves the way he came.

The other man bypasses the baggage carousel and follows suit.

Tell Chief Simms we have a new arrival. Mick secures a baggage trolley and raises the nameboard for B. GOODING. He scans the crowd and spots Brent—the only person in a motorized wheelchair. His hair is salt and pepper, his jaw is sharply cut, and his brown eyes are alert and penetrating. He's wearing a blue button-down shirt, khaki pants, and brown slip-ons.

Brent rolls to a stop in front of Mick and extends his right hand. Then, after introducing themselves, they head toward the black circling conveyor belt.

Brent asks, "When will the others arrive?"

"We're waiting for three more within the hour," Mick says.

Brent points to a suitcase newly ejected from a rubber-fringed metal throat, tumbling onto the conveyor belt. "There's my baggage now."

Mick loads it on the trolley and then checks his watch. "The next guest is about to land."

As passengers from Las Vegas pour in, Mick holds up a nameboard with J. PRUETT on it.

A tall, slender woman wearing a dark blue pantsuit and black heels makes eye contact with Mick. Black curly hair frames her face, but not so much that he can't see dark eyes crinkle at the edges when she smiles.

As she walks toward Mick and Brent, Brent whispers to Mick, "Isn't she a famous magician?"

Before Mick can answer, the woman steps up to Mick and extends a hand. "I'm Jennifer Pruett."

Mick shakes her outstretched hand. "I'm Sean McPherson—Mick." Then, he introduces Brent Gooding. "He arrived just ahead of you from Daytona Beach."

Jennifer purses her lips and cocks her head to the side, studying the man. "Brent Gooding. Daytona Beach." She taps her chin with an index finger and furrows her eyebrows. Then she smiles. "You're the race-car driver."

Brent pats one of the arms of his wheelchair. "Former NASCAR," he says, smiling.

"Please remind me what NASCAR stands for," Jennifer says.

"It stands for National Association for Stock Car Auto Racing."

"It's a pleasure to meet you," Jennifer says, shaking his hand. "Now, if you two gentlemen will excuse me a moment, I'm going to go collect my luggage."

"We'll help," Mick says as he and Brent follow in the wake of her heels clicking on the polished tile floor.

Mick loads three large pieces of hard-sided luggage on the trolley. Each piece is secured with a TSA-approved lock that security officers can open with a universal master key, if necessary, so it doesn't have to be cut.

Fifteen minutes late, the Houston flight carrying Adam Richmond lands just ahead of Lucy Fleming's flight from Chicago. At Bellingham International, this almost constitutes an air-traffic jam.

Mick lifts the nameboard that says A. RICHMOND and holds it high.

A man with a reddish-brown beard and mustache approaches them. He's wearing jeans, a long-sleeved green polo shirt, and brown chukka boots. Mick guesses he's about six feet tall and wonders if his quick stride signals anything about his personality. His easy smile reveals straight white teeth—*very white*.

Shaking Mick's hand, he says, "I'm Adam. You must be Mick. Your sister said you'd be meeting the writers in residence." His gaze takes in the other two people.

After Mick introduces him to the others, Adam says, "I'll be right back, I'm going to grab my luggage."

"I'll come with you," Mick says. Then turning to Brent and Jennifer, "Would you please keep an eye on the trolley?"

Brent nods. "You bet."

Jennifer's practically studying Brent's wheelchair. What's up with that?

When they return with Adam's luggage, Mick loads it on the trolley and checks the arrival board. The flight from Chicago just landed.

Shortly after, passengers flow in like human lava.

Mick raises the nameboard that reads, L. FLEMING.

Within minutes, a tall, athletic-looking woman joins the group. Her short hair is blond, and her form-fitting black cropped pants and short-sleeve black shirt reveal a toned frame. The calf muscles above her black running shoes are well-defined.

Mick knows that, in theory, muscle weight is a burden and a disadvantage for triathletes because of the drag it generates. However, the longer the triathlon distance, the more muscular the triathletes.

Extending his hand, Mick says, "Welcome, I'm Sean McPherson—Mick."

Lucy shakes Mick's hand firmly. It's easy to gauge her strength in the grip of her handshake.

After introducing her to the other writers in residence, he accompanies Lucy to the baggage carousel and puts her luggage on the trolley.

All of a sudden, Lucy shouts, "Hey, you!" Then she bolts after a man wearing a black pulled-up hoodie heading for the glass doors. But before reaching them, a cloud of white smoke bursts in front of him, stopping him dead in his tracks.

Lucy launches herself onto the man's back. Gripping her bicycle suitcase in his hands, he twists to throw an elbow back. "Get off me!"

Before Mick can even move, Lucy flips the guy on his back and straddles his belly. "You son of a bitch." She cocks her right arm, ready to strike.

He pushes the case toward her.

"Here, take it," he says, shoving the case at her.

She grabs it from him and steps off the guy. "Go on. Get out of here before I call the police."

The guy tears out.

Within moments, two uniformed airport security personnel rush up to them. "What happened?"

Lucy explains the event.

"Why did you let him go?" one of them asks.

"When I was sitting on him, I got a good look at his face. He has 'meth mouth.'"

One of the security officers nods. "His teeth were blackened and rotting?"

"Yes," Lucy says. "And he smelled like death."

Both security officers cock their heads. Then, one asks, "How do you know what death smells like?"

"I'm a crime writer. It's my job to know. A dying person gives off a distinct acetone odor related to the changes in the metabolism emanating from the breath, skin, and bodily fluids. The smell is part of a deteriorating body's chemical breakdown as a person nears the end."

One of the officers points to the case in her hands. "What's that?"

"It's my bicycle. It's what the thief was trying to steal."

The security officer raises an eyebrow. "You've got a bicycle in *that*?"

"Yes, it's a folding bike," Lucy says. "I'm going to do some Ironman training while I'm here. It's worth a lot. I think that's why the guy wanted it. He probably would have pawned it for drug money."

"So why let him get away?" security asks.

"Because I felt sorry for him," Lucy says. "And karma's a bitch. It's going to come back and bite his ass big time."

When security finishes taking their notes, they get Lucy's contact information and head away.

"I'm sorry that happened," Mick says.

"No worries," Lucy says. "It can happen in the best of places. I'm just glad he didn't get away with my bike. I plan to train when my brain needs a writing break."

"Well, you've picked a gorgeous part of the country to do it in."

Brent, Jennifer, and Adam had been watching from close by. When Mick and Lucy join them, Brent says, "Holy shit! That was pretty damn cool the way Jennifer conjured that cloud of smoke and you jumped the guy!"

Lucy smiles at Jennifer. "Thank you," she says, extending her hand. "Are you a ninja, a magician, or a miracle worker? That cloud of smoke stopped the thief from getting away with my bike."

Jennifer returns the handshake. "I'm a magician. And it was my pleasure to help."

Mick introduces Lucy to the rest of the writers in residence and explains that she's an Ironman champion and active competitor.

Mick narrows his eyes and makes a mental note. *Adam is covertly appraising Lucy—like he's sizing up her strength.*

Then, with the luggage trolley in hand, he takes the lead, and the small group heads en masse to the parking lot. As they walk, Mick replays the bicycle incident in his mind:

How on earth did Jennifer pull that off from such a distance? No wonder Forbes *describes her as "One of the most commercially successful magicians in history."*

And Lucy is a physical powerhouse who's not afraid to use it. I wouldn't want to be on her wrong side.

The writer who brings up the rear replays the hideous phone call in their mind. *I have to kill one of these people.*

They eye the group and assess each person. *That one doesn't appear to be an obstacle. But that one could potentially be an issue. And that one? Steer clear—they're a problem.*

CHAPTER 3

*"Layers tell a story; it's how books come to life.
Characters are nothing but layers: emotions and
driving actions. Actions have consequences that
fuel new emotions. Layer upon layer, a story is
told, truths learned, and secrets revealed."*
—JOE HART

Much like a brilliant, multifaceted gem nestled on the ragged hemline of the northern Pacific coastline, Pines & Quill, a wooded retreat for writers, sits zen-like on twenty forested acres overlooking Bellingham Bay in Fairhaven, Washington. It provides respite from the distractions of everyday life so that writers can focus on what they do best—writing.

Seated on the periphery of the historic Fairhaven district of Bellingham, this writing paradise is made of fog-kissed bluffs, great horned owls and red-tailed hawks, winding paths, solitude, and the blissful absence of noise, demands, and chores—an ideal place for contemplating many things.

Providing an environment that offers peace, quiet, and inspiration, the wooded retreat boasts four secluded cottages: Dickens, Brontë, Austen, and Thoreau, each handcrafted by a long-dead Amish man whose skill and devotion to his trade are still evident in his work. When the structures were modernized, meticulous care was taken to reflect the same excellence in craftsmanship.

The awe-inspiring mango-colored sunrises and blood-orange sunsets at Pines & Quill compete in their breathtaking showiness, each vying for the rapt attention of would-be onlookers. One heralds the beginning of the day, the other bids adieu, sending it off into the ink-black night sky.

It was a haven until this past May, when Gambino added Seattle and the surrounding area to his ever-growing kingdom. That's when the wave of deaths at Pines & Quill began.

In the big kitchen of the main house, apron-clad Niall MacCullough, one of the owners of Pines & Quill, stands with his hands on his hips. "I would have sworn that I—"

He laughs at himself as he opens the refrigerator. Filled with joy, he's the type who can find the bright side of anything. Almost. Only one person can ignite his fuse—Gambino.

Anger courses through Niall when he thinks of the swath of destruction left by the monster who uses human beings and then disposes of them like trash. Niall shakes his head to clear it of negative thoughts and tries to replace them with pleasant ones.

Even though his brother was a priest, Niall is not much of a brick-and-mortar churchgoer. He believes that anything done with care and joy is an act of worship. That's why he strives to be a kind presence in people's lives; that's why the cookery and garden at Pines & Quill are his cathedrals. The casual atmosphere of sharing a meal in the spacious open-plan kitchen and dining area of the main house is conducive to *esprit de corps*—camaraderie.

Every scratch and divot—a history of purpose and bustling activity—read like braille on the wide, buttery pine boards of the floor in his sanctuary.

Having checked with the guests during registration for dietary preferences and restrictions, Niall prepared a three-week menu of meals. Tonight's welcome-dinner entrée is venison tenderloin trimmed and wrapped in bacon slices, roasted until the bacon is crispy, and served with creamy garlic, mushroom, and green onion sauce.

Niall backs out of the open refrigerator, closes it, and purses his lips. "Well, I guess I didn't put the venison in there after all," he says to his blurry reflection in the stainless steel door.

He turns at the clicking of nails on the hardwood floor.

From the mudroom, his four-legged companion, Hemingway, watches Niall. The Irish wolfhound's bearded chin rests on the closed bottom half of the Dutch door. The bustling five-year-old rough-coated dog tips the scales at just under one hundred and fifty pounds. An ancient breed, the well-muscled, lean wolfhounds were bred to hunt with their masters, fight beside them in battle, and guard their castles, where they were gentle with family and guests.

After snagging a dog treat from the big glass jar, Niall walks toward the mudroom behind the Dutch door. This is where the MacCulloughs, including Hemingway, stow outerwear, boots, and anything else they might need when venturing outside. It also houses the dog's food, water bowls, leash, and bed.

"Hey, big fella. It appears I left a few things in the freezer in the workshop," Niall says to Hemingway while opening the door. "Would you like to come along?"

Hemingway lowers his front legs and chest, forcing his behind straight up in the air—a play posture—making it clear that he'll go *anywhere* and do *anything* with one of his favorite humans.

Niall opens the exterior mudroom door. But before exiting, he snags a colorful market basket from a peg.

Hemingway bolts ahead, nose low to sniff every bush between the main house and kingdom come.

The weather front had passed, leaving puddles and clarity in the cobalt blue sky. A few remnant clouds, wispy at best, linger.

October is usually the same as September in Bellingham, Washington—a moderate autumn month. The low temperature dips to the mid-forties and reaches a high in the upper fifties.

Niall shivers and rubs the goosebumps on his arms. Not because of the weather—his mind has moved ahead to the chest freezer in the garage. They replaced it last month after discovering a body inside.

Over Labor Day weekend, when Gambino's foot soldiers breached the Pines & Quill property line, US Marshal Jake Porter directed some of the writers and other guests to stay by an outcropping of large boulders on the bluff above Bellingham Bay so they would have a clear view of anyone approaching. Unfortunately, some were too scared and ran back to the main retreat grounds, which didn't end well.

Niall unclenches a fist and uses the back of his hand to wipe tears from his eyes. *And just a few months ago, in June, Gambino had my brother, Paddy, killed. To everyone else in the parish, he was the beloved Father Patrick MacCullough at St. Barnabas Catholic Church. He'd been shot six times through the partition in one of the confession booths.*

I wonder what Gambino has in store for us this month?

Libby drives their all-terrain vehicle to put fresh linen in each cottage. With its rugged stance, canopied top, and knobby tires, the ATV is invaluable for getting around the property, regardless of the weather.

She lifts her face skyward and deeply inhales fresh air before heading north to Dickens cottage. A weathered Adirondack chair sits on the covered front porch. A writer herself, she knows the value of not being confined, of being able to move around, and that nature's breath—fresh air—is an encouraging muse.

With this in mind, during the planning phase of the retreat, she ensured that the porch of each cottage has ample space for quiet reflection. As a result, a handcrafted bent-willow chair with a deep seat, the graceful lines of its arms open in welcome, and plump pillows are ready to receive a weary back at the end of a productive day of writing.

Libby enjoys free rein expressing her natural flair for style and interior design in the four writers' cottages. And while the original Amish builder saw that each cottage was similar in size and design, surrounded by its own type of tree, she ensures that they each have unique personalities: color scheme, furnishings, and hand-selected artwork created by local artisans.

In addition to electricity and internet access, each cottage has air-conditioning, a wood-burning stove, and a bathroom with a shower. They're also equipped with an efficiency kitchen that includes a minifridge, microwave, toaster oven, coffeemaker, and a fat-bellied teakettle, ideal for a long day of writing.

On each desk is a phone. Retro, each is bulky and square, from an era before cell phones, even before cordless. Its sole purpose is to connect with the main house. A guest needs only to lift the receiver and dial zero to ring through to the MacCulloughs' kitchen.

After making the beds with crisp, clean linens and setting out fresh towels and washcloths in each cottage's bath and kitchen areas, Libby leaves a cheerful monogrammed note-card with P&Q, the retreat's initials, on each kitchen counter. Inside is printed:

Pines & Quill offers writers a peaceful, inspiring, wooded setting to pursue the work they love. We aim to encourage artistic exploration, nurture creative thought, and forge bonds between diverse thinkers. Our vision is for you to find inspiration and make progress in your work.

Located between the main house and the garden is a common area with laundry facilities and supplies, a printer and paper, and assorted office supplies should you need them. There are also bicycles with covered saddle baskets if you feel adventurous and would like to explore the surrounding area or pick up sundries in town. Each basket contains a map of historic Fairhaven, a brisk twenty-minute walk or a five-minute bicycle ride from Pines & Quill.

Satisfied that everything is in place for their guests' arrival, Libby returns to the main house. Large and rugged, it's inviting in a down-home sort of way. Built for comfort, not grandeur, it sits at the center of Pines & Quill.

While each writer has the option to have breakfast and lunch delivered from the main house to their cottage door, they gather for dinner each evening at the enormous pine table Libby acquired at an auction in Seattle. Said to have seated a dozen threshers at mealtime in the early 1900s, it now serves writers who've come to escape the distractions of life—writers who've come to gift themselves with time and space, let go and connect with nature's muse, find their creative rhythm, and write about the intersections of humanity, both real and imagined.

With each group, Libby and Niall nod to each other under copper-bottomed pots that hang from the rustic beams in the kitchen ceiling. In over thirty years of marriage, they've built an extensive repertoire of facial expressions that only they are privy to the meaning of.

Every month they settle back like satisfied cats washing their whiskers as they watch a small community form, bonds deepening through conversation. Their guests share stories, histories, breakthroughs, and roadblocks, offer advice and feedback, and challenge each other to take risks. This month's group of writers—October—should prove no different.

With its bevy of comfortable, overstuffed chairs, the living room is the after-dinner gathering place for guests to continue visiting over dessert while enjoying drinks from the small but well-stocked main house bar, the Ink Well. The floor-to-ceiling bookshelves and massive fieldstone fireplace are ideal focal points, with the large mirror above the mantel gathering the entire room in its reflection.

The retreat's journal resides in this community space, a journal where guests are encouraged to make notations during their stay. With entries dating from 1980, the Pines & Quill journal is a living legacy, a tangible way for writers to connect with those who came before and those who'll come after. On more than one occasion, it's served as a way-shower, yielding clues that helped solve mysterious occurrences that have taken place at this writer's haven over the years.

Some of the script is small and tight; some is fiercely slanted. Other handwriting is long and loopy, while some is printed with precision, each letter like a soldier marching across the page. Last month, they'd found a message written in red ink: I warned you. My people can infiltrate even the most inaccessible places to do my bidding. When you least expect it, expect it—The Bull. *That's how we discovered that Gambino not only breached our property line, but he, or one of his thugs, invaded our home.*

Libby purses her lips. *If Gambino does something during this month's retreat and we get bad publicity, it will be our last month of business. Niall and I promised each other that if anything terrible happens again, we'd close Pines & Quill, sell it, and move. It would be too painful to stay close by. But it would also tear our hearts out to leave.*

Between fiction and nonfiction, every possible genre is written at Pines & Quill. But in October, all writers who attend the retreat are here to pen crime, suspense, thriller, mystery, or horror in celebration of Halloween.

Libby peers around the entrance to the kitchen. *I wonder where Niall and Hemingway have gotten off to?* She admires the commercial-sized stainless steel appliances and vast grayveined marble counters. *Something smells spicy and delicious.* She turns on the oven light and peeks through the glass window. Four round pans grace the middle rack.

On the counter next to the stovetop, Libby picks up a recipe card dotted with splatters—Sticky Jamaican Ginger Cake with Butterscotch Sauce. Niall was able to get ahold of the recipe back in 2022 when it was created for Her Majesty Queen Elizabeth's Platinum Jubilee. It's become a favorite since then.

Libby's mouth waters. *Niall will sandwich together layers of deliciously sticky spiced Jamaican ginger cake with a salted butterscotch sauce and smother it in orange mascarpone cream. It's a perfect dessert for our guests to celebrate their first evening at Pines & Quill.*

Libby sets the card back down. *And though Niall would never say it himself, he's a culinary artist.*

In addition to Niall's gourmet cooking, another popular feature at Pines & Quill is Libby's movement meditation sessions—tai chi. Many guests avail themselves of this misty-morning offering as a beautiful way to prime the pump for a productive writing day.

I wonder how many of our guests will sleep in and how many will join me in the tai chi pavilion at six o'clock tomorrow morning?

Libby shivers involuntarily at a memory. *Last month, while decorating the pavilion for the Labor Day festivities, I climbed a ladder to hang crepe paper. But because I'm afraid of spiders, before sticking my hand in a dark corner, I used the flashlight feature on my cell phone to check the dark recess. What I saw was much more frightening than any spider. I was staring into the fishbowl lens of a surveillance camera.*

———

Mick brings the van to a stop before a massive wrought-iron entry gate. *If recent history has taught me anything, Gambino won't quit until he's killed us or put us out of business. And he's not above using writers in residence as a means to our end.*

He glances at Adam sitting in the front passenger seat and then in the rearview mirror to scan the other faces. *Not one of them looks like a killer. Then again, looks are deceiving—never judge a book by its cover.* Mick grips the steering wheel, and his stomach clenches.

The overhead sign silhouetted against the sky beckons WELCOME TO PINES & QUILL. He presses a button on the remote attached to the visor, and the huge entrance gate swings open. He knows the vehicle sensor has buzzed in the main house, notifying Libby and Niall of their arrival. *They'll let Emma know.*

When the passengers remark about the lovely forested surroundings, Mick uses the automatic controls to lower their windows, then slowly takes the lengthy drive to the main house so Brent, Jennifer, Adam, and Lucy can drink in the beauty.

Adam says, "I know I read it on your website, but I can't remember how many acres Pines & Quill is."

"All together, there are thirty acres," Mick says. "The retreat grounds, with the cottages, main house, garage, workshop, tai chi pavilion, and the cabin where my wife and I live, are twenty acres. The adjoining bluff that overlooks Bellingham Bay is an additional ten."

Adam hikes his eyebrows, pulls a cell phone from his pocket, scrolls to the calculator app, and starts tapping buttons. "I checked real estate prices before coming here, and *my God*, you're sitting on a gold mine!"

The comment amuses Mick.

Adam keeps tapping away.

"So the bay explains the faint hint of salt in the air," Jennifer says, then points at the trees. "And the pine scent smells wonderful."

"I agree," Lucy says. "It's a lovely combination."

"In addition to pines," Mick says, "there are several other types of trees. For privacy's sake, we planted a copse around each cottage. Austen has blue elderberry, Brontë has Douglas fir, Dickens big-leaf maple, and Thoreau western red cedar."

"Is the foliage changing color for autumn?" Jennifer asks.

Mick nods. "The big-leaf maples are beginning to turn yellowish-orange. And the elderberry leaves are just starting to change. The leaves of western red cedar trees are like scales. They grow in opposite pairs in four rows. One pair is folded while the other isn't. Because of this, they look like overlapping shingles. The leaves are arranged on flat, fan-like sprays on a twig. They have a strong spicy aroma and are evergreen.

They're glossy green on the upper side and white striped on the lower side."

Brent leans forward. "What kind of wildlife do you get around here?"

"We get the usual suspects—squirrel, raccoon, possum, the occasional skunk, and deer," Mick says. "But now and again, a black bear, bobcat, cougar, or coyote meanders through. And on *rare* occasions, we see moose."

At the end of the drive, the trees open into a natural space, and the main house comes into view. The two-story home sits on a gentle rise, accentuated by a large circular drive surrounding low well-maintained shrubs and bushes.

Pointing out the open window, Lucy says, "I know that's quince, but what's that?"

"It's flowering currant," Mick says, "but most people refer to it as hummingbird bush. Red flowers bloom in early spring, making them a first stop for the hummingbirds following the Pacific Flyway on their northern migration."

Casual yet elegant, the drive widens at the front door where Emma, Libby, and Niall, with Hemingway between them, wait.

Mick pulls to a stop and activates the sliding side doors on the van. Then he opens the barn-style doors on the back, presses a button, and lowers Brent in his motorized wheelchair to the ground on a specially designed lift.

Brent holds the back of his right hand toward Hemingway, who shifts into a happy full-body wag and steps forward to sniff the offered extremity. When Brent turns his hand over, Hemingway plunges his whiskered muzzle into his hand.

Brent lets out a belly laugh as the big dog's cold wet nose makes contact. "I can see we're going to be good friends," he says to the dog, who sniffs his bionic arm before strolling over to Jennifer.

She scratches under his chin and then moves to his ears. When she brings her hand away, she's holding a large biscuit. "Well, for goodness' sake," she says to Hemingway. "Look what I found behind your ear."

Hemingway's long wiry tail shifts into propeller mode.

"If you whip that thing any faster, you're going to take off," Jennifer teases the big dog, handing it to him.

Mick hugs Emma and kisses her on the nose. "I swear you get prettier every time I see you." He introduces the guests to Libby and Niall.

When he gets to Jennifer, she steps forward, extends both hands, and cups each proffered hand in turn—Emma first, then Libby. As she gets to Niall and reaches forward, a bottle appears in each hand.

Gasps of delighted surprise ring in the air.

Speechless with pleasure, Niall examines the offerings— two bottles of Abracadabra, a red wine blend from Brian Carter Cellars in Washington State's Columbia Valley.

He turns one of the bottles around and reads the back label aloud. "'A pinch of the unpredictable. A splash of the divine. A bunch of extraordinary tastinesses. And there is magic in the wine.'"

"I was hoping they'd pair well with dinner one night," Jennifer says.

"Thank you," Niall says. "They most certainly will."

Everyone is slack-jawed, including Mick. *How on earth did she conjure two bottles of wine? Where had she concealed them? It would be damn hard to hide two bottles of wine, especially with so many pairs of watching eyes. Abracadabra, indeed.*

CHAPTER 4

"My only job is to tell the story. I think that if more writers focused on that, they'd be better off and probably more successful."
—NORA ROBERTS

L ibby scans the faces of the new arrivals. *Mick said that running a criminal background check on our guests is a good stopgap measure but doesn't guarantee that one of them doesn't work for Gambino. We can't take any more negative publicity. Please let October be an uneventful month. I don't want to leave Pines & Quill.*

Extending her arms in welcome, she says, "I'm so glad you're here at Pines & Quill. It's going to be a productive month of writing. Now let's get everyone sorted." She smiles at each face in turn. "Lucy, you're in Dickens cottage. Jennifer, Brontë. Brent, Austen. And Adam, you're in Thoreau."

She hands Mick the color-coded luggage tags. "For those who'd like a ride, Mick will give you a lift in the ATV while he takes the luggage to the cottages and puts it on the porch, or you can come with Emma and me on the pathways."

"Just point me in the right direction," Adam says. "I want to explore my way there."

"Same with me," Lucy says. "After sitting on a plane for four hours, I want to stretch my legs and explore a bit."

"I'd love a guided tour on the way to mine," Jennifer says. "Same here," Brent says.

Emma steps toward Brent. "Hemingway and I will show you the way."

"While you're getting settled in," Niall says, "I'll put the finishing touches on dinner. We'll see you back here at six o'clock." He glances at his watch. "That gives you just about an hour to catch your second wind."

After Libby points the way to Adam and Lucy, she and Jennifer head toward Brontë. "Conjuring two bottles of wine out of thin air was quite impressive," Libby says.

"I'm glad you enjoyed it," Jennifer says. "Making things appear and disappear is what I do best." She twists the gold wedding band on her left hand. "Now if there was just a little bippity boppity boo to make cheating husbands disappear." Her laugh is humorless.

The flash of menace on Jennifer's face isn't lost on Libby.

———

Emma and Brent make their way toward Austen cottage.

Hemingway, in the lead, whips his long tail in slap-dash figure eights.

Tall trees flank the smooth pathway—like soldiers—their canopied shade expansive, with a few rays of light piercing the foliage in certain spots. The gentle breeze carries an evergreen scent, a mellowness that only pines bestow. The overall effect is mystical.

Emma mentally shudders when they reach the place on the pathway where she was kidnapped by Jason Hughes and then held captive in a cave in El Cañón del Diablo—the Devil's Canyon—so named because of the boulder field at the bottom of a hundred-foot rock wall. Emma shakes herself free of the image.

"All of the pathways at Pines & Quill have solar-powered walk lights that come on at dusk and go off when the batteries deplete," Emma says. "That time differs daily, depending on the amount of sunlight. We want our guests to feel as comfortable in the evening as they do during the day."

A large tree limb blocks the pathway ahead of them.

"It must have come down during last night's storm," Emma says. "I'll drag it out of the way."

"Oh, no, you don't," Brent says, raising his left arm.

A vision of being attacked grips Emma's heart in her ribcage.

"Let me put this bionic arm to good use," he says, smiling.

Relief almost buckles Emma's knees.

Brent moves his wheelchair close to the downed limb and bends forward. "I'd say it's about five inches in diameter and just short of five feet long." Then quick as a blink, he uses his bionic hand to sever the limb, leaving it in five eighteen-inch sections. He sits back, smiling. "There. Perfect for firewood."

Wide-eyed, Emma shakes her head in disbelief. "Whoa! I've never seen anything like that. How did you do it?"

"Although I'd rather have my natural arm and hand back," Brent says, "I've got to say that bionic limbs are amazing. In the clinical trial I'm part of, we're testing technology similar to that of NASA's space robots, with incredible dexterity, finesse, stability, and strength. A flip of a switch"—he points to a small lever inside the wrist area—"and I select the option I want: hammer, cut, crush, and so forth."

Hemingway lifts one of the limb sections in his massive jaws, then bolts toward Austen cottage with his prize.

After Emma moves the remaining pieces to the side of the pathway, she and Brent follow in the big dog's wake.

"I knew that as a wheelchair-friendly facility, Pines & Quill would have smooth surfaces, but this is exceptional," Brent says.

"Libby and Niall learned a lot when Mick was in a wheelchair," Emma says.

Brent looks up, surprised. "I saw that he walks with a limp but didn't realize that he'd been in a wheelchair."

Emma nods. "Yes, and so was I." She turns and spreads her hands toward a ramp leading to the porch of a cottage. "But we're here now, so we'll save that conversation for another time."

Nestled in a glade of blue elderberry, Austen cottage features womb-like seclusion. Brent's luggage is already there, lined up neatly to the right of the door.

Emma gives a sit-and-stay hand signal to Hemingway. Then, after he drops to his bottom, she presses a round silver metal button on the outside wall, and the door swings open. "There's a matching one on the inside," she says. "But it works manually as well."

Brent rolls up the ramp easily, continuing right through the extra-wide doorframe.

"Well, I'll be darned," he says, turning around with a face-splitting grin.

Emma is already backing out, pulling the door closed with her. "See you at six o'clock," she says with a smile in her voice as the door shuts behind her, and she heads toward the main house. In the distance, Emma sees Mick.

Hemingway bolts past her. When he reaches Mick, he sits beside him and dusts the pathway with his tail. The chunk of tree limb is still in his mouth.

Baffled, Mick raises his eyebrows as he looks between Hemingway's prize and four matching pieces on the ground. "What's going on?"

"You aren't even going to believe it," Emma says, stepping into his open arms. "It was the most amazing thing I've ever seen."

———

Brent gazes at his surroundings as he spins his chair in a three-sixty, appreciating the wheelchair-friendly design. The interior elements are spaced for smooth transitions. The wood floor reflects the same warm, honeyed tones of a massive beam that runs the length of the structure—parallel to the pitch of the vaulted ceiling.

I wish my wife were here, he thinks. *Ellen would love the sage and lavender colors. If I'd known she would lose her job, I wouldn't have come to Pines & Quill. It was a want, not a need. An expense I could have avoided. But I'm here now, so I'll enjoy it for all I'm worth, finish my manuscript while I'm here, and hopefully get a sizable advance from the publisher.*

Following a scent, he moves his wheelchair to the kitchen. On the granite counter, he finds a glass bottle with a handwritten note: Designed to enhance creativity, the top note is Caribbean pink grapefruit, the middle note is amber, and the base notes are Jamaican lemon, Tobago lime, and green florals. Enjoy!

Brent feels warm with welcome. A battered and loved square oak desk with ample clearance space faces sliding glass doors that reveal a smooth-tiled patio of faded terra cotta with an abundance of potted plants. He recognizes marigolds and chrysanthemums. The rest are lost on him.

With a west-facing view, he has an ideal vantage point from which to gaze at the sun as it bows farewell, making way for its alluring mistress, the moon.

He slides the glass door open, wheels out, and draws a deep, refreshing breath. The pre-evening stillness is peaceful—a far cry from the hustle and bustle of Daytona Beach.

In the quiet, he hears the hum of a distant boat. *I read on the Pines & Quill website that Bellingham Bay is just to the west. I wonder how close Austen cottage is to the cliffs that overlook the inlet?*

Brent seizes the right arm of his wheelchair; his knuckles turn white. *I was never afraid of the water before my accident.*

Adam pulls the door to Thoreau cottage closed behind him. Instead of heading straight to the main house where the van dropped them off, his curiosity gets the better of him, and he takes a circuitous route to investigate the other buildings and cottages.

As a real estate agent, he knows that "location is everything." *So Pines & Quill, sitting on significant acreage above Bellingham Bay, is worth a fortune!*

After checking out what he guesses to be Mick's and Emma's cabin—*Built to last*—followed by the garage and workshop—*The upstairs addition is new*—Adam slips through the tree line.

The forest floor is blanketed with prickly scrambling vines, shrubs—*Berry bushes? And ferns.* Adam has to fight through the thicket to locate each cottage.

One by one, he notes they're surrounded by a copse of trees, making it difficult to see much but providing him with camouflage. *That's right, McPherson said they did it for privacy.*

Adam's architect training shifts into gear as he admires the exterior aesthetics of the structural work. *If the other cottages are anything like mine—impeccable craftsmanship—they add even more to the value.*

He glances at his watch. *Shit!* Exiting the tree line, he brushes bits of foliage from his shirtsleeves and pant legs, checking to ensure all debris is gone.

At five minutes till six, Adam arrives at the main house. Before mounting the steps, he turns, places his hands on his hips, and surveys the surrounding area. *Damn, what I wouldn't give to get my hands on a piece of this pie.*

Lucy and Jennifer arrive at the main house together. "Hi, Adam," they greet the man standing at the bottom of the steps looking for all the world like he's surveying his kingdom.

Lucy had taken an immediate dislike to Adam at the airport. *Let it go,* she tells herself, but his cocksure stance reinforces her original assessment. *He's a self-absorbed ass.*

"Did you knock already?" she asks, trying to keep the edge out of her tone.

"Nope," he says, seemingly preoccupied with something beyond the tree line.

Lucy passes Adam, ascending the broad stone steps to the rustic, paneled oak door, and uses the heavy polished brass knocker.

Within moments, Libby opens the big door. "Welcome to our home," she greets them warmly. Then, Libby steps back into the foyer, inviting them into the casual elegance of the main house. "Niall says dinner's almost ready. Let's head back to the kitchen."

The yeasty smell of fresh-baked bread, the earthy aroma of venison—some would say "gamey"—and a combination of mysterious spices tease Lucy's nostrils, and she inhales deeply.

She walks on gleaming hardwood floors, passing rooms on either side with wide windows that boast beautiful views. On the way to the dining area, they notice a west-facing terrace that leads to a garden of native plants where at least a dozen colorful birdhouses hang. *I wish I had a home in the country instead of an apartment over our bike shop in the city.*

Libby interrupts Lucy's thoughts. "I love them," she says. "Each year, I add a new birdhouse. Local artisans craft them."

When they arrive at the massive open-plan kitchen and

dining area, Lucy and Jennifer appreciate the cathedral ceiling and large picture window with southern exposure.

"Welcome to my domain," Niall greets them, removing a towel from his shoulder and bowing at the waist.

"This is where all of the culinary magic takes place," Libby adds. Then, pointing to the picture window that Adam—hands on hips—is admiring, she continues, "That's Niall's garden. Much of the food he prepares comes from right here. The rest he sources locally."

And I'll just bet that conceited ass has never gotten his hands dirty in his life. Lucy chides herself, trying to tamp down her competitive streak. *Drop it; this isn't a competition.* But the more she watches Adam, the angrier she gets. *I can hear my analyst now: "Lucy, you've made Adam a substitute for your husband, and you're transferring your anger and aggression at him."*

Mick and Emma walk hand in hand along the pathway toward the main house. Her free hand rests protectively on her barely showing baby bump.

Mick squeezes her hand. "How do you feel?"

Emma looks into his eyes. "Well, I'm sure glad to be past the morning sickness part. But now, at fifteen weeks, all I want to do is eat." She laughs. "When I helped Niall gather vegetables from the garden for tonight's meal, he told me what's on the menu, and my mouth has been watering since."

I'm so excited to be a dad, Mick thinks. *And I'm scared. What if I'm not a good father?*

In the distance, they spot Brent moving at a good clip in his motorized wheelchair.

"Hey, wait up," Mick calls out.

"You're hard to catch," Emma says when they reach him. "May we join you?"

"Yes, please," Brent says. "Your company ensures I won't get lost. That wouldn't be good because I'm ravenous."

Mick rests a hand on the back of Brent's wheelchair. *At the airport, I noticed Jennifer studying the back. Now I know why. It has all sorts of pockets and storage areas, ideal for a magician to hide something for later. And perfect for concealing—*

Emma squeezes Mick's hand, rousing him from his thoughts.

"That's a pretty snazzy set of wheels you've got there," Mick says.

"Once a race car driver…" Brent pats an armrest. "Seriously though, it's an Air Hawk portable. The one I use for travel. The one I use at home puts this one to shame. It's got ATX suspension and can almost qualify for the Indy 500."

Mick laughs. "The one I had was manual—a horse and buggy compared to yours." He glances at Emma. "Emma's too."

"She mentioned you'd both been in wheelchairs," Brent says. "I'd like to swap stories sometime."

Reaching the main house, Brent uses the ramp on the side of the porch, and then they enter the foyer.

"That's the smoothest threshold I've ever had the pleasure to cross," Brent says.

Mick leads the way to the country kitchen. Polished cutlery flanks sangria-red plates and hand-painted serving pieces on a massive dining table—the light reflecting gleaming stemware complements the glazed dinnerware.

Hemingway—his bearded chin resting on the bottom half of the closed Dutch door—thwacks his tail against the washer and dryer, letting God and everyone know that the new arrivals haven't gone unnoticed by him.

Brent moves his wheelchair over to give Hemingway a scratch behind an ear. "Well, hello again, Big Fella."

Eyeing the clear container of biscuits set out of Hemingway's reach, Brent asks, "May I give him a biscuit?"

"Yes, but only one," Niall says from in front of the stove, where he's stirring something that smells delicious. "Did you hear that, Hemingway? I said *one.*"

Hemingway stretches his neck over the lower half of the door.

We probably don't have to worry about Brent working for Gambino. Hemingway's a good judge of character, and it's clear he's enamored with the man.

Jennifer casually observes the spacious open-plan kitchen and eating area, noting nooks and crannies—ideal places for a magician to pull props from and equally perfect for making things disappear.

Then she turns her attention to the others gathered in the room. She notes Emma's baby bump and the proud look on Mick's face. *The papa-to-be look. I remember when my husband looked at me like that. Now he looks at other women that way.*

She studies the siblings, Libby and Mick. Libby's shoulder-length hair, a captivating shade of sable with a few strands of silver, is tucked behind ears adorned with faceted teardrop earrings. *The dangling stones are yellow and green—my guess is citrine and peridot.* A silver necklace studded with identical gemstones lies on the neckline of her white peasant blouse, and a matching bracelet circles one of her wrists.

Jennifer turns her head to observe Mick speaking with Lucy and Adam. She takes in his striking green eyes and the little quirk in the corner of his close-lipped smile. A few silver threads at his temples look distinctive in his otherwise jet-black hair.

She notes that while the resemblance between brother and sister is strong, there are striking differences. Unlike Libby's straight, delicate nose and flawless facial features, Mick's nose is crooked, making him look rakish. In addition, a thin scar creases his forehead at an angle, from his hairline down through his left eyebrow. Both imperfections complement his square jaw and chiseled features.

"Dinner's ready," Niall announces, adding two more covered dishes to the already-laden table. "Belly up to the bar, or table as the case may be."

After everyone's seated, Niall walks around the table with two glass decanters—one in each hand. He pauses behind each person to pour.

Jennifer watches the red wine purl against the glass inside her long-stemmed Bordeaux glass.

"I decanted this Château Berliquet about thirty minutes ago," Niall says. "And though it takes a long time for it to fully open, I believe it'll be well worth the wait."

"What kind of wine is it?" Adam asks.

"It's a blend of merlot and Cabernet Franc. It has a fine chalky thread running through the middle of gently crushed plum and black cherry fruit flavors while sweet tobacco and bay accents hang in the background—perfect with venison tenderloin."

Jennifer thinks, *I remember the Pines & Quill website noting that Niall's not only a gourmet chef but a wine connoisseur.*

After a toast ("To inspiration and the flow of creativity"), they begin their meal.

Jennifer remembers when she first spoke with Libby on the phone. She said, "We learned long ago that sometimes perfectly plated food can create silos and often seems dull. Everyone eats, but you miss out on some of the great conversations and the connection that comes with sharing a meal. That's why we serve meals family style. It invites discussion, and everyone gets to try as little or as much as they want."

Oohs and aahs erupt from the guests around the table as bowls and platters pass between their hands. The colorful glazed pottery is laden with venison tenderloin, maple Dijon roasted carrots, mushroom risotto, pan-fried zucchini, crispy prosciutto-wrapped asparagus fries, garden-fresh organic salad, and garlic and Grana Padano cheese dinner rolls.

"If you were stranded on a desert island," Libby asks, "and could only have one book, which book would it be?"

Jennifer admires how Libby—an adept hostess—orchestrates the conversation. *The woman's a magician. From a single well-placed question, she started an avalanche of animated conversation.*

As Jennifer sips from her glass, Mick—sitting directly across the table—sets down one of the forks he'd used. When he turns to Lucy to answer a question, she watches as Adam uses his napkin and surreptitiously removes it, placing it under the table out of view. *On his lap?* She studies him as he leans back in his chair with a smug, cat-that-ate-the-canary look.

I wonder what the hell he's up to? He bears watching.

CHAPTER 5

*"Writing is the high alchemy of the soul that
combines words and ideas to create magic."*
—SHARIF KHAN

Niall beams at the compliments he receives for the meal. *I wish I felt the same way on the inside. But I've had a nagging sensation that something's wrong since the writers in residence arrived.*

He glances around the table, trying to pinpoint the source of his unease. Finally, when he gets to Libby, he stops. *She's the best thing that's ever happened in my life.* He leans back in his chair and watches her in action. *Her gift of hospitality never ceases to amaze me.*

Libby presses her hands together and leans forward. A spark of challenge kindles in her eyes. "I'd like each of you to share the title of the book you're currently reading, the author, and a one-paragraph summary. We'll go around the table"— she motions in a clockwise fashion—"starting with Adam."

Temporarily derailed from his anxiety, Niall scoots his chair back and subtly begins to clear the table. Then, hands full, he heads toward the kitchen but can still hear the discussion.

Adam says, "I'm reading *The Look of Architecture* by Witold Rybczynski. It's about the role of fashion in architecture. The premise is that clothes make the mansion, as well as the man."

Niall waits for comments, but no one joins in. *That's odd.* He presses his brows together. Silence permeates the air.

Niall sets the platters on the counter and returns to the table. Lucy and Jennifer are staring daggers at Adam.

Adam raises his hands questioningly. "What?"

"As well as the *man?*" Lucy emphasizes the last word.

Jennifer turns to Lucy. "It's always about the *male* of the species."

"Well, excuse me," Adam says. "Let me amend my summary. The premise is that clothes make the mansion as well as the man *or woman,* as the case may be." Then exasperated, he sets his palms on the table.

The unease Niall felt earlier returns as a pretzel-like knot in his stomach. He pulls the red-and-white striped dishcloth from his shoulder and diffuses the situation. "Okay, everyone. It's time to adjourn to the Ink Well. Libby and I will join you soon."

"Thank you again," Brent says. "The meal was delicious."

"Yes, thank you," the others chime in.

"Niall, if you share your recipes," Jennifer says, "I'd love the one for the venison tenderloin. I've never had it wrapped in crispy bacon slices before. I think that's what keeps it so moist—that, and the creamy garlic sauce with mushroom and green onion."

"I agree," Lucy says. "It practically melted in my mouth."

"I'm glad you enjoyed it," Niall says. "I'm happy to share the recipe." Then, to his brother-in-law, he gives an unspoken but well-conveyed look.

Mick nods acknowledgment, then he and Emma shepherd the guests to the Ink Well.

When they're out of earshot, Niall turns to Libby. "Well, that was uncomfortable."

———

Brent, his appetite satisfied, surveys the Ink Well—a large, cozy room with floor-to-ceiling bookshelves on either side of a massive fieldstone fireplace. It serves as the after-dinner gathering place for guests to continue visiting over dessert while enjoying drinks from the MacCulloughs' bar.

A silver-framed photograph featuring a much younger Libby and Niall in wedding attire draws his attention. Their glowing faces bring to mind his own wedding day.

Brent rests his hands on the thighs of his paralyzed legs. *I'm fortunate that Ellen meant, "For better, for worse, for richer, for poorer, in sickness and in health, until death do us part." I wasn't in a wheelchair when we married, and now I am. And to add insult to injury, we're closer to the poorer end of the financial spectrum than ever.*

He glances at Adam, and his mood lightens. He has to press his lips together to stop a smile. *Lucy and Jennifer handed him his ass in a basket with his chauvinistic "man" comment. Being the only boy with four sisters, I learned long ago that it's not always about the male of the species. I wonder what Adam's story is—why is he so damn cocky? Of course, it could be a cover-up for being insecure.*

I know from experience that in the racing world, people sometimes try to hide the fact that they have certain insecurities by putting on an act, hoping that they and everyone else will believe it. I'll invite him to Austen cottage for a drink one evening and try to get to know him better.

Brent moves with ease between thoughtfully placed overstuffed chairs to an oak pedestal with an open book. After removing it from the stand, he sets it on his lap, then turns to Mick. "Is this the journal I read about online?"

Mick nods. "Yes, it is."

As Brent starts at the beginning and turns the pages slowly, Mick continues. "We encourage guests to make entries during their stay. We have entries dating from 1980, when my sister and brother-in-law opened the doors of Pines & Quill."

"Hold on a second," Brent says. "There's an entry dated *today*."

"Wow, that was fast," Mick says. "What does it say?"

Brent reads it out loud:

Some people see a magic trick and say, "Impossible!" They clap their hands, turn over their money, and forget about it ten minutes later. Other people ask how it worked. They go home, get into bed, toss and turn, wondering how it was done. It takes them a good night's sleep to forget all about it. And then there are the ones who stay awake, running through the trick again and again, looking for that skip in perception, the crack in the illusion that will explain how their eyes got duped; they're the kind who won't rest until they've mastered that little bit of mystery for themselves. I'm that kind.

Brent closes the journal thoughtfully and turns to Jennifer. "It's signed by Jennifer, who also wrote that the quote is from Leigh Bardugo's book, *Six of Crows*." *We all came into the Ink Well at the same time, right after dinner, so when did she write this?*

"And if I remember right," Jennifer says, "doesn't the Pines & Quill website also say that the journal has provided clues that have helped solve mysteries that happened here?"

"That's right. And Hemingway has, too," Mick says.

"Speak of the devil," Libby says, entering with one of her hands around the big dog's leather collar. She looks around the room. "Unless there's an objection, we typically let Hemingway join us for this part of the evening."

Brent taps his thigh. "Come here, fella. You're welcome to sit next to me."

"Thank you," Libby says, releasing Hemingway.

Hemingway pads over, his tail waving figure eights. After inspecting Brent's hands for goodies, he circles several times, then *harrumphs* onto the floor in a tight coil by Brent's footrest.

Brent swallows a sob in his throat and struggles to control his emotions. *Just last month, we had to put Blade down. We got him as a puppy fourteen years ago. The kids—Bradley and Kelly—had so much fun naming him. We knew it had to be something to do with racing, and Blade—a term race drivers use for a rear spoiler—stuck. A Cairn terrier, he was a great family dog and my closest companion when I was finally allowed to come home from the hospital after the wreck.*

Jennifer takes a seat in the chair near Brent. "It looks like you've got a friend for life."

Brent clears his throat. "I love dogs. Well, all animals really, And they seem to sense it."

"I wonder why dogs circle before lying down?" Lucy asks.

"My kids begged their mother and me for another dog, and before we said yes, we had them write a paper on their care and keeping. We figured if they'd be willing to write an essay, they'd probably be more likely to take responsibility.

"But I digress. It covered the circling topic. When they presented it to us, I learned that turning in circles before lying down is an act of self-preservation in that the dog may innately know that he needs to position himself in a certain way to ward off an attack in the wild. Some wildlife biologists believe that wolves sleep with their noses to the wind to pick up on a threatening scent quickly."

"Did they get a dog?" Emma asks.

"They sure did," Brent says. "They got a husky."

Emma leans forward. "Oh, I'm glad. What did they name it?"

Brent smiles. "Timber. When they call for him, it sounds like they're felling a tree."

"Now, *that's* clever," Emma says.

"On that note," Mick says, picking up a tablet and pen from an end table, "Emma and I are going to take drink orders."

Libby eases the group back to their previous conversation. "Brent, let's pick up where we left off. Please tell us the book you're currently reading, the author, and give us a one-paragraph summary."

"I'm reading *Racing the Devil*, by Charles Todd," Brent says. "It's a part of a mystery series, and in this installment, Scotland Yard's Ian Rutledge finds himself caught in a twisted web of vengeance, old grievances, and secrets that lead back to World War I."

Once they've all had a chance to share, Libby picks up a slender box. Holding it so everyone can see, she says, "This is called the Observation Deck. It was created by Naomi Epel as a tool for writers; it helps prime the writing pump." Libby removes the lid from the box, revealing a book and deck of cards. She walks over to Lucy and says, "Will you please start? The idea is that you draw a card from the deck and get a short assignment that helps jumpstart inspiration, writing, and storytelling."

"I'd love to," Lucy says. Her hand hovers over the deck before removing a card.

Brent leans forward. "What does it say?"

"It says, 'Create a Conflict.'"

"If the shoe fits," Adam says.

Brent gives him a "Don't start up again" look.

Adam holds up his hands. "Sorry."

Libby gives Lucy the book. "Now, use the table of contents to find 'Create a Conflict,' and then read it out loud for us."

After finding the spot, Lucy reads, "'It's a writer's job to stage conflict and confrontations so the characters will say surprising and revealing things,' says novelist Kurt Vonnegut. 'If a writer can't or won't do that, he should withdraw from the trade.'"

Talk about "conflict," Brent thinks. I love being here at Pines & Quill so much, but it's expensive, and we can't afford it. Then again, when I made the reservation and paid for it, we didn't know Ellen would lose her job—that completely blindsided us. I told her I would cancel, but Ellen insisted I come. She said, "A month of protected writing means this will be the best book yet in the Burnt Rubber *series."*

After Lucy reads the rest of the short passage, they discuss the suggested writing tips for creating conflict.

"Brent, tomorrow night it'll be your turn to draw a card," Libby says.

Oh, great. I hope I don't draw a card that opens me up to a verbal jab like Adam gave Lucy— "If the shoe fits." And I sure don't need any additional stress. I'm already under enough pressure to produce while I'm here— "It'll be the best book yet in the Burnt Rubber *series."*

Suddenly, Hemingway lifts his head from his paws, sticks his large wet nose in the air, and thumps his tail against the floor.

Brent smells it too. His maternal grandfather was a perfumer, and as his mother said, "My dad passed his 'sniffer' down to you." And like his grandpa, he was often referred to as "Nose" because of his fine sense of smell.

But you don't need a good sense of smell at a racetrack. You can be nose-blind and still smell the nitro that burns out of header pipes at over three hundred miles per hour and the burning smell of the tires when they strike the asphalt. That's why I named my book series Burnt Rubber.

Brent pats the arm of his wheelchair. *If I'd become a perfumer, I wouldn't be in this chair.*

Heads turn in unison when Niall enters the room carrying a large tray with plated dessert. "Can I interest anyone in a slice of Sticky Jamaican Ginger Cake with Butterscotch Sauce?"

Lucy rubs her hands together. "Bring it on."

"I'm going to have to jog in the morning," Brent jokes, taking a plate and fork from the proffered tray. Then he turns to Jennifer. "If I'm out of line, please say so, but I'd love to see another one of your magic tricks. I can't stop thinking about what you did with the wine bottles when we arrived. It blew me away."

Jennifer smiles. "Well—"

"She can't do tricks on such short notice," Adam says around a bite of cake. "She has to have time to prepare because magic is nothing but a gimmick."

Brent white knuckles his fork and imagines driving it into Adam's carotid artery. *That guy has a stick up his ass, and somebody needs to remove it.*

———————

Jennifer pins Adam to his chair with a glacial stare. *You can't hide under your beard and mustache from me. Why are you being a killjoy and trying to ruin things for everyone else?*

Adam can't hold her piercing gaze and turns away.

"I was going to say if Libby and Niall have a card table, a big bag of loose candy or nuts, and a large glass bowl, I'd love to do a bit of magic."

"I just bought a huge bag of M&M's," Niall says. "Will that work?"

"That's perfect," Jennifer says.

"Coming right up," Niall says.

"And I know right where the card table and punch bowl are," Libby says.

When Libby and Niall return with the items, Jennifer says, "I usually ask for a volunteer, but because Adam has doubts"— she turns and looks at him—"*you* can help me. That way, you can watch what I do up close. It's already obvious that this is spur of the moment and I haven't had the opportunity to prepare a *gimmick*, so we've eliminated that concern." Jennifer motions toward the candy, table, and bowl. "And none of the items we're about to use—we call them props in the industry—are mine."

"You're on," he says.

After Niall places the card table in front of Adam's seat, Brent moves closer, and the others lean in.

"We're going to start with something easy," Jennifer says. "But I need a penny and a nickel."

Adam digs in his pants pocket and pulls out his change. "I've got a penny, but no nickel." Mixed in with the coins is a small silver pocket cross.

Jennifer is surprised. *I sure as hell didn't expect that.*

"I've got a nickel," Mick says, handing it to Jennifer.

"Adam, I'd like you to hold out your hand, palm up." When he does, Jennifer places the nickel in his palm. "Now, make a fist and extend your arm over the table."

Adam follows her instructions.

"Turn your fist over so that your thumb is underneath." He complies with her request.

"For the sake of confirmation, which coin is in your fist?"

"The nickel."

Jennifer touches the edge of the penny to the back of Adam's closed fist and circles it three times before laying it flat on the back of his closed hand.

"Now, keeping your fist perfectly level, Adam, I want you to release the nickel."

Adam opens his fingers.

A penny drops onto the table, and a nickel rests on the back of his hand.

Gasps of astonishment fill the room.

Brent's eyes are wide. "That was amazing!"

Hemingway barks with enthusiasm as applause and a chorus of "Oh, my gosh!" "How did you do that?" and "Unbelievable!" fill the air.

Adam's eyebrows are nearly in his hairline. "How the *hell* did the coins trade places?"

"You tell me," Jennifer says. "You're the one who said, and I quote, 'Magic is nothing but a gimmick.'"

Adam leans back against his chair and crosses his arms. "Do another one. What are the candy and bowl for?"

"I'm glad you asked," Jennifer says. "I'd like you to open the bag of M&M's and pour them into the glass bowl."

After completing her request, Adam asks, "Now what?"

"Using one hand or two, sift your fingers through the bowl to establish that there's nothing but candy in there."

Adam sifts through the bowl several times. "It's clear."

"Are you sure?"

Adam nods. "Yes, I'm sure."

With her right hand, Jennifer gets a fist of candy and then turns her fist sideways like she'd hold the handle of a mug.

With her left hand, she scoops a few more pieces into the opening between her thumb and index finger on her right hand.

When it's full, she places her left hand, palm up, under her candy-filled fist.

Then she opens her fist, and a Rubik's Cube drops into her left palm. No chocolate.

Adam sits back with his mouth agape.

She hands the cube to Adam. "Please scramble all of the colors."

Adam takes the cube from Jennifer and then twists and turns it until the colors—white, red, blue, orange, green, and yellow—are thoroughly mixed. Then he hands it back to her.

Jennifer sets the cube on the table, then tents her hands over it and has Adam cover her hands with his, similarly. "In a moment, I'm going to slip my hands out from under yours. Please keep yours there."

Jennifer slips her hands out.

Now, only Adam's hands cover the cube.

Jennifer sifts her hands through the bowl of M&M's twice. Then, on the third time, a Rubik's Cube with scrambled colors appears in her hands.

"For the love of God!" Brent says.

She holds the cube for Adam's examination, then waves it back and forth in a figure-eight motion several times. When she brings it to a stop, all six sides are solved.

Everyone leans in closer. The air is thick with astonishment.

"Adam, please remove your hands from the cube, then place it in one of your palms."

When he does, his cube—the one he'd scrambled—is also completely solved.

When everyone starts to clap, Jennifer holds up a hand. "We're not quite done."

She leans forward and blows across Adam's palm, and the Rubik's Cube turns into M&M's again.

"Un-fucking-believable," he says with admiration in his voice. "I've got to hand it to you."

Oh no, you don't. You're not getting off that easy. "Let's do one more," Jennifer says. She steps toward Emma. "Please make two fists and then place your wrists together."

Once done, Jennifer says, "Now, extend your arms in front of you and open your hands, palms up."

Emma's eyes widen with disbelief. There's a piece of red silk in her hands. She picks it up by a corner so everyone can see that it's about twelve inches square.

Jennifer has Emma give the silk to Brent.

"Please tuck it into your shirt pocket," Jennifer says.

Once it's no longer visible, she asks Brent to remove it. When he pulls it from his pocket, it's double in length. One square is red, the other one yellow.

"How on earth?" he asks, shaking his head.

Jennifer takes the silk and hands it to Adam. "Please tuck it into your shirt pocket."

Once it's no longer visible, she asks him to remove it. When he does, it's rolled in a cylindrical shape.

"Adam, please place it on the card table and unfurl it." *What I wouldn't give for a drumroll.*

Adam nods. When it's open, there, in all its glory, is the fork he'd secretly taken from the side of Mick's plate during dinner.

"Well, I'll be darned," Niall says, bewilderment lacing his voice. "That's one of ours. How'd you get it in here all the way from the kitchen?"

Jennifer looks at Adam. Keeping her tone sweet, she says, "It's magic." But her eyes say, *Don't fuck with me.*

CHAPTER 6

*"The four words of power. Obey, Kill, Protect, and
Die. Words so primal, so dangerous, so powerful
that they commanded the raw magic itself."*
—ILONA ANDREWS

Adam heads from the main house to Thoreau cottage
under a crescent moon surrounded by hundreds of
shimmering stars.

His cell phone rings, alerting him to a video call from
"Unknown."

An orchestra of startled crickets becomes instantly silent.

Remembering the last call from "Unknown," Adam's
stomach clutches up to his throat. He stops walking. The
display informs him that it's midnight. Barely trusting themself
to speak, he whispers, "Hello."

There's no face on the display. Instead, there's an enormous
fish tank in the foreground.

"People who obey my orders are rewarded. If you continue to do as I say, I won't kill your daughter."

"May I—"

"Did I say you could speak?"

Adam remains silent.

"That's better. Now, let's get down to business." An arm enters the screen; the hand is white-gloved. A suit-coat sleeve eases back, revealing a Rolex watch.

"The purpose of this call is twofold. First, to remind you that the clock is ticking."

His watch face shows midnight, so the guy's calling from the same time zone as Pines & Quill—Pacific Time.

"Second, to assure you that I mean what I say, and I say what I mean. Answer the next call."

The phone disconnects.

An owl's low-pitched hoot sends a shiver down Adam's spine.

Moments later, he receives another video call. The display is almost black when he answers, but then a soft light illuminates the *Houston Chronicle*, from the city where his daughter, Brittany, attends Rice University. It has today's date and headlines.

Adam's heart bangs against his chest. He breaks into a cold sweat.

"You know where I am," a man's voice says. "This isn't a bluff."

The camera pans to the left and zooms in.

A person is sleeping, face up, in a bed.

Oh, my God. That's Brittany. That man's in her dorm room!

"I'll do anything—*anything*—to protect my daughter."

"That's good," the off-screen voice says. "Otherwise, she'll die."

The call disconnects.

The scream of a small creature pierces the air. *The owl caught its dinner.*

Tight-lipped with resolve, Adam clenches his fists.

As Adam slips into Thoreau cottage, he checks the time on his phone. *A quarter past midnight.* Sick over what he has to do, he knows that sleep won't come easy, but on the off chance he gets some, he sets the alarm on his cell before getting into bed.

I can't believe Libby was serious when she said she'd meet us in the pavilion at six o'clock for a tai chi session to prime the day's writing pump.

He crosses his arms over his chest and stares at the ceiling. *I'm running out of time. I have to decide which writer to kill. And frame Mick for their death. The only question is, who?*

Lucy's a former Olympian and current Ironman competitor and champion. Her muscles rippled when she was going to pulverize that guy at the airport who tried to steal her bicycle suitcase. And though I'm in decent shape, she can probably beat the shit out of me.

Jennifer's a world-renowned magician. She stopped the bike thief from escaping by conjuring a smoke cloud. And the magic she did tonight was incredible. Adam relives the embarrassing moment when Jennifer had him unroll a piece of silk fabric at the dinner table only to reveal the fork he'd swiped from the side of Mick's plate. *Busted! I should choose her to kill for doing that, but who knows what other tricks she has up her sleeve?*

Brent's a former NASCAR driver. He's in a wheelchair after a tragic racing accident. He's paralyzed from the waist down, and one of his arms and hands is prosthetic, so it's not like he can run away or overpower me.

Mick presses the stem on his watch to illuminate the time. *Five o'clock.*

He rolls over in the warm bed in the main bedroom of their cabin and kisses Emma on her forehead. "I told Libby I'd light the patio heaters in the tai chi pavilion this morning."

"I'll be there a little before six," Emma mumbles before rolling onto her side and falling back to sleep.

After dressing, Mick slips out the front door. The crisp air is as still as held breath, absolutely without motion. It raises goose bumps on his arms.

A distant foghorn sounds its deep, reverberating hum.

Mick's breath rises in front of him as he walks toward the pavilion. It reminds him of the prior month when he, Joe, and Rafferty staked out the cabin on Mount Baker where Emma, Joe's two daughters, and several other women were held captive by Gambino's thugs as they prepared to traffic them to a Russian buyer.

Damn, that was a close call. Mick clenches his fists.

A small creature scuttles in the thick foliage off the pathway.

Reaching the tai chi pavilion, Mick slips his shoes off next to the entrance ramp and stairs that are situated next to each other. Then barefoot, he crosses the smooth wood floor and flips a switch that turns on the overhead light in the center of the open-beam ceiling. Flipping another switch illuminates a strand of white lights around the roof's perimeter.

He takes a long fireplace lighter from the cabinet and lights tall propane patio heaters, one on each side of the open structure, and then, relishing his alone time, he limbers his body while he waits for the others.

Lost in deep stretches, Mick lets his mind wander. *Last night during dinner, the tension between Adam, Lucy, and Jennifer hung in the air like a cold fog. And how and when did Jennifer have the opportunity to write in the journal in the Ink Well?*

Thinking about her entry brings to mind another one. Libby found it last month just before Gambino's foot soldiers breached their property: "I warned you. My people can infiltrate even the most inaccessible places to do my bidding. When you least expect it, expect it—The Bull."

*And though my family's safe right now, I know that
Gambino's not done with us, not by a long shot.*

––––––––––

Lucy rolls over, reaches out a hand, and stops the alarm on her
cell phone. No stranger to rising early for training, she checks
the time. *Five thirty. It feels later than that.*

She rolls onto her back, squeezes her eyes shut, and
recalls where she is. *Pines & Quill is in Washington State.
That's a two-hour time difference from Chicago. At home,
it's seven thirty.*

Lucy opens her eyes and stares at the dark ceiling. *When
I left the main house last night, someone was on the pathway ahead of me. Just after they veered off, they must have
gotten a call because whatever they held in their hand lit up
their face—a cell phone. But I couldn't determine who it was
because of the thin light and tree branches shrouding them.*

She turns onto her side. *I can rule out Brent because he's
in a wheelchair, and I would have at least been able to tell
that much. So that leaves Adam, Jennifer, Niall, Libby, Mick,
or Emma. Okay, now you're just making excuses to lay here.*

In her mind, Lucy hears her coach's voice. "There's no
excuse for champions." She groans, pulls the covers back, and
rolls out of bed. *There's no point in showering because, after
tai chi, I'll grab my bike, hit the road, and get in an hour or
so before I write.*

She slips into her sweatpants and shirt. *Phone calls in the
middle of the night are never good news. I wonder what was
so important, or so bad, that it couldn't wait until morning?*

––––––––––

Jennifer enjoys the brisk walk to the tai chi pavilion. Through
the white puff of her breath, she sees that Libby, Emma, Mick,
and Brent are already there.

She removes her shoes and adds them to the neat row of other shoes by the entrance ramp and stairs. *Seeing them lined up reminds me of a trick where I disappeared a pair of shoes from the feet of a front-row audience member in my Vegas act, and they reappeared on my assistant's feet on stage.*

Jennifer smiles. *Making things appear and disappear is what I do best.*

Adam presses the snooze button a third time. He's exhausted from killing people.

In his twisted dreams, he strangled Lucy with a bicycle inner tube on the side of a busy road while motorists honked their horns and waved enthusiastically. He sawed Jennifer in half on stage in front of an audience who clapped their approval as he stood in a pool of blood. And after disabling the braking system on Brent's wheelchair, he shoved him over a sheer cliff into Bellingham Bay while the other writers in residence stood by cheering him on.

Bone-weary, Adam rolls out of bed. *The idea of early morning tai chi doesn't entice me, not one little bit.*

He doesn't brush his teeth. *No one should get close to someone who hasn't had coffee yet. It'll serve them right if they do.*

He walks out the door of Austen cottage and stops short. *Oh, for fuck's sake, it's still dark!*

When he nears the tai chi pavilion, he hangs back. Then, not wanting to give himself away, he crouches behind bushes and peeks through the thick foliage.

The raised pavilion has a pagoda-style copper roof, patinated with age, with corners flaring over Chinese-red supports. Its design is distinctly Asian. String lights around the roof's perimeter add to the glow from the main light in the center of the ceiling. Patio heaters spaced evenly on each side of the open-air structure provide warmth in the chilly morning air.

Adam watches several people moving inside the space. With her back to them, Libby is at the front of the group in loose-fitting, pale blue pants and a matching jacket. She moves through the tai chi forms with graceful energy.

The others—Brent in his wheelchair, Jennifer, Lucy, and Emma—imitate her lithe movements, Brent from the waist up. In the back of the group, Mick wears garb similar to Libby's, except black.

Adam's stomach churns at the thought of what he has to do, at the horrific images that kept him awake all night.

He shakes his head. *I can't do it; I just can't do it.*

Then the image of his daughter's peaceful face asleep in her dorm room fills his mind.

Adam clenches his fists and sets his resolve.

Next to the steps and ramped entrance, a line of shoes catches Adam's attention.

He looks back at the group and sees that, except for Brent, they're all barefoot on the smooth wood floor.

Adam glances over each shoulder. *Niall and Hemingway must be at the main house. Niall's probably making breakfast. He said he would deliver it to our doors after this morning's tai chi session.*

He rubs his throbbing forehead. *That giant dog could be a problem. I might have to kill him too.*

In his mind, he hears the instruction he received on the phone. "Kill another writer and make it appear as if Sean McPherson did it—frame him for the death. It's your job to ensure that he has a motive, opportunity, and means. And that there's enough of his DNA at the scene to arrest and convict him. Everyone, especially the police, must believe that he's guilty. If you fail, your child dies."

Adam swallows a combination of fear and bile that rises in the back of his throat.

———

In the warm kitchen of the main house, Niall pours vanilla glaze over the warm pumpkin spice pull-apart bread—one of his favorite autumn breakfast recipes and always a hit with their guests. *It's easy to pack in glass containers with airtight lids and deliver to the cottages in insulated totes. And I've been told it stays warm for a long time.* He smiles. *Not that I'd know from personal experience. We gobble ours up.*

As he gathers items, he remembers the tension that Adam's chauvinistic comment created at dinner last night. *Fortunately, his "gimmick" comment—which started as a challenge before Jennifer's impromptu magic show—turned out well. She blew everyone away, including Adam, with her impeccable performance.*

With his arms full, Niall and Hemingway walk to the garage to get the ATV. It makes the deliveries fast and easy.

He looks at his four-legged companion. "And *you*, you big lummox, never turn down a chance to ride shotgun."

Hemingway barks in agreement before bolting toward the garage.

It's true that with their muscular hindquarters built for speed, Irish wolfhounds don't run; they gallop.

After depositing everything in the open back of the vehicle, Niall checks his watch and tells Hemingway, "Perfect timing, Boyo. It's just after seven. They should be done with tai chi by now."

Niall turns his gaze and looks above the treetops on the east side of the property. He knows the sun has started its ascent because of the uplight. And even though it's October, the sky is the oyster-shell white it gets in July. *That can only mean one thing—rain's on the way.*

They pull out of the garage and head toward Brontë cottage to deliver Jennifer's breakfast.

Hemingway whips his tail when they see Mick, Emma, and Libby on the path up ahead.

I swear he's smiling under those whiskers.

Pulling alongside them, Niall looks at Mick's bare feet. "I always knew you loved nature, but isn't that going a bit far?"

"I started out with shoes this morning," Mick says, scratching Hemingway under his proffered chin, "but they disappeared."

"What do you mean, *disappeared?*"

"Before tai chi, I toed them off by the stairs and set them next to everyone else's. After the session, they were gone."

"And we looked around the entire area," Emma says.

"Anyone else's shoes missing?" Niall asks.

"No, just mine," Mick says.

"Were *all* of our guests there this morning?"

"Everyone except Adam," Libby says. "He must have slept in."

"He was the first person to leave the main house last night," Niall says. "He said it's rare anymore that he stays up that late."

"Hemingway probably took them," Mick says, scratching behind one of the huge dog's disproportionately small ears. He presses his forehead to Hemingway's. "He's always up to some type of shenanigans. Aren't ya, Boy?"

"No," Niall says. "He was with me the whole time making pumpkin spice pull-apart bread."

Emma's eyes widen as she places a hand on her baby bump. "That's one of my favorites."

"I know it is," Niall says. "I was going to drop some off at the cabin for you two."

Mick rubs his hands together. "Thank you. We'll take it with us and save you a trip." He looks in the back. "Which one's ours?"

"The big one because there's two of you."

"Make that three," Emma says, laughing. "I could eat it all."

"Will we see you guys for lunch?" Niall asks.

"No, I've got a skip trace today."

Niall furrows his brows. "What's that?"

"It's when you track someone down who's particularly hard to find," Mick says.

"Isn't that what a bounty hunter does?" Niall asks.

"Skip tracing is a distinct procedure," Mick says. "And while it's sometimes used in conjunction with bounty hunting, the two activities aren't the same. Bounty hunters can work as skip tracers, but skip tracers can't work as bounty hunters."

"Who are you tracking down?"

"In this case, it's a member of the Sureños gang. He's a person of interest in a homicide case who skipped bail. Joe's been on light duty since he was shot last month, so Chief Simms asked if I'd help Joe out." Mick turns to Emma. "Honey, are you having lunch at the main house?"

"No, I'm working on a piece of pottery I promised for a customer." She turns to Niall. "But we'll see you for dinner if that's okay?"

"It's perfect," Niall says.

As the parents-to-be walk hand-in-hand toward their cabin, Libby turns to her husband. "Can I make the deliveries with you two handsome guys?"

Niall looks at Hemingway and throws his thumb over his shoulder. "Time to scoot your buns into the backseat, Big Fella."

Once Hemingway is seated on the back bench seat, Niall pats the seat next to him. "Hop in, Love, we're glad for your company. Besides that, I want to run something past you."

Mick sits across from Emma at their dining table. *I don't believe for a minute that Hemingway took my shoes. Not that he wouldn't—he has. But every time he does, he brings them to me in hopes of a "finder's fee"—a reward.*

He watches Emma lick sticky vanilla glaze from one of her thumbs. *It's true that pregnant women glow.*

She looks into his eyes. "Please be extremely careful today. You're going after a Sureños *gang* member who's a person of interest in a *homicide*. I don't want to be a widow, Mick. I don't want to be a single parent."

Mick scoots his chair back and holds up a finger. "Excuse me for just a minute."

Walking down the hall to the main bedroom, Mick remembers when Sam, his partner and best friend, was killed on the job and was gone from his life. Mick still feels responsible. *No matter how much regret I pour into that single moment, it never changes the outcome. Still, if the day's coin flip had come up tails, I would have been the one driving our cruiser. Not Sam. I would have been killed. Not Sam.*

A few minutes later, Mick returns to the dining room. He's added shoes and a denim jacket to his wardrobe. "I don't want you to be a widow or single parent either."

He opens the jacket revealing his Glock 22 in a leather cross-draw shoulder holster.

Then he lifts the cuff on a pant leg and shows Emma his ankle carry—a Sig Sauer P938.

Mick reaches across the table and places a warm hand over Emma's. "I promise to take every precaution I possibly can, Mrs. McPherson. I love being your husband, and I'm excited to be a dad."

"Thank you, Mick."

Mick shrugs off his jacket, places it on the back of his chair, and sits back down. "Now that we've got that taken care of, is there anything else that's worrying you?"

"It's not a worry, but a request," Emma says.

"What is it?"

"I talked with Marci on the phone," Emma says. "She said she can tell that Joe's getting better because he's cranky as sin."

Mick laughs. "Joe doesn't like being still."

"Let's talk with Libby and Niall about inviting Joe, Marci, their girls, and Rafferty and Ivy to the magic show that Jennifer's going to do." Emma takes another bite of the pull-apart bread. "And your mom too. Maeve would love it."

"Not only are you beautiful," Mick says, "you're brilliant. I'll check with Libby first and then Jennifer to make sure it's okay with both of them. And if it is, we'll set it up. I'm glad we have the new addition over the workshop. That way everyone can stay the night."

"Another thing," Emma says. "I can't overlook the fact that your shoes are missing."

Mick nods. "I agree that it's strange. I can't imagine why anyone would take another person's shoes. The next obvious possibility is Hemingway. But Niall said he was in the kitchen with him. So that leaves . . ."

"My point exactly," Emma says. "There's no explanation. Which is precisely what I'm having a problem with. Your shoes didn't grow legs and walk off by themselves. Someone took them. And I want to know who and why."

Mick squeezes Emma's hand. "When Libby was pregnant with Ian, I learned from Niall to never disagree with a pregnant woman."

"He's a smart man," Emma says. "So we won't let it go? We'll try to figure it out?"

"This afternoon, when I'm done with the skip trace," Mick says, "and you're done with the pottery piece, we'll set about searching for the shoes. And we'll take Hemingway with us. He'll probably lead us right to them." Mick stands up, leans across the table, and kisses the vanilla glaze from Emma's lips. "I promise that in addition to the skip trace, I'll do my best to solve the case of the missing shoes."

I'm not about to worry Emma with my suspicions, but my gut says something's going on, and Dad always said, "Trust your gut, son. Always trust your gut."

His heart racing, Adam sits in a chair holding a pair of shoes in Thoreau cottage in front of a south-facing wall constructed entirely of glass. It frames a breathtaking view of the Bellingham Bay National Park and Reserve, home to El Cañón del Diablo — the Devil's Canyon.

If someone blew on me, I'd splinter into a broken heap on the floor.

CHAPTER 7

"Writing a novel is like driving a car at night.
You can only see as far as your headlights, but
you can make the whole trip that way."
—E. L. Doctorow

The clouds looming behind Whatcom County's slumbering giant, Mount Baker, emerge as black storm clouds, spawning a wall of darkness ahead of Lucy. It mirrors her mood—angry.

She uses the back of her right hand to swipe raindrops from her eyes, then returns her grip to the handlebar. The road's vibrations irritate her despite the silicone pads in her bike gloves.

After tai chi this morning, I shouldn't have checked my phone for text messages.

In her mind's eye, she rereads the text from Rick, her husband:

You shouldn't have gone. We're shorthanded in the shop. It's one thing for you to go places to compete because there are potential sponsorship funds. It's a whole different thing to go to a writing retreat that costs a lot of money. You better get a hefty advance on the manuscript you're working on.

The tar-like smell of wet asphalt assaults Lucy's nostrils as she high-force pedals along Chuckanut Drive, a popular scenic road in Bellingham. Her calves burn, and her quads scream—they feel like they're clamped in a vise.

Tires from a too-close passing car hit a rain-filled rut that cascades water and road crud over her, temporarily blinding her. She wipes her eyes again.

Anger at her husband and the driver combine. Fury stokes her momentum. She gains speed and catches the car ahead of her as they approach a sharp bend in the road. Lucy pulls on the brakes a few times, preparing to corner. Her front wheel comes within a foot or two of the car's bumper. Her eyes meet the driver's in the rearview mirror before he accelerates out of the turn. She dances on the pedals to do the same as the gap between them grows, and the car disappears around the next curve.

Last night in the Ink Well, Mick told me that this bend, about ten miles south of Bellingham on Chuckanut Drive, is one of the rare spots on this road where bikes, for a brief moment, are faster than cars. "It's a one-hundred-and-eighty-degree blind turn at the bottom of a hill where the road narrows. A sign before it indicates a sharp corner and suggests fifteen miles per hour."

As soon as Lucy realizes she's doing twice that, she slows down and loosens her death grip on the bars. With a short-lived straightaway ahead, she thrusts her chest forward, tilts her head back, and closes her eyes. *The rain feels good on my face, arms, and legs.* Then, taking a deep breath through her nose, she opens her eyes and lets it out. Some of the anger flows away with it.

She remembers a few years ago when she talked with her mom about being unhappy in her marriage to Rick. Her mom's advice had been: "Stay married for the sake of the children. Your father and I did, and it eventually turned out."

Lucy shakes her head. *Yeah, Mom, but I don't know if I can take it that long. I don't wish I was dead—nothing like that—but I wish I could disappear.*

Rain streaks the Jeep's windshield muddling Mick's view as he drives. *I'm worried about Joe Bingham. He was shot in the right shoulder last month when we—Joe, Rafferty, and I—rescued Emma and Joe's two daughters from Gambino's thugs in a cabin on Mount Baker.*

Mick taps his fingers on the steering wheel. *The kicker is that Joe's right-handed, and the doctors don't yet know if the bullet caused any permanent damage to his ability to shoot—a requirement for a homicide detective. Aside from Joe's wife and daughters, his job is his life. To be removed from law enforcement would kill him—like it almost did to me.*

Mick turns on the defroster, and a pleasant earthy scent fills the air. His mind keeps time with the swipe of the windshield wipers as he puts himself in Joe's place, knowing full well about the painful recovery period, physical therapy, and most of all, the boredom. *And Joe's even worse at sitting still than I am. I bet he's going stir-crazy. Besides his 1980 Chevy Camaro, which he can't work on right now, he doesn't have any hobbies.*

I would have lost my mind if one of the doctors on my team hadn't suggested that I take up whittling. He smiles to himself. *What started as a pastime turned into carving that evolved into a small side business called Bespoke Wood: Handmade—Lovingly Crafted—Unique. I'm glad that Current & Furbish, in the heart of Historic Fairhaven Village, and Hyde & Seek Gift Shop, in Bellingham, feature my pieces alongside other artwork made by local artists.*

He catches his reflection in the rearview and grins. *After all, I'll be a dad soon and need to save for my daughter's college tuition.*

As Mick wraps his head around an idea, he clicks the directional lever, changes lanes, and turns right at the next intersection. *Joe can work the skip trace with me. But Marci and Chief Simms can't know, or they'll stop us, saying that Joe's not recuperated yet.*

A few minutes later, he pulls the Jeep into Joe's driveway, parks, and steps out into the rain. *I'll tell Marci that I'm going to borrow Joe for a little while and pick his brain about a case. She'll be okay with that.*

Mick runs to the porch and presses the doorbell, shaking off drops of water as he waits.

Joe opens the door like a man grabbing a lifeline. "I thought I saw your Jeep pull into the drive." He pulls Mick into the house. "Come in where it's dry. What's up?"

"Emma told me that when she spoke with Marci on the phone, she said that you're not a good patient and that you're going stir crazy. Any truth to that?"

"I'm the epitome of a good patient. But I *am* going to lose my mind if I don't get back in the saddle soon."

Marci wipes her hands on a dishtowel as she joins them in the foyer. "Saddle? You're not thinking about going horseback riding, are you?"

Mick shakes his head. "Not today, but I'd like to borrow him for a couple of hours if that's okay."

"I'll get my jacket." Joe makes a beeline down the hall toward the main bedroom.

Marci furrows her brows. "But your jacket's in the coat closet."

"I'm getting a different one," Joe calls over his shoulder before disappearing through a doorway.

"The other reason I'm here, Marci," Mick says, taking her elbow and guiding her toward the kitchen to keep her mind off her husband, "is to invite you, Joe, and the girls to Pines & Quill for the weekend. One of the writers in residence is Jennifer Pruett; she — "

Marci grabs his arm. "As in *the* Jennifer Pruett?" Her eyebrows skyrocket. "The famous magician?"

Mick nods. "The same." He snags a chocolate chip cookie from a cooling rack on the counter and points it at Marci for emphasis before taking a bite. "She's going to give a private show this weekend. Libby said the whole family is welcome to come after the girls finish school on Friday, and then plan to stay through the weekend."

Warm chocolate dances on Mick's tastebuds.

A brilliant smile lights Marci's face.

Mick mentally congratulates himself. *Joe could have fallen in the well for all she knows. I successfully redirected her focus to Jennifer Pruett's up-and-coming private magic show.*

Mick takes another bite of the cookie and talks around it. "On the drive over, I called Rafferty. He said that he, Ivy, and Maggie would love to get out of the city for the weekend. Then I called Emma and told her they accepted. She's excited and said the only thing that could make it even better is if the Bingham family can make it too."

Marci flips the dishtowel onto her shoulder. She nods while she listens to Mick as he guides her back to the entryway.

"They'll head up to Bellingham right after school gets out on Friday. And my mom's coming too."

"But with this month's writers in residence, do you still have enough room for all of us?"

"You bet. Remember? You guys camped out in the new addition over the workshop before it was done. Now that it's finished, you and Joe will stay in one room, Rafferty and Ivy in another, and the girls will each have their own. Mom called dibs on the guest room in the main house."

Marci stands on tiptoes and pecks Mick on the cheek. "We'd love to!"

"We'd love to what?" Joe asks, joining them.

Marci's eyes are effervescent. "We've been invited to Pines & Quill for the weekend, and guess why?"

"I give up. Why?"

"One of their guests is Jennifer Pruett. *The* Jennifer Pruett, the famous magician. We've seen her on *television*. She's doing a private show, and *we* get to be in the audience."

Joe kisses the top of his excited wife's nose. "That'll be fun."

"I'm going to go call my sisters." Marci practically bounces through the living room toward the kitchen. "They're going to be *so* jealous!"

Mick talks to her retreating back. "Will you call Emma while you're at it and tell her you guys are coming? It'll make her day."

"I'm on it." Marci disappears into the kitchen.

Joe leans in. "Let's get out of here quick before she forgets I'm an 'invalid' and makes me stay."

They pull the front door shut behind them and momentarily stand under the gable roof. Rain gushes through the downspout connected to a long drainage pipe that diverts it from the house's foundation.

The sky is an ominous blue-gray.

The branches on the oak tree in the front yard droop with rain.

Joe nods at the slight bulge in Mick's jacket where his shoulder holster is. "When you arrived, I saw that you came prepared."

Mick raises a hand, aims his keys at the Jeep, and fobs the door locks open. "I could say the same about you." He juts his chin toward Joe's waist.

"That's why I didn't grab a coat from the closet. I saw that you're packin' and got my gun from the safe in our closet and then covered it with this." Joe pats his jacket. "I hope to hell we're heading somewhere to work a case. I'm desperate."

Mick nods. "We are. I'll tell you about it on the way. You up for a run?"

"Damn straight."

The men dash for the Jeep.

After they click their seatbelts, Mick checks the surrounding area, then backs out of the drive. "Chief Simms asked for my help with a skip trace on one of your homicide cases."

"Which one?"

"A person of interest in the Henderson murder case jumped bail on a different case and has disappeared off the radar."

Joe glances at Mick. "That would be Rico Canchola, a member of the Sureños gang."

"You got it." Mick pulls to the curb down the street. Leaving the engine running, he turns to Joe. "You've got to agree to two things before we start."

"Anything."

"Chief Simms doesn't know I enlisted your help."

Joe nods, "My lips are sealed."

Heavy drops splatter the windshield like pebbles. Mick turns the wipers on high.

"And you can't die on my watch." *Like Sam did five years ago.*

Joe holds up two fingers in Boy Scout fashion. "I promise."

"Because then I'd have to face Marci, and we both know she'd kill me."

Brent pulls on a slicker and pulls the hood up before heading out of Austen cottage. He came to Pines & Quill prepared. After he made his reservations, he researched the area and read that Washington State has three types of weather: It's about to rain. It's raining. It just finished raining.

The wheels of his chair hiss as rubber speeds over the smooth, wet pathway in the unrelenting rain. The weather app on his cell phone displays a crisp fifty-two degrees. Brent inhales the sharp, pungent scent of the rain-soaked earth and surrounding foliage.

On his way to Brontë cottage, he thinks, *I hope I don't make a fool of myself, but I want to offer my assistance to Jennifer for the big magic show she's going to do.*

When he called his wife, Ellen, to run it past her, she encouraged him. "Go for it, Brent. It's a once-in-a-lifetime opportunity."

Bolstered by her optimism, Brent continues on the pathway between the back of the main house and Niall's garden. As he clears the house, something in his peripheral vision catches his attention.

He looks north. The workshop is about fifty yards away. One set of sliding barn-style doors is wide open.

Inside the building, Emma sits at her potter's wheel with Hemingway sprawled on the floor—*Stretched out like that, he must be eight feet long.*

Libby steps into view from the right. A basket is cocked on her hip.

The women throw their heads back, and laughter ripples through the air.

Hold on a sec.

Unmistakable with his reddish-brown beard and mustache, Adam walks toward the front of the workshop along the covered left side of the building.

Suddenly his body language changes.

What the hell?

Adam eases forward. His shoes squish water with each step, leaving a trail of wet prints behind him. He flattens his back against the building and peeks into a window. *Libby, Emma, and Hemingway. Oh, shit! I hope that dog doesn't hear me.*

He crouches and ducks under the first window, then the second, and comes to a standstill at the corner of the building. He barely breathes as he listens.

"And it's going to be even more fun with Joe, Marci, the girls, Rafferty, Ivy, Maggie, and Mom," Libby says.

"How the heck did Jennifer do it?" Emma asks. "I mean, she had no time to prepare. Zero. Yet she blew us out of the water with her magic."

"I have no idea, but she's amazing. That's why she's considered world-renowned and does television appearances. And why her mystery novels are bestsellers. They include magic, illusion, and sleight of hand."

"I imagine that the people who see her shows turn into avid readers of her books," Emma says. "By the way, what are the sleeping arrangements for the extra guests?"

"Everyone will stay in the new addition except Mom. She'll sleep in our guest room."

"What can I help with?" Emma asks.

"Not a thing. You should see Niall. He shifted into overdrive now that we've more than doubled the guest list. He loves planning as much as he does cooking. That's why I've got a basket full of goodies from the garden."

"I'll come over this afternoon and help him prep," Emma says. "I love being his sous chef because I learn so much. I'm hoping he'll teach me how to make baby food. I read online that it's so much better than store-bought."

"Just ask him. He'll say yes. When Ian was a baby, he made all of his food and loved every minute of it."

Uncomfortable in the damp weather, Adam pulls the cuffs of his rain-soaked sleeves. He shivers as the fabric releases from his arms, and cold air slips in.

How on earth can I frame a pregnant woman's husband for murder? I can't, that's how. Last night during after-dinner drinks, I learned that Mick's a woodworker and does his carving in this workshop that he shares with Emma. I need to get in there, find a pair of gloves, and steal one of his knives or sharp tools. Then, when that psychopath calls me again, I can show him what I've got so far—Mick's shoes and a weapon with his fingerprints—to buy a little time while I think of a plan to save my family without killing anyone.

Adam hears what sounds like a chair scraping across the floor.

"I wanted to get your opinion on something," Libby says.

"Ask away."

"What do you think about having a costume party with the writers in residence this month? After all, it's Halloween."

"I think it's a great idea."

"When I bounced it off Niall, he pooh-poohed the idea because we didn't give anyone notice so they didn't have a chance to come prepared."

Just then, Adam lets loose an unexpected sneeze. Too late, he slaps a hand across his mouth to stifle it. *Damnit, Grandpa!* His mom told him he inherited his grandfather's sneeze. Back in the day, when there were party lines, his grandfather eavesdropped on people's phone conversations until his hellacious sneeze gave him away. "Get off the line, Henning," his neighbors would say.

Hemingway bolts around the corner. A ridge of raised hair like a Mohawk runs the length of his spine.

Holy shit! Adam holds the back of his hand out for Hemingway to sniff. "Hello, Hemingway. It's me, Adam."

The big dog wags his tail as he nudges Adam, herding him into the workshop.

"Look what the cat dragged in," Adam says. He feels blood rush to his cheeks. "I got turned around, and then I followed your voices."

Libby furrows her brows. "You're drenched. You must be a pluviophile."

Adam pulls back slightly and grimaces. "A *what?*"

"A pluviophile—a person who loves rain."

Adam regains his composure. "I like rain as much as the next guy, but I *don't* love getting caught in it and soaked to my skin. As a matter of fact, I'm heading to Thoreau cottage to change into dry clothes." He pauses. "But before I do, I think I heard you mention a costume party. Unfortunately, I didn't bring anything like that with me."

He shifts his gaze to the piece of pottery Emma's working on. As the wheel spins, she moistens her hands and shapes the clay. The continuous rotation is mesmerizing. It reminds him of teaching Brittany how to ride a bicycle, and the moment she gained enough momentum, he let go, and she made the wheels go round and round by herself.

His belly releases acid, curdling its contents in fear. *I can't let Brittany die!*

Emma looks up at Adam. "It doesn't have to be elaborate. You and the other three writers in residence can each bring a clue that alludes to a famous author, and the rest of us have to guess who it is."

Adam nods, "That sounds doable."

"And in the spirit of 'the more, the merrier,' a few close friends will be joining us this weekend." She turns to Libby. As Emma's voice gains enthusiasm, her potter's wheel spins faster. "And the rest of us will keep it simple too. For example, the guys can be what they are in real life."

"You mean Niall would come as a chef," Libby says, "Mick as a private investigator, Joe as a homicide detective, Rafferty as an FBI special agent . . ."

The rest of the conversation is lost on Adam as he homes in on what Libby just said—*a private investigator, homicide detective, and FBI special agent will be here at Pines & Quill.* The penny drops. *They could be the solution to my problem.*

CHAPTER 8

*"Write freely and as rapidly as possible and
throw the whole thing on paper. Never correct
or rewrite until the whole thing is down."*
—JOHN STEINBECK

Jennifer's stomach has been in knots since reading her
daughter's early-morning text. She hears the *ba-boom
ba-boom* of her heartbeat and feels the burn of tears. Unable
to hold them back, she lets them flow.

Elaine, a student at the University of Michigan, Ann
Arbor, wrote:

> I told Bill, my professor, that I'm pregnant with
> his child. Not only did he say we're through, he
> grabbed his briefcase and nearly ran out the door.
> Mom, what should I do?

Jennifer removes the teabag from a thick ceramic mug and holds it over the sink. Pinching the tag between a thumb and index finger, she studies the dripping bag as it dangles from the string. She circles her other hand in a widdershins motion beneath it, and it disappears. She nods in satisfaction. *As they say, practice makes perfect.*

Then, passing through the living room, Jennifer snags an afghan from the back of an overstuffed chair before going out to the front porch of Brontë cottage to think through everything weighing on her heart and mind.

And though it's stopped raining, it's gotten even chillier since I spoke with Brent. I'm glad he stopped by because I needed a break from worrying.

Before settling in one of the Adirondack chairs, she rotates her head and rubs the back of her neck to work out the kinks. *There, that's better.* Next, she takes a sip of hot ginger tea, hoping it will soothe her stomach.

I need to be careful not to take the helm of Elaine's life like my mom tried to do with me. It's her life, so it's her decision, one she has to live with for the rest of her life. I'm here to listen and offer support, not take over. I remember when my therapist first used the word "enmeshment" concerning my mom. She explained, "Your mom has difficulty allowing you to have your own life outside of her."

Jennifer shakes her head. *I never want to do that to my daughter.*

Needing a respite from that scenario and all it entails, she compartmentalizes her thoughts and mentally shifts gears to revisit her conversation with Brent. *He volunteered to be my assistant for the private magic show I'm doing Saturday.*

And whether it was intentional or not, he let slip that he saw Adam eavesdropping on Emma and Libby in the workshop. That confirms my suspicion that something's up with Adam. But what?

Jennifer takes another sip of tea, hoping it will loosen the tendrils of unease that squeeze her stomach.

———————

Adam lets himself into Niall's garden through the gate, pulling it closed behind him. He ducks behind what's left of tall sunflowers between him and the main house, hoping they'll conceal him from any watching eyes.

His heart thumps fast against his chest. It's that feeling you get in an emergency when you have to figure out what to do. *First, I have to find gloves so I don't leave fingerprints on the woodworking tool I'm going to steal from the workshop. Oh, God, please let a pair be on the potting bench I saw.*

A six-foot-tall, half-inch woven-wire fence surrounds the garden to keep intruders out. *Or pen me in!* Adam wipes his palms on his pants and swallows.

Answering a question about his garden last night at dinner, Niall said, "Deer and rabbits are the aboveground critters I worry about most. They can devour a garden overnight.

"As to the underground critters, I do my best to keep moles, voles, and gophers out with wire mesh that I installed vertically around the garden to a depth of thirty-six inches. I also use a combination of wind-spinners, cayenne, walnut leaves, and Neem oil."

Crouch-walking, Adam makes his way toward the potting bench. Identification stakes inform Adam that the garden is divided into three sections: roots, leaves, and other.

He carefully steps between the still-muddy rows of newly planted garlic, onions, shallots, carrots, turnips, beets, spinach, and kale before he reaches the bench. *Bingo!* A pair of gardening gloves nestles next to a roll of twine and pruning shears under a neat hanging row of tools: trowel, hand fork, and hand rake.

Adam shoves the gloves in his back pocket and untucks his shirt to cover them. And though it's chilly, he feels sweat trickle down his back. His heart races as he backtracks across the garden.

The bottom drops out of his stomach when he sees Hemingway waiting for him on the other side of the gate. Adam dry swallows.

The big dog stands on his hind feet and places his front paws on the top of the gate. He has a ratty tennis ball in his mouth.

"Hi, Fella." Adam scratches behind one of Hemingway's ears and then opens the gate. "Where are your parents?" He peers about. "Are they with you?"

Hemingway's body wags his delight at finding a friend to play with. He nudges Adam with his muzzle.

"You want me to throw the ball?" Adam takes the ball from Hemingway's mouth and heaves it toward the workshop. *That'll at least get me in the direction I need to go next and looks innocent enough if anyone sees us.*

Several heaves and fetches later, they arrive at the workshop. Both of the sliding barn-style doors are closed. Adam tries the handle on the pedestrian door. *Unlocked.* They enter—Adam with his heart in his throat, Hemingway with the ball in his mouth.

The upper windows on the barn-style doors provide enough light for Adam to find his way to Mick's workbench, where he eyes a selection of tools.

He pulls the gloves from his pocket and slips them on before choosing a wicked-sharp sloyd knife with a four-inch ridged blade that excels at removing wood quickly. *If push comes to shove, this'll work.*

He picks it up by the smooth oakwood handle, creates a makeshift sheath with a workshop rag, and eases it in one of his back pockets, the gloves back in the other.

"Come on, Hemingway. Let's go play some more." They leave the workshop.

The moment Adam pulls the door shut, he throws the ball, this time toward Thoreau cottage. Throw, fetch. Throw, fetch.

Wispy pewter-hued clouds dot the sky.

I'm glad it stopped raining. That was a nasty downpour earlier. Adam inhales the scent of pine and sweet wet earth.

When they pass Brontë cottage, Jennifer waves. "Hi, you two."

Hemingway bolts toward the friendly voice, vaults over the porch steps, and gives the beautiful woman his ball.

"Well, thank you," she says, scratching under Hemingway's chin before focusing on Adam's muddy shoes. "It looks like you two are having a good time."

Adam nods. "We've been playing fetch, and he's worn me out. So I'm heading to my cottage for a shower and a nap before dinner." He glances at the ball in her hands and then points south toward Thoreau. "Give it a toss, and we'll be on our way."

Jennifer stands and throws the ball.

Hemingway takes off like a shot.

"You've got a good arm," Adam says before jogging after the big dog. To himself, he said, *She's been crying. I wonder why?*

Mick and Joe track Rico Canchola to the waterfront near the Harris Avenue Shipyard cleanup site. Five acres of contaminated in-water marine sediment and five acres of contaminated upland soil and groundwater are a result of shipbuilding and other industrial operations in years past.

A six-foot chain-link fence surrounds the acreage. The drive-through entrance is padlocked, but someone, undeterred, used wire cutters on the linking to the left of the gate as a workaround.

Mick holds the fencing back while Joe eases through.

Joe reciprocates for Mick.

The men survey the area. Everything is weathered-gray or lackluster-brown except for a dozen overflowing green dumpsters near the docks.

"That's where the rancid smell is coming from," Mick says.

Squawking seagulls overhead take turns dive-bombing the contents.

"Yes," Joe says, "but they'll provide perfect cover for us."

Mick nods. "Let's go."

The men crouch run to the dumpsters. The ground—covered with seagull droppings—is slippery.

"This is a lot of area to cover," Joe says. "But the binoculars will help."

"We've narrowed it down to two possibilities," Mick says, gesturing toward a row of dilapidated warehouses. "He's either in one of those, or"—he juts his chin toward three sleek-looking boats, their lines wrapped around cleats on a dock—"he's on one of those."

"Warehouses first," Joe says. "They're in our jurisdiction."

Keeping to shadows, they work their way to the first building—two stories of rust-pocked steel. The first floor is windowless; the second floor has dark holes where windows had once been.

Mick points to the metal door. It's ajar about six inches.

Joe nods.

Both men draw their weapons and hug the wall on either side of the door.

Mick's heart hammers in his chest. *How recently was this opened? Are there people inside? How many? Should we have brought backup?*

He raises a hand and counts down with his fingers—three, two, one—then he toes the door open.

Mick enters first, his elbows locked, weapon out front.

Joe's on his heels, gun at the ready.

A sea of dank air and gray envelops them as light from the upper window holes reveals rows of steel I-beams supporting a roof that sags between steel trusses. Gleaming shards of window glass wink from the floor of the gutted building. A shiver races up Mick's spine.

He sweeps the abandoned space from left to right, Joe from right to left. Finally, they meet in the center of the building's eerie skeleton. *It's at least seventy feet wide and a hundred and fifty-feet long.*

They continue their inspection and discover that one of the corners is littered with a stained sleeping bag that reeks of urine, a hypodermic needle, a spoon, the stub of a candle, and a shoelace.

Both men whip their weapons around at a shuffle. A brown wharf rat, the size of a cat, scuttles into the shadows.

After clearing the first floor, Mick ascends the narrow metal stairs on one side of the building while Joe climbs the other.

Shafts of light from broken windows near the roof trap dust motes like flies in amber.

The center of the entire building is open to the ceiling.

Joe's side is loft-like, unobstructed except for a steel rail that runs the length of the building through the I-beams.

Mick's side is nothing more than a suspended catwalk. *This must have been the perch where management watched their workers, much like guards watch prisoners.*

Their steps echo as they walk the length of the long, empty building.

Just then, an ear-piercing roar blasts through the silence.

Mick and Joe race down the stairs to the door. With the benefit of the binoculars, they confirm Canchola's ID and location—a Skater 46 twin-turbine Hellfire powerboat tied to the dock. Two of the four men they can see—all wearing royal blue bandana headbands, the Sureños gang identifier—are casting off lines. The aft part of the sleek boat begins to drift from the dock.

Only three more cleats to go.

"Shit," Joe says.

The Skater 46, as touted by the company Skater, is truly the "Rolls Royce of powerboats." It's fitted with twin Teague Custom engines of 1,500 horsepower each giving a total of 3,000 horsepower. In addition, it features dual fuel tanks that hold a capacity of a thousand gallons and can easily cruise at more than a hundred miles per hour for long hours. And its hull is designed to cut through turbulent water.

"That beast," Mick says, pointing to the powerboat, "can accelerate up to one hundred and fifty-two knots."

Joe raises his eyebrows. "That's like one hundred and seventy-five miles per hour."

Mick nods.

"Well, it's in the water," Joe says. "So we have to call the Coast Guard. At least for backup."

They make their way and duck behind a dumpster over-flowing with rotting litter—fishing gear, debris from lobster traps, cigarettes, plastic bags, broken glass, fast-food bags and plastic foam containers, beer bottles, and soda cans.

Speculative bullets ping the dumpster, toppling garbage. A round pierces the metal, barely missing Mick's thigh. "They made us," he says.

Joe makes the call. After relaying the information, he's told, "Stand down. Don't show yourselves or compromise your location. We've got this."

"They already know our lo—"

A bullet whistles next to Joe's ear.

Both men round the dumpster's edge with their guns drawn—Mick left, Joe right.

A bandana-wearing man shoves a hooded person, hands bound behind their back, onto the deck.

"Joe, they've got a hostage. Cover me."

Adrenaline pumping through his body, Mick runs forward, zigzags, then rolls. He draws his knees up, steadies his Glock 22 between crossed ankles, and squeezes off a shot. One of the two men casting off lines hits the water—the other dives into the boat.

Bullets strafe the ground around Mick. Most of the Sureños shooting is spray and pray—the kind that can get you killed.

Mick dives into the water.

Joe dives in after him.

When they surface, Joe asks, "Where are you hit?"

"I'm not hit," Mick says. "I dove in because I wanted to keep it that way."

"Well, shit," Joe says. "We're going to stink."

Two Sureños men pull the floating member over the gunwale into the boat. As seagulls squawk the news overhead, the sound is temporarily drowned out by another rev of the Skater's engine.

As the last line's cast from the final cleat, a Coast Guard cutter comes into view.

"A cutter?" Mick sputters while treading water. "Unbelievable! Why the hell didn't they send something that can *move?* A Defender Class Boat can outrun and outmaneuver the Skater."

As Mick and Joe hoist themselves onto the dock, a massive glob of seagull poop—like full-scale human diarrhea—plasters Mick's shoulder.

Joe tries to stifle a laugh. "Getting pooped on by a seagull is supposedly good luck."

"Well, then I wish *you'd* been the lucky one."

"No, seriously," Joe says, "with countless birds in the sky and numerous people, getting pooped on by one is extremely unlikely. In fact, it's said to be even more unlikely than winning the lottery ticket, but the bird chose *you,* my friend." Joe points to Mick's left hip. "Hey, I thought you said you weren't hit."

Mick's eyes are on the boat. "I wasn't."

"Then why are you bleeding?"

Mick looks at the area where Joe's pointing—a red stain blossoms on his left hip.

"How bad is it?" Joe asks.

"It must be a graze," Mick says, unzipping his pants to check. The powerboat's engine booms like thunder.

Mick and Joe feel the reverberation and watch in stunned disbelief as Canchola's boat shoots into Bellingham Bay. It plays nip and tuck, taunting the unwieldy Coast Guard cutter before rocketing into the open water leaving a growing wake between them.

"Damn it!" Mick says. "If Canchola makes it past the shipping lanes, he's home free."

"It's the Coast Guard's problem now," Joe says. "Let's have a look at that wound."

As Mick slides his pants over his hip, he sucks air in through clenched teeth.

Joe shakes his head when he sees the four-inch-long gash. "Damn, that's got to hurt."

"Now that you mention it," Mick says, "it feels like someone's holding a red hot piece of metal against my hip and won't take it off."

Joe juts his chin at the filthy water where quakes from the Skater lap at the dock. "When was your last tetanus shot?"

Mick purses his lips in thought. "Five years ago when Sam and I had the accident."

"Let's get you to a hospital to see if you need any stitches and maybe a shot."

Mick eases his pants back up and nods. "All right. And Joe, do me a favor."

"What's that?"

"I was lucky that time. Remind me to never again complain when a seagull craps on me."

CHAPTER 9

"Never wait around for inspiration. It's your job to sit down in the chair and figure out what to write. There is no muse. There is no writer's block. There's only writing."
—NORA ROBERTS

Two hours, one tetanus shot, and a couple of hot cups of coffee later, Mick drives the Jeep past the massive Pines & Quill gate, drives up the long pine-shaded lane, pulls into the garage, then bolts for the back of his and Emma's cabin.

His anger rises to the surface. *I can't believe Canchola and his men got away. Jurisdiction be damned. Joe and I shouldn't have called the Coast Guard. "Stand down," they said. "We've got it," they said. And then Canchola and his men laughed as their powerboat left the cutter in its wake.*

I'm glad I texted Emma to let her know I'm running late and need to shower before I join everyone at the main house for dinner. I never want to cause her to worry, especially when she's pregnant. And she doesn't need to know, at least not right away, that a bullet grazed me.

Mick scans the area at the back door before stripping off his filthy clothes and shoes. *God, I reek!* Once naked, he lets himself inside and heads straight for the main bathroom, where he turns on the shower. After letting it run a minute, he steps under the hot spray.

He grits his teeth when the hot water hits the gauze dressing. The doctor had said, "When you take a shower, you can remove this dressing. Be sure to keep the wound clean. Then once your skin is dry, use the ointment I'm going to prescribe and redress it." After a few minutes, the pounding water begins to ease the tension in Mick's shoulders.

Joe and I tracked Rico Canchola to the Harris Avenue Shipyard cleanup site. He tips his head forward, closes his eyes, and rests his forehead on the shower wall tiles. *And then we lost him—and the hostage along with him. The glimpse I got was so brief I'm not even sure if it was a man or a woman. But if I had to guess, I'd say female.*

Mick wrinkles his nose at the lingering odor of decay. *Hemingway would have loved the waterfront cleanup site because it stunk of dead fish and rotten seaweed.*

After Mick shampoos his hair, he grabs the soap, lathers his body, and rinses off. He rotates his shoulders. The pounding hot water has eased the tension. He turns off the hot water, steps out of the shower, and looks into the steam-clouded mirror. *I don't know what Emma sees in me, but I'm glad for whatever it is.*

When he's dry, he dabs ointment on the searing red graze and then tapes gauze over it. After dressing in clean clothes, he heads to the main house.

Hemingway nearly topples him with an exuberant greeting when he enters through the mudroom door. "If you think

I smell good *now,*" Mick says, "you should have smelled me *before* I fell in the drink."

Hemingway's nostrils quiver. Then like a magnet, his big wet nose is drawn straight to Mick's left hip.

I don't know if the ointment, blood, or both got his attention. Mick scratches behind one of the big dog's ears and then leans in close. "I'm okay, Hem. I'll tell you all about it later."

Before heading to the dining area, Mick snags two biscuits from the big glass jar.

The bottom of the Dutch door between the mudroom and dining area is closed; the top is open. Most people prefer not to have a curious, tail-wagging, pony-sized dog in their midst while eating, so Hemingway is relegated to the mudroom. With only the bottom shut, he can pop his head over the half-door with his awning eyebrows and mop-like beard—and still be part of the gatherings without being directly among them.

Mick slips through the bottom half-door and closes it behind him before handing the treats to Hemingway over the ledge.

"Don't pout," Mick says, "you can join us after dinner."

Mick beelines for Emma. After kissing her, he turns to the guests. "Hi, everyone. I'm sorry I'm late."

It's been quite a day, but we survived. And for that, I'm incredibly grateful. He recalls Joe's remark about being pooped on by a bird. *Good luck, indeed.*

Mick glances at the faces around the table. *There's a much better vibe than there was last night. Let's hope it stays that way.*

———

"You're just in time," Niall says when Mick takes the empty seat next to Emma. "We've only had appetizers."

Mick groans. "Don't tell me I missed the antipasto kabobs. The ones with cheese tortellini, onion-stuffed green olives, black olives, pepperoni, and salami."

Niall nods. "Yep, those are the ones. But I packed a few skewers for you to take home."

Mick smiles. "That's why you're my *favorite* brother-in-law."

"I'm your *only* brother-in-law."

Brent, seated next to Adam, picks up the conversation Mick's arrival interrupted. His brows furrow. "But I *still* don't understand."

Adam uses silverware to explain. "When the work is done correctly," he says, picking up a fork, "the homes and buildings are a win-win for both the home flipper and the new buyer. Assuming the flipper sells the house at a higher price than they paid for it, they make money even after taking renovation expenses into account. Likewise, flipper homes allow new buyers," he says, picking up a spoon, "to get a bargain on a property where everything is new and fresh."

Talk around the table is animated as Niall and Libby head to the main kitchen area to get platters.

"Need any help?" Mick calls out.

"Thank you, but we've got it," Niall calls over his shoulder.

Delicious aromas—a combination of herbs, spices, and browned butter—precede the pair as they return, stopping all conversation except for a chorus of *oohs* and *aahs*.

Niall nods to Libby, "Ladies first."

With each bowl placement, Libby gives a description. "This is leafy garden salad tossed with Niall's homemade Dijon mustard vinaigrette. The majority of the salad is from Niall's garden. What he doesn't grow himself, he sources locally. And these," she sets another bowl on the table, "are grilled vegetables with a side of braised button mushrooms with garlic, parsley, and grated lemon peel."

Jennifer places her hands on her stomach and shakes her head. "There's not a magician on earth who can make those calories disappear."

Everyone laughs, and Libby continues. "Now that my hands are empty, I'll get the wine."

Niall places a large bowl on the table. The beguiling scents scream autumn. "Down here, we have cubed butternut and acorn squash glazed with butter and brown sugar. And this," he says, placing a huge platter and large bowl on the table, "is German beef roulade with homemade pickle slices, and a side of red cabbage sautéed with apple and onion."

"I think I died and went to heaven," Brent says.

"I'm right there with you," Lucy says.

"You offer liposuction with the residencies, right?" Adam teases.

Libby returns, holding two uncorked bottles by their necks in each hand. She hands two to Niall. As they pour wine into their guests' glasses, Niall says, "I paired this evening's meal with a wine from our neighbors to the north. The Canadian border is less than twenty-five miles from Bellingham, home to British Columbia, Canada's wine region.

"This lovely red," he says, holding up a bottle, "is Lightning Rock Pinot Noir from Elysia Vineyard in the Okanagan Valley. A ripe pinot, it has aromas of cherries and leather with a chalky graphite texture and some raspberry jam. Very earthy and brambly. It's perfect for October nights and autumn food."

Niall raises his glass, and everyone else raises theirs, too. "Here's to autumn, comfort food, and productive writing. Cheers!"

And in this month of Halloween, I hope you left your skeletons in your closets at home and didn't bring any ghosts or ghouls with you. We've already had enough scares to last a lifetime.

Mick's mind swings back and forth like a hypnotist's watch as he thinks through the day's events. Even though Niall's meal is exceptional, his stomach churns with anger.

I'm sitting here with family and friends, acting as if nothing terrible has happened. Pretending all's well with the world when Canchola and his men got away. With a hostage, no less.

Mick glances down at the table. *I have a delicious plate of food in front of me when who knows if the person Canchola took will ever get to have another meal.*

Regret joins anger in Mick's belly, curdling the food he's already eaten.

Emma squeezes his hand and leans into his shoulder. "Is everything okay?" she whispers.

I don't want to upset her. Mick's hand drifts to his left hip. *Or scare her.* He squeezes her hand in return and smiles. "Everything's fine."

Just then, Hemingway's wiry muzzle wedges between Mick and Emma.

"You stinker," Niall says, rising from his chair. "How did you get in here?"

Mick lays a palm on Hemingway's back. "Down."

Hemingway disappears from everyone's sight, but enthusiastic tail thumping is a dead giveaway that he's still in the thick of things.

Mick turns to his brother-in-law. "Niall, I must not have latched the door. If no one objects"—he looks at the faces around the table—"and Hemingway stays put, do you mind if he stays this once?" *I could use some dog love right now to help me calm down and think about how to stop a killing machine.*

———

Libby gazes around the dining table to gauge their guests' reaction to having Hemingway in the dining area. She stops at Mick and Emma, her brother and sister-in-law. *I was worried sick about him today. Tangling with a Sureños gang member has proven deadly, as any newscaster will tell you. Then when I saw Marci's name come up on caller ID and Mick still wasn't home, my mind jumped straight to the worst-case scenario with my heart on its heels.*

She remembers the relief that flooded her body when Marci said Mick dropped Joe off in one piece. Marci told her, "Had I known what they were going to do, I wouldn't have let Joe go. But, even though neither is worse for wear, something went wrong. The skip trace, Rico Canchola, skipped *again*. This time through the Coast Guard's fingers.

"Joe blames himself," Marci went on. "He's the one who said that because Canchola was on a boat in the water they had to follow protocol and call the Coast Guard for backup. But there wasn't any *backup* about it. They were told to stand down, that the Coast Guard would take it from there. And take it they did—straight to hell in a handbasket. How's Mick doing?"

Now, Libby looks at her brother, who's beaming at his pregnant wife. *He seems to be taking Canchola's escape in his stride. I'll get him aside later and talk with him about it. I don't want to worry Emma.*

As dinner winds down, Libby catches Niall's eyes and silently conveys that it's time to move their guests to the Ink Well. After over thirty years of marriage, they possess the ability to speak volumes with a glance.

Niall nods. "Folks, Libby and I are going to take a moment to clear the table. We'll meet you in the Ink Well shortly. I hope you saved room for dessert." He looks at his sister-in-law. "I made Emma's favorite—caramel-pecan cheesecake pie."

Brent leans against his chair. "Holy Mary, Sweet Mother of God. There's *more*?"

Emma laughs. "You'll come to learn that there's *always more* at Pines & Quill."

"Speaking of *God*," Jennifer glances at Brent, "it sounds heavenly."

Emma nods. "If heaven tastes like a mix of sweet, buttery crunch with a savory nutty aftertaste, then yes, it does. And Niall makes the caramel from scratch."

Jennifer turns to Niall. "You *make* it?"

Niall nods. "It's amazing what you can do with a little sugar, butter, and heavy cream."

Lucy says, "It looks like I'm going to have to start doubling the daily mileage on my bike. If I don't, I'll sink during the swimming portion of the Ironman competition."

When the guests adjourn to the Ink Well, Hemingway circles the warm, inviting room a few times, his tail waving back and forth like a conductor's baton. Satisfied with his inspection, he makes a final circle, tucks his tail, and settles himself on the rug, resting his chin on his front paws. Ever vigilant, he keeps his eyes open and scans the room in case anything drops.

Libby and Niall bring in dessert-laden trays, and the rest of the evening goes off without a hitch.

Libby smiles to herself. *Dessert was devoured. A card was drawn from the Observation Deck. And the conversation was lively.*

"No magic tonight?" Adam asks.

"Not tonight or Friday, tomorrow night, when our nonwriting guests arrive," Libby says. "Which reminds me, everyone needs to bring something—a clue of some type—that alludes to a famous author. And the rest of us will guess who it is. For those who aren't writers, they'll bring a clue that points to what they *do*—or in a retiree's case—what they *did* in real life."

She looks toward Jennifer. "Between now and then, our resident magician is saving all of her mystical, magical wonder for the big show Saturday evening in the tai chi pavilion."

And I hope there won't be any disasters between now and then.

Adam strolls through the bucolic woods of Pines & Quill on smooth, low-lit pathways between the main house and Thoreau cottage. The evening air is chilly. An early-October breeze brushes his skin like a cold feather.

He lifts his gaze. The stars are hiding behind thick cloud cover. Only the slight glow of the moon is visible, like a light behind a curtain. A break in the distant tree line reveals a silhouette of purple-black mountains—a jagged line across the backlit sky.

When Adam reaches Thoreau cottage, he steps inside and closes the door behind him. He strips out of his clothes and brushes his teeth. Then, leaving the bedroom light on but the rest of the cottage dark, he walks into the living room and sits in an overstuffed chair facing the glass wall that overlooks El Cañón del Diablo—the Devil's Canyon.

As his mind goes back and forth, contrasting the pleasant evening with the brutal assignment he's been tasked with, the delicious meal curdles in his stomach.

Kill a writer in residence and frame Sean McPherson . . . or your daughter dies.

Apart from the great horned owl perched on a high limb in one of the Western Red Cedar trees on the south side of the property, no one else is aware that Pines & Quill has an uninvited guest.

The owl watches the short-haired man step with care between tree trunks, stopping periodically to survey the sur-roundings. Then, after pressing his needle-sharp talons into the tree's flesh, the owl rotates his head on his flexible neck to get a better look with his large yellow eyes.

He isn't the only one schooled in the predator-prey dynamic. The man hugs the shadows, blending with the night, easing over root heaves and through fern shoots as he makes his way toward Thoreau cottage. He climbs the steps gingerly. Once he's on the porch, he disappears under the overhang.

The Lhaq'temish, the tribe of local Native Americans who live on the nearby Lummi reservation, believe that owls think like humans—only far better.

A coyote releases a series of high-pitched cries and yelps that echo through the canyon.

The owl knows the coyote is a predator but wonders if the man is predator or prey. Then, with its impressive wing-span, the large bird lifts off and glides silently through the branches into the sky, a better vantage to hunt his next meal, aware that the night will tell what carnage unfolds at Pines & Quill.

CHAPTER 10

> *"In writing about evil, writers must uncover the heart of darkness that reaches out from so many to wreck lives and destroy our ways of life over and over again in the fulfillment of a shadowed, unspoken secret."*
> —ALAN DEAN

At eleven fifteen, the sun has long since set. Opal moonglow filters through the pine trees creating an eerie effect on the north-facing porch of Thoreau cottage—even more so when Carmine Fiore, Gambino's right-hand man, climbs the steps, and his shadow creeps across the wall.

He pauses to open a small foil packet and tip a few small black squares into his dry mouth. *Being here without Gambino's knowledge is the first act to set the rest of my plan in motion.*

Anticipation quickens his heart with adrenaline.

Before removing the lock pick from his pocket, Carmine tests the doorknob. When it turns with ease, he shakes his head. *People are so careless.*

Snakelike, he slides inside the dimly lit cottage.

Adam sits with his back to Carmine in an overstuffed chair facing the cliff and canyon below. The moonlit glass wall silhouettes his head and shoulders.

Carmine rarely carries a gun. The noise draws too much attention. More importantly, he enjoys the satisfaction of work that's up close and personal, the intoxication of watching the light extinguish from his victim's eyes.

But that's not what's drawn him here this evening. It's far more dangerous than that.

If Gambino discovers I've betrayed his trust, that I'm here without his permission, he'll have one of his foot soldiers try to kill me.

Carmine lets a rare reptilian smile play across his face.

If he finds out I intend to replace him as head of The Family, he'll try to kill me himself.

—————

Adam startles at the backlit reflection in the window.

A man stands behind him—one hand holds a knife, the other presses a finger to his lips.

Adam's heart jackhammers his breastbone. *Was I too slow on the job? They said I had twenty-one days to kill one of the other writers. Oh, God! Did he kill Brittany? Is he here to kill me, too?*

The shadow-clad figure steps around Adam's overstuffed chair and faces him.

And though Adam's body is frozen in fear, his mind whirls like turbo-driven windmill blades flashing images of Brittany, then him, dead—their throats slit with the double-edged knife in the man's hands.

The man points the knife toward a matching chair angled for conversation.

"Do you mind?" he asks, his voice a raspy whisper.

Adam knows the question is rhetorical and shakes his head. "It's practically dark in here." The man reaches out and turns on the table lamp. "There, that's better." He leans forward, forearms on his knees. The distance between them narrows to a foot.

Adam smells black licorice and something else on the intruder's breath, then winces at the sudden change of light. "Who are you?"

After his eyes adjust, he inventories the man's face: *Except for a receding chin, his features are pointy, like a ferret. His hair's buzzed so short it looks like salt-and-pepper whisker stubs on a cue ball. He has a three-inch scar that runs along the hairline over his left eye. His ruddy complexion and vein-lined nose suggest a long and loving relationship with alcohol.*

Adam's heart lodges in his windpipe. *Oh God, Oh God, Oh God! It hasn't been twenty-one days. Why is he here?*

"I'm the man who was in your daughter's classroom and dorm room; the man who's going to kill her if you don't do exactly as you're told."

The laser penetration of the man's ice-gray eyes raises the hair on the back of Adam's neck. Looking into them feels like staring at a giant gray wave about to crush him. The sea has no regard for souls. Adam knows this to be true. James, his twin brother, drowned in the ocean when he was a sophomore in college. The menace in the man's eyes confirms that he, too, has no regard for souls.

Tears run down Adam's cheeks, and his voice thickens. "I'm working on it," he says. "I can show you that I've already got Mick's shoes and one of his woodworking knives." His heart feels on the verge of bursting. Adam swallows. "And I didn't leave any fingerprints."

"Well, aren't you the fastidious one," the man says. "There may be hope for you after all."

Adam blinks furiously. *There's no hope for me. I know*

*what you look like—I can identify you. And I know what
that means.*

Brent hit a roadblock in his manuscript earlier in the day.
*I need to clear the cobwebs in my mind, and I do my best
thinking when I'm out "walking" in nature—or rolling, as
the case may be.*

He glances at his watch. *It's almost eleven thirty, but that
doesn't matter. I doubt I'll run into anyone. Although I may
swing by Thoreau cottage, and if Adam's still up, set a date and
time for that drink I promised him. That, and I want to learn
more about flipping houses.*

And though the smooth pathways throughout Pines &
Quill are low-lit with Malibu lights, Brent tucks a headlamp
into the pouch inside the arm of his wheelchair. *Just in case I
decide to do a bit of off-roading.*

He closes the door to Austen cottage behind him and
glides down the ramp.

The keen sense of smell he inherited from his maternal
grandfather—the perfumer—kicks in as the wind picks up a
notch and moans through the pines. It carries the flinty scent
of wet rocks and freshly sawn pine boards.

The scream of a small animal pierces the night and sends
shivers down his spine. *Somebody just caught their dinner. At
this time of night, it's probably an owl.*

While waiting for an appointment at his physical therapist's office, he picked up a *National Geographic* magazine
and learned that owls have special feathers on their wings that
enable near-silent flight by altering air turbulence and absorb-
ing noise. Once locked onto its target, the owl flies toward it,
then in a swift strike, it pulls back, thrusting its razor-edged
talons forward and spread wide. It simultaneously pierces
flesh with the sharp beak and kills its prey.

Brent peers into the darkened surroundings as he moves along at a good clip. Spindly moonlight serves to backlight the trees, and ground-breathed mist wafts ghostlike across the pathway as he heads south. The stanchions supporting the roof of the tai chi pavilion appear skeletal in the dark.

The Halloween season must be getting to me. If I'm not careful and let my imagination run away, before long, I'll see a witch flying through on a broomstick.

As he approaches Adam's cottage, he sees a soft glow from the back. *A light's on. He must still be up.* When he reaches the front porch, he veers to the right of the steps, remembering what Libby said: "All the structures at Pines & Quill have wheelchair access. Most are located to the right of the traditional entry."

At the top of the ramp, Brent's nostrils flare. *I'd know that scent anywhere—Sen-Sen. Grandpa—Dad's dad—used the tiny black licorice and anise-flavored squares to cover the smell of smoking and drinking. He let me try a piece, and I nearly gagged.* Brent wrinkles his nose at the memory. *It tasted like freshly sealed asphalt smells. I thought they stopped selling that nasty-tasting stuff years ago.*

About to knock on the cottage door, Brent halts his hand when he hears a muffled conversation coming from inside. *I wonder who's here with Adam? Well, I certainly don't want to interrupt.*

He turns to leave. When he reaches the bottom of the ramp, he hears a stifled cry.

Without hesitation, he puts on his headlamp and follows the path to the back of Thoreau cottage. *I'll peek in the window to make sure everything's okay.*

———

Adam's throat grows tight, and his heart pounds as he grips the arms of the chair. He bounces one of his knees with nervous energy.

As the man leans toward him, he taps the flat side of the blade on his left palm. "There's about to be a coup. And you're the first person outside The Family that I'm taking from the boss and making my own."

Adam tries to push back the tears threatening to choke him. He looks at the intruder. "I don't understand."

The man's eyes are emotionless. "Let me explain. The person I currently work for doesn't know it, but he's on his way out. In fact," he says, tapping the blade against his palm again, "he's going to die. I'm taking over, and every person who works for me will bear *my* mark."

Lightning-quick, the man grabs Adam's left hand, twists it palm up, and slices the veins across his wrist.

"Oh, my God!" Adam falls to the ground, curls into the fetal position, and clamps his right hand over his bleeding wrist.

"You're going to live," the man says. "It's a surface wound, just deep enough to leave a scar. If I'd wanted to kill you, I'd have slit your veins lengthwise." He walks to the kitchen, grabs a dishtowel, and tosses it to Adam. "I'll be in touch."

Pressing the towel against his wrist, Adam watches the man, through tear-filled eyes, turn to leave.

He stops and looks over his shoulder. "One more thing. Keep this between us." He juts his chin toward the bloody dishtowel. "If you tell anyone what happened, I'll come back, and next time, it won't be your wrist I slit. It'll be your throat. And then your daughter's. Do we have an understanding?"

Adam's heart vaults into his throat, and he nods.

"I can't hear you."

Fear fills Adam's mouth. "I won't say anything." His voice comes out as a whisper.

The man opens the cottage door and then slithers into the night.

Clenching his eyes shut, Adam writhes in pain on the floor as he tries not to pass out.

Brent douses the light on his headlamp before peeking around the rear corner of Thoreau cottage.

His heart accelerates, and he widens his eyes in horror when he looks through the glass wall. Adam's tear-streaked face is contorted in pain as he curls on the floor, pressing a bloody cloth to his left wrist.

Oh, my God, he tried to kill himself!

Brent spins his wheelchair around, flips on the headlamp, and beelines for the front entrance. His heart continues its anxious pounding. *Why on earth would he try to kill himself?*

At the top of the porch ramp, his nostrils pick up the scent of Sen-Sen again before he barrels through the already open doorway.

Then the unmistakable metallic smell of blood assaults Brent's nostrils.

"Hang on, Adam," he yells before picking up the receiver on the desk phone. Niall told them at their first dinner gathering that the bulky and square retro phones on each cottage desk connect with the main house. *"Just lift the receiver and dial zero to ring through to our kitchen."*

Libby picks up the line, and Brent blurts, "Libby, it's Brent. I'm calling from Thoreau cottage. I just found Adam. He tried to commit suicide."

Libby screams up the stairs to Niall, who's at the midway point with Hemingway at his side. "Stop! That was Brent on the phone. He's at Thoreau cottage. Adam tried to kill himself."

"Oh, my God!" Niall bolts down the stairs with Hemingway on his heels. "I'll grab the first-aid kit, secure Hemingway, and head over there now. Call Mick and 911."

Niall and Hemingway disappear behind the Dutch door to the mudroom.

Libby calls Mick and explains the situation.

"I'll take care of 911," Mick says, "then meet you at Thoreau."

Libby sprints out the front door and heads south. Her heart's in her throat. *Why on earth would Adam try to kill himself?*

Almost there, she intersects with Mick, whose cabin is the closest structure to Thoreau. He's running with a first-aid kit in one of his hands.

Libby first, they bolt through the open doorway.

Niall squats next to Adam, assessing the situation.

Adam pulls his arm back from Niall. "You shouldn't be here," he cries. "No one can know about this." His eyes fill with fresh tears.

"There's nothing to be ashamed of." Libby grabs an afghan from the back of the couch and places it around the bare shoulders of the now-sitting Adam, who's shaking. From cold, nerves, or both, she can't tell.

"It's not what it looks like," Adam says through chattering teeth. He shakes his head. "I *didn't* try to—"

The piercing wail of a siren draws close.

Mick squats and looks into Adam's eyes. "That's Skip. He's a paramedic who works out of St. Joseph Hospital. And he's a good friend. Nobody has to find out about this if you don't want them to."

"If anyone finds out, he'll kill me. And then he'll kill my daughter, Brittany."

Libby, Niall, Mick, and Brent exchange puzzled glances over Adam's head.

Adam's chin drops to his chest, and his shoulders rack with sobs. "Now we're *both* going to die."

Skip rushes into Thoreau cottage. If he's surprised at the size of the audience, his face doesn't show it. He's all business.

"I'm going to ease you onto the floor to elevate the wound higher than your heart. That will help slow the bleeding." Skip examines Adam's wound, then turns to Libby, who's closest. "I need you to continue to apply pressure here," he says, pointing to the supplying artery, "while I get a few things."

Once he has the necessary items, he uses a calm tone as he works. "Whoever applied pressure did a fine job. It must have been constant, and that's a good thing."

Adam's jaw tightens as he sucks air in between clenched teeth.

"Sorry about that necessary evil," Skip says. "But I'm more worried about the germs on the dishtowel than I am about what cut you." He looks around. "Speaking of which, what did you use?"

Libby and the others look around the room, too.

"That's what I've been trying to tell you," Adam says. "I *didn't* cut myself. I *didn't* try to commit suicide. A man came into the cottage while I was sitting here enjoying the evening view. *He's* the one who sliced my wrist with a knife."

Brent rolls his wheelchair closer. "When I first arrived and was on the porch, I didn't knock because I heard a conversation, and I didn't want to interrupt. But when I started to leave, I heard crying. So I went to the back wall to look through the glass, and that's when I saw Adam. He was by himself, writhing in pain on the floor, holding a bloody towel to his wrist. I never saw anyone else, but I heard them."

Who was here with Adam? Libby wonders. *Was it one of the other writers?*

"I can transport you to the emergency room at St. Joseph," Skip says, "where the on-call will stitch you up. But it's their job to ask questions." He nods toward Adam's wrist. "And considering the nature of the wound, they'll most likely keep you for observation. Or I can do it myself. Either way, there's going to be a scar."

Adam nods. "I'd like you to do it. The fewer people that know about this, the better."

When Skip finishes his ministrations, he and Mick help Adam sit in the chair.

"My undershirt and pajama bottoms are on the bed," Adam says. "I'd get them myself, but I'm feeling a little light-headed. Would one of you mind getting them for me please?"

"I'll get them," Mick says.

"While you do that," Niall says, pointing at the blood on the hardwood floor, "I'll take care of this."

Libby looks toward the fat-bellied kettle on the stove in the kitchen. "Adam, I'm going to make you a hot cup of tea, then I hope you'll tell us what happened."

Libby tightens a fist around the kettle's handle. *I bet Gambino's at the bottom of this.*

———

Adam's wrist pulses in time with his accelerated heartbeat. *It hurts like a son of a bitch!*

He closes his eyes and takes another sip of the hot tea. "Thank you, Libby."

"Folks," Skip says, "I need to get back to the hospital, or they'll wonder what happened to me." He looks at Adam. "Follow the instructions I gave you. It's going to hurt for a while, but it'll heal."

"Thank you. I appreciate everything you did for me."

"No problem." Skip lets himself out.

"Please tell us what happened," Libby says to Adam. "You can trust me when I say we're here to help you."

Adam purses his lips. His chest constricts.

"Would you prefer if I wasn't here?" Brent asks.

"No. Since it involves you, I'd like you to stay."

Brent's eyebrows skyrocket. "*Me?* What does any of this have to do with me?"

Adam sets the chunky ceramic mug on the side table. "I guess I'd better start at the beginning."

With Adam and Brent already seated, Mick pulls over the desk chair, turns it around, and straddles the seat. Then leans his arms on the wood trim.

Libby sits in the empty overstuffed chair, and Niall sits on the floor between her knees. She places her hands on his shoulders and nods at Adam. "Take your time."

Adam clears his throat and then recounts everything from the initial phone and video calls—"You're going to frame Sean McPherson for the murder of another writer in residence. I don't care which one, nor do I care how you do it. If you fail, your daughter dies," to this evening's attack—"There's going to be a coup. And you're the first person outside The Family that I'm taking from the boss and making my own."

At the words "The Family," Libby, Mick, and Niall exchange wide-eyed glances.

"He said, 'The person I work for doesn't know, but he's on his way out—he's going to die. I'm taking over, and every person who works for me will bear *my* mark.' That's when he grabbed my arm and slashed my wrist."

Adam swallows to keep from crying, then explains about taking shoes from the tai chi pavilion, gloves from the potter's bench, and a knife from the workbench.

His heart hurts—his stomach twists. "I'm sorry. I didn't know what else to do.

"Before the man left, he said, 'I'll be in touch. Keep this between us. If you tell *anyone* what happened, I'll come back, and next time it won't be your wrist. I'll slit your throat and then your daughter's.'"

Mick leans forward. "Why didn't you call the police right away?"

Adam's throat grows tight with tears. "He said that I'm under surveillance and my technology's being monitored and that if I even *consider* involving the police, he'll kill Brittany." Renewed fear rushes through Adam. "Now you know why I don't want *anyone* to find out about this."

Mick nods. "Would you be able to identify him? Could you describe him to a sketch artist?"

"Yes," Adam says. "He didn't bother to cover his face. And I know what that means." His heart thuds harder and harder. "I'm expendable."

"If you don't mind my asking," Niall says, "How far had you'd gotten in your plan? Who were you going to kill?"

Adam feels warm color bloom on his cheekbones as he turns to Brent. "That's where you come in," he says, his voice filled with shame. "I was going to kill you."

CHAPTER 11

*"Write the kind of story you would like to read.
People will give you all sorts of advice about
writing, but if you are not writing something
you like, no one else will like it either."*
—MEG CABOT

A floorboard moans down the hallway outside the main bedroom. Emma glances at the digital display on the nightstand. *Two o'clock—it's already Friday morning.*

A chill kisses the back of her neck. *The last time I heard footsteps in the middle of the night, I had to defend myself and shoot an earlobe off one of Gambino's foot soldiers.*

She opens the nightstand drawer. Her hand hovers over the Glock 26. She flat-palms her belly with the other. At almost sixteen-weeks pregnant, Emma feels the tiniest movement. *Oh, my gosh, this is Connie's first kick! The adrenalin rush probably woke her up.*

"Mick, is that you?"

"I'm sorry, honey," Mick calls out. "I was trying not to wake you."

Emma closes the nightstand drawer as Mick walks through the open doorway.

He steps out of his clothes and lays them across a chair before slipping into bed beside her.

Emma's excitement is effervescent. "I just felt Connie kick." She places one of Mick's hands on her belly, and they both hold their breath, waiting for the baby to do it again, but nothing happens.

"She's a smart girl," Mick says. "It's time to sleep, and she knows it."

He presses a kiss to the top of Emma's head and then kisses the constellation of freckles splayed across the bridge of her nose. "Why are you still up?"

"I was worried. What happened at Thoreau cottage? Is Adam okay?"

Mick draws Emma into a warm embrace and explains what transpired over the last couple of hours.

She snuggles deeper into his chest. "Well, I'm glad you're home," she says, sliding a hand over his hip and down his thigh. She halts her caress when her fingers encounter the wound dressing. Feeling it gently with her fingers, she tries to identify what she's discovered.

Mick's body tenses. and he sucks air between his teeth.

"What's wrong?" Emma says, reaching over and turning on the bedside lamp.

"It's noth—"

Emma draws back the covers, then scrambles onto her knees as she bends over the gauze and tape to get a better look. "What on earth happened?"

"It's just a graze," Mick says.

"What *kind* of a graze?"

Mick twists his wedding band. "A bullet graze."

Emma's eyes taper into slits. "You were hit by a *bullet* and didn't tell me?"

"It happened this afternoon when Joe and I were at the docks tracking down Rico Canchola, the skip trace I told you about. When I got home, I showered and joined you at the main house for dinner. I didn't want to say anything in front of the guests."

Fueled by fear, Emma draws her mouth into a thin line of fury. "Sean Braden McPherson, you *could* have—no, you *should* have—told me the minute we got back to our cabin. Do I have to excavate every single thing out of you? We're a team. Or at least we're supposed to be."

Mick tucks a strand of unruly hair behind one of Emma's ears. "I was going to tell you, but then the phone rang, and I had to go to Thoreau cottage. This is the first chance I've had to say anything."

"You could have been *killed*, Mick. I need my husband, and our daughter needs her father." Emma turns out the bedside lamp, pulls the covers up, and curls on her side, facing away from the man she loves. Clenching down on her whirling thoughts, she grapples for emotional footing. *I knew what I was getting into when I married Mick.* Emma takes a deep, cleansing breath. *One of the reasons I fell in love with him is his sense of justice and desire to do good and contribute to society.* She takes another deep breath.

Mick's strong arms circle Emma's waist. He pulls her back against his front, moves his knees behind hers, and buries his face in her hair. "Everything's going to be okay."

Fear sheathes Emma's heart.

The Sureños gang this afternoon and Gambino—or one of his henchmen—this evening. Oh, God. What's going to happen to us? To our baby?

At just after five in the main house kitchen, Niall stares at the stainless steel coffeemaker, willing it to work faster. The bittersweet aroma wafting from the carafe fails to soothe him this morning. Instead, the taut thread of tension that began in Thoreau cottage last night continues to tug through his stomach.

He pinches his bottom lip with two fingers and puckers his brow in thought as his mind works through the evening's events: *Pines & Quill was breached. Again. Someone who works for Gambino slit Adam's wrist to mark him as his own. He said there would be a coup, Gambino would die, and he was replacing him.*

Niall drums his fingers on the gray-veined marble counter. *I'm anxious for Joe and Rafferty to arrive today so we can make a plan. And Maeve, too. If anything, retirement has only sharpened my mother-in-law's abilities. That, and Gambino had her husband, Connor, killed. She wants what we all want—justice. And then there's Adam's daughter, Brittany. To save her, everyone must believe that Mick has killed a writer in residence.*

Niall's hand shakes as he pours coffee into his thick ceramic mug.

He takes it, walks to the glass patio slider, and looks out at the still-dark sky. *Today's forecast calls for a high of fifty-six degrees, a low of forty-three, and a guaranteed chance for rain.*

Niall turns at thudding on the stairs.

Hemingway bounds over the remaining steps and then slides across the hardwood floor like Tom Cruise in *Risky Business*, stopping inches before Niall's feet. As he scratches the giant dog behind a floppy gray ear, one of Hemingway's rear feet starts pedaling.

"It looks like you found the spot," Libby says, joining them. She eyes Niall's mug. "I need one of those."

Even with purple hammocks from sleeplessness under her eyes, she's beautiful. Niall opens the slider to let Hemingway out for his morning ritual, then follows Libby into the kitchen. "I can use another one myself."

While getting cream from the refrigerator, Niall also pulls out individual breakfast quiches he made the day before. A retreat favorite, they're delicious, easy to deliver to the writers' cottages, and perfect for reheating in the microwave.

Libby's eyes widen. "Are those the ones with bratwurst sausage, spinach, mushrooms, and black olives?"

Niall nods. "The quiche, along with toast, plate-sized hash brown patties, and chilled containers of diced mixed fruit, makes a hearty meal."

"A *tasty* hearty meal."

Niall opens the refrigerator door and points. "Not to worry, Mrs. MacCullough. I made enough for us and Mick and Emma to enjoy after you teach tai chi this morning. I'll deliver everything as you wrap up the session, then meet you guys back here. We need to talk about last night and create a skeleton plan before Maeve, Joe, and Rafferty arrive."

He puckers his brows in thought. "We know that no one's *really* going to be killed, but it has to look convincing. So much so that Mick's arrested for murder and goes to jail. And who better to aid in the deception than a former and current FBI agent, a homicide detective, and an ex-cop turned private investigator no longer bound by the same rules and red tape?"

Libby's heart is heavy as she lights the tall propane patio heaters on each side of the tai chi pavilion. *To save Adam's daughter, Brittany, Mick has to be framed for murder. The news outlets will have a field day:* Ex-cop Turned PI Kills Guest at Writing Retreat. *That kind of publicity will destroy everything we've worked so hard to accomplish. No one will ever want to come to Pines & Quill again.*

Adam is the first to arrive at the pavilion. He checks over

his shoulder, ensuring no one else is around, and then points to the navy-blue hoodie he's wearing. "With cuffed sleeves, it'll keep the dressing on my wrist covered."

Libby nods. "How are you feeling?"

"Physically, I feel okay," Adam says. "But mentally, I feel like I'm in the middle of a shit storm with no chance of getting out."

Libby places a reassuring hand on his shoulder. "Once our friends arrive and the magic show is over, I think we can help you." She sees a tiny spark of hope kindle in Adam's eyes.

"I'd like to believe that."

"Here are the others now," Libby says, squeezing his shoulder. "We'll talk more about it later."

As Libby welcomes Jennifer and Lucy, she sees Brent roll up the ramp. He nods at Adam and gives him a "Your secret's safe with me" look.

After Mick and Emma remove their shoes and climb the steps, Libby pulls them aside and invites them to the main house for breakfast. *Something's wrong. Their smiles are strained.*

She walks to the front of the group, turns so that her back is to them, and begins moving through the tai chi forms with graceful energy.

And though her body is there—her slow movements impeccable—her mind replays part of what she said to Adam: *"Once our friends arrive and the magic show is over." That's it! Jennifer Pruett is a world-renowned magician. As a master of illusion, she makes people believe they see things that aren't real all the time. I wonder if she can help us pull off a murder without anyone getting hurt?*

<hr />

Mick checks his watch. It's just after seven when he, Emma, and Libby wish their guests a productive day of writing and head from the pavilion to the main house.

He looks up. Though the sky is a layered parfait of faint pastels, the weather forecast promises rain.

Mick inhales through his nostrils. The scent of pine and dirt with a hint of woodsmoke saturates the crisp morning air.

Hemingway greets the trio as they pass the garden. He faces them in an excited crouch, ready to play.

Mick picks up a pine cone and throws it for him.

It comes right back in the big dog's mouth like a four-legged boomerang. *Just like Gambino keeps coming back for me. And he won't stop until I'm out of his way—dead or behind bars—where I can't interfere with his business.*

Near the main house, Mick sees a tennis ball on the ground and trades out the pine cone, heaving it instead. "I'm going to toss this a few more times for Hemingway," he says to Emma and Libby. "I'll catch up with you in a couple of minutes."

Mick heaves the ball. As he waits for Hemingway to return, he mentally picks at the problem like a scab. *The trafficking of drugs, weapons, and humans will continue to spread unless Gambino and his foot soldiers are shut down. We've got to stop them.*

Mick pats his thigh. "Hemingway!" *Where the heck did that big lummox go?* Mick heads in the direction he heaved the ball.

In the distance, the big dog sniffs something on the ground—his tail whips back and forth.

When Mick approaches, he says, "Leave it."

And though Hemingway sits, his tail dusts the ground.

Mick squats to look at a small red, blue, and gold foil square printed with the words Sen-Sen. *This is what Brent said he smelled at Thoreau cottage last night.*

Careful not to add his fingerprints, he picks it up with a leaf and tucks it into a front pants pocket. *Maybe it has the prints of whoever plans to kill Gambino and take over his organization.*

Excitement energizes Mick's steps. A waft of rich, nutty coffee aroma teases his nostrils when he and Hemingway enter the main house through the mudroom.

Mick ruffles the wiry hair on top of Hemingway's head. "Thanks to your nose, you may have just discovered a lead." He opens the lidded dog food container and scoops some into his furry companion's bowl. "There you go, you big lug."

Hemingway tucks into the kibble as if he hasn't eaten for days, inhaling his food with gusto. His long gray tail, flecked with a bit of white to match his bib and one white sock, wags the entire time.

Mick washes his hands in the deep sink, dries them on a hand towel, and then enters the dining area through the open Dutch door.

Emma, Libby, and Niall stand next to the massive pine table. Emma's arms are crossed over her chest. Libby's hands are fisted on her hips. And Niall leans against the table with an "I'm sure glad I'm not you" look on his face.

"Exactly when were you going to tell us you got shot?" Libby asks.

Mick raises both hands in resignation. "I *would* have told you, but there hasn't been an opportunity when I could say something without guests also hearing the news." He purses his lips. "We all know that risk comes with the territory. Joe is still recovering from a bullet wound. Rafferty was shot in July. And now I was grazed. But here's some good news." Mick pats a front pocket on his pants. "Hemingway may have found a lead. Remember last night when Brent told us he smelled licorice and anise both times he approached the front porch of Thoreau?"

Emma looks bewildered. Libby and Niall both nod.

Mick scans the room, holds up an index finger, then says, "Excuse me a moment. I'll be right back."

He returns from the kitchen a minute later with a pair of tongs, then extracts the foil Sen-Sen square from his pocket and places it on the table.

"If they can lift clear prints from this, we may learn the identity of the person who plans to overthrow Gambino. And we might be able to stop him and Gambino from terrorizing Pines & Quill and save it from having to close."

At three o'clock, retired criminal psychologist and FBI profiler Maeve McPherson pulls her Prius up to the Pines & Quill entry gate. Rain sluices down the windshield as she removes a Walther PPS from the glove compartment. She releases and checks the magazine that holds seven 9mm rounds. Satisfied, she reinserts it and then tucks the gun in her waistband and a second magazine in her hip pocket.

Before stepping out of the car, she swivels her head, surveying the surroundings through the rain-coated windows, then continues to scan the area as she walks to the gate and inputs the code.

A twig snaps.

Maeve whirls. Gun drawn and ready.

A trio of deer wanders on a berm behind rain-drenched trees.

She lowers her weapon and thinks of her husband, Connor, and of the countless hours they spent at the shooting range even after he retired from the FBI. He was Special Agent in Charge of the Marin, Napa, and San Mateo County offices and the main office in San Francisco.

After inputting the gate code, Maeve gets back in the car. As she drives up the long tree-bordered lane toward the main house, scanning the landscape as she goes, she has a mental conversation with Connor—a habit she began in July when Gambino had him killed in a parking garage in San Francisco.

Our daughter Libby and son-in-law Niall are doing well with Pines & Quill. And our grandson, Ian, and his wife, Fiona, are making a go of their veterinary business at our old house in San Francisco. Mick and Emma have a baby on the way. It's a little girl, and she's due in late March. They're naming her Constance after you.

Hank Dupree, who stepped into your role at the FBI when you retired, has permitted me to come out of retirement to work with Mick, Joe, and Rafferty on the Gambino file. He's given me access to databases that provide information to help me determine the likelihood and timing of his next crime. From what I've gathered, I think it's going to be soon and close to home—our son Mick has a target on his back.

Maeve takes her weekender bag from the front passenger seat and exits the car. But she doesn't make a mad dash for the front door of the main house. Instead, she enjoys the feel of the rain on her skin. She told her kids when they were growing up what her mother told her: "You're not sugar. You won't melt."

Libby opens the front door and grins at her mom. "You're not sugar. You won't melt," she says.

"I just thought the same thing," Maeve says.

Libby pulls her mother into her arms for a hug. "The vehicle sensor buzzed, so I knew it was you."

"How did you know it wasn't Joe or Rafferty who set off the sensor?"

"I wish I could say I'm psychic like our friend Cynthia Winters. But the truth is, neither of them can come until after school lets out, and that's not until three forty-five. I suspect the Bingham family will arrive about four thirty. But Rafferty, Ivy, and Maggie won't arrive until six thirty or so. It'll take them at least two hours to get here. On a Friday, and with the rain, maybe even longer."

Maeve runs her fingers through her silver hair. "That'll give me time to blow-dry this wet mop." She tips her head up and sniffs as they walk toward the dining area, then flares her nostrils in appreciation as they take in the delicious scent of Niall's kitchen wizardry. "What's my son-in-law up to? It smells incredible."

Niall pops his head around the corner. He has an eyebrow cocked and a slight grin on his face. "I'm about to stuff some Cornish hens. What you smell is the stuffing I just made—butter, bacon, onion, a diced Granny Smith apple, toasted baguette cubes, chicken stock, a dash of cinnamon, a pinch of sage, salt and pepper to taste, and one egg to bind everything together."

Maeve matches Niall's cocked eyebrow with one of her own. "Cinnamon?"

He steps around and kisses his mother-in-law's cheek. "Shhh, don't tell anyone. It's the secret ingredient."

Maeve crosses her heart. "I'll take it to my grave." *Just like Connor did with the information he was going to share with me when he got home but was killed instead. He was helping "The Boys"—how we referred to Mick, Joe, and Rafferty—with a case. The last text he sent said,*

> Maeve, I think I may have hit pay dirt. I'll explain when I get there. Do you need me to pick anything up on my way home? I love you.

———

Nerves coil tightly in Niall's gut as he stuffs Cornish hens. His mind, not on the task at hand, keeps wandering to the rusty coffee can he tucked behind some cleaning supplies under the kitchen sink.

When he'd gone to the workshop to get a few items from the chest freezer, he found a royal blue bandana crumpled on the floor. Hairs raised on his neck as he looked into the shadows for an intruder, remembering what Mick had said:

"The Sureños gang identifies with nearly all shades of blue, but they're best known for royal-blue bandanas worn around the neck, tied around the wrist, or as a headband. As brutal as the Sureños are, they're child's play compared to Gambino. God help us if they ever start working together."

With no one in sight, Niall used a rag by Emma's pottery wheel to pick up the bandana and drop it into a half-empty coffee can of nails. He stuffed the rag on top for good measure.

After Mick's and Joe's run-in with Rico Canchola at the docks yesterday and Adam's encounter with one of Gambino's foot soldiers last night, I wonder if the two factions have teamed up to combine their efforts.

I won't tell Libby about the bandana I found; she's already worked up about her brother getting shot and not saying anything. And Maeve has enough on her platter, what with losing Connor. So I'll keep it to myself until Mick gets here and I can pull him aside.

Niall sets out ingredients to prep for the rest of this evening's British-themed menu: deviled eggs—each topped with his signature whole roasted cashew and basil leaf. And cheese, veggie, and prosciutto pastry roll-ups. To go with the main, succulent Cornish hens, he's planned garden salad, roasted potatoes and carrots, gravy, and Yorkshire pudding—a savory pastry perfect for soaking up gravy. The pièce de résistance will be sticky toffee pudding for dessert.

Once Maeve settles her things in the guest room of the main house and dries her hair, she joins Niall and Libby in the kitchen. Removing a bib apron from a hook, she loops it over her head and ties it in the back. "I want something to do. So put me to work."

Niall sets a paring knife on a cutting board and takes in his mother-in-law. Her still-damp silver hair is pulled up in a messy bun. Mutinous wisps frame a face that blooms with a smile. Her round eyes kiss at the edges and crinkle into crescent moons.

He remembers the adage: "If you want to know what a girl will look like when she gets older, take a look at her mom." Niall turns to Libby. Her cheeks are flushed from the warm kitchen. *The apple didn't fall very far from the tree. Her beauty is from her mother.*

Niall picks the knife back up and hands it to Maeve. "I'm always glad to have a sous chef alongside me in the kitchen—two's even better."

Niall readies the pastries for the roll-ups on one side of the center island as his wife and mother-in-law dice vegetables for the garden-to-table salad on the other. A previous writer in residence had teased about its size, saying, "It's not an island; it's a continent!"

As they work, Niall and Libby take turns conveying last evening's event in Thoreau cottage. "So we have our work cut out for us," Niall says. *And now, with that bandana, maybe even more than we realized.*

Maeve splays her hands flat on the granite counter and twists her lips to the side in contemplation. "First and foremost, we must keep Adam's daughter—for that matter, everyone's children—safe."

She looks into Libby's and then Niall's eyes. "And I understand your concern about losing writers from the fallout of negative publicity. But if we can pull off a sting operation, make it appear that Adam's compliant with Gambino and his goon, then we can put *two* guys behind bars. The kingpin of three regions—New Orleans, San Francisco, and the greater Seattle area. And his double-crossing right-hand man."

Niall wipes his hands on a dishtowel. "And save the future of Pines & Quill while we're at it."

CHAPTER 12

*"For your born writer, nothing is so healing
as the realization that he has come upon the
right word."*
—Catherine Drinker Bowen

Rafferty loosens his death grip on the steering wheel and
tries to tamp down the growing sense of dread in the
pit of his stomach.

He glances away from the windshield and gridlock traffic
on I-5 North to the hand that Ivy, his fiancée, places on his
right arm as they drive toward the Pines & Quill writing retreat
in the Fairhaven Historic District of Bellingham, Washington.

Until the phone call from Mick, he'd been looking
forward to a relaxing weekend with their friends and the
private show that Jennifer Pruett—writer in residence and
world-famous magician—is giving tomorrow night.

Instinctively, Rafferty pats the shoulder holster under his
jacket. *It's going to be a working visit after all.*

"I may not be able to see you," Ivy says, "but I can feel your energy. And something's wrong. I'm blind, not fragile. So please tell me what it is."

Ivy's guide dog, Maggie, pops her head between them over the seat at the sound of Ivy's voice. Ivy scratches the curly hair under the black-and-white Standard poodle's chin.

Maggie angles her neck so Ivy can get an even better reach.

"Mick called while you were in the shower," Rafferty says. "He conferenced in Joe and Maeve so the four of us could talk." He shares with Ivy what happened to Adam at Thoreau cottage the previous night and the threat of what will happen to Adam's daughter Brittany if he doesn't kill a writer in residence and successfully frame Mick for the murder.

Ivy contemplates the information for a few minutes, then says, "You said that one of Gambino's foot soldiers plans to kill him and take his place. Does that help matters any? I mean, can you leverage that to your advantage and use it to put them all out of commission?"

While at a standstill behind the car in front of them, Rafferty takes the opportunity to look at Ivy. Concern etches her features. And though her gray-tinted glasses all but obscure her eyes, he loves their attractive pale gray color.

"In addition to being beautiful, you must be a mind reader," he says. "I'm wondering the same thing. By the time everyone leaves the after-dinner conversation in the Ink Well this evening, it'll be late, so tomorrow morning after tai chi, when the writers go back to their cottages, the rest of us will strategize over breakfast in the main house."

Tension coils in Rafferty's gut. More than anything, he wants to put Gambino out of commission. In addition to countless other deaths, he's responsible for the death of Rafferty's almost-sixteen-year-old son, Drew. Gambino saw to it that he died in a car accident five years ago. Then he had Niall's brother, Paddy—Father MacCullough to everyone else in the parish—killed in a confession booth at St. Barnabas Church in June. And he had Maeve's husband—Mick and Libby's father—Connor, killed in a parking garage in San Francisco in July. Connor had been helping Rafferty, Mick, and Joe follow a lead on Toni Bianco, a dirty cop who worked for Gambino and turned out to be his daughter.

The beginnings of a migraine scrape a jagged nail across Rafferty's temples. *I'd do almost anything to eliminate Gambino and his crime family from the equation.*

———

While sitting at the head of the dining room table, fear gnaws the edges of Niall's heart. *I hope the opportunity to share with Mick and the others about the royal-blue bandana—the Sureños gang identifier—I found on the floor in the workshop presents itself soon.*

Just then, the vehicle sensor buzzes, taking Niall's thoughts in a different direction. *That must be Rafferty and Ivy.*

The couple lets themselves in through the mudroom a few minutes later.

Niall stands and opens his arms in welcome.

The cacophony of thumping, bumping, and delighted yelps as Hemingway and Maggie greet each other is deafening.

"Let those four-leggers outside to run free," Niall shouts. "Maybe they'll work off some of that energy."

After the dogs zoom off, Rafferty hangs his and Ivy's wet jackets on pegs in the mudroom. Then he opens the closed portion—the lower half—of the Dutch door, and they enter the dining area to greetings from their friends.

"It smells delicious," Ivy says.

"I'm starving," Rafferty says.

"It's a good thing you texted to let us know you were almost here," Niall says, hugging Ivy first, then Joe. "As you can tell from the growling stomachs around the table, we were about to start without you."

Niall pulls out a chair for Ivy. Once seated, she folds her collapsible white cane and sets it on the floor beneath her.

Rafferty glances at the wall clock as he takes the empty seat beside her. "It's almost seven o'clock. I'm sorry to have kept everyone waiting."

"No problem," Niall says. Then pointing to bottles in ice buckets on the sideboard, he continues. "Joe, will you please pour the wine while Libby, Mick, Emma, and I bring in dinner? I paired tonight's meal with Wente Vineyards Morning Fog Chardonnay. A nice accompaniment to the Cornish hens, it bursts with aromatics of melon and green apple, complemented by hints of tasty oak and vanilla from barrel aging."

"I'd be happy to," Joe says, standing.

"You'll also find sparkling cider for Carly and Brianna and a bottle of Emma's favorite sparkling water."

As Joe fills glasses, Adam leans across the table and eyes Rafferty's leather cross-draw shoulder holster and the butt of a Sig Sauer P229. He lets out a low whistle. "We were all supposed to bring a clue this evening. The four writers in residence, a clue that alludes to an author. And the rest of you, a clue that hints at your job. Or if you're retired," he says, looking at Maeve, "to what you used to do. If I didn't already know, *that*"—he points to the gun—"is a darned big clue."

The two couples return from the kitchen carrying large serving platters and bowls, two gravy boats, two dressing cruets, and a huge tray and place them on the table.

Niall hears the tail end of Adam's comment to Rafferty. *I know there are at least three guns at the table—Rafferty's, Mick's, and Joe's. And while that makes me feel secure, it also breaks my heart that family and friends at Pines & Quill have come under attack and warrant that kind of protection.*

"Tonight's menu is British-themed," Niall says. Then he points to and names each item: "Stuffed Cornish hens, deviled eggs, prosciutto pastry roll-ups, garden salad with carrot ginger dressing, roasted potatoes and carrots, gravy, and Yorkshire pudding."

Lucy furrows her eyebrows as she scrutinizes the last item. "I thought Yorkshire pudding was a dessert?"

"Many Americans do," Niall says. "But British and American definitions of pudding are quite different. In the States, the word pudding often evokes thoughts of creamy chocolate or vanilla dessert that Europeans call custard. However, people in the UK think of pudding as a savory dish that often includes meat topped with gravy. And when sausage gets involved, Yorkshire pudding is called 'Toad in the Hole.'"

"Are you from the United Kingdom?" Brent asks.

"Yes." Niall nods, then cranks up his Scottish burr and rolls his r's. "I'm *frrrom* Scotland."

The wine and conversation flow as everyone enjoys the meal, shares about the writing triumphs and disasters of the day, and then tries to guess each other's clues.

Niall lets his gaze drift to each face around the table. *Could one of this month's writers in residence be a fake? Unfortunately, it wouldn't be the first time Gambino planted an impostor in our midst. Even though Libby ran a background check on each of them, Gambino has a long reach. Like cockroaches, his minions infiltrate the most inaccessible places to do his bidding, and manipulating data for his benefit is mere child's play.*

Niall brings his thoughts back to this evening's game. The non-writers in residence go first. Their clues are easy as everyone already knows what they do for a living—except for Maeve. They're blown away that she's come out of retirement to work on a case for the FBI. As they pepper her with questions, she holds up her hands and says, "Sorry, but I'm not free to elaborate."

"Okay," Niall says, "now it's time for the writers in residence to share their clues. Adam, let's start with you."

Adam holds up a black feather representing Edgar Allan Poe's poem *The Raven*.

Libby is the first to guess correctly.

After much inaccurate speculation, Lucy has to explain her clue. A bicycle chain. "One of my favorite books is *Across African Sand* by Phil Deutschle. It's an incredible story of his three-thousand-mile bicycle trek across the world's largest stretch of sand—the Kalahari and Namib Deserts of Southern Africa."

Brent pats his bionic arm, both of his thighs, and the arms of his wheelchair with his natural hand. "These are my clues," he says.

"Does it have to do with being in a wheelchair?" Adam asks.

Brent nods. "Yes."

But that's as far as the guessers get. They're stumped.

"My clue is for the book *Beauty Is a Verb*. It's an anthology of poetry by thirty-seven authors with disabilities. Each section begins with the artist's statement about their work, followed by a selection of poems in experimental styles. Every time I start to feel sorry for myself, that book snaps me out of it."

Jennifer Pruett is the last writer to share her clue. "And while the subject of my clue is an acclaimed storyteller, he's even better known as a filmmaker." She stands and walks to the sideboard with an empty six-foot expanse of wall above it. Once there, Jennifer turns sideways, the light from the dining area casting her slender shadow against the wall. As she steps forward, continuing to take slow steps, her shadow morphs into the well-known silhouette of Alfred Hitchcock.

Amazed gasps come from those seated at the table before an eruption of questions, with "How on earth did you do that?" being the most prominent.

Ivy says, "Will someone please tell me what Jennifer just did?"

Everyone tries to explain at once. "She did magic without any props." "Hands-free, no tricks." "Jennifer's shadow on the wall changed from her own to the memorable silhouette of Alfred Hitchcock."

Niall takes in the delighted faces around the table. Many of them are slightly flushed. He's thrilled when Jennifer sits back down to rousing applause.

Tomorrow night's magic show will be in the tai chi pavilion. It's open on all four sides and surrounded by woodland—easy for someone to hide in the thick foliage. But it's the location that Jennifer's been preparing for, so it's too late to change. His heart clenches. We need to cut this evening short so I can tell the others about the bandana. We don't just have Gambino to worry about; now we have the Sureños gang, too.

───────

Mick claps bits of loose bark from his hands after adding a few more logs to the fire in the massive Ink Well fireplace. He focuses on the flames, watching them dance in undulating orange, red, and blue licks as the fire crackles in the hearth.

It feels like an anchor drops in his stomach. *Last month Emma was trapped inside a burning cabin on Mount Baker— an inferno.* He shakes his head to clear the memory and then turns back to face the room. The wall clock indicates that it's just after nine. *Tonight is Friday night. In less than twenty-four hours, we'll all be in the tai chi pavilion watching Jennifer's big show.*

He surveys the faces in the large room. Most people are seated in well-worn overstuffed armchairs arranged in conversational groupings. Joe's daughters—Carly, age thirteen, and Brianna, age eleven—sit together on a loveseat. Wearing Bluetooth headphones, they're oblivious to everything around them as they listen to an audiobook, *The Girl Who Drank the Moon*, by Kelly Barnhill. Ivy brought it for them knowing how much they love to read. Their faces are flushed with happiness.

But that was far from true last month when the girls were held hostage along with Emma. Gambino had contracted to sell the three of them and nine other women. Mick tucks his hands into his front pockets and clenches his fists. *When Joe, Rafferty, and I arrived, they were about to be transported to a container ship heading to Gambino's counterpart in Russia — the human trafficking side of his business. Joe was shot twice while saving Brianna — once in his right shoulder and a second bullet grazed his forehead.* Mick thinks about his unborn daughter. *If anything —*

Niall enters, wiping his hands on a dish towel, and addresses the room. "Before I serve dessert, does anyone mind if the dogs join us?"

Niall's face is tight. He looks anxious. Mick catches his glance and gives him a "What's wrong?" expression.

Niall mouths, "Later."

When none of the guests oppose having the dogs join them in the Ink Well, Niall departs to let them in.

Moments later, Hemingway and Maggie, exhausted from their untethered romp around the property, greet everyone with lolling tongues and wagging tails. As their wet noses inspect each person's hands for treats, the guests dole out scratches and pats. Finally, when they realize no juicy tidbits are forthcoming, the two big dogs wander over to the fireplace and collapse on their pillow beds.

"Your dog is beautiful," Jennifer says to Ivy. "This is the first opportunity I've had to get a good look at her. I don't remember ever seeing a two-toned poodle before. In fact," Jennifer says, pressing her hands together in delight, "her markings make her look like she's wearing a nun's habit."

Ivy smiles. "When her trainers described her coloring to me — 'black with a white wimple, like a traditional nun's habit' — I couldn't resist giving her a nun's name."

"Maggie's a nun's name?" Jennifer asks.

"That's her nickname," Ivy says. "Her full name is Sister Margaret Mary McCracken."

"Oh, my gosh," Jennifer says. "I love it."

Maggie lifts her head from her front paws at the sound of her name and wags her exclamation-point tail.

"And Maggie loves coming to Pines & Quill," Rafferty says. "It's one of the few locations where she's not on duty and gets to play with her best friend." He nods toward Hemingway.

"I'm going to help Niall bring in the dessert," Mick says. "I'll be right back."

As he steps through the doorway, he hears Emma say, "This is a great time to pull cards from the Observation Deck."

In the kitchen, Mick says, "I've come to help carry the sticky toffee pudding."

Niall looks up. Worry blanches his face; there's rising panic in his eyes.

A chill fishtails up Mick's spine. He places a hand on his brother-in-law's shoulder. "But first, tell me what's wrong. Maybe I can help."

"I was going to wait until after the writers in residence left, and it was just the rest of us. Then, I was going to tell you all at once."

"Tell us what?" Libby says, joining them in the kitchen.

Niall's shoulders seemed to deflate, and a look of defeat settles on his face. "It'll be easier if I just show you." He opens the cupboard under the sink, squats down, reaches behind the trash can, and pulls out an old coffee can.

Mick and Libby exchange puzzled glances.

Niall stands back up. "When I went to the garage to get some ingredients out of the chest freezer," he says, removing the crumpled rag, "I found this on the floor." He holds out the can.

Alarm bells clang in Mick's head like a train signal when he sees the royal-blue bandana.

It's no longer raining when Lucy and the other writers leave the main house. *I wonder why we were rushed through drawing cards from the Observation Deck and eating dessert. Then Libby announced that tai chi was canceled in the morning because, "It's going to be a long day with the magic show, so take the opportunity to sleep in." I'll put the time to good use and hit the road with my bike even earlier. Why didn't the other guests, the nonwriters, leave when we did? Something's up.*

She follows the lit pathway north toward Dickens cottage. The digital display on her cell phone informs her that it's just before ten—shadows shift and fall. Silhouettes of tall pines stretch toward the sky. In the distance, a foghorn's deep base wails.

After entering her cottage, Lucy walks to the center and inhales deeply. Then she follows her nose to the beautiful glass fragrance diffuser with a handwritten note from Libby. She reads it, not for the first time: This blend is designed to invoke a feeling that anything is possible. The top notes are fresh-picked Honeycrisp apple and smooth oat milk. The middle notes are warm cinnamon, cardamom, and sweet-spicy clove. And the base notes are rich sandalwood and warm vanilla. Enjoy!

The Pacific Northwest could be my new home if I dared to leave Rick. Greg, our oldest son, would be okay; he's in college with a life of his own. But Doug's still in high school. A senior, but nonetheless . . .

After changing into her pajamas, Lucy slips into bed, sets the alarm on her cell phone, then turns out the remaining light. In the dark, she curls onto her side, closes her eyes, and replays Jennifer's clue this evening. *How the hell did her shadow change to Alfred Hitchcock's silhouette?* She thinks about the other magic she has watched Jennifer do. *How does she make things appear and disappear?* Then she contemplates the essential oil blend that Libby designed to invoke a feeling that anything is possible.

Lucy pictures herself pedaling her bike into thick Pacific Northwest fog—disappearing.

———

Niall's stomach churns as he carries a large stainless steel carafe of hot coffee to the dining area. The massive pine table is no stranger to the people gathered around it—Libby and her mother Maeve, Mick and Emma, Joe and Marci, and Rafferty and Ivy.

Hemingway and Maggie nestle on their pillow beds in the Ink Well, where Carly and Brianna are asleep with their headphones on—an afghan placed over each of them.

"I'm sorry I didn't say anything earlier," Niall says, tipping the coffee can to show everyone the royal-blue bandana he found crumpled on the workshop floor. "But I didn't want the writers in residence to know there's a potential threat from the Sureños gang."

Next, Libby shares what happened to Adam at the hand of Gambino's man, the promise of what will happen to his daughter if he doesn't frame Mick for murder, and the threat of a coup. "The goon said he's going to kill Gambino and take his place."

On the tabletop, Ivy's hand tightens around Rafferty's.

In a plastic sandwich bag, Mick holds up the small foil Sen-Sen package that Hemingway found. "I think it's worth trying to get prints."

Rafferty calls Stewart Crenshaw, his Seattle office commander, explaining everything and getting a green light to move forward. Next, he arranges for the Sen-Sen package to be picked up and run for prints and for the bandana to be tested for possible DNA—dander, hair, anything that might help.

Niall brings fresh coffee to the table and a platter of snickerdoodles. He made the cookies to deliver tomorrow morning with the guests' breakfasts. The cinnamon-sugar cookies with crispy edges and chewy centers are a retreat favorite.

Joe calls Bellingham Police Chief Bruce Simms, wakes him from a sound sleep, briefs him on the situation, informs him of Stewart Crenshaw's approval, and gets Simms's backing. Then he arranges for a police sketch artist to work with Adam in the morning.

Niall endorses Libby's suggestion to ask Jennifer Pruett to help them pull off the illusion of murder. When he sees doubt in some of their eyes, he says, "She's a *world-renowned* magician. She makes her living by deceiving the eye."

But even though Jennifer's clue of changing her shadow to Hitchcock's silhouette earlier was beyond impressive, Joe, Rafferty, and Maeve haven't seen her in action like the rest of them, so they're not convinced.

Maeve pats the top of her daughter's hand. "Honey, I think we should wait until after tomorrow night's magic show to decide whether to approach her or not."

Joe nods his agreement. "It's always a risk to bring in a civilian."

"An even bigger risk," Maeve adds, "when we bring in civilians—plural. We have to get buy-in from the rest of the writers to go along with it."

"I agree," Libby says. "But once they realize what's at stake—Adam's daughter—I'm sure they'll be willing to be witnesses and point the finger at Mick to help Adam frame him."

Niall scrapes a hand through his hair. *Were the Adam and blue bandana events initiated by two separate factions, or are they connected?*

His heart knocks against his ribs and dampens his palms when he remembers the thought Mick shared when he spotted a gang member at the airport while waiting for this month's batch of writers. "As brutal as the Sureños are, they're child's play compared to Gambino."

Metallic fear slides to the back of Niall's throat when he thinks of Mick's closing words. "God help us if they ever start working together."

CHAPTER 13

"Each writer is born with a repertory company in his head. Shakespeare has perhaps 20 players . . . I have 10 or so, and that's a lot. As you get older, you become more skillful at casting them."

—GORE VIDAL

At one o'clock on Saturday morning, Maeve secures the Walther PPS in her belly band, then pulls her blouse over it as she enters the Ink Well. *Between Gambino, his traitorous foot soldier, and potentially the Sureños gang, we have to be prepared.*

Hemingway and Maggie lift their heads when she crosses the room. Two tails thump against pillow beds when she slips them each a dog biscuit.

Before extracting an afghan from a wooden chest by the pedestal that holds the Pines & Quill journal, Maeve adds a few more logs to the fire. They make a kind of singing sound, like happy bees. She knows what Connor would say. She can practically hear his voice: *"They're not dry enough."*

On her way to one of the recliners, she checks to ensure that Carly and Brianna are still asleep. Their faces are peaceful in slumber—her heart grips. *The children come first; we must protect them. I'm glad that Mick, Joe, and Rafferty agreed with my suggestion to put a tail on Adam's daughter, Brittany.*

Starting tomorrow—Maeve looks at her watch—*make that today—a female FBI agent who can pass as a college student will shadow her wherever she goes. All of Adam's, Jennifer's, Brent's, and Lucy's family members will also be shadowed by agents. We're not taking any chances where Gambino is concerned.*

As a criminal psychologist and FBI profiler, Maeve is no stranger to people with an antisocial personality disorder— psychopathy. *They're exquisite planners who don't make important moves without studying all the angles. And though they're capable of off-the-cuff triage, they prefer to examine a problem from every angle before taking a course of action. That's one of the reasons Gambino has never done time. He's a relentless planner.*

Maeve pulls the afghan up to her shoulders and focuses on the dancing flames in the fireplace. She thinks about her own plan as the logs crackle and spit.

In the morning, I'll contact Adam's cell phone carrier to get the numbers from which he received the phone and video calls. With that information, I'll contact the carrier of those numbers. I can get the historical cell-site location information if the phones haven't been turned off or destroyed. That will give me an indication of where those phones have been. And if they're still viable, I'll get a warrant for real-time CSLI.

The hypnotic dance of the marmalade-colored flames makes Maeve's eyelids heavy. Her last conscious thought before drifting off to sleep is of her late husband. *I miss you, Connor. Good night, Love.*

Libby wakes with an uneasy feeling in the pit of her stomach. She dreamed that Jennifer Pruett made everyone disappear during tonight's magic show but couldn't bring them back.

She glances at the "electronic rooster"—Niall's term for their alarm clock—and groans inwardly. *It's not even five o'clock.* Then Libby flares her nostrils at the bittersweet smell of coffee.

Niall snores next to her.

Who's making coffee?

She slips out from under the warm covers and pads barefoot to the bathroom. Then she closes the door before flipping on the light to avoid disturbing her husband. Squinting against the brightness, Libby looks in the mirror. Deep lines embrace her eyes.

She splays both hands on the bathroom vanity and leans in to look closer. Libby twists her lips to the side in contemplation. "You're not getting enough sleep," she whispers to her reflection. "And you know why? It's because you're afraid that Pines & Quill will have to close because of Gambino and maybe the Sureños gang too."

She smells the aroma of coffee again. Then, curiosity piqued, Libby makes quick work of her morning routine. The last thing she does is run a brush through her hair. Then she sweeps it up in a loose chignon, captures it with the crane hair slide Mick carved for her from rosewood, and skewers it with the matching eight-inch-long hair stick—one end sharpened to go through her thick hair with ease.

She smiles at the memory of his cherished gift almost being confiscated by TSA at Bellingham International Airport. Though no alarms went off as she stepped through the body scanner, a female officer asked her to step out of line. When Libby did, the woman pointed to the hair slide on the back of her head. "Please remove those for me and set them here," she said, pointing to a plastic container.

The officer examined the items and then held up the stick. "Because this can be used as a weapon, I'm afraid I can't let you take it onboard the flight." The only reason Libby got to keep it was because she agreed to put it in her carry-on and check that piece of luggage.

As Libby descends the stairs, her mother enters the dining area from the mudroom. "It smells like you made coffee," Libby says.

Maeve nods. "Niall told me to make myself at home in the kitchen, so I did. And while waiting for it to finish brewing, I let the dogs out for their morning romp. Want to help me start breakfast? I found Niall's menu, the recipes, and the ingredients."

"I'm game," Libby says. "But not till after my first cup of coffee."

"Carly and Brianna are still asleep," Maeve says. "I just put another log on the fire to keep them toasty until they wake up."

Libby steps to her mother—two tall, willowy bookends. "Mom, I'm worried."

Maeve links her arm in her daughter's and steers her toward the kitchen. Then, always a good listener, she says, "Tell me."

Libby shares her concerns. And though she doesn't mention last night's dream, she shares her fear for the safety of her family, friends, and the writers in residence. Angst gnaws Libby's guts. "Mom, you know Niall and I have worked our *entire* married lives to make Pines & Quill the sought-after writing retreat it's become. But no one will want to come here anymore if the violence continues. Murder is bad for business."

After breakfast in the main house, Joe and Marci, his wife of fifteen years, enjoy a few hours of free time, strolling the property hand in hand. Joe surveys their surroundings as they walk. *Just last month, Gambino's thugs kidnapped my two girls and Emma. Now he's back again. His brand of evil is relentless.*

"It was sweet of Emma and Mick to invite the girls to their cabin to see the baby's nursery," Marci says.

Joe squeezes her hand. "It sure was. They know we don't get a lot of alone time." He waggles his eyebrows. "Let's make good use of it." First, he wraps himself around her and basks in the feeling of safety and love as she holds him. *Home—Marci is my home.* Then his mouth finds her mouth, and they kiss as if they depend on each other for oxygen.

The breeze ruffles their hair as their tongues collide. "You're the best thing that ever happened in my life," Joe says into Marci's hair when their mouths finally part. *And I would do anything, and I mean anything, to protect you and our daughters.* His eyes are hazy as he looks down at her and rubs her bottom lip with his thumb.

"We need to come to Pines & Quill more often," Marci teases.

Over her shoulder, Joe continues to scan the surrounding forest for movement. *Until a few months ago, Pines & Quill had always been a safe place to bring my family, a haven. Now Gambino is trying to take that away.*

As they walk toward the bluff, Joe places a hand on the spot under his jacket where his Sig Sauer P229 rests in his cross-draw holster. *I hope I don't have to use it this weekend.*

A few hours later, when everyone except the writers in residence meets for lunch at the main house, the girls chat nonstop about the McPherson baby's nursery.

"Mom," Brianna says, "I think *you* should have another baby."

"Yeah, Mom," Carly agrees. "It would be so much *fun!*"

Caught off guard and midsip, water shoots out Joe's nostrils, and he nearly chokes.

Marci pats his back.

The vehicle sensor buzzer sounds, and Joe glances at the wall. He winks at Marci and mouths, "Saved by the bell." Then, standing from the dining room table, he says, "It's two thirty. That'll be Rebecca Snyder, the forensic artist. She's right on time."

Marci changes the subject to the upcoming event. "What kind of tricks do you think Jennifer Pruett will do tonight?" she asks her daughters.

"I hope she'll saw me in half," Brianna, age eleven, says.

"And can't put you back together," Carly, her older sister, teases.

"Knock it off, you two," Joe says. Then without missing a beat, "I'll buzz Rebecca in, then meet her in the drive." He turns to Mick. "Would you please call Adam to let him know we'll be at Thoreau cottage in a few minutes?"

Rebecca parks her car in the circular drive opposite the main house door. When she opens the driver's door, Joe says, "I'm sorry to call you out on a Saturday. Thank you for coming."

Rebecca steps from the car. Her hair is a mass of gray Brillo-tight curls around her rotund face. "It's not a problem, Joe. In all the years I've been doing this, I've never known criminals to take weekends off." She opens the back passenger door, gathers two large tote-style bags with handles from the backseat, and hands one to Joe. "I'm ready."

"Did you have a chance to read the report I emailed you about what happened?"

"I did," she says. "*Damn*, that was brutal. He slashed his wrist?"

Joe purses his lips and nods. As they walk south across the property, he scowls at the sky. It's the color of wet cement. "I didn't check the weather report today."

"I always expect rain," Rebecca says. "That way, if it doesn't, I'm pleasantly surprised."

"I'll have to try that," Joe says, climbing the porch steps of Thoreau. He knocks on the door.

Adam opens it and steps back in welcome. "Come in."

After Joe makes the introductions, Rebecca sets up an easel by the south-facing glass wall. She places a large flip-pad on it and then arranges two chairs in front of it. Forensic artists, especially seasoned ones like Rebecca, know what to ask to cull the most accurate information. "Adam, take your time as you try to remember the details," she says.

He places his forearms on his thighs, leaning closer to the easel. "I'll *never* be able to forget his face. Even if I tried."

"Let's start with the shape of his head," Rebecca says. "Was it round, oval, squ—"

"Round," Adam responds, fast, like he's on a game show. "That's why his features stood out to me. They're pointy, like a ferret. Except for his chin; it's receding."

Joe steps behind the two and watches Rebecca's right hand fly across the page as Adam answers her questions. She uses her left thumb periodically to smudge areas as she brings the portrait to life.

"Stop," Adam says. "That's him."

"This is the guy who slashed your wrist?" Joe asks, pointing to the sketch.

"I'd bet my life on it," Adam says, leaning back in his chair. "So, *now* what happens?"

"I'm going to photograph the completed sketch," Joe says. "Then run it through a face image database to see if we get a match. If we do, it'll help us nail the son of a bitch!"

Niall's hands shake as he lifts a ladle from the counter in the main house kitchen. *Tonight we're all going to be in one convenient spot. And in an open-air structure, to boot.* His heart constricts. *Easy pickings for Gambino, his thugs, or the Sureños gang. One or all of us could be hurt or killed.*

Like a hamster on a wheel, Niall's mind races ahead. *The holidays are just weeks away. Will all of us still be alive to celebrate? Last year my brother Paddy and father-in-law Connor were with us. But Gambino had them both killed. I wonder who's next in his sights?*

As he opens the oven door, the smell of red wine-braised short ribs fills the kitchen, creating a natural stress reliever. Niall inhales as he ladles the thick sauce of red wine and beef stock over the ribs. *Cooking, baking—and memories of my grandmother, who taught me all things culinary—always bring me comfort. I can hear her voice as if it were yesterday. "Niall, don't let the bullies terrorize you. If you're scared, they win. When you refuse to be afraid of them, they lose."*

Closing the oven door, he pastes a resolute smile on his face and enters the dining area. Wiping one hand on his striped bistro apron and brandishing long-handled tongs in the other, he says, "The meat's going to slip right off the ribs when they're done. But with the extra-long braising time, I'm glad everyone voted to have dinner *after* tonight's magic show instead of before."

"What's on the full menu?" Mick asks.

"Well, since you asked." Niall smiles. "In addition to the beef short ribs, we're having braised cabbage with caraway seeds, grilled corn, garden salad, buttermilk biscuits, garlic mashed potatoes, and scratch gravy made from the red wine braising liquid."

Joe enters the dining area through the glass slider.

"Did Adam give Rebecca enough information to sketch the guy?" Rafferty asks.

Joe holds up his cell phone. "Done. And according to Adam, it's spot on."

He walks to the massive pine dining table, brings the photo up on his cell phone, and hands it to Rafferty.

Though Niall is in the kitchen, the spacious, open-plan design allows him to see the others and hear their conversation. *I'm thankful Adam was able to describe the guy. Maybe they can issue an all-points bulletin, catch him, and put him behind bars.*

Rafferty studies the portrait and shakes his head. "I don't recognize him." Then he passes the cell phone to Maeve.

"Doesn't ring any bells with me either," she says, handing the phone to Mick.

By the time the cell phone makes it back to Joe, it's clear that no one in the room is familiar with the face.

"I'm sending it to facial recognition now," Joe says. "I hope we get a hit."

"While you were at Thoreau," Rafferty says, "The Sen-Sen wrapper and bandana were picked up. I know there's a backlog, but I asked Crenshaw if *he* would put a rush on it. The directive carries more weight coming from him."

Brianna puffs out her cheeks and blows air through her lips. "You told us about dinner, Niall. But what's for dessert?"

Niall grins. "How's that for a subject change?"

"Honey, it's not polite for guests to ask about the meal," Marci says, quirking an eyebrow at Niall as if to say, "But I want to know too."

Everyone at the dining table laughs.

"Carrot cake," Niall says. Then pointing the tongs at Brianna, he continues. "With thick, ooey-gooey frosting."

"Just shoot me now," Mick says, grabbing his chest with both hands, "because I've died and gone to heaven."

Fear's cold hand squeezes Niall's heart despite his recent reflection on his grandmother's words. *Death and dying. Please, God, don't let anyone die tonight.*

· CHAPTER 14 ·

"Give the reader magic,
but don't explain the trick."
—Elizabeth Zelvin

At six forty-five, Maeve climbs the steps of the pavilion. She's the first to arrive for the evening's big event.

The sun set fifteen minutes ago, so she flips a switch that turns on the overhead light in the center of the open-beam ceiling. Then another switch illuminates the strand of white lights around the roof's perimeter. It makes the thick surrounding woodland seem even darker—*A perfect place for someone to hide.*

Despite her years of experience with the FBI analyzing some of the most heinous criminals in the underbelly of society, electric fear snaps its way up her spine, causing the hairs to rise on her flesh.

Hemingway and Maggie bound up the steps, each with a bully stick clenched in their jaws. They settle at the back of the pavilion, happy with their task.

Maeve removes a long fireplace lighter from the cabinet and lights the tall propane patio heaters. *I'm glad I wore a jacket.*

She rests a hand on the Walther PPS hidden in the belly band beneath her layers and takes comfort in knowing that Mick, Joe, and Rafferty are armed too. She thinks about "The Boys"—their similarities and differences.

Mick, age thirty-eight, is the youngest of the three. He thrives outdoors and would just as soon sleep under the stars in a hammock slung between two trees as in a comfortable bed. Give him a fishing pole, and he'll happily catch dinner. Give him a knife and a block of wood, and he's content to carve.

Joe, age forty-two, is a devoted family man. He's been married to his high school sweetheart, Marci, for fifteen years and is proud to tell anyone that he's a "girl daddy." In addition to Carly and Brianna, his third "baby" is a Carousel Red 1980 Chevrolet Camaro Z28, which he loves to work on and take to car shows.

Rafferty, age forty-five, enjoys the creature comforts of life. His idea of camping is having to stay in a motel instead of a hotel. Niall's cooking is the only thing he loves more than dining in five-star restaurants. He loves classical music, collects first-edition books, and wears tailor-made suits.

As different as they are, each of them desires to make the world a better place. They want to protect people before they even know there's a threat. And each of them has a "tell"—an unconscious action. When worried, Mick rubs his left thigh or fiddles with the whale fluke pendant he carved. Joe presses the muscle at the corner of his right eye. And Rafferty removes his glasses and pinches the bridge of his nose.

Yet, each of them remains cool, calm, and collected under fire and would lay down his life for the other.

Maeve surveys the layout—three rows of chairs are split in half to create a center aisle. *I want the best vantage point to keep an eye on Jennifer Pruett, the magician, and all the guests.* She rests her hand on the back of a chair. *From here, I can also see out three sides of the pavilion. Unfortunately, the fourth side is behind my back—a blind spot.*

Having weighed the alternatives, she takes the aisle seat in the left back row in front of the two dogs.

Niall takes the seat on Maeve's left. Then Libby joins to his left on the outside of the row.

Emma and Mick sit directly in front of them. *Like his dad Connor,* Maeve thinks, *Mick is courageous and self-sacrificing. But I'm worried about my daughter-in-law and Constance, my unborn granddaughter. I wish Emma wouldn't have come this evening, but we couldn't convince her otherwise.* Just as Maeve is about to turn away, she notices Mick fiddle with the whale fluke pendant on the leather cord around his neck.

Brent pauses next to Maeve with a wide smile. "I get to be Jennifer's assistant for a few of her tricks this evening."

"Oh, that'll be fun," Maeve says.

Then he continues forward and parks his wheelchair just a few feet from where Jennifer will perform.

Maeve surveys the other side of the aisle: Marci Bingham is seated directly across to her right, with Carly and Brianna next to their mom. *I wish the girls weren't here either. I'm terrified for their safety. Thankfully, their dad, Joe, is seated at the end of the row. Connor always said, "Joe is protective and fueled by conviction."* Maeve notices Joe lift a hand and press the muscle at the corner of his right eye.

Rafferty guides his fiancée, Ivy, to a seat in front of the Bingham family. *Connor described Rafferty as determined and selfless.* Ivy nods when he angles toward her and whispers something in her ear. Then leaning back in his chair, Rafferty removes his glasses and pinches the bridge of his nose.

Adam and Lucy are seated in the front row, having an animated conversation.

Maeve laces the fingers of her hands together. *This whole thing worries me. At least Mick, Joe, and Rafferty have weapons under their jackets.* She does a head count. *When Jennifer arrives, there'll be fifteen. That accounts for each person.*

Everyone hushes as the speakers come to life with "Smoke & Mirrors"—a mix of electronic music with natural instruments composed by conductor and magician George Arkomanis. The pitch-perfect crescendos and decrescendos build a sense of anticipation, causing the audience to sit upright in their seats.

All heads turn at the rhythmic clicking of Jennifer's stilettos as she walks up the center aisle in a tea-length black gown. Then, just past the front row, she turns to face the audience, holds her empty hands out in front of her, and then presses her palms together. When she separates her hands, there's a brand new, unopened box of cards in one of them.

She walks to Maeve and asks her to break the seal and draw out a card. "When I turn around, look at the card and then show it to everyone else. Make sure not to say what it is. Then once they've seen it, place it face down on your lap and let me know you're done."

Jennifer turns around and closes her eyes.

Maeve flips the card over, shows it to everyone, then places it face down on her lap. "Okay, Jennifer, it's face down on my lap."

As Jennifer turns back to Maeve, she conjures three items out of thin air: a small pedestal table with a vial of oil and a small bowl containing silver glitter sitting on top. Jennifer wets the tip of an index finger with the oil and draws on the back of Maeve's hand. Then she sets the vial on the table and picks up the glitter, sprinkling it over what she drew. After placing the bowl back on the table, she blows the excess glitter from the back of Maeve's hand.

The music crescendos.

Everyone leans toward Maeve as she gasps in astonishment. Her heart races at the sight of the back of her hand. The remaining glitter is in the shape of a lightning bolt—the exact shape on the card she drew.

Jennifer says, "Now, please take the rest of the cards out of the box to make certain they're not all lightning bolts."

Maeve tips the deck on her lap and turns them face up. Every card has a different shape on it.

Jennifer snaps her fingers, and the table, vial, bowl, cards, and box disappear. All that remains is the shape of a lightning bolt on the back of Maeve's hand.

As Jennifer walks back to the front of her audience, the music changes and the speakers pour out "Lights in the Night." This piece of music, also composed by George Arkomanis, is characterized by syncopated rhythmic patterns with prominent sub-bass frequencies. Jennifer lifts her arms and tips her head back, and the lights go out.

Maeve can't believe what just happened. Stunned, she shakes her head. *If I hadn't seen it with my own eyes . . .* Now, more worried than ever about what might happen to those around her, she rests one hand on her hidden gun.

Joe blinks when the lights come back on. He's still stunned at what he just witnessed. He turns to Marci and mouths, over the girls' heads, "Holy Crap!"

Marci nods in wide-eyed agreement.

"Carly and Brianna," Jennifer says, "I noticed how much you enjoy listening to *The Girl Who Drank the Moon* audiobook."

The girls nod.

"I like the part when the witch in the Forest, Xan, is kind. She shares her home with a wise Swamp Monster and a Perfectly Tiny Dragon. Xan rescues the children and delivers them to welcoming families on the other side of the forest, nourishing the babies with starlight on the journey."

"You've read it?" they ask, astonished.

"Of course." She smiles. "Now, will you please do me a great big favor?"

"Sure," they say in unison.

"Stretch your arms out and put the edges of your hands together like this." Jennifer demonstrates, making a small tray with her hands.

The girls mimic Jennifer.

"Perfect," she says. "Now, in a minute, the lights are going to go out. When they do, you're each going to feel something in your hands. It'll tickle a little, but don't be scared. And no matter what, keep your hands together, okay?"

"Okay," they say.

Oh Lordy, Joe thinks, *I hope we're not going home with puppies. I'll be the one designated to poop patrol duty.*

As the music builds, Jennifer raises her hands, and the lights go out.

Joe turns in his seat toward his daughters. And though he can't see them in the dark, his heart races in anticipation of whatever will happen when the lights come back on.

But they don't.

Instead, his daughters' faces—filled with pure delight—glow from the palm-sized fire-breathing dragons standing in their hands.

"What's happening?" Ivy asks.

"Carly and Brianna are holding fire-breathing dragons," Joe says.

"Stuffed animals?"

"No, they're alive. At least they look like it. They're blinking and flexing their little wings."

Joe reaches a hand to pet one of the little creatures. "Christ!" he shouts, pulling his hand back. "It scorched me."

Jennifer snaps her fingers. When the lights come on, the tiny dragons disappear. All that remains are two tendrils of gray smoke where they'd been.

As Jennifer walks back to the front of her audience, the music changes again. This time the speakers play "The Magician"—emotional symphonic rock—another piece composed by George Arkomanis. The tempo escalation has everyone brittle-tight on the edge of their seats. She lifts her arms, tips her head back, and the lights go out.

Joe sits slack-jawed. *Holy Mother of God!*

———

Joe blinks when the lights come back on. Stunned, he remains still, but Rafferty turns in his seat and makes eye contact with Maeve, Mick, and Joe. There's no mistaking the message he conveys—*I no longer doubt Jennifer's ability to create the illusion of murder.*

"Brent, would you please come up front?" Jennifer points to the area next to her.

Brent maneuvers to the spot.

"That's a darned fancy wheelchair," she says. "I know that you were a race car driver at one point. I suspect this set of wheels," she says, touching the arm of his chair, "can move pretty fast too."

Brent grins. "Yes, indeed."

"Are you game to find out just how fast it can go?"

He nods. "You betcha!"

Jennifer surveys the audience. "Rafferty, would you mind lending us a hand?"

Rafferty stands and then walks to the front. "How can I help?"

Jennifer points to a dull silver metal slab about forty-eight by forty inches and two inches thick, leaning against a pavilion joist to her left. "Would you please bring that over here." She points to a spot on the floor. "And then hold it as steady as you can?"

Rafferty walks to get the large metal sheet, but it's so heavy he can hardly lift it. So he drags it over instead.

"Please inspect that sheet of metal and tell the audience if there are any dents, cracks, weak spots, or secret openings of any kind."

Rafferty inspects both sides of the heavy piece of metal. "It's a solid piece."

Jennifer turns to Brent. "Do you trust me?"

Brent nods.

"Okay then. I'd like you to back up as far as you possibly can and then go full throttle, right through that solid sheet of metal."

The audience gasps.

Nonplussed, Brent backs his chair to the edge of the raised pavilion floor. "I'm ready when you are."

Jennifer raises her hand, racing style, then drops it. "Go!"

Brent takes off.

Rafferty grips the metal, and he braces himself. He watches as Brent draws near and then is seemingly absorbed into the piece before he comes out the other side with a face-splitting grin.

Jennifer walks to the center of the floor as the audience erupts into thunderous applause. She lifts her arms, tips her head back, and the lights go out.

This time when they come back on, there's no music.

Instead, there's a guttural cry from Niall. "Oh, my God!"

He stands, pointing to the chair next to him. Libby has disappeared. On the seat of the chair where she'd been sitting just moments before is a crumpled royal-blue bandana.

The heavy metal slab thunders when it hits the floor as Rafferty runs toward the back of the pavilion.

CHAPTER 15

"You always start a fight scene or an action scene with, 'What are we learning about this character at the moment, and how are we going to arc him or her in the next three minutes,' and it's no different with Deadpool or Atomic Blonde or John Wick."
—DAVID LEITCH

Ivy's immediate goal is not to get trampled. But from the rapid foot thuds on the tai chi pavilion's wood floor and the metal chairs banging, it sounds like that is what will happen if she gets in the way. Reaching under her seat, she grasps her collapsible cane, sets it on her lap, and stays put, simmering with fear and uncertainty. *Without Rafferty or Maggie, I don't dare move right now.*

Like a radar atop a ship's mast, she rotates the top of her body and absorbs information. In the chaos around her, her nostrils catch the lingering scent of mineral salt and spicy ginger—*Rafferty's cologne from when he stopped momentarily on his way to help Niall when he shouted, "Oh, my God!"*

A metal folding chair tips over and bangs on the floor in front of her. Her mind jumps to the bangs on the night of the Fourth of July. They'd been watching fireworks with their friends on the bluff overlooking Bellingham Bay. Then, during the explosive booms and bangs of the grand finale, Toni Bianco shot Rafferty. Ivy shudders at the memory. *If it hadn't been for the Life Flight helicopter that airlifted him to St. Joseph Hospital, he might have died.*

Ivy leans forward. "What happened?" she asks Lucy and Adam.

"When the lights came back on," Lucy says, "Libby was gone. She's disappeared. And in her seat, there's a blue bandana."

"I thought it was part of the show," Adam says.

"It's *not* part of the show," Jennifer barks as she runs by, her stilettos clicking the floor like a crazed woodpecker.

"Will you be okay here?" Adam asks.

The scent of vanilla and lavender wafts toward Ivy.

"She'll be fine," Maeve says, placing a comforting hand on Ivy's shoulder. "I'm taking her and the girls back to the main house."

"Okay, then," Adam says. "Then we're going to catch up with the others and help find Libby." Adam and Lucy's footfalls diminish in the distance.

Ivy unfolds her collapsible cane and locks it into place. Then standing, she says, "Maeve, what's going on?"

Maeve's explanation is brief and reassuring. "I'm sure she probably just had to use the restroom." But Ivy hears thickness in her words. *She's swallowing back tears. Libby is this woman's daughter, Mick's sister, and Niall's wife.*

Ivy swallows the lump in her own throat at the magnitude of heartache.

Determined not to be caught unaware, she feels the lump at the waistline under her blouse where her fiancé's ankle carry, a Sig P938 with six rounds of 9mm Luger ammunition, is nestled. *As Rafferty says every time I practice using it, "No one expects a blind woman to have a gun. It's the ultimate element of surprise."*

———————

Libby struggles to consciousness. When she opens her eyes, everything is black, and her breathing is labored. *Was I knocked out?* Icy fear slides up her spine. *I was at the magic show in the pavilion, and now I'm here. But where's "here," and how long have I been gone?*

Her arms and legs are limp as her body is dragged across rough ground and gnarly roots. Libby is tall, and her muscles are well toned—a heavy burden for someone to drag any distance. Tree trunks—one, two, three—blur by. Bramble bushes and thorns bite at the flesh of her hands. They tear at her clothes. *I need to get on my feet.*

Something presses hard against her throat as she's pulled deeper into the woods. Black spots pop in Libby's vision as she tries to control her ragged breathing. She fights a wave of nausea, brings her hands up, and clamps her fingers into the thick forearm under her chin. She inhales through her nose—*a tang of salt in the air and pine. I think I'm still at Pines & Quill.*

"Who are you? What do you want?" Libby's voice is muffled. She feels fabric at the base of her chin and rubs it between a thumb and forefinger. *It's a hem. There's a covering over my head.* Then, using every bit of her strength, she rips it off and bites into the flesh of a muscled arm. She tastes warm, slick blood as her teeth pierce the skin, and she struggles in his vice-like grip.

A low growl precedes a rock-solid fist that slams into the side of her head.

Blinding light blooms before Libby's eyes. She squeezes them shut against the pain and bears down harder with her teeth.

Another blow to the side of her head.

———

All the horrible possibilities of what might be happening to his sister fill Mick's mind. *How the hell could Libby disappear right out from under our noses?* He wipes sweat from his forehead with the sleeve of his jacket. "We'll find Libby faster if we split up," he says to the group assembled at the base of the pavilion steps.

The writers—Adam, Lucy, Brent, and Jennifer—stand together.

"Do any of you know how to use a gun?" Mick asks.

Jennifer and Brent nod. "I do," they say in unison.

Mick and Joe give their ankle carries to the pair.

"The four of you will scour the main property. Stay on the pathways," Mick says. "They're smooth and well-lit."

He rakes a hand through his black hair. "Head south until you reach the ridge that overlooks the national park and reserve. Then follow it east. When you get to Thoreau cottage, turn north and work your way up to the garage and workshop. We'll head northwest to the bluff, work our way back, and meet you at the main house."

The writers turn as a group and head toward El Cañón del Diablo—The Devil's Canyon National Park and Reserve.

Mick, Niall, Joe, and Rafferty walk north in a straight line at four-foot intervals. They use the flashlight apps on their cell phones to scour the ground and spill light into the forested area around them.

Mick takes in the dark surroundings. The air's so cold it feels like he's inhaling needles. *We've got to find Libby.*

Emma and Marci, who refused to stay at the tai chi pavilion, are on their heels. Their cell phone flashlights are activated as well.

Just past Austen cottage, Mick stops and holds up a hand signaling his group to halt. He holds a finger to his lips. They listen to the quiet sounds of the woods around them—skittering in the undergrowth as small creatures dart around looking for food.

They hear a soft whine and bolt toward the sound.

———

The moon casts a much-needed yet muted glow when Libby can open her eyes again. She glances into the surrounding trees, but everything is black. The darkness is so thick that she's unsure if her eyes are actually open.

Deeper they go. The air is damp and dank. The moon can't penetrate the thick canopy of trees, and blackness swallows them whole.

The man's terrifyingly calm breathing slithers over her skin with the confidence of a man who's done this before. Her palms, armpits, and the nape of her neck are sweaty. Libby's chest tightens as fear's sharp talons grip her tighter. *He's going to kill me—I'm going to die here.*

She starts pedaling backward with her feet to keep her spine from grinding into the uneven ground. Her mind races along with her legs as she braces to fight for her life.

Libby has practiced slow and gentle tai chi movements for over thirty years, usually as a moving meditation and whole-body exercise. But she's equally skilled in the combat modules—that powerful and effective form of tai chi is called Taijiquan. Quan means *fist*, or boxing as a martial art.

Libby counts the steps to the tree line. *Ten maybe. He's strong, but I'm fast. I might be able to take him by surprise if I move now.* She kicks her legs out but doesn't catch on anything. Her fingernails find skin. She rakes deep furrows from elbow to wrist, drawing blood.

He stops. "Bitch!" His voice rasps out in a rough scrape of sandpaper and gravel. He releases his chokehold, bends over, and places his hands on his knees. His attention is momentarily diverted.

As Libby sucks in desperate gulps of air, oxygen floods her lungs and bloodstream. She presses herself up on her elbows, bends her knees, and plants her feet on the ground. Counting her breaths, she tries to control them. An attempt to make sure her lungs are ready for what she's about to do.

One deep inhale. Then another.

Libby rolls to her side, pushes herself up, and, surging all the strength she can muster into her legs, flies like a racer exploding from a starter's block.

The light from Mick's cell phone flashlight joins similar beams bouncing on the ground ahead of the small group until they land on Maggie and Hemingway.

Both dogs are four legs sideways on the dirt. The gnawed remains of large meat bones lay close to their bodies.

"Oh, my God! They've been poisoned," Mick yells.

They drop to their knees by their furry companions.

Mick's stomach is in knots as he lays an ear against Hemingway's chest. "His heart's still beating. He's alive."

"So is Maggie," Rafferty says. "She's whimpering."

Mick lifts one of Hemingway's eyelids, but there's no response. The big dog lays limp on the ground. He calls Dr. Kent Sutton, who picks up on the second ring. "Doc, it's Sean McPherson. Hemingway and Maggie have been poisoned."

"Are you where you can induce vomiting?" the vet asks.

"We're in the forested part of the property. What does it take?" Mick asks.

"A watered-down solution of hydrogen peroxide and a turkey baster. Unless they already present signs of pois—"

"What kind of signs?" Mick breaks in.

"Elevated heart rate, tremors, coma—"

"Hemingway's out cold, and Maggie has tremors."

"Then get them here immediately," Doc Sutton says. "Fairhaven Veterinary Hospital is only ten minutes away. Molly and I will be waiting with the equipment to pump their stomachs."

"Thanks, Doc," Mick disconnects the call, fishes his keys out of his front pocket, and tosses them to Rafferty. "With four-wheel drive, the Jeep can get close. We'll hear you and help lift them into the back."

Rafferty bolts toward the garage.

"I've got this," Joe says, looking at Mick and Niall. "I'll help Rafferty lift them into the Jeep. You two keep searching for Libby."

Mick turns to Emma. "*Please* stay with Marci and Joe. Whoever's done this," he says, gesturing to Hemingway and Maggie, "is twisted—evil. And if anything happens to you or the baby," he says, swallowing hard, "I wouldn't be able to live with myself."

Emma slips her arms around Mick's waist, stands on tiptoes, and pulls his head down to hers. She whispers in his ear. "Come back to me, Mr. McPherson, because I wouldn't be able to live without you either."

He hugs her fiercely and whispers back. "I promise."

Then he and Niall take off in the direction they'd been heading when they found the two dogs. *Please, God, let my sister be okay.*

There are heavy footfalls behind Libby—*right* behind her.

Then a deep resounding thud between her shoulder blades as a thick branch knocks the wind out of her and propels her face down on the ground.

The man looms over Libby. First, he kicks her in the ribs, then snakes his forearm around her throat again, pressing against her windpipe as he yanks her up.

When her shoes hit the ground, Libby feels her pulse beat in the soles of her feet.

With an arm still around her throat, closing off her windpipe, the man pulls her back against a heaving chest. Her adversary's strained breathing is warm against her ear. *Why doesn't he say something—anything?*

At that moment, all of the senseless deaths over the past months—especially her father's and brother-in-law's—and the sleepless nights from fear of losing Pines & Quill contract to a laser-point of rage.

She remembers what the TSA agent said about the eight-inch carved skewer that holds her chignon in the crane hair slide Mick made for her. *"Because this can be used as a weapon, I'm afraid I can't let you take it onboard the flight."*

Libby feels her stomach churn. *This is it; there's no room for error.* Lightning quick, she pulls the stick from her hair, fists it, and thrusts it down and back with a roar, piercing pants fabric and then the thigh of the man behind her. Then, when it meets with resistance, she twists and shoves it for all she's worth into his front left quad muscle.

The man's howl reverberates in Libby's head.

He tightens his grip and leans forward. Then, growling, he takes her right ear in his mouth and bites down through the cartilage.

Libby sucks air in through clenched teeth as she switches the skewer from her left to right hand, ensuring the sharp end protrudes out the thumb end of her fist. Then, in one swift motion, she surges her fist up and plunges the skewer past her right ear.

This time, there's no resistance.

Something warm and wet trickles down her neck.

The man unclamps his teeth from her ear and spews venom. "You fucking bitch!"

Globules of spit land on the back of her neck.

As her assailant loosens his chokehold, she thrusts herself forward out of his grasp, falling onto the ground. She turns around on all fours. Without her to support him, the man slips face down to the ground, driving the entire length of the hair stick through his right eye and into his brain.

———

Niall's heart rips at every vulnerable seam as he runs alongside his brother-in-law. *I've got to find my wife!*

The thud of each footfall brings with it the names of people killed in recent months: *Jason Hughes, alias for Andrew Berndt; his brother Paddy MacCullough; Vito Paglio, alias for Salvatore Rizzo; Pam Williams and her impersonator Shelly Baker; Kyle Williams; Kevin Pierce the valet at Mick and Emma's wedding; Connor MacCullough, his father-in-law, and Toni Bianco, Joe's ex-partner who turned out to be a dirty cop. God, please don't let Libby's name be added to that list.*

In the distance, their lights pick up a figure crawling out of tangled foliage. As the space closes between them, Niall sees that it's Libby. She's on all fours, panting. The side of her head is covered in blood, and her right eye is swollen shut.

"Libby!" Niall yells, running forward and throwing himself on the ground beside her.

Libby's teeth chatter. Her body shivers uncontrollably.

"She's in shock," Niall says, tearing off his jacket and placing it around her. Tears of relief course down his cheeks. His voice is thick. "What happened, Love?"

He feels the silent sobs wracking Libby's body.

Mick squats down beside them. "Do you know who did this to you?"

Libby shakes her head. "I don't know who he was." Her voice cracks and then shatters. "But he's dead. I killed him." She buries her face in her hands.

Niall and Mick look at each other wide-eyed over her head.

She lifts her head. "His body," she says, pointing over her shoulder to the thicket behind her, "is back there."

"Right now, we need to get you to the hospital," Niall says.

Libby shakes her head. "I'll go in just a minute. But first," she says, looking up at her brother, "Mick, will you please go check and make absolutely certain that he's dead? I don't *ever* want to worry about him coming after me or our family again." She burrows deeper into her husband's chest. "I want Niall to stay here with me."

Mick draws his gun and disappears into the thicket.

Niall wraps his arms protectively around Libby, the love of his life. Then, as the adrenaline rush starts to wear off, he rocks her gently back and forth—as much to soothe himself as her.

———

It doesn't take long for Mick to locate the body. Keeping a steady aim, he toes it over with the tip of his boot and directs the flashlight onto the face. *Holy Mother of God!*

He bends down to look closer at the end of an object barely protruding from the dead man's right eye. He sees his sister's initials. *It's the rosewood stick from the crane hair slide I carved for Libby.*

Mick moves the flashlight around the rest of the man's face. *Not at all familiar; he appears to be in his early to mid sixties. A bulbous nose webbed with spider veins dominates his ruddy face. A heavy brow counters it. He has a thick mat of white hair and a matching white mustache. He's large and looks to have possessed physical strength.*

Mick picks a fallen branch off the ground, slips it under

one of the man's wrists, and lifts it. He leans closer. *Why would he wear white cotton gloves?*

Standing back up, he calls Joe's cell phone. "We found Libby. She's banged up pretty bad, and I think she's in shock, but she's alive."

Joe's loud exhale is weighted with relief as if he'd been holding his breath. "Oh, thank God."

"But we've got a body."

"Whose?" Joe asks. "Is it the guy that Adam described to the police sketch artist?"

"No," Mick says. "It's not him. I don't recognize the guy."

"What happened?"

"Libby killed him in self-defense," Mick says, explaining the hair stick.

"Holy shit!"

"Since we have no idea who he was," Mick says, "I'm going to photograph his face and send it to you. Forward it to Chief Simms, bring him up to speed, and ask him to send the medical examiner and her team to pick up the body.

"And in the meantime, I'm going to help Niall get Libby back to the main house. Then I'll come back out here and stay with the body so it doesn't get dragged away by any wildlife."

"Okay," Joe says. "And now that you found Libby, I'll round up the rest of the group. They're going to want to know what happened."

"Right," Mick says. "Take them to the main house. We can explain everything to everyone at the same time and answer their questions as best we can. Have you heard from Rafferty about Hemingway and Maggie?"

"He just called," Joe says. "Doc Sutton pumped both of their stomachs. He's keeping the contents for forensics to examine. He also said he's keeping Hemingway and Maggie overnight so he can keep an eye on them, but he's pretty sure they're both going to be okay."

A whoosh of palpable relief escapes between Mick's lips. "Thanks, Joe," he says. Then, turning around, he starts toward Libby and Niall through the scrub. "I'll see you shortly."

He pauses for a moment, tips his head back, and looks at the night sky through an opening in the canopy of trees. And though clouds obscure the moon, he thanks his lucky stars.

Carmine Fiore, Gambino's underboss, blends in with the shadows outside Brittany's dorm at Rice University and mutters under his breath. "Goddamned bastard. This is the *last* fucking time I'll have to ask 'How high?' when he says 'Jump.'"

He checks the time on his cell phone and does a quick mental calculation. *It's midnight here in Houston and ten o'clock in Fairhaven, Washington. I'm right on time.*

He presses the button on his cell phone to call Gambino, then lifts it to his ear.

It rings once, twice, three times.

He pinches his bottom lip. *The bastard always answers on the first ring.*

He pulls the phone from his ear and squints at the display, puzzled, to ensure he'd pressed the right button.

Carmine disconnects the call and redials. He runs a fingernail between his teeth while he waits to leave a voicemail. But there's no outgoing message. Gambino's phone continues to ring.

Carmine disconnects the call again. *What the fuck?*

CHAPTER 16

*"Don't be paralyzed by the idea that you're
writing a book. Just write."*
—Isabel Allende

Mick struggles to control his emotions as he and Niall
carry Libby between them toward the circular drive.
Her face grimaces in pain as she sucks air through clenched
teeth, squeezes her unswollen eye shut, and clenches her fists.

Arriving at the car, the two men settle Libby into the
front passenger seat. Mick notes the time on the dash—*Ten
thirty*—before shutting the car door. *That was a close call. Too
damn close. I almost lost my sister tonight. And Hemingway
and Maggie too.*

He balls his hands into fists. *Who is the dead guy? One
of Gambino's thugs? A member of the Sureños gang? I need to
find out. Fast. Before anyone else gets hurt or killed.*

Mick tips his head back and draws a deep, ragged breath
of brine-scented air. Clouds, backlit by the moon, slither across

the inky night sky. *How did that man get Libby right out from under my nose? I failed my sister.* Guilt gnaws at his gut.

There's a loud snap in the distance.

Mick swallows hard as an icepick of adrenalin shoots through his body. *One of the dead man's partners?* He draws his gun and squints between the surrounding tree trunks, but his eyes fail to pierce the stygian woods.

A deer snorts when Niall turns on the headlights. It bounds deeper into the thicket snapping more twigs as it goes.

Relief floods Mick's veins, and he holsters his weapon.

Before Niall can pull the car out to take Libby to St. Joseph Hospital, a set of headlamps pierces the long, dark tree-flanked lane that winds from the entrance gate.

A white van with MEDICAL EXAMINER stenciled on the side pulls behind Niall's car in the circular drive. A thin layer of ice outlines the windshield where the wipers and heat from the defroster haven't reached yet.

Off to the side, in his peripheral vision, Mick detects movement. The silhouettes of several people—backlit with a soft yellow glow from the dining room light—stand inside the glass patio slider, watching the activity in the circular drive. *Each of them is accounted for. I wonder if the dead guy was working alone or if others are still lurking in the woods?*

Chief Medical Examiner Dr. Jill Graham opens the driver's door of the van and steps out.

Three other people on her team exit the vehicle as well.

Dr. Graham walks toward Mick.

The others open the doors on the back of the van and retrieve a body bag, stretcher, lighting equipment, and two large hard-sided silver cases.

In the distance, darkness devours Niall and Libby's tail-lights. *At least they're on their way to the hospital, and thank God it's close.*

Dr. Graham says, "Your mom answered the gate intercom and buzzed us in."

Mick nods. "Thank you for coming. I'm sorry to call you out so late and on a Saturday night, to boot."

She shakes his extended hand. "Don't worry about it. I might need a favor someday."

Another set of headlights appears in the dark lane.

Mick tucks his cold hands in his pockets. "It looks like my Jeep. That'd be Rafferty coming back from the vet. Two dogs were poisoned." Nuclear pissed, Mick rolls his head between his shoulders to relieve the tension. "Thankfully, we found them in time."

Rafferty parks and steps out. He greets Dr. Graham, who introduces him to the others on her team.

Mick calls Joe's cell. "Rafferty's back from the vet. We're heading to the body now." Then, disconnecting, he informs the others, "Joe's joining us. He's just in the main house, so he'll be here in a moment."

While they wait, Rafferty passes Dr. Sutton's message along to Mick. "Right now, they're a little worse for wear, but Hemingway and Maggie are going to be okay."

Joe joins them, and Mick leads the group through the forested property to the body.

"Do you know the identity of the corpse?" Dr. Graham asks Mick.

Mick shakes his head. "No. I've never seen him before."

"Do you have an idea of how he died?"

Mick pauses momentarily and looks at the ME. "I'd tell you, Doc, but you wouldn't believe me. You have to see this for yourself."

Carmine bites the cuticle on one of his thumbs. His repeatedly unanswered calls to Gambino have him on edge. *What the hell is going on?* He pulls a foil Sen-Sen pack from his pocket, pops a few into his mouth, then calls a strategically placed associate at the Bellingham Police Station to see if Gambino—or one of his aliases—was arrested. No.

He twists his lips in thought, then calls another associate—this one at the Whatcom County Morgue—to see if Gambino's body turned up there. No.

The display on Carmine's cell phone indicates that it's ten fifty. He calls a contact in admissions at St. Joseph Hospital to see if he's been admitted. No. But that call yielded some interesting information. His contact says, "Libby MacCullough is in the emergency room right now."

"Why?" Carmine asks.

"No idea. All that shows on my screen is the patient's name, the time of admittance, which was just a few minutes ago at ten forty-five, and her location in the hospital."

"Find out more and call me back," Carmine says. He disconnects and drives his rental car to Karl Young Park—wooded grounds near the Meyerland area of town, close to Rice University, where he'd been hiding in the shadows outside Brittany's dorm a short time ago, waiting to call Gambino as instructed.

In addition to mature trees, the park boasts public restrooms, a baseball field, tennis and basketball courts, a playground, and a large gazebo with tables and benches where he'd sat several times watching young mothers—*Oh, what I could do to them*—while waiting for a call from Gambino. But the most crucial feature of this park is the absence of security cameras.

After parking, he removes a carry-on case from the backseat. Then he walks into the men's restroom, checks the stalls—*empty*—and enters one, pulling the door shut behind him. After changing his clothes, he puts on a brownish-red man's wig, mustache, and beard. Then he changes the ID in his wallet before leaving the stall, taking the carry-on with him.

Back in his rental car, he uses his cell phone to book a ticket on the next flight to Seattle. *I'll check the penthouse first. Then if Gambino's not there, I'll fly to Bellingham and check his house that overlooks Whatcom Lake.*

Carmine slams his fist against the steering wheel. *Where the fuck is Gambino, and what's he up to?*

⎯⎯⎯⎯⎯⎯

At just before eleven o'clock, Mick leads the group through thick moonless woods to the body. Wet leaves and pine needles slap his face, but he doesn't care. His gut wrenches that one of his greatest fears—being unable to keep the people he loves safe from harm—has been realized. Again.

First, my partner, Sam, was killed. Next, Paddy, Niall's brother. Then my dad. Gambino's thugs tried to get Emma twice. And now Libby. Thank God they're both still alive.

When they reach the dead man, Mick, Joe, and Rafferty stand on the periphery to avoid disturbing the crime scene. Their breath comes out in vapors. The ground, wet from recent rain, frames their shoes with mud. Mick's left leg aches and his hands feel numb from the cold. And though they're a good six feet from the corpse, the smell of blood and sweat seems to permeate Mick's mouth.

"When I found the body," Mick says to Dr. Graham, "I was careful not to disturb anything."

Dr. Graham nods, and then she and her team start to work. First, they set up lights.

Autumn-colored leaves and pine needles glisten and drip.

A chill marches across Mick's arms and back.

The photographer takes multiple photographs of the prone body in the now-lit area.

As the team members place numbered cones next to their findings, Dr. Graham squats and pats the corpse's back pockets for a wallet. None. The cold paints a stain on her cheeks and nose. Her eyes water in the frigid air. "It's miserable out here," she says. "But the cold is a great preserver. At least it's not rain."

She rolls the body to a supine position and checks the front pockets. None. As she extracts a cell phone from an interior breast pocket, the phone rings.

Dr. Graham's eyes go wide, and everyone freezes in their tracks.

It rings again.

Mick leans forward. "What does the display say?"

"One word," she says. "Judas."

It rings a third time.

"*Judas* means betrayer or double-crosser," Joe says.

"Should I answer it?" she asks.

Rafferty hikes his brows. "It could provide answers."

"Yes," Mick says. "But it could also—"

The phone stops ringing.

"Well, it doesn't matter anymore," Dr. Graham says. "Either they hung up, or the call went to voicemail." She bags and labels the phone.

"We'll have a forensic information technologist access the phone and copy the data," Rafferty says.

The photographer continues to take more photos, especially of the face. When he finishes, Dr. Graham leans in for a close look. "Well," she says, turning to Mick, "I see what you meant. Do you know what the object in the right eye is? It looks like the end of a chopstick but with lettering—LM."

Mick nods. "It's an eight-inch carved rosewood stick— like a skewer—that goes with the hair slide I carved for my sister, Libby MacCullough."

Dr. Graham angles closer still. She tilts her head to the side and purses her lips. With gloved hands, she lifts and feels the back of the corpse's head. Then removing a measuring tape from her pocket, she checks the distance from the eye socket to the back of the head. "The hair stick is eight inches long?"

"Yes," Mick says.

"Then it must have broken when it hit the occipital bone. Otherwise, there'd be an inch sticking out the lower back portion of his skull. But I'll know more after the postmortem."

When Dr. Graham and her team finish their crime-scene tasks, they zip the corpse in a body bag and place it on the stretcher, then pack up their equipment and follow Mick, Joe, and Rafferty back out of the woods.

Once everything's loaded into the back of the van, Mick turns to Dr. Graham. "By any chance, are you working tomorrow?"

She places a hand on a hip. "You should know by now that I'm married to my job. So yes, I'm working Sunday."

"Would it be okay," Mick asks, "if we come by to learn about your findings? We're going to need to get the guy's cell phone, his fingerprints, and DNA to see if a match pops."

"Come by about noon. And if you bring me a hummus platter from Keenan's at the Pier," she says, cocking an eyebrow, "I should have something definitive."

"You got it, Doc," Mick says. "We'll be there on the dot."

CHAPTER 17

*For the writer, the serial killer is, abstractly,
an analogue of the imagination's caprices and
amorality; the sense that, no matter the dictates
and even the wishes of the conscious social self,
the life or will or purpose of the imagination is
incomprehensible, unpredictable.*"
—JOYCE CAROL OATES

In the main house, Maeve checks on Carly and Brianna in the Ink Well. While placing a few more logs on the fire, she mentally replays the discovery of Libby's disappearance at the end of the magic show. The blue and orange flames dancing in the fieldstone hearth do nothing to relieve the soul-biting chill of fear at almost losing her daughter, Libby.

Oh, how I wish Connor were here. We worked so well as a team. Without him, I feel—she pauses to think of the right word—*inadequate.*

Her throat clenches as a wave of sadness at the loss of her husband nearly smothers her. Then she mentally shakes herself. *What would Connor do? Well, one thing's for damn sure; he wouldn't just stand here and wallow in sorrow. Instead, he'd figure out how to help The Boys. And that's what I'm going to do too.*

As Maeve returns to the dining room with fresh resolve, a swath of savory scents greets her—the beguiling aroma of herbs and spices from Niall's delicious meal. She takes her seat at the massive pine table. A glance at the wall clock informs her that it's eleven fifteen. She looks at the worried faces of the others sitting there too—Adam, Lucy, Jennifer, Brent, Ivy, Marci, and Emma.

They all glance up when Mick, Joe, and Rafferty enter through the patio glass slider, where they toe off their mud-covered shoes and shuck off their wet coats, placing them on a wrought-iron coat rack.

Emma, Ivy, and Marci each pull out a chair next to them and pat it. The relief on Emma's face is palpable.

Maeve gestures at the dishes around the table. "We ate the meal that Niall made before the magic show. Your dinners are warming in the oven. So get your plates, and then when you come back, we'll talk."

When the guys return from the kitchen, their plates are loaded with beef short ribs, braised cabbage, grilled corn, mashed potatoes and gravy, and buttermilk biscuits.

"It smells delicious," Mick says. "Thank you for saving dinner for us."

"Yes, thank you," Joe and Rafferty say.

"I wish Niall and Libby were here to enjoy it with us," Mick says.

As the three men tuck into their meals, Maeve says, "If Carly or Brianna come in here from the Ink Well, where they're listening to their audiobook, I'm going to change the subject."

Everyone nods their understanding.

"While you guys eat, I'll share some new information. Hank Dupree called me after Chief Simms contacted him about the police sketch the artist created from Adam's description."

Mick furrows his brows. "Why would Simms contact Dupree?"

Maeve swallows back the metallic taste of fear. "There was a match."

Mick snaps his head up. "Who is it?"

Maeve raises a one-moment finger, then explains to the writers in residence. "Bruce Simms is the local police chief. He brought Hank Dupree—FBI Special Agent in Charge of Marin, Napa, and San Mateo County offices and the main office in San Francisco—into the loop when he discovered the identity of the man Adam described this morning for the police sketch artist."

Maeve turns back to Mick. "He's not only wanted by the police, but by the FBI. His name is Carmine Fiore."

"Are we talking about the guy they found in the woods?" Brent asks. "Is it the same guy?"

Mick sets down his glass. "It's not him."

Jennifer tilts her head to the side. "Then who's the guy in the woods?"

"We'll know more tomorrow," Mick says, "when the medical examiner finishes the postmortem."

Joe rubs the whiskers on his jaw. "The name Carmine Fiore rings a bell, but I don't know why."

Maeve places her palms on either side of her plate. "He's a serial killer. And like Ted Bundy, he escaped from custody before his final arrest."

Lucy leans forward wide-eyed. "I didn't know that Ted Bundy had escaped."

Maeve does a quick mental calculation. "That's probably because you were so young—or not even born yet. He started killing in the 1970s, possibly earlier. Not only did he escape, but he escaped *twice*."

Shock paints Brent's face. "But *how*?"

"Hard to believe, but Bundy's first escape happened when he jumped out of a second-story law-library window." Maeve shakes her head. "For his second escape, he lost thirty pounds and squeezed through a hole in the ceiling of his cell."

"That had to take some time and serious planning," Adam says.

"You're right." Maeve stands and picks up the stainless steel coffee carafe from the center of the table. "Especially about the planning." She glances at the thick ceramic mugs by each place setting on the table. "Who else can I top off?" Adam proffers his cup, and she fills it with steaming coffee, then Mick's and Lucy's, before sitting back down. "Let me explain," she continues. "Before I retired, I helped create the FBI's dichotomy approach to better understand serial killers. Based on an extensive database of closed serial killer cases, law enforcement began inferring patterns from past cases to catch current serial killers on the loose."

Jennifer leans forward. "A serial killer is someone who kills three or more people, right?"

"That *used* to be the definition." Maeve touches Connor's gold wedding band on a chain at her throat. "But over the years, it's changed. The FBI's current definition of a serial killer is 'the unlawful killing of two or more victims by the same offenders, in separate events.'

"From the killing patterns, we learned that there are four types of serial killers that fall within two categories— organized and disorganized.

"The *organized* killer is cunning, charismatic even. A planner. He can lure you into his car, like Ted Bundy. Or meet you through Craigslist, like the Long Island serial killer. He's meticulous, has contingency plans, and cleans up after himself, often transporting the body from the crime scene. They seem normal, so you don't see them coming."

Emma places a protective hand over her belly.

Mick puts an arm around her shoulders and pulls her into his side.

Maeve peers down at the dark liquid inside her mug, collecting her thoughts. "The *disorganized* killer is socially awkward. He won't be able to get you to have a conversation with him. He jumps out from behind a bush and strikes out of nowhere. Think of a Jack the Ripper type. These killers don't plan, so they often leave the body where they attacked and flee the scene."

"You keep saying *he*," Lucy says. "Are all serial killers male?"

Maeve shakes her head. "Not at all. There are lots of female serial killers. But the majority of them are male."

"You said that there are four 'types,'" Brent says. "What are they?"

Maeve counts them off on her fingers. "Visionary, mission-oriented, hedonistic, and power seekers."

Lucy shakes her head. "I don't understand. Will you define those for me?"

That's her third question, Maeve thinks. *Either she's highly interested in serial killers, or perhaps there's more to it. Lucy's almost six feet tall and looks to be solid muscle. And she travels a lot. While neither of those is unusual for a professional athlete, they would be helpful for a serial killer's cover. And because they're narcissists, they enjoy hearing about themselves. Or their styles—hence all the questions.*

Maeve nods. "The *visionary* serial killer believes that a person or entity is commanding him to kill. A prime example is Herbert Mullin. He killed thirteen people as a blood sacrifice."

Jennifer shudders.

"The *mission-oriented* serial killer kills to rid society of a particular group—for instance, drug dealers or prostitutes."

"Who would be an example of that?" Brent asks.

Maeve thinks for a moment. "Joseph Paul Franklin targeted black and Jewish people. He believed that race mixing was a crime against God. This led him to focus mostly on interracial couples."

"That's sick," Adam says.

"What about the third type?" Jennifer asks.

Maeve steeples her fingers in thought. "The *hedonistic* serial killer kills for personal pleasure. This type has three groups: lust, thrill, and profit."

"Will you explain?" Lucy asks.

Maeve nods. "The *lust* killer is driven by sex. Rape, torture, and mutilation give them sexual gratification. The *thrill* killer thrives on his victim's terror. And the *profit* killer kills for the sake of money and wealth."

"Who is an example of a hedonistic killer?" Brent asks.

"Jeffrey Dahmer is a high-profile example." Maeve sips from her mug. "He raped and then killed seventeen men in the Milwaukee area."

"What about the fourth type?" Lucy asks.

"*Power* serial killers are motivated by the process of murder." Maeve glances across the room at the black expanse through the patio slider. "They fantasize about having power and seek to dominate and control their victims. They tend to be organized. A high-profile example is John Wayne Gacy, who killed at least thirty-three young men and boys. He regularly performed at children's hospitals and charitable events as 'Pogo the Clown' or 'Patches the Clown.' Ted Bundy and Gary Ridgway—'The Green River Killer'—both fall into the power serial killer type."

Maeve presses her palms together, then laces her fingers. "And *that's* the type of killer that Carmine Fiore is."

There's a collective gasp around the table.

"He's wanted for at *least* seven murders—three women and four men—in three states: Louisiana, California, and

Washington. They also happen to be the states where Gambino's headquarters are located—New Orleans, San Francisco, and the greater Seattle area, including Fairhaven and Bellingham."

Maeve looks at Adam's blanched face and cups a warm hand over one of his.

"You're extremely lucky to be alive," she says.

———

Frustrated and tired, Lucy jams her hands into her armpits. The wall clock across from her indicates that it's eleven forty. "What do you mean that Adam's lucky to be alive? What happened?" Her voice is shrill, rising to a crescendo at the end. *I've been trying to figure out how to extend my stay at Pines & Quill so I can avoid the drama at home. I need a break. I can barely stand the sight of Rick anymore. But this is worse. I saw the medical examiner's van outside earlier—this is death.*

Adam glances at Mick, who nods. Then Adam lifts the shirtsleeve on his left arm to reveal a blood-seeped dressing over a wound. "The man in the sketch, Carmine Fiore, visited me at Thoreau cottage last night and slit my wrist."

Aghast, Lucy looks at the faces around the table. "Jennifer, you're the only person who seems as surprised as me." Lucy's anger mounts at the situation—at being uninformed. She turns to Brent and gives him a withering stare. "You *knew* about this?" She feels heat rise in her cheeks as she speaks through clenched teeth.

Brent nods. "Yes. I was the one who found Adam last night. I thought he tried to commit suicide. That's when I called the main house. Libby, Niall, and Mick came immediately."

"So they took you to the hospital?" Lucy asks.

"No," Adam says. "A paramedic friend of Mick's came because"—his voice breaks—"because *no* one"—he looks around the table—"not a *single* soul can find out about this."

An explosion of questions erupts around the dining room table as everyone talks and gesticulates at the same time.

Lucy stands and shouts. "For the love of God, will you please be quiet so someone"—she looks pointedly at Mick—"can tell us what the *hell* is going on? We saw the medical examiner's van earlier. Was Carmine Fiore the dead person they took away?"

"No. It wasn't," Mick says.

"Then who was it?" Lucy asks.

"I'm going to explain everything we know," Mick says. "Not only so you'll be informed, but because we need your help."

As Lucy takes a seat, she gestures with a hand around the table. "Why should we help you? Why shouldn't we just pack up and leave? How much danger are we in?"

Mick wipes his mouth with a napkin. *I need to keep everyone calm.* "That's an excellent question, Lucy." He places the napkin on the side of his plate. "If we don't help Adam, his daughter, Brittany, will die.

"But there's good news. And the best person to share it is Joe Bingham." He nods toward his friend. "As you know, he's a homicide detective and has information that involves all of us."

"In the interest of safety," Joe says, "the Bellingham Police Department has posted officers not only around the property, but an officer has been assigned to each cottage as well."

Next, Mick gestures to Rafferty. "You also know that Sean Rafferty is a special agent with the FBI. He also has information to share."

Rafferty pushes his glasses up higher on his nose. "You can rest assured that not only you but your families—including students living away from home—are safe. Each of them is being shadowed by an FBI agent to keep them from harm."

Mick stands and looks at each of the writers. "Here's the part where we need your help. Adam has been instructed to kill a writer in residence and frame me for the murder. If he doesn't, his daughter, Brittany, will die." He turns to Jennifer. His mind is uneasy. *What'll we do if she won't help?* "After your incredible show earlier this evening, I have to ask. Is it possible for you to create a realistic illusion of murder without anyone getting hurt?"

Jennifer crosses her arms and presses her eyebrows together. "I've never done anything like that. But if someone's life depends on it," she says, looking at Adam, "your daughter, Brittany, then I'll do everything I can. But I need *time*—time to plan and acquire props. Then Adam, the victim, and I will need to rehearse and refine the trick to ensure the ultimate possible impact—the illusion of reality."

"Adam told us the guy on the video calls said the murder has to happen before the twenty-first," Mick says. "The date the October writers in residence return home."

He looks at the date and time on his watch. "It's almost midnight—almost tomorrow, Sunday the ninth. And everyone leaves on the twenty-first. So that gives you twelve days."

Jennifer bites her bottom lip. "That's not a lot of time, but I'll make it happen."

"Then only a single thing remains." Mick searches Brent's and then Lucy's faces. "One of you needs to die."

CHAPTER 18

*"You rely on a sentence to say more than the
denotation and the connotation; you revel in
the smoke that the words send up."*
—TONI MORRISON

Libby slits her unswollen eye open when the swoosh of
metal rings supporting thin green cloth draped around
the sterile cubicle reveals the return of Dr. Gail Berman, the
on-duty emergency physician at St. Joseph hospital. *I want
to go home.*

Tubes of overhead fluorescent lighting stab Libby's vision.
The omnipresent smell of antiseptic, bleach, and sickness fills
her nostrils. Hurried footsteps, whispered conversations, the
beep of monitors, and distant crying merge to create a buzz
in Libby's ears like a swarm of wasps. *It feels like I'm in hell.*

Niall's warm hand squeezes hers three times, telegraph-
ing "I love you." But it doesn't alleviate her fear. *I don't want
to die. And it wouldn't be the first time Gambino has had*

people killed in this hospital. But if Dr. Berman's on his payroll, she could have killed me before she left to check on the X-rays.

As Libby pulls the hem of her flimsy hospital gown toward her knees, pain pulls her back from her mental reverie.

The doctor holds a clipboard and pen in one hand and two capped syringes in the other. The wall clock indicates the time to be twelve fifty-five—*almost one o'clock Sunday morning.*

From the plastic chair beside the bed, Niall releases Libby's hand and stands. "Are her ribs broken?" His voice chokes with anguish.

Libby tries to sit up, but the motion unleashes an explosion of pain. She grabs her right side, groans, and eases back down on the bed.

Dr. Berman sets down the syringes and places a hand on Libby's shoulder. "Lie still. You have two broken ribs." She looks at her clipboard. "The thing that's equally concerning to me is the puncture wound I found on the back of your neck. I saw it when we capped your hair before I stitched your ear." The doctor twists her lips to one side. "Based on its appearance and the incident you described, I think it might be from a tranquilizer dart. We'll know more when the results of your blood work come back."

The physician walks to a wall-mounted display screen. After turning it on, she makes a few keystrokes on the keyboard beneath, then positions herself so that Libby and Niall can both see the X-ray.

"The rib cage has twelve paired rib bones, each symmetrically paired on the right and left side." Dr. Berman steps closer to the image and points with a pen. "Libby, as I said, you have two broken ribs on your right side—numbers four and five. And though it's not visible with an X-ray, that most certainly means that the intercostal muscles in that area are bruised."

A knot bulges in the crook of Niall's jaw, and a vein pulses in his forehead. "How do you treat broken ribs?"

Dr. Berman pulls on a pair of latex gloves and then picks up the syringes. "Most broken ribs heal on their own within six weeks. Restricting activities and icing the area promote healing. But I'm also going to prescribe medication for pain relief. First though," she says, turning to Libby, "I'm going to give you two injections. The first one is an anesthetic to the nerve area that supplies the ribs. The second is to help you sleep—our bodies heal during sleep. The combination of these, plus the anesthetic I injected by your ear before stitching it, will provide relief. But only until they wear off. That's when you'll start taking the one-week prescription of co-codamol I'm writing. It's a strong pain killer."

Libby feels the chill on her skin from the isopropyl alcohol Dr. Berman uses to cleanse the first injection site. "Why only a week's worth if it takes six weeks for ribs to heal?"

"Because codeine—the opioid in co-codamol—is a central nervous system depressant. And though I *want* you to reap its benefits, I *don't* want you to become addicted."

Libby winces as the doctor administers the injection. "What are the benefits?"

Dr. Berman inserts the used syringe through a narrow slit in the biohazard box on the wall. "It causes feelings of relaxation and drowsiness, which help alleviate anxiety, panic, stress, and sleep disorders." The doctor locks eyes with Libby over the top of her glasses. "But it's *only* to get you over the first-week hurdle." After giving the second injection, she adds the syringe to the biohazard box, pulls off her latex gloves, and drops them in a trash can. "I want to see you for a follow-up in a week."

Dr. Berman gathers her pen and clipboard in one hand and tucks the other in a pocket on her white lab coat. "You can make an appointment at reception when you pick up the prescription at the twenty-four-hour pharmacy on your way out. They're next to each other," she says before drawing the flimsy curtain to the side and leaving.

Libby turns to Niall, who's rubbing his beard-stubbled jaw. His face sags with exhaustion, and there are purple hammocks under his eyes. *He's beautiful, and I'm so glad he's here with me.*

"It's going to be okay, Love," Niall says. "You didn't die, and that's what matters."

It's all Libby can do to nod. *I feel like a wrung-out dishrag.*

A wave of hopelessness engulfs her. *The attacks on my family, friends, and guests at Pines & Quill are relentless. And so many deaths, including my brother-in-law Paddy and my dad. Now I'm in the hospital. One minute, I was watching a magic show. The next, a man dragged me through the woods. We fought, and I stabbed him with the skewer part of my hair slide. He died. I killed a man.*

Libby's head is heavy. She lets it drop to her chest. *The medication must be taking effect. Either that, or whatever the doctor gave me is meant to kill me after all.*

Carmine Fiore extracts his carry-on from the overhead compartment, slips it over his shoulder, and stands in the aisle with the other passengers waiting to exit the flight from Houston to Seattle. *I need to find out where Gambino is and why the hell he's not answering his phone.*

While waiting, he resets his watch to Pacific Time—five thirty Sunday morning. He feels antsy, cooped up on this plane with all these people. *The driver I called before boarding my flight had better be waiting outside. And though I believe he's one of mine, I don't trust anyone.*

Frustration mounts as passengers jostle in the aisle—*like a bunch of cattle*—waiting for the flight attendants to open the door. To maintain calm, Carmine imagines slitting their throats.

The five-hour nonstop flight had given Carmine time to think, plan, and strategize. *If Gambino's onto me, the driver could be an assassin. So instead of sitting next to him, I'll sit behind him. When he dropped me off at the airport, I remembered I couldn't take my gun on the flight, so I left my Sig Sauer P226 chambered in 9mm with a fifteen-round magazine under the driver's seat.*

The airplane door opens, and the passengers disembark, making their way into United's Arrival Terminal at Sea-Tac.

Carmine checks his cell phone. *It's forty-fucking-three degrees. At least it's not snowing.* He turns up the collar on his black peacoat and pulls down his cuffs.

Cold air envelops him when he exits the building. A black Cadillac SUV idles curbside. The driver leaves the vehicle, walks around, and tips his head. "Boss."

Carmine nods back. "Marco, I'll sit in the back."

Marco opens the back passenger door.

Carmine slips in, slides across the seat to the other side, and reaches beneath the driver's seat. He finds the gun, checks the magazine—*still loaded*—and pockets it before Marco is seated behind the steering wheel.

"Where to, Boss?"

Carmine looks at Marco's reflection in the rearview mirror. "Third Avenue. The penthouse."

Black car and black windows—it's like a damn coffin in here. With his right hand on his gun, Carmine uses his left to lower the tinted window to ease his claustrophobia. The cold air whipping in bolsters him. He gazes up at the anvil-black sky. At this time of year, October, it won't morph to steel gray until closer to eight o'clock.

The distance between Sea-Tac and Third Avenue in downtown Seattle is fifteen miles. And though traffic is already starting to congest, the drive is smooth and uneventful.

When the SUV enters the underground parking area of Gambino's high-rise, Carmine closes the window.

Marco brings the vehicle to a stop next to silver elevator doors marked PRIVATE—PENTHOUSE SUITE.

Carmine exits the vehicle before Marco can and taps the roof twice. "I've got it from here."

Marco nods and pulls away.

Carmine eases the Sig Sauer from his pocket as he scans the area and watches until the taillights are no longer visible.

Then he walks over to the retinal scanner and lets it scan his eye. Though it's the latest technology, that's not why Gambino had it installed.

Carmine recalls the evening Gambino told him that he'd lost most of the feeling in his fingertips decades ago when he tried burning his prints off with cigarettes. When that didn't work, he used hydrochloric acid. "It hurt like a son of a bitch, and I couldn't use my hands for days."

A green light lets Carmine know he's clear and the elevator car is on its way. *Another fucking coffin.* But he's willing to ride in it for the prestige. As Gambino's underboss, he's one of the few people with that type of access.

He slips his gun into the pocket of his peacoat when the doors slide open, then steps inside. Aware of the security camera, he looks straight ahead. His image is a man of determination.

And though I'm going to kill Gambino, I don't want to kill McPherson. Not just yet. I want him to suffer. Last month, he killed Tank on Mount Baker, where our hostages were being held before shipment. Tank was one of mine; he was going to be my underboss. No one takes from me without retribution. And with everything that's already happened to McPherson, his family, and their precious Pines & Quill, he's like a hairline crack in glass.

Carmine smirks at his reflection. *Eventually, I'll shatter him.*

Showered and dressed, Niall sits on the bedside rocker next to Libby in their primary bedroom upstairs in the main house. He glances at the digital numbers on the nightstand clock — *five fifty-five.*

Last night in the ER, it felt like a runaway freight train was in my chest, ready to derail at any moment. I'm so glad to be back home with Libby. The next step is to get her well. He telegraphs a three-hand squeeze message to his wife—*I love you.*

Gentle chirps outside the still-dark window indicate the birds are waking up.

Her hand, in his, is warm as he takes up a one-sided conversation with God.

Just because my brother, Paddy, was a priest doesn't mean I have the same amount of faith in you. You let him die. And Libby nearly died.

The smell of antiseptic cream on Libby's ear clogs Niall's nostrils. And the muscles in his jaw spasm as he clenches his teeth.

The increased speed of the rocker—back and forth, back and forth—matches his agitation.

I don't understand why you allow bad things to happen to good people. It doesn't make sense. But if you are there and you're listening, I'd appreciate it if you'd watch over my family, our friends, and our guests at Pines & Quill.

Niall stops rocking to check Libby's pulse. Again. *She's alive but still out cold since I carried her in from the car at two o'clock this morning—less than four hours ago. She needs more sleep. Dr. Berman said, "Our bodies heal during sleep."*

His mother-in-law, Maeve, sick with worry about her daughter, met them at the main house door. Everyone else had gone to their quarters to get some much-needed sleep. Once they got Libby upstairs, changed, and tucked into bed, Maeve said, "Niall, I know the best medicine for you when you're upset is to be in your kitchen cooking and baking. So I'll come up at six o'clock and stay with Libby while you make breakfast."

Before Maeve returned to the guest room downstairs in the main house, Niall asked, "We were sitting in the same back row as Libby. Did you see or hear anything unusual?"

Maeve shook her head. "I've gone over it a dozen times. I was focused on what Jennifer, Joe, and Brent were doing at the front of the pavilion. I didn't see or hear anything else."

Niall's hands grip the rocker's arms as he mentally reviews last evening's events and the kaleidoscope of feelings that consumed him. *Dread engulfed me when I realized Libby had disappeared. Horror washed over me when we found her crawling from the bushes covered in blood. Angst shadowed me throughout the emergency room visit.*

There's a light tap on the bedroom door.

Niall glances toward the nightstand. *Six o'clock. Maeve's right on time.*

Armed with a flashlight and an e-reader—*And if I know Maeve, she's got a gun somewhere on her person too*—his mother-in-law tiptoes into the room and takes his spot in the rocker.

"Emma, Marci, Ivy, and I will take two-hour shifts so you can feed your guests and manage the retreat. We'll let you know the minute she wakes up."

Niall squeezes Maeve's hand. "Thank you. I don't know what we'd do without you."

"And don't worry about delivering breakfast to the cottages. Joe said he'd do it while Mick and Rafferty pick up Hemingway and Maggie from Dr. Kent at Fairhaven Veterinary Hospital."

"You've thought of everything."

Maeve smiles up at him. "It's not just me. *Everyone's* pitching in." She gestures toward the door. "Now off you go."

Niall kisses Libby's forehead and whispers, "I love you," before leaving.

When he descends the stairs, his belly craters. *Hemingway's not beside me.* He misses his four-legged companion. *He's as much a part of my morning routine as sunrise.*

Niall enters the kitchen and flips on the pendant lighting over the center island. Then he slips the loop of a bib apron over his head, preps Libby's favorite Peruvian coffee, adds a pinch of cinnamon, then starts the large stainless steel machine.

Once the rest of the group arrives, it'll take a lot of caffeine to figure out what happened last night. How could Libby have been taken without any of us realizing it? And who is the man that took her? The man that's now dead, lying on a cold slab in the morgue.

Then on top of that, we have to create the illusion of murder, frame Mick for it, and have him arrested and taken to jail. Then, most importantly, ensure the media finds out and broadcasts it far and wide. That's what it will take to satisfy Gambino and save Adam's daughter, Brittany.

As the coffee perks, the fragrant aroma reminds him of his grandmother's spice cupboard—nutty with a hint of caramel. He inhales the soothing aroma and tilts his head back. *Gran started teaching me to cook when I was a little boy. As far back as I can remember, cooking and baking have been my way to self-soothe.* His shoulders lower instinctively, and he welcomes the healing energy of his chef's kitchen—his sanctuary.

Niall checks the day's menu board. Sunday breakfast is one of his favorites: buttermilk biscuits with honey-whipped butter and Pacific Northwest Scramble. He makes it with homemade beef chorizo—seasoned, coarsely ground pork sausage—eggs, onions, peppers, white cheddar cheese, cotija cheese, potatoes, and cilantro cream.

Several years ago, Niall and Libby had developed a food questionnaire for writers in residence who'd applied and been accepted for a three-week stay at Pines & Quill. Knowing their diet type—vegan, vegetarian, carnivore—and their likes, dislikes, and any food allergies helps Niall prepare menus everyone enjoys.

This morning, I'm also going to add some crispy bacon to the Pacific Northwest Scramble. It's one of Libby's favorite smells. When we were first married, before our son, Ian, was born, she said, "It's one of the only smells that's able to make me magically rise from sleep and float slowly downstairs on a cloud of savory goodness like in the cartoons."

Because I already made the chorizo, the potatoes will take the longest. So I'll start with them. Niall pulls his ten-inch Wüsthof chef's knife from the magnetic strip on the wall. The sharp blade glints in the light as he tests the heft in his hand.

Everyone's asleep right now, but as soon as they arrive for breakfast, I'll ask if anyone noticed anything slightly off or out of the ordinary at the magic show last night. For the love of God, there were fifteen of us! So someone had to see or hear something.

Niall rinses the potatoes under the faucet and then gives them an extra good scrub—tearing off much of the skin in his agitation.

Jennifer, Joe, and Brent were at the front of the pavilion. They would have had a good view of the audience. Then again, they were probably so focused on the illusion that everything else slipped into the background.

His movements are brusque as he halves and then quarters the potatoes lengthwise before making long thin slices.

Joe, Marci, the girls, Lucy, Adam, and Ivy were on the other side of the aisle from me. They were all facing forward, intent on the trick.

Maeve, Emma, and Mick were on the same side of the aisle as Libby and me.

He starts dicing the long, slender slices of potato.

Then guilt, which has a way of spoiling everything, taps *him* on the shoulder and attacks. *"Niall, you were sitting right next to Libby. How was she taken right out from under your nose?"*

Carmine exits the elevator when the silver doors hush open on the fifty-fifth floor—the penthouse suite. The plush foyer has mahogany walls, a marble floor, a large gilded mirror over a hall table, and a sleek black-framed wall clock with beautiful brass hands — *six fifteen.*

He draws the Sig Sauer P226 from his pocket. *I'm going to kill Gambino and take over.* And though he moves panther-like with slow deliberation, his heart accelerates with excitement as he corners the interior walls — checking behind doors, under beds — clearing each room.

He tries calling Gambino's cell phone again to see if it rings in the penthouse. But there's no sound. *Where the fuck is he? And why doesn't he answer his phone?*

When Carmine is confident that Gambino is not on the premises, he settles back in a leather chair in the living room. Nearby is a three-hundred-gallon aquarium with red-bellied piranha swimming back and forth, looking for prey. He shakes his head in approval, not disgust. *I've watched Gambino execute some nasty punishment with those fish.*

Carmine shifts his gaze to the exterior walls — floor-to-ceiling windows that boast a three-hundred-and-sixty-degree panoramic view of Seattle. The Space Needle, one of the most recognizable landmarks in the world, presents an imposing figure at any time of day. But uplit against a still-dark morning sky, it's awe-inspiring.

Gambino often says, "I'm King of the Hill — close to the city but above it all." But now, it's going to be mine.

Carmine returns to the main bedroom, opens the well-appointed walk-in closet, and starts opening drawers until he finds what he's looking for. Dozens of neatly folded royal-blue bandanas — the Sureños gang identifier. *And,* he muses, *calling cards we leave behind when we need to divert suspicion and place it elsewhere.* He grabs a dozen.

Next, he calls Tommaso, the man in charge of Gambino's fleet of cars. When Tommaso answers, Carmine says, "It's Fiore. Send a car to Third Avenue. Something that looks sedate but can haul ass if needed. I don't need a driver. I'll be waiting by the elevator in the underground parking garage in ten minutes."

Carmine disconnects, walks to the foyer, and shoves the bandanas in his carry-on.

Then he heads to the kitchen. Thanks to Gambino's chef, the refrigerator contains multiple containers of prepared food and a board covered with clear plastic wrap. He grabs the charcuterie board, peels back the wrap, and shovels cooked cold meats and cheeses into his mouth.

When his hunger's satisfied, he pulls a bottle of Chimay Blue from the door, finds an opener, pops the top, and starts slugging it down. At another time, he might appreciate the dark Trappist-style ale. But not today.

Ten minutes later, at seven o'clock, he takes the elevator to the parking garage.

When the doors slide open, the driver of a cream-colored Taurus SHO walks over to Carmine and hands him the keys. "It may not look like much, but it's the ultimate sleeper car that nobody expects. It's ruthlessly fast with all the capabilities of a hardcore sports car—but none of the persona."

Then the driver gets in the front passenger seat of a similar vehicle, and it pulls away.

Carmine places his carry-on behind the driver's seat, gets in, and turns the key. The V8 engine roars to life. He pulls out of the parking garage and heads to Gambino's luxury home on Lake Whatcom in Bellingham. *Traffic is lighter on Sunday mornings, so it should only take about ninety minutes.*

He imagines seeing Gambino in his crosshairs. Then, as adrenaline courses through his veins, he grips the steering wheel harder and presses the gas pedal. *And that location— only ten miles from Pines & Quill—is the perfect place to orchestrate the rest of my plan.*

CHAPTER 19

*"You never have to change anything you got up
in the middle of the night to write."*
—SAUL BELLOW

At seven fifteen, just minutes before first light on Sunday morning, Mick, Joe, and Rafferty meet in the workshop. Already in warm outerwear, each dons a headlamp and carries a tactical flashlight they retrieved from their go-bags.

"If Libby was shot with a dart gun like Dr. Berman suspects," Mick says, "and there weren't any darts or a dart gun found by the ME's team where Libby killed her captor, those items have to be *somewhere* between the pavilion and where the body was found."

Joe holds up a hand. "We can't rule out the possibility of an accomplice. Maybe he or she already collected those things. And the uniforms who scoured the perimeter of Pines & Quill didn't find a vehicle. Maybe they walked, or a second perpetrator drove it away."

"Speaking of *she*," Rafferty says. "I wonder if Jennifer Pruett, the magician, is the accomplice. When you think about the illusions we watched her do, making Libby disappear right out from under our noses is something she could pull off."

Mick presses his lips together. "I hate to think that, but I've thought about it, too. But *why*? What on earth would be her motivation?"

"Maybe she's being manipulated like Adam," Joe says. "Maybe she was threatened that if she didn't cooperate, someone she loves would be killed."

Mick nods. "You're right. But no matter what, we still need to check for evidence." He taps his headlamp. "Our LEDs will penetrate the thick foliage on each side of the pathway. I'll start where I found the body. You guys start at the pavilion. And we'll meet somewhere in the middle." He looks at his watch. "We've only got forty-five minutes before we promised to collect our families for breakfast at the main house. But at least it's a start. Then we can continue combing the area when we get back from the morgue this afternoon. If one of us finds something this morning, text the other two."

Joe and Rafferty nod, then head southwest toward the pavilion.

Mick heads northwest. His mind reels with questions. *Who's the guy that Libby killed? Where is Carmine Fiore? Does Jennifer have anything to do with Libby's abduction?*

Empty-handed, Mick meets Emma at their cabin at eight o'clock. Inside their warm living room, she pulls on her hat, gloves, and coat, then zippers her baby bump inside the fleece lining.

Mick adds a mental snapshot to his collection. *I'm so grateful to have Emma as my wife and the mother of my child.*

Concern fills Emma's face as she looks into Mick's eyes. "Did you guys find anything?"

Mick shakes his head. "I didn't. And since Joe and Rafferty didn't text me, they didn't either. But we'll pick up again after we get back from the morgue."

They step outside, and Mick pulls their cabin door closed behind them.

"It's freezing," Emma says, stifling a yawn before leaning into him and pulling her knit cap lower to cover her ears.

Mick puts an arm around her shoulders and pulls her close. "I'd guess low to midforties." He points east to the cotton-candy pink clouds that crested the Cascade Mountains a short while ago. "The sun's right on their heels, so it should warm up soon."

Mick's breath blows fog clouds as they walk from their cabin to the main house. They enter through the exterior mudroom door, where they peel off their outerwear and hang it on pegs.

An anchor drops in Mick's stomach when he doesn't receive a tail-wagging reception from his four-legged companion. "I can hardly wait until Dr. Kent calls to say we can pick up Hemingway and Maggie."

The moment they enter the open Dutch door into the dining area, the smell of coffee, sausage, bacon, and yeasty dough for buttermilk biscuits teases their nostrils. They make a beeline for the kitchen, passing the wall clock on their way—eight ten.

Niall looks up from his sauté pan; he looks exhausted. His shoulders slump. "Oh, Emma. My mind's all a jumble this morning. I set the ingredients out for hot chocolate—including the miniature marshmallows that you love." He points a wooden spoon to the counter area next to the ingredients for buttermilk biscuits and honey-whipped butter. "But I forgot to make it. I know you're not drinking coffee while you're pregnant. Speaking of which, how's little Connie doing this morning?"

Emma places a hand on her stomach. "She's been kicking. How's *Libby* doing this morning?"

Niall chuffs out a breath. "She has two broken ribs, and that guy nearly bit her ear off. Dr. Berman gave her a tetanus shot, stitched her up, and then gave her a sedative injection to help her sleep. She's still conked out. Maeve's with her right now."

A wave of guilt washes over Mick. *That guy would have killed Libby if she hadn't killed him first. If Gambino's behind this, he knows that hurting my family and friends is a much more effective torture than killing me, or he'd have done it by now. How many people is it going to take until he's satisfied? Who's next?*

"Mick, I'll set the table," Emma says, "if you make my hot chocolate. I bet Carly and Brianna would love some, too."

Mick nods. "Deal."

Emma turns to Niall. "How many place settings?"

Niall wipes his hands on his apron. "Let's see now. There's Joe, Marci, and the girls. Rafferty and Ivy. And the three of us. That's nine. I'll take plates up to Maeve and Libby."

"What about the writers?" Emma asks.

"Joe's going to deliver breakfast to their cottages when Mick and Rafferty pick up Hemingway and Maggie."

"Got it," Emma says, heading to the massive sideboard that houses the dinnerware and cutlery.

Once she's out of earshot, Mick says, "I don't want to worry Emma any more than she already is. Was Libby able to tell you how the guy took her without any of us noticing?"

Niall shakes his head. "No, but Dr. Berman said that when she capped her hair to stitch her ear, she found a puncture wound on the back of her neck. She said based on its appearance and the incident, she thinks that it might be from a tranquilizer dart and that they'll know more when her blood-work results come back."

"I don't know much about tranquilizers, especially when they're administered with a dart gun," Mick says. "But I know who does—Dr. Sutton at Fairhaven Veterinary Hospital. Joe and I will see him this morning when we pick up Hemingway and Maggie. I'll see if we can learn something that might help us figure things out.

"Regardless, a huge question remains," Mick says. "If Libby was tranquilized right there in the pavilion with the rest of us nearby, wouldn't *somebody* have seen her collapse and then taken away?"

Not wanting to voice a potentially false accusation, Mick keeps his thoughts to himself. *Jennifer Pruett is the only person at Pines & Quill who could pull off that kind of diversion.*

An hour after sunrise, at eight twenty, Joe, Marci, Carly, and Brianna walk from the guest quarters over the workshop to the main house. It doesn't matter to him that there are police stationed on the grounds—Joe still scans the surrounding tree line. The space between the trunks is still thick with shadow. He touches the butt of the Glock 22 in his clip holster.

When they arrive, they enter the front door, shed their outerwear onto the coat tree, then the girls ditch the adults and head to the Ink Well to watch television while they wait for breakfast.

Marci joins Emma, and they pour two mugs of coffee— one for Maeve and one for Libby in case she's awake—then climb the stairs to the main bedroom.

Joe drapes an apron loop over his head and ties it in the back. "What can I help with?"

"Ever make honey-whipped butter?" Niall asks.

Joe pours himself a cup of coffee. "No, but there's no time like the present."

"It's easy," Niall says, pointing to the ingredients on the counter. "Put the softened butter in that bowl, pour the honey over it, and beat with the mixer until creamy."

Joe sets to the task at hand. As the beaters blend the ingredients, he mentally replays last night's events. *The magic show was nothing short of astounding. Then Niall's yell sent up the alarm—"Libby's disappeared!"* The word "disappeared" rolls around in his mind. *Jennifer, the magician, made things appear and disappear. You don't suppose—*

"How's that honey-whipped butter coming along?" Niall's question ends Joe's mental reverie.

Joe dips a spoon into the bowl and then tastes it. He smiles at the delicious goodness. "Light, creamy, and sweet."

"Well, save some for the rest of us," Mick teases.

Niall continues working on the Pacific Northwest Scramble.

Mick rolls out Niall's homemade buttermilk biscuit dough and then uses the floured rim of a drinking glass to cut out circles.

As Niall coaches Mick on what to do, Joe returns to his thoughts. *When I deliver breakfast to the cottages this morning, I'll question Jennifer—not interrogate. Mick told me that with the violent events at Pines & Quill since May, they started, with permission, to run background checks on the writers they accept for residency. But like anything else, that kind of information can be manipulated to appear different than it is—an illusion.*

"The dogs were poisoned," Niall says.

Joe perks up his ears.

Mick nods. "So that explains why they didn't bark."

Rafferty and Ivy arrive. "Where are the gals?" Rafferty asks.

Joe recognizes the look on Rafferty's face. *He has news. But he probably doesn't want to scare Ivy.*

"Carly and Brianna are in the Ink Well watching television," Joe says. "And Maeve, Marci, and Emma are upstairs with Libby. I know they'd love for you to join them, Ivy."

"I'd like that," Ivy says. "How is she?"

"The doctor gave her an injection to help her sleep," Niall says. "She was still out cold when Maeve relieved me at six."

"I'll take you upstairs, Ivy," Rafferty says. "Would you like a cup of coffee?"

"Yes, please. It smells wonderful."

Rafferty pours a cup. "I'll be right back, guys." Then he leads Ivy upstairs to the main bedroom.

When he returns, he shakes his head. "Libby's still sleeping, but man, she took a beating."

Joe summarizes the puncture wound on the back of her neck. And what the doctor said about it potentially being from a tranquilizer dart.

"Do you think she was tranqued before or after she disappeared?" Rafferty asks.

"It had to be before," Mick says. "Libby would have kicked, screamed, and fought like a demon if she wasn't out cold. Then, after Brent rolled his wheelchair through the metal sheet you were holding, the lights went out. That's when the guy must have taken her."

"And it always takes a second or two for vision to acclimate to bright light when it comes back on," Niall says. "That, and the music was loud. It probably covered any sounds of her abduction."

Joe twists his lips to the side. "Right now, we're speculating. We won't know with certainty that Libby was darted with a tranquilizer until her blood-work results come back."

"Speaking of results," Rafferty says, "they didn't get any hits from the bandana, but they got a hit on the fingerprints on the Sen-Sen package."

"I *knew* you had news to share," Joe says.

Rafferty nods. "They belong to Carmine Fiore. Now all we have to do is find that son of a bitch."

"After we divided our effort this morning, Rafferty, did you find anything on or near the pavilion?" Joe asks.

"Not a thing."

"Mick, did you find anything out at the body site?"

Mick shakes his head. "Nothing. How about you?"

"Zilch," Joe says, pulling the apron over his head. "It's like we're chasing a ghost."

———

At eight thirty, Carmine pulls the cream-colored Taurus SHO into the driveway of Gambino's home on Lake Whatcom in Bellingham. A doll house compared to his high-rise in Seattle, this well-hidden, multilevel luxury residence nestled in the woods has a helo pad on the roof, though it's currently vacant.

Carmine cants his head to the side. *That's Gambino's favorite way to travel, so I doubt he's here. But if he is, the security cameras have already announced my arrival.* He lets his right hand casually brush against his peacoat pocket, confirming the presence of his Sig Sauer P226. Then he steps to the retina scanner. When the light changes from red to green, he turns the handle and lets himself into the foyer.

"Boss," he calls out. "You here?" When there's no answer, he pulls out his cell phone and calls Gambino's cell number. *No ringing. No pickup. No outgoing voicemail.*

He draws his gun from his pocket. Then keeping his back to the wall and his gun out in front, he steps into the living room, sweeping his weapon left, then right. He continues moving from room to room until he's cleared the entire house and then the four-car garage. Finally, he presses a button on the wall to open a door in front of an empty stall. Then he pulls the Taurus inside to hide it. *The fewer people who know I'm here, the better.*

Carmine sits in Gambino's favorite leather wing chair in front of a massive plate glass window that overlooks Whatcom Lake. The water is the same steely gray as the sky. He picks up a crystal decanter from the antique side table and pours two fingers of Lagavulin 16 into a matching crystal glass. The first slug goes down like fire, but a smooth warmth follows, reaching down into his belly.

His gaze wanders to the long dock where two of Gambino's boats moor. *At the end of the month, they'll be hauled from the water and stored for winter.* After slugging the remaining scotch, Carmine lets his mind wander to a boat of much greater interest to him. Georgio "The Bull" Gambino's namesake, *Il Toro. It's moored on a dock at the Harris Avenue Shipyard cleanup site.*

Carmine pours himself more scotch and takes another slug. *That boat is guarded by two of Gambino's men—Luca and Mario—and their allegiance is now mine. No one knows except me that hidden inside the hull is a cache of heroin.* He smiles at his ingeniousness. *Gambino's been ripping Sean McPherson's ass for over five years. He's even killed members of Mick's family, thinking he knows its whereabouts.*

Five years ago, Gambino's previous underboss, Alex Berndt, who used the alias Jason Hughes, killed McPherson's partner, Sam, to create an "officer down" situation. It drew just about every law enforcement officer on duty and within radio range. Then, with an almost-empty stationhouse, we stole a huge cache of heroin seized from a crime-ring bust out of lockup. The street value was well over ten million dollars.

Alex Berndt's twin brother, Andrew, was one of Gambino's minions who was caught and imprisoned. He was the person responsible for hiding the heroin. But before he could tell his brother the location, he "committed suicide." Due to a bit of encouragement, he squealed the location before my inside guys strung him up in his cell. That's when I snagged the heroine and hid it inside Il Toro's hull, where it's been financing my coup ever since.

Carmine's right index finger roves up and down the nearly empty glass. His breathing accelerates with the excitement of the hunt. He uses a technique Alex Berndt taught him years ago to compose himself, exhaling long, slow breaths until his heartbeat is within an acceptable range.

Then I picture my prey—in this case, Gambino—in my crosshairs. I know I can't miss at this range, not with the ammo I'm chambering. I can almost feel the pull of the trigger. Then my target's head jerks back—a look of surprise on his face— before falling to the ground.

Carmine sets the glass on the antique table, checks his pulse, and smiles. *It never fails to calm me. Now then, where the hell are you, Gambino?*

· CHAPTER 20 ·

*"Figure out what exactly is at stake, and how to
establish it quickly. That's your conflict."*
—KATIE LIEF

Mick watches his beautiful pregnant wife as she, Marci,
and Maeve walk down the stairs and join everyone at
the table. At Emma's sixteen-week appointment, Dr. Freeman,
the OB/GYN, had told them, "You're officially four months
pregnant. Welcome to the second trimester! This is the fabled
sweet spot of pregnancy when you can put all the yuckiness
of the first trimester behind you and coast for a little while.
But not too long, because months six and seven are coming,
and they're a bit more uncomfortable."

I've never felt like this before, Mick thinks, pulling out
the chair next to him for his wife. *My love for Emma and the
baby is equivalent to my fear of losing them—enormous. I'd
do anything to protect them, to keep them safe and happy.*

"Libby's still asleep, Rafferty, so Ivy's sitting with her
for a while."

"Niall," Marci says, "can I please have your recipe for the Pacific Northwest Scramble? It's delicious."

Niall smiles. "That's the highest compliment you can pay a chef. Absolutely."

Mick's cell phone rings. He glances at the display before answering. *Fairhaven Veterinary Hospital—eight forty-five.* "McPherson." He rubs the top of his left thigh as he listens. "Yes, we can be there shortly after nine. Thank you so much!" Then he disconnects. "We can pick up Hemingway and Maggie."

"Perfect timing," Niall says. "I told the writers that breakfast would be delivered about nine." He looks at Joe. "Are you still game to make the deliveries?"

Mick is anxious not only to get Hemingway and Maggie—to see for himself that they're okay—but to ask Dr. Sutton about dart guns and tranquilizers. *I'm sure he's used them during his career.*

Maeve waves at the guys. "Go on. I'll clear the—"

The patio glass slider opens, and Lucy leans in, wearing a bicycle helmet and gear. One of her gloved hands is on the seat of her high-end triathlon bike. "No need to deliver breakfast to my cottage this morning. I had an energy bar. I'm going to hit the road for an hour or so before I write."

Lucy leans back out of the open slider, but before closing it, she says, "And *I* want to be the one who Adam murders. I know it'll only be an illusion, but I don't want anyone to know that because I'm *not* going back to my family. I want to remain dead to them." Then she hops on her bike and pulls away.

Mick looks at the stunned faces around the table. *What the hell?*

———

Joe's frustration mounts after his third and final breakfast delivery to the cottages. *Not one of the writers saw or heard anything unusual.*

And while I initially suspected that Jennifer Pruett, the magician, might be an accomplice, I don't think so anymore. I've interrogated people for almost two decades, and Jennifer didn't display any body language we're trained to look for that conveys guilt. She didn't cross her arms or rub her hands together. Her breathing didn't shift, and her blink rate didn't increase. Instead, she was calm and maintained eye contact with me the entire time.

During the magic show, her full attention was on Brent in his wheelchair, barreling toward the metal sheet that Rafferty was holding in place. And while I'm not going to completely eliminate her as a possible accomplice, she's no longer at the top of our nonexistent list. Damn it! I wish we had a lead.

Brent Gooding, the former NASCAR driver, was intent on making it through the sheet of metal unscathed.

Adam Richmond, the real estate investor and professional house flipper, was in the front row, hell-bent on figuring out how Jennifer did the trick.

Lucy Fleming, the professional athlete, was sitting in the front row next to Adam, equally intent on the magic show. And she just announced that she wants to remain dead; she doesn't want her family to know it's an illusion.

By the time he gets back to the main house, it's almost ten.

Mick's red Jeep is in the circular drive.

Joe lets himself in the front door and follows the voices to the dining area.

Ivy's here, but Marci's not. They must have traded places sitting with Libby.

Hemingway and Maggie are in the spotlight. Their tails are wagging—*maybe a bit slower than usual*—but their tooth-filled grins show their happiness as they lap up vast amounts of attention.

When the dogs notice Joe, they dash over to him so he can sing their praises too.

Joe ruffles Hemingway's ears. "Who's a good boy?" Then Maggie's. "Who's a good girl?"

Both dogs press their wet noses to Joe's mouth as he talks with them.

"What so interesting about my breath?"

"Dr. Kent said their tummies are still sensitive," Mick says. "They can't eat until lunchtime. And then only half their usual amount. They've systematically checked everyone's breath." He chuckles. "I think they're living vicariously through food fumes."

"Emphasis on *living*," Joe says. "That's what matters. That they *lived* to tell about it."

Mick rubs the stubble on his jaw. "Dr. Kent sent Hemingway and Maggie's stomach contents for examination. He ruled out antifreeze, a common way to poison dogs, saying they would have already died.

"He also said that a drug used to sedate livestock, xylazine, is creeping into the illicit drug supply. When people mix it with opioids, it's called 'tranq dope,' and often leads to death. He said if Libby was shot with a tranquilizer dart, the shooter might have dosed her with xylazine because it's an extremely effective, fast-acting sedative."

"That's brutal." Joe shakes his head. "I *also* learned some things while delivering breakfast to the writers. The good news first. I don't think Jennifer's an accomplice." After briefing them on why, he says, "She's been mulling over an illusion for murder and thinks she has an idea. She said she'll run it past us at dinner tonight. The bad news is, like us, none of them saw or heard anything out of the ordinary." Joe pulls out his cell. "We said we'd be at the morgue by noon. And we promised to stop at Keenan's at the Pier on the way. Maybe the ME will have some answers for us."

A licensed physician certified in forensic pathology, Dr. Jill Graham is the chief medical examiner at the Whatcom County Morgue in Bellingham. She pulls off her nitrile gloves, drops them in the trash can, and looks at the display on her ringing cell phone. *Joe Bingham.*

Jill glances at the wall clock and smiles—*eleven fifty-nine.* Then she answers, "You're right on time. I'll come out and let you in."

She grabs her keys before heading to the entrance. It's locked because they're closed on Sunday. When she opens the door, Joe—with McPherson and Rafferty behind him—holds out a bag from Keenan's at the Pier, and she takes it. "That's a better key than any of these." She holds up her key ring. "Come on in, guys, follow me."

The fluorescent lights hum inside the autopsy suite. *I wasn't kidding when I told them I'm married to my job.* Jill inhales the mixture of antiseptic and alcohol in the air. She thrives in the clean, orderly white and stainless-steel surroundings. *I love this job. It was made for me.*

After setting the bag on a counter, she pulls on nitrile gloves and a protective mask. "Okay," she says, "even though you're not assisting in the postmortem, I want the three of you to put on gowns, shoe covers, gloves, and protective masks."

When the guys are ready, she says, "Before we discuss the body, I want to show you a few items of interest." She leads them to a stainless steel counter with several clear plastic bags, each tagged with details. "He didn't have a wallet, keys, or any type of identification on him. But there was a thousand dollars cash in one of his pockets, which I documented and put in the safe."

She gestures to the first bag. "This cell phone has rung several times. I looked at it the first few times, and in each instance, the display said 'Judas.'"

Then she points to a second bag. "This contains three royal-blue bandanas. I found them in separate pockets on his clothing."

Her hand moves to the third bag. "These are white cotton gloves—think footmen or butlers in days gone by. Today they're usually only worn with police and military dress uniforms. Or by male waitstaff at high-end functions. You'll have to see for yourself why John Doe wore them."

Her hand moves to the fourth bag. "I had to do a bit of research for this item. It's a Pneu-Dart Type U RDD device. Type U the most versatile and universal tail design for Pneu-Dart projectors. Type U tails for 6cc to 10cc darts are the standard tail design for any projector. As an option, Type U tails also support 0.5cc to 5cc darts."

"So it's like the casing, the brass part, of a bullet?" Joe asks. "It holds the propellant that delivers the projectile?"

Jill nods. "Exactly. Only in this case, the projectile is a dart that's tipped with a hypodermic needle and filled with a tranquilizer, vaccine, or antibiotic meant for animals."

"Or in this case," Mick says, "my sister, Libby MacCullough."

"How is she doing?" Dr. Graham asks.

"She has two broken ribs. And this guy"—Mick points at the sheeted corpse—"nearly bit off her ear. But Dr. Berman in the ER was able to stitch it back together."

"I'm happy to hear that. Glad, too, that she was on the winning side of that fight. Come on," she says, nodding to the table behind them, "you'll see that he got the worst end of it."

Dr. Graham stands on one side of the sheet-covered corpse. Next to her is a portable stainless-steel surface with several tools. An autopsy saw—the blade gleams under the harsh fluorescent lights, its serrated edge designed for precision. An assortment of scalpels, each with a different blade shape—a #10 for delicate work, a #22 for deeper cuts. Metzenbaum scissors, their curved blades snip through tissue effortlessly. Adson forceps with tiny teeth at the tips. A Liston bone cutter—the heavy sheers can slice through bone. A sail-maker's needle and suture thread to stitch up incisions with neat closures. A chisel for removing bone fragments and a hook that allows her to manipulate organs without damaging them. Last but not least, industrial tweezers. Their robust design enables her to grasp tiny fragments—a bullet casing, a shard of glass—critical evidence in her investigations.

Mick, Joe, and Rafferty stand on the opposite side of the sheet-covered cadaver. The autopsy table is centered under a surgical lamp suspended from the ceiling.

Dr. Graham draws back the sheet, exposing the corpse's ashen face, his bloodless skin. It's a man in his midsixties with a bulbous nose webbed with spider veins, countered by bushy eyebrows that look like well-fed caterpillars. He has a thick mat of white hair and a matching white mustache.

The ME traces her finger along the jawline. "His jaw broke from the force of a dead-weight face-forward fall onto the ground. That's a perfect segue to what killed him." She moves her finger to the right eye area. "Death was caused by the eight-inch rosewood 'skewer'—your term"—she looks at Mick—"that you carved for your sister.

"Based on the trajectory, that skewer pierced the right eye, then the frontal lobe, the corpus callous, the fornix, the cingulate gyrus, and the cerebellum. When it struck the occipital bone on the back of the skull, the skewer broke in the center of the cerebrum, further damaging the corpus callous."

"Holy shit!" Joe says.

"Now, before I pull back the rest of the sheet," Dr. Graham says, "I'm going to show you why I believe he wore gloves."

She walks to their side of the table and lifts the sheet at the midpoint, revealing a hand splayed on a metal block. She turns it palm up, showing severely disfigured fingertips, including the thumb. "You asked me to print him. This corpse has no prints. Both hands are the same."

She raises the sheet a little farther, revealing deep bloody furrows from the elbow to the wrist. "Libby MacCullough is a fighter."

Mick nods. His eyes glisten.

She walks back to the other side of the table and pulls the sheet down to the corpse's waist, revealing a fresh, stitched-up Y-shaped incision in the chest.

But even more arresting is the massive, shoulder-width tattoo across the sternum depicting steer horns with the words "The Bull" immediately below.

CHAPTER 21

Upstairs in the main bedroom of the main house, Libby tries to crack her eyelids open. She fists the quilt as pain gallops around the inside of her skull. She tries again, but only one eye opens. Barely a sliver at that. Her right ear and the back of her neck feel hot. Like stinging flames, they pulse with her heartbeat. *I need to get up to help Niall with Pines & Quill and our guests.*

She turns her head. The digital readout on the nightstand clock informs her that it's one forty-five. Relief floods Libby's system, and she releases her talon grip. *Oh, good, there's still plenty of time to sleep.*

Spears of pain radiate from the right side of Libby's rib cage when she rolls onto her back. A moan of pain escapes her lips.

Niall's warm hand squeezes hers. "I'm right here, Honey. You've been sleeping for a long time."

"It's only one forty-five," Libby says. "We just left the hospital a few minutes ago."

"It's one forty-five in the *afternoon*," Niall says. "On *Sunday*. You've been asleep for almost twelve hours."

"Then why is it dark in here?"

"Your mom pulled the shades over the windows so the light wouldn't wake you."

Memories of last night flood Libby's mind, and she tries to sit up. "Oh, my God, Niall. I *killed* a man."

Niall stands and turns the night table lamp on low. Then he cups his wife's shoulders with his hands and looks into her eyes. "It was self-defense, Libby. He would have killed you if you hadn't killed him first."

"Was it the same man who slit Adam's wrist?"

Niall shakes his head. "No. It's a different guy. Mick, Joe, and Rafferty are at the morgue, hoping the medical examiner can shed some light on who he is.

"In the meantime, Joe said that Chief Simms put out a BOLO—be on the lookout—for the guy who slit Adam's wrist. Every police department and three-letter agency in the greater Seattle area and along the Canadian border has a copy of the sketch and is trying to find him."

Niall bites down on a yawn, and his cheeks balloon like a puffer fish.

"Have you gotten *any* sleep?" Libby asks.

Niall nods. "After Maeve helped me get you into bed, I got in too and slept until it was time to make breakfast. Since then, your mom, Emma, Ivy, and Marci have been taking turns sitting with you."

Tears well in Niall's eyes, then one slips down a cheek. He leans in close to Libby and speaks into her neck. "Libby, the fact that you were next to me when you were taken is something I won't ever be able to forgive myself for." His voice is thick.

Pain sears Libby's torso as she lifts her arms, wraps them around her husband, and pulls him closer. "Niall, there's *no* reason to feel guilty. *None* at all. But if you need my forgiveness, you have it. Remember the sermon on forgiveness your brother Paddy preached at St. Barnabas one morning? I've never forgotten it. He said, 'At some point, each of us will need to extend forgiveness to someone for something they did or failed to do. And at some point, each of us will need to receive forgiveness for something we did or failed to do.' Where would any of us be without forgiveness?"

Niall nods between Libby's head and shoulder. His beard nuzzles her skin.

She pushes him back a bit so she can look into his eyes. "I need to tell you something."

"What is it?"

"If I don't get to the bathroom *right now,*" Libby says, "I'm going to wet the bed."

Niall grins. "Now, *that's* something I can help you with." He pulls back the covers and helps Libby sit up and then stand.

When the floor beneath her grows unsteady, she leans against Niall for support.

Once he situates her in the bathroom, he says, "It's time for more meds. But you can't take them on an empty stomach. I'll text Maeve and let her know you're awake and ask her to bring up the lunch plate I saved in the oven for you."

"What is it?" Libby asks, washing her hands.

"It's one of your favorite comfort foods—macaroni and cheese with ham. I used Gruyère and sharp white cheddar, my secret ingredient Dijon mustard, and added a few grates of fresh nutmeg, just the way you like it."

"I've died and gone to heaven," Libby says.

Niall locks eyes with her in the mirror. "Don't even tease about that. We could have lost you last night."

Once Libby's tucked back into bed, there's a soft knock on the door. "I brought your lunch," Maeve calls out.

"Come in, Mom," Libby says.

Maeve smiles as she enters carrying a bed tray table. On the center is a plate with a domed cover to keep the food hot. Off to the side is a crystal vase with a small colorful bouquet—a *posy*, her mother calls it—of wildflowers: Echinacea, black-eyed Susan, and Bluebeard.

"How are you feeling, Honey?"

"Like Dad used to say, 'I'm going to live to tell about it.'" *But he didn't. Gambino had Dad killed. I wonder if he put a hit out on me too?*

Niall plumps several pillows behind Libby's back.

Then Maeve opens the tray's legs and adjusts it across her daughter's lap. "That was a close call, my dear." Her eyes glisten. "*Much* too close for comfort." When Maeve lifts the cover off the plate, steam billows into the air carrying a delicious aroma—savory, cheesy, with a hint of butter and the woody notes of nutmeg.

Libby's stomach rumbles. *That's right. I didn't eat last night because dinner was going to be after the magic show.*

Maeve stays until Libby has taken several bites, then gives her the next dose of medication with water from a glass on the nightstand. Before leaving, she kisses her daughter's forehead. "Sweet dreams," she says, pulling the door shut behind her.

When Libby tells Niall she can't take one more bite, he removes the tray and sets it on the dresser. Then except for one, he removes the pillows behind her back and helps her lie down and get settled.

After turning out the lamp, Niall sits in the rocker and takes one of Libby's hands in his.

She feels her eyelids droop and then close as the meds

creep past last night's terror and hold it at bay. Then drifting in comfortable bodiless darkness, the world's hard edges go soft, and Libby along with it.

Excitement builds inside Mick's chest. "Doc, when you collect DNA samples from this guy"—he gestures to the corpse on the autopsy table—"please send them for comparison to Toni Bianco."

Joe's eyes widen with comprehension. "My dirty cop, now dead, ex-partner Toni Bianco was Gambino's daughter. Her DNA's on file. All we have to do is have their samples compared. If they match, and the dead guy's Bianco's father, then we know with *certainty* that it's Gambino."

Dr. Graham nods.

Mick paces the length of the autopsy table back and forth, back and forth. "For *years*, we've looked for Gambino's fingerprints, facial, and DNA identification and found *nothing*. It was like he didn't exist. Now, though, it looks like we may have hit pay dirt." Mick strides over to the stainless steel counter with the corpse's personal effects tagged and bagged in clear plastic. He picks up the one that contains the three royal-blue bandanas the ME found. "We need to contact Rico Canchola."

Joe stares at Mick. "Of the Sureños gang?"

Mick nods. "Yes. I think we may be able to assist each other."

"How so?" Rafferty asks.

"If the dead guy *is* Gambino, and he was using Sureños gang bandanas to divert blame," Mick says, "don't you think Canchola would want to know?"

Joe nods. "Especially if there's still another one out there pulling the same stunt."

"I think we have an informant," Rafferty says, "a guy who knows a guy who knows a guy, who might be able to get word to Canchola." He pulls out his cell phone. "I'll get on that *now*."

The beginning of a smile plays on Mick's mouth. "I bet Canchola will be interested in helping us nail Fiore's hide to the wall."

"Thank you for everything, Doc," Mick says as Dr. Graham escorts the men from the autopsy suite to the front door.

"I'll put a rush on the DNA test and let you know the results as soon as I do," she says before locking them out.

Back in the Jeep, Mick glances at the clock on the dash—*two o'clock*. He feels equal parts satisfaction and frustration. *It looks like Gambino's dead, but Fiore's still out there.*

In the rearview mirror, Mick sees Rafferty listening to someone on his cell phone.

He turns to Joe. "Can we throw *more* resources at the BOLO to intensify the search for Fiore? He said he'll kill Adam's daughter, Brittany, if Adam doesn't murder a writer at Pines & Quill before the twenty-first. And if Fiore can't get to Brittany because of her FBI shadow, he'll place someone else in his crosshairs. We need to get Fiore into custody *now*."

Rafferty leans forward between the two front seats. Excitement heightens his voice. "I've got a location and a name. Manny's expecting us at four o'clock."

"Where to?" Mick asks.

"South State Street MGP—Manufactured Gas Plant." Rafferty lifts his eyebrows. "It's just north of the Harris Avenue Shipyard, where you two had a shootout with Canchola."

Mick touches his left hip, where a Sureños bullet grazed him, and nods. "It's another one of the twelve cleanup sites in the Bellingham Bay area. All of them are on or near the waterfront. It looks like we're going back for more." He catches Rafferty's eyes in the rearview. "But *this* time, we've got more firepower."

Lucy disconnects after video chatting with her husband, Rick, on the phone. *It's two thirty. We were on the phone for an hour, and now I'm exhausted. He's like a vampire, but instead of sucking blood, he drains energy. What happened to us? I used to love talking with him. The man is insanely knowledgeable about all things bike. But that doesn't mean he's good at running a business—unless it's running it into the ground.*

She pinches her lips together. *I can't believe he just asked me to come home and get a refund on the remainder of my writing residency. Nope, it's not going to happen. Not only because I don't want to but because that's not how a good business operates. If I leave Pines & Quill now, it'll be without a refund.*

Lucy stands and stretches her quads. *I'm so glad Rick doesn't know about the savings account I started years ago when I began earning money for Olympic endorsements. If he did, he would have bled it dry. Now it's the financial foundation for me to start over. This time without excess baggage—Rick.*

She runs a hand through her short blond hair. *I feel bad about the boys, though. But Greg's already out of the house at college, making a life of his own. And Doug's a high school senior ready to fly the coop. He hardly comes home as it is because Rick takes advantage of him.* "It's not unpaid labor," she'd heard him argue with Doug. *"I put a roof over your head and food in your mouth. That's your compensation."*

Lucy sits down and toggles to a bookmarked internet site on her laptop. She triple-checks the requirements for becoming a permanent Canadian resident: "You must be 18 years old to become a Canadian resident. Minors must have a parent or legal guardian fill out the application on their behalf. You are not eligible for immigration if you have committed a crime, have a serious health issue, are in financial trouble, or you (or someone you are related to) have been barred from Canada. You must speak either English or French." *Check, check, and check.*

She toggles to another bookmarked page and confirms that the distance between Bellingham, Washington, and the Canadian border is twenty-three miles. *That's less than the distance I run in a triathlon. And I'll have no problem crossing. As a professional athlete, I travel extensively, so I always carry my passport and supporting ID.*

Lucy closes the lid of her laptop. *Everything's falling into place. The only thing I don't know is how Adam will kill me.*

Rico Canchola orders the man at the helm of the Skater powerboat to take them to the dock at the Harris Avenue Shipyard cleanup site. "Get us there by four o'clock, Diego."

"I thought Manny was at South State Street MGP."

"He is," Rico says. "I want to be close, but far enough away to turn on a dime and haul ass if it's a trap."

Diego nods as two of the four men, all wearing royal-blue bandana headbands, cast off lines and then jump over the gunwale into the sleek boat where it's moored at a little-known dock on Blakely Island about thirty miles west of Bellingham.

As the twin inboard Teague Custom engines, 1,500 horsepower each, roar to life, the four external propellers, aft and under, churn the water into a roiling tsunami behind the *Southern Comfort. Most gringos assume the name refers to whiskey. Not so.* Rico smiles. *It means Confort Sureño to honor the gang.*

His gaze travels from his watch—*three o'clock*—to the tattoo on the back of his left hand—X3. *Sur is the Spanish word for south among Sureños. It also stands for Southern United Raza. Sureños use the number thirteen. It represents the thirteenth letter of the alphabet, "M," to mark our allegiance to the Mexican Mafia.*

Although Sureños use many tattoos, only one validates membership—the X3 tag. The one I have. When a Sureño is asked what being a Sureños means, members answer, "A

Sureño is a foot soldier for the Mexican Mafia."

I wonder what McPherson and his two buddies—the homicide detective and the FBI agent—want? When Manny contacted me, he said they have some information I'd be interested in.

I know two things. First, they're trying to take down the Gambino crime family, one of our trafficking rivals. So are we. Second, they'll take me down if given a chance.

Rico cracks his knuckles. *So, stay smarter and faster, and keep your eye on the prize—a lieutenant position in the Mexican Mafia.*

———————

Adam Richmond checks the time on his laptop screen in Thoreau cottage—*Three fifteen.* He stands up from the desk chair where he's been working on his manuscript, *Good Bones,* a crime thriller involving a body found in a structure during renovation. Then he walks over to the south-facing glass wall to enjoy the view of El Cañón del Diablo. And though it's stopped raining, fog blankets the treetops below. From this bird-like vantage, spiked pine crowns pierce the otherwise smooth grayish-white blanket now and again.

He stretches his back, rotates his head, and then works the kinks from his shoulders. *Dinner's not until six. I've got plenty of time to take a long hot shower, change my clothes, and do a bit more work.*

On his way to the bathroom, he intentionally detours through the kitchen and inhales deeply to enjoy the smell of the fragrance diffuser that Libby left. The handwritten note says, I designed this blend to leave you warm and toasty. The renewing top notes are sweet orange peel and tart bergamot. The middle notes are honeyed pumpkin, spiced masala chai, and fresh ginger root. And the base notes are sweet vanilla bean, toasted caramel, and rich coconut milk. Enjoy!

The mattress dips under his weight when Adam sits on the foot of the bed. As he toes off his shoes and unbuttons his shirt, his cell phone rings. He'd tried to call his wife earlier and had to leave a message. He smiles. *It's probably Helen calling me back.*

But when he picks up the phone, the display indicates it's a video call from "Unknown." *The last time this happened, that monster told me my daughter, Brittany, would die if I didn't murder another writer in residence and frame Sean McPherson for it.*

Dread seeps into every pore of Adam's goose-pimpled skin. When he swipes the "slide to answer" button to the right, he sees the man who'd slit his wrist. Even though the man is wearing a brownish-red man's wig, mustache, and beard, Adam would recognize him anywhere. His pointy ferret-like features, beady eyes, and three-inch scar over his left eye are unmistakable.

"There's been a change in plan," Carmine Fiore says. "You're going to have to rip the Band-Aid off."

Even if I hadn't recognized his face, I'd have recognized his voice. It'll haunt my dreams until I die. Adam's face is in a small square in the bottom right corner of his cell phone screen. His brows are knit together in distress. "I don't understand."

"There's been new developments, and it accelerates the timing of our previously discussed agreement."

Adam's pulse is on fire. "What do you mean?"

"Instead of having until the twenty-first to kill another writer and frame McPherson for the murder, you now have until midnight tonight."

Silent fear screams inside Adam's head as he stands from the foot of the bed. "What?" His voice sounds strangled. "But—"

"No buts," Fiore says, then ends the video call.

Panic surges through Adam. He yanks his shoes back on and bolts out the front door.

CHAPTER 22

*"The unread story is not a story; it is little black
marks on wood pulp. The reader, reading it,
makes it live: a live thing, a story."*
—URSULA K. LE GUIN

"Guys," Mick says. "We've got a tail. He's been following us since we left the morgue."

Joe checks the Jeep's right side-view mirror. "There's four cars behind us. Which one?"

"The white panel van," Mick says.

"My money's on Fiore—the Gambino wannabe—or one of his goons," Rafferty says. "Panel vans are their style. That's what they abducted Emma, Carly, and Brianna in."

"Or," Joe says, "it could be the Sureños gang making sure we don't bring backup to the meeting with Canchola's guy, Manny." His cell phone pings. "Good news. I texted Chief Simms earlier. He sent two plainclothes officers we've worked with before, Chris Lang and Herb Johnson, to the meeting site. They're posing as a romantic couple out for a stroll."

Mick's pulse accelerates as he sails through an amber-turned-red light, guns it, then slips the Jeep in front of a semitruck out of the pursuer's line of sight.

The white van is stuck behind two cars stopped at the intersection.

Mick screams off the next exit, pulls into a parking garage, and slams on the brakes—the antilock braking system pulses beneath his foot. A minute later, the van barrels past in hot pursuit.

Mick continues driving under a cloud-laden sky toward South State Street Manufactured Gas Plant. When he opens his window to dry the adrenalin-induced sweat from his neck, his nostrils pick up the scent of petrichor—the smell of rain. *When I first came to Pines & Quill to recover from the accident that killed my partner Sam, Libby told me that the word petrichor comes from two Greek words:* petra, *meaning stone, and* ichor, *meaning the ethereal blood of the gods. I hope there's no blood today.*

Mick's cell phone rings. The display indicates the call is from his mom. His mind leaps to concern for his pregnant wife, Emma, and his recovering sister, Libby. He answers hands-free. "Mom, you're on speaker. Is everything okay?"

"Libby's fine. Ivy's sitting with her right now."

"And I'm fine too," Emma's voice interjects.

Mick lowers his shoulders in relief.

"We've got you on speaker too," Maeve says.

Mick hears tension in his mom's voice.

"Niall, Emma, Marci, and I were prepping tonight's meal," she says, "when Adam arrived. He—"

Adam's voice breaks into the conversation. "That monster, Fiore, video-called me again." Raw panic propels his voice. "I had until the twenty-first to kill another writer." A sob catches in his throat. "But now he's moved up the deadline."

Mick tightens his grip on the steering wheel. "To when?"

"I have until midnight."

Rafferty leans forward. "*Tonight?*" His bass voice booms.

"Yes," Adam cries.

Mick looks at the dash clock—*Three thirty*—and clenches his jaw. "That's only eight and a half hours from now." Urgency pulses through him at this new information. Like the countdown at the ball drop in Times Square on New Year's Eve, Mick is hyperaware of the ticking clock.

"I *know*," Adam says. "What are we going to *do*?" His voice is pleading.

Joe's cell phone pings again. He reads the text message from Marci and then holds the phone between Mick and Rafferty for them to see.

> It's chaos here. Everyone's panicked for Adam's daughter, Brittany. Fiore will kill her if Adam doesn't kill another writer before midnight. Is there anything you can say or do to calm the situation?

"Adam," Mick says, "we're on our way right now to speak with someone we think can help us catch Fiore."

"Do you think they will?" Adam's voice is filled with hope.

"We have information he wants. It's a strong motive for him to help. So I think we can work a deal." *Unless, of course, we're driving straight into an ambush.*

Mick white knuckles the steering wheel as he thinks about the greater good—the benefit of others at the potential cost to himself. *I never questioned it in the past. But now that I'm married with a baby on the way, I have to think of them too.*

"What do you *mean* you fucking lost them?" Carmine Fiore barks into his cell phone. "I told you to tail anyone who leaves Pines & Quill. You said you followed McPherson, Bingham, and Rafferty, unseen, to the morgue. Now you're telling me that when they left the morgue, you lost them. You're a moron!" *A dead moron.*

Fiore checks his watch—*Three forty-five.* "What direction were they headed when they left the morgue?"

"They were heading southwest on Bayview Drive."

Fiore's mind shifts into overdrive as he pictures the area. *The Gambino crime family—soon to be the Fiore crime family—does a lot of business along the bay. Twelve cleanup sites make it fairly easy to move around in plain sight.*

The cleanup sites are the legacy of municipal and industrial practices that preceded modern environmental laws. Soil, marine sediment, and groundwater were contaminated by operations at the former Georgia-Pacific pulp and paper mill, municipal landfills, wood treatment plants, shipyards, and a coal gasification plant.

With so much to be done, workers focus on the task. They don't have the time or inclination to mind somebody else's business. *The hardest location to stay undetected in is South State Street MGP because the northern portion of Boulevard Park—a heavy-use recreation area—is part of it. People at play are relaxed. They love to watch other people.*

"Franco, are you listening?" Fiore asks.

"Yes, Boss."

"Here's what I want you to do. I want you to stake out South State Street MGP. Don't get too close. Just park, observe, and report what you see to me. Do *not* act. Do you understand me, Franco?"

"Yes, Boss."

"I'll be a mile and a half from you at the Harris Avenue Shipyard cleanup site. I need to check on *Il Toro* anyway. *The fucking crew on the Sureños boat keeps testing the boundary on my turf. That dock is mine.* "And Franco?"

"Yes, Boss."

"You're out of chances," Fiore says. "One more strike and you won't be out. You'll be dead."

Jennifer can't suppress a look of surprise as Adam thrusts the glass slider open and thunders out. "What's wrong?" she asks the group sitting around the large pine table in the dining area of the main house.

Hemingway's and Maggie's tails wag as they step up to their favorite treat-conjuring writer. One minute Jennifer's hands are empty. The next, they're doling out dog biscuits.

Jennifer kneads their ears and then joins the others at the table, where she's flanked on each side by two pairs of vigilant eyes. Hemingway's long tail thumps the floor haphazardly while Maggie's metronome tail beats a silent allegro vivace tempo.

"Why is Adam angry?" she asks.

"He's not angry," Maeve says. "He's scared."

"But why?"

As Maeve relays the drastic change in Fiore's timeline, Jennifer feels a prickle of sweat at the back of her neck. She looks at the wall clock—*It's almost four o'clock.* Her heartbeat accelerates at the ramification. "Oh, my God. That's only eight hours." Fire-hot tentacles squeeze her lungs, making it hard to take a deep, calming breath. "I met with Lucy and thought we had a plan involving a knife with a spring-loaded retractable blade and special effects blood pouches. We were going to run it by the rest of you at dinner tonight. But there's no way we can pull it off in eight hours without the right props. And the closest place to get them is *maybe* Seattle. Then we have to test the illusion. *If* it works—and that's a big if—we need to practice. In order for Mick to be arrested for murder, Lucy's death has to be believable."

A young woman's life is at stake. Instead of defeating her, the timeline change acts as a catalyst. Jennifer sets her resolve and stands. "I'm going to gather the other writers and take them to my cottage. I don't know how we'll pull this off, but one way or another, we'll kill Lucy."

At four o'clock—the designated meeting time with Canchola's guy, Manny—Mick drives past substation transformers. A fence and green landscaping hide the lower portion while the upper part etches against a cloudy sky. *The voltage in there has to be astronomical.*

He pulls the Jeep to a stop alongside the curb on the west side of the street. It runs parallel to the block-long gas plant. A massive mural covers the entirety of the windowless back side of the building. The artist used blue, purple, and gray hues to create mountains, raw against a vivid persimmon-colored backdrop. Five wind turbines painted in purplish-gray stand sentry at the north end of the mural.

There's a smattering of people on the sidewalks on either side. In his rearview mirror, Mick sees a couple walking with their arms around each other's waists in the distance—*Chris and Herb.*

On the east side of the street, directly across from the Jeep, a man exits a glass door in a gray and blue industrial building. It's the same length as the gas plant but not as tall. It has high windows, two feet from the rooftop—that run the entire length, with a few shoulder-height windows between glass doors.

The man is wearing a royal-blue bandana tied like a durag around the top of his head. And though it's cold, he's not wearing a coat. Instead, the sleeves of his flannel shirt are rolled to his elbows. He walks toward the Jeep. As he draws close, Mick sees an X3 tag inked on his left forearm.

"No weapon in sight," Mick says. "Apparently, he doesn't think we're a threat."

"Look at the ten and two o'clock windows behind him," Rafferty says.

Two of the roof-high windows are open with guns trained on the Jeep.

Mick starts to open his door, but the man raises a hand. Then he motions for Mick to lower his window.

Mick powers down the window.

The man nods. "McPherson, Bingham, and Rafferty." It's a statement, not a question.

"Manny," Mick says, noting the black dagger inked under his right eye. The downward blade has a single drop of red blood near the corner of his mouth.

Two gunshots pierce the air.

Three guns clear leather.

"I got Manny," Mick shouts. "Rafferty, take ten. Joe, two."

Manny holds up his hands, palms out, and shakes his head. "I wouldn't if I were you. Those shots weren't a threat. They were a precaution. If this meeting goes south, a couple of flat tires ensures you won't get away. You'll be dead." Manny shouts to the people who'd been walking on the sidewalks. "You can get up now. There's nothing to see here. Go on about your business."

In his peripheral vision, Mick sees Herb and Chris continue past the Jeep, then turn right at the end of the block-long plant, no longer visible.

―――――

Parked at the curb just past the end of the gas plant, fifty yards ahead of McPherson's Jeep, Franco is on his cell with Fiore making his first report of what's unfolding in his rearview mirror when there are two loud cracks.

"Shit!" Franco shouts as he slides down in the driver's seat. "That was gunfire."

He sits up enough to look in the side-view mirror. The Sureños guy says something to the people who'd flattened themselves on the sidewalks when the shot rang out. They get up and run away. He notices a movement near the top of the building behind the Sureños guy. *Two of the windows are open with guns trained on the Jeep.*

If I use the cars parked along the curb behind me as cover to get closer, maybe I can take out the Sureños guy. Better yet, I can take out McPherson. That'll go a long way in moving up the ranks. All I have to do is make it to the end of the plant unseen, then I can use it as cover. I can get back to my car and haul ass out of here before they can get down the stairs and catch me. Fiore doesn't have to know a thing until it's over.

He checks the rearview mirror. *Shit! There's a couple leaning against the wall at this end of the plant. The man's groping the woman.* He checks his Ruger 9mm pistol. *Not a problem. But I can't shoot them from here without drawing attention.*

Fiore is midsentence when Franco disconnects the call and silences his phone. Before slipping it into his pocket, he notes the time—*Four fifteen. By the end of this day, I'll be promoted.* He smiles at the thought.

Sliding into the passenger seat, he checks the side-view mirror. *The couple's still at it. This time the man's back is against the plant wall, and the woman's leaning her full length against him. I'll kill the guy and use the woman as a body shield.*

Franco opens the passenger door and slips out. Ducking low, he eases the door shut. Then using the cars parked along the curb as cover, Franco heads toward the end of the building. Hand gripping the gun in his pocket, he approaches the couple. But before he can draw it, the man grabs his collar and smashes his head into the wall.

The woman claps one hand over Franco's mouth and shoves a badge into his face with the other. "Give me a reason," she hisses into his ear as the man jerks his arms behind his back and cuffs him.

Fuck! Fiore's going to kill me.

Fiore pulls the cell from his ear and glares at the display. *What the fucking hell? Did that bastard Franco hang up on me? Manny's as good as dead.* The clock on his phone shows four twenty-five. *At least something's working in my favor. In less than seven-and-a-half hours, McPherson'll be on the hook for murder. And if he's not, I'll kill Brittany. Everyone will learn that I mean what I say and I say what I mean. Everyone will fear me.*

Seagulls squawk overhead as he looks over the helm of *Il Toro* at the aft part of the *Southern Comfort*. It's moored at the front of the dock. His boat's much farther back. *So far, I haven't seen any signs of life. But they wouldn't leave it unguarded. Not a chance. Maybe they're in one of the warehouses.*

"Lorenzo," Fiore barks, pointing at the row of dilapidated warehouses.

"Yes, Boss?"

"Start with the warehouse closest to the entrance gate and clear the buildings. Make sure there's no one hiding in them." *Like a coal-mine canary, it's much better if he dies than me.*

Lorenzo clears the gunwale, draws his weapon, and heads toward the first warehouse.

Fiore watches the *Southern Comfort* for any signs of movement. *Why are McPherson, Bingham, and Rafferty meeting with the Sureños gang? Are they dirty? Have they got something to do with Gambino's seeming disappearance? They hate him and would do just about anything to take him—now me—down. But would they team up with the Sureños gang to do it? I need to get the upper hand here.*

Rico Canchola and his men lay low on the *Southern Comfort.* He's fully aware that *Il Toro* has moored at the end of the pier. More than piqued, his curiosity and anger skyrocket when one of Gambino's men leaves the boat and, gun drawn, makes his way to the first dilapidated warehouse. *The one I'm supposed to meet McPherson, Bingham, and Rafferty in.*

Those bastards are setting me up!

Guns holstered, Mick, Joe, and Rafferty wait for Manny to make the first move. Mick's sure the others can hear his heartbeat.

Manny's gaze is cool and appraising. "I understand you have information for Rico."

Mick nods. "We do."

Manny curls the fingers on his right hand and gestures. "Give it to me."

"The information is for *Rico,*" Mick says. "We need to speak with *him.*"

"You've got some *grande cajones,*" Manny says, jerking his head back over his left shoulder. "All it takes is a flick of my wrist and you're dead."

"That may be the case," Mick says, "but then Canchola wouldn't get the information we have. It's about a rival who's hell-bent on acquiring his turf. Do you want to take the chance of forfeiting that type of intel?"

Manny rubs the dark stubble on his jaw, then pulls a cell phone from his pocket. He turns, presses a button, and speaks rapid-fire Spanish. "*McPherson dice que solo te dará la información a ti. ¿Quieres que lo desperdicie?*"

Mick does a mental translation. *McPherson says he'll only give the information to you. Do you want me to waste him?*

Silence from Manny as he listens. Then, "*Si entiendo.*"

Yes, I understand.

"*¿Cuántos hombres tienes contigo?*"

How many men do you have with you?

"*Cuatro está bien. Puedes sacarlos si lo necesitas. Incluso si no lo haces.*"

Four's good. You can take them out if you need to—even if you don't.

Silence again as Manny listens. Then, "*Bueno. Los enviaré al primer almacén que encuentren en el astillero de Harris Avenue.*"

Okay. I'll send them to the first warehouse they come to at the Harris Avenue Shipyard.

Manny turns back to the Jeep. "Go to the Harris Avenue Shipyard. His boat's moored there. But he doesn't want your stink on it, so he'll meet you in the first warehouse you come to."

He starts to walk away, then turns around. "Oh, and if you're not there by four forty-five—in twenty minutes—the meeting's off." He juts his chin to the two flat tires on the left side of the Jeep. "Good luck with that, Gringos." Then he walks away and disappears into the building through the door he'd come out of earlier.

"There's only one spare tire, and that won't do it," Mick says. Even with his limp, he knows he can outrun the other two men. "I'll run to the shipyard. There are at least a dozen cars parked along the street. Hotwire one if you have to, and then meet me there."

Before they separate, six men wearing royal-blue bandanas step out onto the sidewalk and laugh. Then Manny shouts, "*Será mejor que te apures!*"

"You speak Spanish," Rafferty says to Mick. "What did he say?"

"He said, 'You better hurry.'"

Mick bolts down the street. As he passes the end of the gas plant, a voice calls out. "McPherson!"

He glances over his shoulder.

Herb has his knee in the back of a handcuffed man face down on the ground.

Chris holds up a keyring. "Need a ride?"

Mick runs back to her. "I owe you. Which car?"

"The blue Dodge Charger five vehicles behind your Jeep. Herb and I will call the station for a ride." She toes the shoulder of the guy on the ground. "We've got a deposit to make."

"Joe. Rafferty." Mick yells, holding up the keys.

The three of them jump in the unmarked car. As they tear away from the curb, Mick says, "When Manny was talking on the phone, I learned that there are five of them at the shipyard—Rico and four other men."

"Let's hope we're not walking into a death trap," Joe says.

My thoughts exactly, Mick thinks.

"I hear that," Rafferty says. "At least we'll be in a warehouse and not on a boat. We'll have a better chance."

"And it's the *first* warehouse we come to," Joe says, looking at Mick. "The one you and I were already in, so at least we have a bit of an advantage in that we scoped it out earlier."

"Bring me up to speed," Rafferty says.

Joe is in the middle of detailing the warehouse layout when a horn blares and brakes squeal.

Their vehicle is T-boned on the passenger side, throwing the three of them forward until whip-stopped by their seatbelts.

The front airbags deploy. The one in the steering wheel hits Mick in the face. He reaches up and touches his face. His fingers are bloody when he pulls his hand away. He shakes his head to clear his vision. "You guys okay?"

"I'm okay," Joe and Rafferty say.

A man dressed in a business suit runs to their car. "Oh, God," he says, wringing his hands as he peers in the passenger window. "Are you guys all right?"

Mick and Rafferty get out on the driver's side of the car.

The passenger side doors are smashed shut, so Joe slides over the console and the driver's seat to get out.

"I'm running late for a job interview," the man says. "And I thought I could make it in front of you."

"We can't leave the scene," Joe says to Mick and Rafferty. "Go ahead on foot. He'll call it off if you're late. I'll be right on your heels."

Joe flashes his badge at the man.

"Oh, shit!" he says as Mick and Rafferty bolt toward the shipyard.

Mick doesn't let the searing pain in his left thigh slow him down.

The soles of Rafferty's shoes thud on the pavement right behind him.

They run past the padlocked entrance to the workaround Mick and Joe had discovered before. Both men bend, hands on knees, to catch their breath.

Rancid smells from a nearby dumpster blow their way. Seagulls squawk as they ride air currents overhead.

After a moment, Mick holds the fencing back while Rafferty eases through. Then he slips through behind him. *Manny said we had until four forty-five to get here or the meeting with Canchola's off.* He checks his watch—*four forty-three. Two minutes to spare.*

CHAPTER 23

"Good stories are not written,
they are rewritten."
—Phyllis Whitney

"Just because you *want* us to kill you," Jennifer tries to reason with Lucy, "doesn't mean you're the best choice."

Jennifer looks at the wall clock—*Four forty-five. Time is running out. If we're going to save Brittany's life, Adam needs to kill another writer before midnight. I wish Lucy would get over herself and realize this isn't about her.*

Lucy leans forward in her chair and thumps her sternum with her fisted right hand. "But I *need* to be the one who dies."

Jennifer glances at Adam, then Brent, the other two guests in the living room of Brontë cottage. "No offense to either of you," she says, then turns back to Lucy. "But I don't think Adam's a match for a professional athlete. You're the epitome of physical strength. It's not believable that he could overpower you."

Adam nods. "To be honest, I've been scared shitless at the idea of taking you on. Even pretending."

I don't want to hurt his feelings, but it needs to be said. Jennifer directs her gaze at Brent in his wheelchair. "I believe you're a more plausible choice."

Brent nods. "I get it. I don't have the ability to run away." He raises his left arm. "Even though my mechanics are bionic," he says, turning to look at Adam, "for me to stand a chance against you, at least three criteria would have to be met: You'd have to be on my left side. I'd have to see you coming. And you'd have to remain still." Brent shakes his head. "It's not believable because, in reality, it would never happen that way."

Lucy's breath whooshes out as she slumps against the back of her chair. "Damnit! I wish you weren't right, but you are."

Adam stands and begins to pace. "After the first time that *psychopath*, Fiore, video-called me and said he'd kill Brittany if I didn't kill another writer, I had a dream—a nightmare." He turns to Brent. "It might be the key for *how* to kill you. And we don't need to waste time acquiring special props."

Jennifer leans forward. "What was your dream?"

"I've got to warn you," Adam says, "it was strange."

Brent nods. "That's true with most dreams. They're odd at best. After losing my legs in the accident, I dreamed I could fly. Not in a plane, but like Superman."

Jennifer nods. "It was probably your brain's response to being in a wheelchair."

Brent shrugs. "I don't know." He turns to Adam. "Tell us what you dreamed."

Adam sits back down. "I dreamed I strangled Lucy with a bicycle inner tube on the side of a busy road while motorists honked their horns and waved enthusiastically. Then I sawed Jennifer in half on stage in front of an audience who clapped their approval as I stood in a pool of blood."

He turns to Brent. "Then after disabling the braking system on your wheelchair, I shoved you over the cliff by the bluff into Bellingham Bay while the other writers in residence stood by and cheered me on."

"Well, that's twisted," Lucy says. "But at least I got to die in that scenario."

"That could work." Jennifer's voice is excited as she looks at Brent.

His eyes are wide. "You wouldn't really shove me over the cliff, right? Somehow, we'd get me down there safely." He taps the arms of his chair. "And this bad boy cost a bloody fortune." He presses his brows together in concern. "It can't really get smashed up like it would have to be for it to be believable."

Jennifer holds up an index finger. "Wait a second. I'm sure you've seen them too."

"Seen what?" Adam asks.

"In the workshop, there are two wheelchairs parked against the wall between the pottery and woodworking stations. I was watching Emma at her potter's wheel one afternoon and asked her about them. She said they belong to her and Mick. 'They were our wheels while we were learning to walk again.'" Jennifer rubs her palms together in anticipation. "I'm willing to bet they'd let us sacrifice one of those wheelchairs for the sake of believability."

———

Mick looks over his shoulder at Rafferty as they slip into the shadows alongside the first two-story building. *Two hours until sunset.*

He remembers the building from when he was here with Joe a few days ago. The second floor resembles a toothless grin with gaping holes where windows had once been. He worries a hand through his hair. *Once we step inside, our tactical exposure is high.*

The air, perfumed with brine, is pregnant with change. *A storm is on the way.* Seagulls squawk as they circle low over a dumpster, angling for scraps. A smattering of sail birds anchor in the water beyond that.

Mick points to the metal door. It's ajar.

Rafferty nods.

Both men draw their weapons and hug the wall on either side of the door.

A cold chill rises from Mick's heart to his throat. He swallows hard. *Has this door been opened since I was here last? Is someone inside there now? How many? I wish Joe were here to add firepower.*

He raises a hand and counts down with his fingers—three, two, one—then he toes the door open.

Mick eases into the gray interior. Dank air fills his nostrils. He feels the familiar slowing of time he often experiences at the initiation of conflict. The mental clarity, the visual focus, the pulse in his neck, a slight dissociation, as if he were watching what was unfolding rather than actively participating.

Rafferty is on his heels.

With his focus distilled to a single point, Mick reviews their goal. *Rico Canchola said he'd meet us in this warehouse so we can personally deliver our information. Namely, Carmine Fiore and his men leave Sureños bandanas at their crime scenes to deflect blame.*

This information might persuade Canchola to help us catch Fiore and put him away. The elimination of his competition is a good incentive.

Fiore is like a tick. If we don't stop him, he'll bury his head into the greater Seattle area—just like Gambino did—and feast until he's drained the life out of it. Mick fists his empty hand. *And hurt my family and friends while he gorges himself.* The combination of dread and anger fuels Mick's purpose.

Across the threshold, Mick and Rafferty separate. Backs to the wall and guns out front, Mick goes right, Rafferty left. They sweep the abandoned space with their weapons—finding the points of egress and possible cover—the way they were trained to do whenever they enter an enclosed area.

Mick mentally repeats his mantra: *The key to recon is to be the observer, not the observed.*

He stops. *Something's not right.* Fear wraps icy fingers around his throat and squeezes as his gaze locks on the littered corner. *The last time I was here, the sleeping bag was in a heap by the hypodermic needle, spoon, candle stub, and shoelace. Now it looks to be cover—*

Mick sees a glint of metal at the open end of the filthy drab-green bag. He dives at Rafferty, knocking him to the cement floor as a shot rings out.

A bullet grazes his head, slapping it sideways as he lands next to Rafferty.

Shit! Blinding colors bloom before his eyes. Mick reaches a hand up and touches the graze. Fresh blood mingles with dried blood from the airbag's punch. Warm, it trickles down his face and neck.

Rafferty clasps Mick's shoulder. "That was meant for me. Thank you."

"You'd have done the same." Mick shakes his head to focus, then looks around. The dilapidated warehouse is at least seventy feet wide and a hundred and fifty feet long. "Our best bet for cover is behind the metal stairs on each side of the building."

Rafferty nods.

Shafts of light from the broken windows near the roof reveal rows of steel I-beams supporting a roof that sags between steel trusses. "There's nowhere else for us to take cover in this colossal skeleton," Mick says. He points to the closest set of stairs. "I'll cover you until you get *there*. Then you cover me until I get *there.*" Then he nods toward the steps on the opposite side of the building.

As Rafferty commando crawls across the cement floor, the warehouse door bangs open with a kick, and another man enters, gun drawn. "Lorenzo," the newcomer shouts, ducking behind the door for cover.

Mick rolls to the stairs on his side of the building.

"You still alive?" the man shouts from behind the metal door.

"It's good to hear your voice, Matteo. Yeah, I'm okay. But I'd be better if you help me take these guys out. And quick. This sleeping bag smells like piss."

Mick motions at Rafferty. *You take Sleeping Bag. I'll take Newcomer.*

Rafferty nods.

The center of the entire building is open to the ceiling.

Rafferty's side is loft-like, unobstructed, except for a steel rail that runs the length of the building through the I-beams overhead.

Mick's side has nothing more than a suspended cat walk overhead. *If I climb the stairs, I'm a wide-open target.* His will to survive takes Mick to a primal place. *I want to live to be a husband, a father, a brother, a son, and a friend.*

He bolts for Newcomer, still hidden behind the door. Then, crouching low, he grabs the handle and wrenches the door toward him.

A shot rings out where his head would have been if he were standing.

Mick drives the heel of his right hand into Newcomer's kneecap. He feels it fracture. Then he strips him of his .45 as the man screams, tilts, and falls to the ground.

"Behind you!" Rafferty shouts.

Standing upright, Mick catches another man with an elbow that crushes the cartilage of his nose, sending him to the ground. He pivots, steps on the man's wrist, and disarms him, shoving the gun into the back of his waistband. Then with a knee in his back, he pulls the man's arms behind him, and cuffs him with one of the zip cuffs he always carries. Then he cuffs Newcomer's wrists behind his back. "You move, you die."

Mick rushes to Rafferty, whose left forearm is wedged under the now-standing Sleeping Bag's chin. The man's weapon is on the floor. With his gun in his right hand, Rafferty manages a glancing blow above Sleeping Bag's ear. But rather than crumple, Sleeping Bag plunges the syringe he found in the filthy corner into Rafferty's neck.

Like a bucket of ice water, shock hits Rafferty's face.

A user wouldn't have left their hit here, Mick thinks, *so hopefully, the syringe was empty. But anything could be on the needle. And if it was fentanyl, it could be deadly. It only takes two milligrams to kill an adult.* Mick's thinking clots with rage. His left hand grasps Sleeping Bag's throat, and he squeezes.

The man goes rigid, then arches his back, gasping. His eyes are wide.

Rafferty pulls the syringe from his neck and looks like he's going to throw it on the ground

"Stop!" Mick shouts, still squeezing the man's windpipe. "We need to have it analyzed to find out what was in it. You could be in serious trouble."

Rafferty tears a sleeve from Sleeping Bag's shirt and wraps the syringe before slipping it into his pocket. Then he pulls Mick's hand away from the man's throat. "He's not worth it," he says, his voice low and raspy. He presses the guy's carotid artery until he passes out. Muscles slack, Sleeping Bag falls to the floor, where his wheezing lungs start to suck air again.

"Are you *sure* you're okay?" Mick asks. "You sound strange."

Rafferty gives Mick a chin lift. "I'm all right."

When they turn around, Mick and Rafferty are facing the barrel of a gun. "Drop your weapons and come with me. Mr. Fiore would like to speak with you."

"They're not going anywhere."

Mick, Rafferty, and the gunman's heads snap up like hatch covers to where the voice came from.

The gunman whirls the barrel of his weapon toward Joe.

With split-second timing, Joe fires a shot, chinking the concrete an inch in front of the startled man's shoes. "The next one will be between your eyes." His bass voice is serious and strong.

The gunman drops to the ground, rolls on his back, and empties half his magazine at the catwalk.

Joe double-taps his trigger. The prone shooter jerks and goes still. When the gun clatters from his hand, Rafferty tucks it into the back of his waistband.

"Man, am I ever glad to see you," Mick says.

Rafferty glances at his watch. "It's just after five. That didn't take you long."

"I bolted as soon as the uniforms arrived." Joe juts his chin toward Mick. "What the hell happened?"

"Same thing that happened to you when you body-dove to save Brianna," Rafferty says. "Only this time, I was the intended target."

Joe stays on the catwalk, gun at the ready, while Mick and Rafferty round up the two survivors.

"How do you feel now? Still no adverse effects from the syringe?" Mick asks Rafferty.

Rafferty shudders. "You know I hate needles. And I can only imagine what had been in this thing," he says, patting his pocket. "I'm just glad it wasn't a blade."

"We'll have you both checked out at the hospital when we're done here," Joe says, descending the stairs.

My head is pounding. With a sleeve, Mick swipes away blood pouring from the wound on his forehead into an eye as it travels down his face. He covertly glances at Rafferty, looking for any negative effects from the needle Sleeping Bag jammed into his neck. Then, satisfied that there's nothing apparent—*At least not yet*—he says, "We might as well head outside. Canchola probably decided to wait until the dust cleared when he heard gunshots."

When they reach the open door of the warehouse, they shove the handcuffed pair through first. "Just in case anyone's trigger-happy," Mick says.

When no shots are fired, they step through the door behind them.

In the near distance, two boats are docked. *Il Toro* is farthest away. *Southern Comfort* is closest. Both of their bows point toward open water. *Easier for fast getaways.*

A man is standing between the dock and them. Gun in hand, he slaps a rhythm against his thigh. He's close enough to recognize. *Carmine Fiore.*

Mick homes in on the movement. *Nervous or cocky? To stand out here like a wide-open target, he must think he's invincible. My money's on cocky—none of us are invincible.*

"We've got a couple of your guys," Mick calls out.

"I see that," Fiore says. "Where's the third one?"

"He's currently having a chat with his maker," Mick says.

"That's gonna cost you," Fiore says.

Mick, Joe, and Rafferty walk their human shields forward, closing the distance.

Behind Fiore, Rick Canchola and three of his men rise from the deck of their powerboat where they'd been hiding. They fold their arms across their chests. Two of them wear bandolero-style blade holsters.

They're close enough that Mick hears the shush of the water against the hull. He shakes his head. "The cost will be *yours*, Fiore, when the Sureños gang finds out you've been leaving royal-blue bandanas behind to divert suspicion and place it on them."

"Those beaners," Fiore sneers, "will never find out. They're too stupid." He jerks a thumb over his shoulder. "They even left their boat unattended."

A rope encircles Fiore's torso, lasso style, cinching his arms to his sides. His gun drops as he's pulled to the ground. "What the hell?" he roars, trying to right himself.

A man with a royal-blue bandana tied around his neck clears the gunwale and, much like rodeo calf roping, trusses Fiore's hands and feet. When done, he pulls a bandana from a back pocket and gags him, tying it behind his head. Then he gathers the fallen gun and steps to the side, awaiting orders.

Canchola's mouth is set sharp and hard. His hands fist and release. Fist and release. The cords of his neck bulge so much they look like they'll burst. "McPherson," he calls out. "Is that the information you wanted to tell me?"

Mick nods. "Yes."

"*Gracias*. Now, I'm going to send two men to the *Il Toro*. We're taking it as payment for what this *wop*"—he juts his chin to the bound and gagged man—"has done."

Another man hops over the *Southern Comfort*'s gunwale. Before heading to the other boat, he and the first Sureños man cast off *Southern Comfort*'s lines. The aft part of the sleek boat begins to drift from the dock. The rope, attached to a winch, starts to drag Fiore toward the water.

Canchola gives a signal, then the twin inboard Teague Custom engines, 1,500 horsepower each, roar to life. The four external propellers, aft and under, seethe the water into a roiling tsunami behind the *Southern Comfort*.

Fiore's body is dragged closer and closer to the water. Then, as realization dawns on him, he thrashes like a beached fish before he's pulled off the dock into the water.

Mick's pulse thumps in his ears. He rushes forward.

Canchola trains a gun on Mick and shakes his head. "Stop."

As the winch winds the rope around the drum, it pulls Fiore under.

"*Hasta luego*," Canchola calls out before the *Southern Comfort*'s engines rev and it pulls away.

Mick watches in horror as the water churns red behind it.

· CHAPTER 24 ·

"When you start writing the magic comes when
the characters seem to take on a life of their
own and write the words for themselves."
—ALICE HOFFMAN

Lucca, Fiore's youngest foot soldier, easily passes as a student sauntering across the dusk-draped campus of Rice University wearing a blue and gray Rice University hoodie, ripped jeans, and high tops.

He passes the massive arch of a three-story dorm and follows, at a distance, three young women—*Brittany and two of her friends.*

Lucca checks the time on his cell phone. *Seven twenty-five. There's a two-hour time difference between Houston and Bellingham. It's nearly seven thirty here, so it's almost five thirty there. Fiore said, "If you don't hear from me by midnight, kill the girl."*

Well, shit! I wonder if Fiore meant midnight Pacific Time where he is or midnight Central Time where I am?

He digs his cell out of a pocket and calls Fiore. It goes straight to voicemail.

The girls barely make it inside the dining hall before the doors are locked and they stop serving for the evening.

Lucca casually leans against a wall while checking his surroundings. His call goes to voicemail. *Well, shit! What am I supposed to do now? Leave a message?* Not knowing what else to do, he says, "Hey, Boss. Just to be clear. I know I'm supposed to kill the girl if I don't hear from you by midnight. But did you mean midnight *your* time or *my* time? Call me back. But if I don't hear from you, I'm going to run with exactly what you said. 'If you don't hear from me by midnight, kill the girl.'"

He disconnects and shakes his head. *Why was I worried? Fiore would have said, "Kill the girl at two a.m.," if he meant midnight his time.*

Lucca pockets his phone, finds an empty table outside the glassed-in dining hall, opens a book, and pretends to read. Then, he adjusts his angle so that Brittany and her friends are in his line of sight. In doing so, he notices another student in the reflection of the glass. She sits a few tables away, slightly behind him, and opens her laptop.

He watches the reflection of the young woman focused on her laptop. Her face glows bluish-white from her laptop's screen.

My youthful appearance is the only reason Fiore chose me for this job. But tonight, I intend to prove that I'm an asset in other ways.

Rivulets of rain pouring down the outside of the nursery window only serve to increase Emma's anxiety. A tiny bud at first, her anxiety has fully blossomed and radiates outward from the center of her chest.

What's taking the guys so long? She rechecks her cell phone in case she missed something. The display indicates that it's five fifty. *I haven't heard from Mick since the guys went to the morgue just before noon. Why hasn't he answered my calls or texts?*

She sets the cell phone back down on the nursery floor, where she and Ivy sit cross-legged, folding freshly laundered newborn clothing for Connie's arrival in March.

Keep your worry to yourself, Emma. There's no need to make Ivy anxious too. She folds another onesie. *Mick always teases me that I get plenty of exercise from jumping to conclusions. But I can't help it. I worry about him and want our baby to have two parents.*

Emma glances at Hemingway and Maggie. Both dogs are stretched out four legs sideways on the floor by the crib. Hemingway is snoring, and Maggie's feet twitch as she chases something in her sleep.

"We'd better get going, Ivy. Dinner's at six, so we've only got ten minutes."

When the women stand, both dogs get up, do deep downward dog stretches, then shake out their coats, ready for whatever's next on the agenda.

Emma grabs an umbrella from the hall tree before opening the front door.

Hemingway and Maggie seize the opportunity and bolt into the downpour, shoving their muzzles into every bush in their trajectory.

Growing up, Emma's family had a collie, Sadie, who loved the rain. Emma's dad said that water vapor holds onto scent molecules longer, causing smells to be stronger and last longer. *Hemingway and Maggie—Nosy Nellies that they are— aren't missing a single scent.*

The clouds looming behind the Chuckanut Mountains for most of the afternoon had finally emerged as purple-black storm clouds and let loose with a vengeance, blanketing Pines & Quill and the surrounding area in fog and rain.

Emma remembers the first time she came to Pines & Quill. Libby said, "No Bellingham visit is complete without checking out the Chuckanut Mountains south of town. *Chuckanut* is a Native American word meaning 'long beach far from a narrow entrance.' A part of the Cascade Range, they're the only place where the Cascades come west down to meet the sea."

Emma inhales deeply. The scent of wet earth, pine, and woodsmoke from the main house chimney fill her nostrils. Then she presses a button at the umbrella's base. The canopy snaps open, and the women tuck under it.

The rain falls on the silk of the black umbrella, and translucent silvery streams flow over the side. The wind, brisk with a hint of winter, raises goosebumps on Emma's skin and tries to yank the umbrella from her grasp as they make their way toward the main house.

Emma squeezes Ivy's hand. "We should have left with Libby and Marci an hour ago."

Ivy stretches an arm out, palm up. A puddle forms in her cupped hand. "I don't mind the rain." She smiles at a remembrance. "I was born blind, and my parents weren't up to the challenge. So they put me in a convent where I was raised. My best friend, Nora, and I used to sneak out when it rained. It was the only time we wouldn't get caught because the nuns wouldn't go out in it."

"Why not?" Emma asks.

"Because their habits were wool and stunk when they got wet."

Emma laughs with Ivy.

The unrelenting rain thunders the umbrella's taut fabric, making it hard to hear anything else as Emma guides them around the worst of the puddles. She peers at the sky, then down at her ever-growing baby bump. "The underbellies of the clouds are full," she shouts to Ivy. "They look pregnant, like me."

Ahead of them, Hemingway and Maggie do their dead-level best to collect as much water in their coats as possible.

"I swear those dogs are smiling," Emma shouts again. "We'll go through the mudroom so they don't track water through the whole house."

"I'm glad they're having fun," Ivy yells. "Maggie's on duty with me twenty-four seven except when she's at Pines & Quill. It's nice for her to enjoy a break with her best friend."

The smell of rain tiptoes in with the women through the mudroom door. Emma barely has time to register that the lower portion of the Dutch door is closed before Hemingway and Maggie barrel in, carrying the smell of wet dog with them. Then before she can throw towels over them, they shake their bodies, and water flies off their coats.

Emma tilts the umbrella to shield her and Ivy, but too late. The women are soaked.

The two dogs are oblivious to what they've done.

Hemingway's long tail sweeps the floor. His wiry coat is a flattened, dark-gray mess.

Maggie's metronome tail wags an allegro beat. Her tight black-and-white curls glisten.

"You should have come with us," Libby says, smiling at Emma and Ivy from the safety of the dining room side of the Dutch door. "And you two," she leans over the ledge and mock scowls at the wet dogs, "will stay in the mudroom until you're dry."

She hands each of the grinning dogs a biscuit as the two women, armed with fresh, dry towels, slip through the door, careful not to let their four-legged companions in with them.

Marci—seated at the table—looks up from putting the finishing touches on the pine cones and greenery centerpiece on the dining room table.

"You two look like you could use some hot tea." She scoots her chair back and stands. "I'll be right back."

Halfway to the kitchen, her cell phone rings. Slipping it from her back pocket, she checks the display, and her face erupts with a warm smile. "Hi, Joe," she says. "Dinner's going to be ready soon. Are you and the guys on your way?"

Marci stops midstep, turns around, and lowers herself back into the chair. In a heartbeat, her face morphs from delight to concern. Deep lines furrow her brow.

"*Both* of them? How bad?" No longer light and breezy, Marci's tone is all business.

Ivy reaches for Emma's hand.

Emma grips it tight. Fear rips through her body like a wildfire consuming everything in its path.

After hanging up with Marci, Joe glances at the large round wall clock in the emergency waiting room at St. Joseph Hospital—*Six o'clock straight up*. He can't seem to sit still. He needs to do something other than wear a path on the highly buffed black-and-white tile floor.

The smell of coffee, floor polish, and nervous sweat fills his nostrils. And like others in the room, his shirt has visible wet crescents in the underarms.

He sits on the edge of a hard seat, elbows on his knees, and steeples his fingers. *The situation could have gone so much farther south. A quarter-inch more, the bullet would have hit Mick's frontal bone. A half-inch more, he'd probably be dead.*

And the empty syringe Rafferty gave to one of the officers who drove us to the hospital after responding to my call at the Harris Avenue Shipyard could have been full of only God knows what. Once the lab analyzes it, we'll know.

Looking up, he notices Dr. Kloss, white lab coat over

blue scrubs, walk by. *He's the surgeon who removed the bullet from my shoulder.*

Joe strides across the room. "Hey, Doc."

The doctor stops as recognition dawns. "Bingham, right?" He extends a hand to shake. "How's that shoulder of yours?"

"It's great, Doc," Joe says, shaking his hand. "Thanks. But I've got *two* friends in the ER who need help, and there's only *one* ER physician on call. Can you take a look at Special Agent Rafferty?"

"Special agent as in *FBI*? What? Were you in *another* shootout?"

Joe juts his chin toward the door with a long narrow window on one side separating the waiting room from the emergency room. "Well, yeah, there's that too. But Rafferty got the business end of a syringe shoved into his neck. We think the filthy thing was empty. It's been sent to the lab to be analyzed. Can you take a look?"

"I'm on my way home," Kloss says. "However, I'll take a quick look."

As the two men push past the swinging door, Joe purses his lips and nods as he walks with the doctor past the nurse who wouldn't give him access before.

They locate Mick and Rafferty in side-by-side cubicles. The thin green curtain that usually separates the small areas is drawn back against the wall.

Dr. Gail Berman, the emergency room physician who took care of Libby after she fought for her life, killing Gambino in the process, has just finished stitching the graze across Mick's forehead. "It must be in your family's DNA or the water you drink," she teases.

Not a fan of needles, Rafferty sits on the opposite gurney and focuses on the floor.

Berman steps back, puts her hands on her hips, and studies Mick. "These should leave a smaller scar than the one you already have running through your left eyebrow. Now, let's take a look at that nose. The angle and two black eyes suggest that it's broken. You said you were in a car accident before you got shot, and the airbags deployed." She shakes her head. "Those things can pack a wicked punch."

She tips Mick's head back, then uses a light to look in each nostril. "Just as I thought. Your nasal bones have shifted out of alignment. I'm going to give you a local anesthetic, then manually push the bones and cartilage back into place."

Rafferty tenses his shoulders.

Joe steps between him and the next gurney to block what's happening to Mick.

As Dr. Kloss pulls on surgical gloves, Joe introduces the two men. Then Kloss examines Rafferty's neck. "The injection site is red, swollen, and beginning to bruise."

When the doctor probes the area, Rafferty winces.

"There's a nasty lump under your skin. I think whoever stabbed you with the syringe shoved it to the hilt." The doctor shakes his head. "That must have hurt like a son of a bitch. On the bright side, it wasn't a knife."

Rafferty nods. "I had that same thought."

Just then, Mick lets out a deep groan.

Joe, Kloss, and Rafferty turn to look.

The worst part—the manual realignment—is over, and Berman is packing Mick's nostrils with gauze.

"Need any help?" Kloss asks.

Berman shakes her head. "Thanks, I've got it. I'm just going to tape on a nasal splint, and he'll be good as new in a few weeks."

Joe and Kloss turn back to Rafferty. "Other than this area being tender," the doctor says, indicating the injection site, "are you experiencing any negative symptoms like nausea, dizziness, or blurred vision?"

Rafferty shakes his head. "No."

Kloss removes a penlight from his lab coat pocket and examines Rafferty's pupils. Then has him stick out his tongue to see if it's swollen. After checking his heart rate and blood pressure, he cleans the injection site, swabs on some anti-microbial gel, and covers it with a gauze bandage. "Keep it clean," he admonishes before leaving.

A short time later, as Joe, Mick, and Rafferty leave the ER, people stare as Mick walks by.

"Is it that bad?" he asks his friends.

Joe grins. "You look like you head-butted a train and lost."

"Well, only time's going to fix that," Mick says. "Right now, we've got to get the Jeep. It'll need to be towed because it has two flat tires and I only have one spare."

Rafferty nods. "And I also want to know what Chief Simms is going to say about Chris and Herb's undercover Dodge Charger that got T-boned."

"Not to worry," Joe says, pulling Mick's keyring from a pocket and tossing it in one hand. "I had the uniforms who responded to the accident radio the chief about the Charger. When he called me for details, he said that Herb contacted him about the situation with the Jeep. After he dispatched a flatbed tow truck for the Charger, he called AAA. They changed your tires and brought the Jeep to the hospital parking lot."

"But how—"

Joe holds up his hand and smiles. "I don't know. Being the Chief of Police has its perks."

"Thanks for handling everything." Mick and Rafferty slap Joe on the back.

Exhaustion works its way into Joe's bones. The day's emotional rollercoaster has taken a toll, plummeting him to worry for his two best friends, then to peaks of gratitude now that they're both going to be okay.

At least for now. But as a homicide detective, I know something's always lurking in the shadows. What I don't know is when and where it will strike.

———

Sitting in the backseat of the Jeep, Rafferty is anxious to see Ivy. *I've probably worried her sick again, and I need to assure her everything's all right.*

In the rearview mirror, Joe's face is low-lit by lights on the dashboard. *I'm glad he's driving because I'm too wound up and Mick's on painkillers.*

Rafferty catches Joe's eyes and nods toward the uniform standing in the last light by the entrance gate at Pines & Quill. He's decked out in raingear, at the ready with his hand on the butt of his gun.

"Until we close this case," Rafferty says, "I feel better about our family and friends knowing that Chief Simms posted uniforms around the property and at each cottage."

Joe stops the vehicle and lowers his window. When the officer recognizes him, he radios ahead, taps the visor on his plastic-covered cap, and lets them in.

The Jeep's headlamps punch two tunnels of light in the long dark lane where tall pines stand sentry on either side. The soporific rhythm of the wiper blades does nothing to calm Rafferty's frazzled nerves.

When they reach the roundabout in front of the main house, Rafferty hops out before Joe pulls to a complete stop. He runs through the pelting rain, past another officer in raingear, and up the front steps.

When he opens the front door, the smell of something delicious envelops him. He quickly toes off his shoes and heads toward the spacious open-plan kitchen and dining area, where the air is resplendent with garlic, onions, and thyme.

Seated around the dining room table are Ivy, Emma, and

Marci, who is flanked by her daughters Carly and Brianna, Maeve, and the writers in residence—Brent, Jennifer, Adam, and Lucy. Niall's standing in front of the oven, stirring something on the stovetop. And Hemingway and Maggie peer at him over the ledge of the lower half of the closed Dutch door.

The conversation around the table stops abruptly, and there's a communal intake of breath as Mick and Joe follow behind Rafferty.

One of Emma's hands flies to her chest, and she jumps to her feet when she sees Mick's face. "Oh, honey."

She and Rafferty rush past each other—Emma to Mick, Rafferty to Ivy.

Joe makes a beeline for Marci.

Rafferty kneels next to Ivy's chair and pulls her in close. He inhales the light mesmerizing scent of her—*Apple and lemon collide with rose and bellflower. Springtime. Home.*

"I've been so worried," Ivy whispers. When she feels the gauze on his neck, she says, "What's this? What happened?"

Like machine-gun fire, questions erupt around the table. "Oh, my God, Mick. What happened to your face?" "Did you guys find Canchola?" "Did you catch Fiore?"

Niall walks over and stands behind Libby's chair. He twists a dishtowel between his hands as he listens to the volley of questions. The wall clock indicates that it's seven fifteen. "Folks, I can't hold dinner off any longer. We need to continue this conversation over the meal."

Rafferty stands from his kneeling position. "I'm starving. And whatever you made smells delicious. It's been enticing me ever since I walked in the door. What are we having?"

Niall winks. "If you help me carry it to the table, you'll find out before everyone else."

"I'm in," Rafferty says, following Niall.

Niall opens the oven door, releasing even more of the delicious aroma of a well-seasoned, slow-braised meal. "We're having lamb shanks," he says, handing Rafferty a couple of hot mitts and then pulling a pair on himself. Pointing to the other covered dishes, he adds, "And roasted sweet potatoes, roasted Brussels sprouts with garlic, mint peas, and rice pilaf."

Libby and Maeve join them. "What can we help with?" Libby asks.

"Libby, if you'd carry in the spinach salad and dinner rolls, that would be terrific. And Maeve, will you please serve the wine? I've paired this evening's meal with a delicious Sangiovese. It teams exceptionally well with spice-driven foods. And though it doesn't need it, I decanted the bottles about a half hour ago."

In the dining area, Maeve pours wine as the other three load the table family-style with brimmed serving dishes.

"Watch your fingers," Rafferty says, setting a platter on a cork trivet. "It's hot."

Once everyone is seated, they fill their plates from the dish or platter in front of them and then pass it to the right. The guys' recollections of the day's events are peppered with questions as the food and wine dwindle.

Adam sets down his fork. "I just thought of something. Since Fiore's not alive to know that a murder's been committed, we no longer have to stage one and frame Mick for it. Right?"

"I'm afraid I have to disagree," Rafferty says. His voice is deep and clear. "We don't have *any* idea what Fiore set in motion. What we *do* know is that he wasn't working alone. And though we don't know their identity, there's still at least one Bellingham cop on Gambino's, probably Fiore's now, payroll. And it could well be one of the uniforms outside this very minute standing watch. We also know that Fiore was physically *here*," —he presses an index finger on the table— "not in Texas. So he must have set someone in place to kill Brittany if Adam doesn't comply. I'm glad we have an agent shadowing her."

Jennifer shares the discussion the four of them—she,

Brent, Adam, and Lucy—had earlier in Brontë cottage about pushing Brent off the cliff based on Adam's dream. "Not really push him off, of course. But stage it to look like that's what Mick did. And use one of Mick's or Emma's wheelchairs from the workshop so we don't ruin Brent's." She taps the arm of his wheelchair next to her.

Everyone has something to say, and the conversation is off and running with a life of its own.

Niall stands. "Let's move this discussion to the Ink Well. Libby and I will join you shortly with dessert."

Jennifer places a hand on her stomach. "I'm so full." She smiles. "But I suspect I can do a little magic and make room."

Lucy leans forward. "What did you make?"

Niall says, "I made a pear frangipane tart using my grandmother's buttery shortbread crust recipe. I bake it with almond frangipane filling, then top it with sliced pears and almonds. We'll bring it in soon."

Taking Ivy's hand in his, Rafferty stands. Nodding toward the wall clock, he says, "It's almost eight thirty. That means we only have three and a half hours to pull off a murder."

After the three young women return to their dorm, Lucca walks the campus to test his exit strategy and plan a backup just in case. Keeping his hoodie pulled over a Rice University ball cap, he looks for and avoids security cameras. The bill keeps his face in shadow.

At ten thirty, he's outside the entrance of Fondren Library. He'd done his homework. *It doesn't close until two on Sunday mornings.*

He slips a keycard from a pocket. *When Fiore gave it to me, he said, "It allows admittance to campus buildings while monitoring the holder's entrance and exit activity for security. Don't lose it. It was hard to come by, and I may need it again."*

Using his hoodie sleeve, Lucca wipes nervous sweat from his brow. *Fiore will have me thrown into the piranha tank he bragged about if I mess this up.* He holds his breath and then uses the keycard—*click.*

Exhaling in relief, he steps inside and surveys the space. There's a sprinkling of students. Some talk in hushed tones in small groups, and others sit alone.

Taking a seat at a distant study carousel, Lucca pretends to read a book while discreetly monitoring a women's bathroom tucked into a corner. He pats the chest-mounted knife sheath beneath his shirt and remembers Fiore's orders. "No guns. You must do it silently."

He wipes his sweaty palms on his jeans and rechecks the time. *Eleven o'clock. No one's entered for the last thirty minutes. So it has to be empty.*

A smile tugs at his lips. *I get to kill the girl if I don't hear from Fiore before midnight. That gives me an hour.* He picks up his backpack containing the gear he needs. *I might as well transform into "Lucina" now.*

CHAPTER 25

"The greatest part of a writer's time is spent in reading, in order to write: a man will turn over half a library to make one book."
—SAMUEL JOHNSON

S ophia Bonetti shivers from the cover of the copse of big-leaf maples surrounding Dickens cottage. As she adjusts her plastic-covered cap, a stream of icy rainwater runs down the back of her neck and between her shoulder blades inside her uniform shirt. *Damn it to hell and back.*

She pulls at the raingear covering her dark blue, almost black, uniform. *It doesn't matter that I've got this piece of shit on. I'm soaked from the inside out. When Fiore lured me from Gambino with the promise of more money, street action, and a swift climb up the ranks, I never dreamed that meant standing in the rain in the middle of the night watching trees grow.*

Sophia kicks a mossy rock and checks her watch. *Nine thirty. I've got over four fucking more hours left in this hell hole.*

A not-so-distant snap draws her attention.

She moves her right hand to the butt of her service weapon and backs with care farther under the tree's sparse October canopy. Many of its leaves have already hemorrhaged onto the ground.

Sophia squints, trying to see better through the deluge. *With their raingear, it's hard to make out the people. But with the limp, McPherson has to be the man pushing the wheelchair.*

And the person in it is gesticulating wildly. I can see that their left hand is glinting. I bet it's that bionic prosthesis I read about in the newspaper articles. So that has to be Brent Gooding, the NASCAR driver who almost died in a fiery crash at Pocono Raceway. He's lucky to be alive. But from the looks of it, not for much longer.

Fiore was wrong about one thing, though. Instead of Adam framing McPherson for murder, it looks like McPherson's going to do it himself.

Dressed and made up as Lucina, Lucca exits Rice University's Fondren Library and strolls toward Brittany's dorm. The brown hair of his shoulder-length wig bounces as he walks. Not used to wearing a purse on his shoulder, he adjusts it a few times until it feels comfortable.

A couple of guys make lewd remarks when they pass him on the walkway.

Keeping his eyes focused straight ahead, Lucca wills them to try something. *Come on. Lay a hand on me, and I'll gut you like a fish.*

The two guys laugh and keep walking.

Stopping just outside the circle of light cast by the dorm's exterior fixtures, Lucca takes out his cell phone. The display indicates that it's eleven forty. He checks to make sure he hasn't missed any calls from Fiore. *Not a thing. It's almost*

Go Time. I'll enter the dorm at eleven fifty-five. That gives me five minutes to get in, kill the girl, and get out.

This isn't Lucca's first kill. It's his third, but his first female. His heartbeat increases as a zing of excitement travels up his spine.

He pats a pocket on the trendy denim jacket he paired with a navy-blue crewneck sweater. *Wait. What?*

He shoves a hand in the pocket. *Empty.*

Then he checks every other pocket on his outfit. *Shit. Oh, shit!*

He checks the purse. *Nothing.* So he dumps it on the lawn to make sure.

I can't get into the dorm without the keycard. Fuck! Fuck! Fuck!

Lucca turns around and bolts back to Fondren Library the way he came, checking the ground as he runs.

"Hey," the two guys call out as he catches up and then passes them. "You change your mind, sweet cheeks?"

When Lucca reaches the library entrance, he pulls the door handle. It doesn't budge. He kicks the wall next to the door. *I can't get in without a keycard.*

His heart is racing, but from fear, not excitement. *If I don't get in there, my ass will be grass and Fiore the mower.*

He walks to the side of the building and motions through the window to a group of students. It takes a couple of tries, but "she" finally conveys that she forgot her keycard and will they please let her in.

Once in, Lucca makes a beeline for the women's bathroom, where he'd changed earlier and left his backpack, thinking he'd never need it again—that it would slow him down. *It's still here, and the keycard's in the pocket of the shirt I changed out of.*

He checks the time. *Fuck! It's eleven fifty.*

Lucca turns around and runs. *I've only got ten minutes to make it back, kill the girl, and get the hell out, or I'm a dead man.*

Rachel Tanner is Brittany Richmond's personal protection detail—PPD—at Rice University for two reasons: her college-age appearance, and she kicked massive amounts of Quantico butt throughout the rigorous close-quarter combat and marksmanship programs, both long and short-range.

Of course, it doesn't hurt that she kickboxed competitively before she joined the agency. Her powerful fighting discipline and devastating power continue to serve her well.

At eleven fifty, Rachel side-steps behind the dorm wall next to a second-floor window. She uses a periscope-type device to watch the building's entrance. Built for stealth and night vision, its matte surface and nonreflective glass ensure that she can observe without being observed.

She cocks her head to the side and furrows her brows. *I've been tailing the guy shadowing Brittany since he arrived. Up to now, he's stuck to her like white on rice. So why the hell did he just take off?*

Using a photo she covertly took earlier, she runs it through a facial recognition program and learns his name is Lucca Armando De Santis. She Googles his surname and discovers it's Italian, derived from *sanctus*, meaning holy or devout. *I doubt that.*

Rachel swipes to a different app and studies Lucca's lengthy rap sheet. *He's a reputed member of the notorious Nuestra family prison gang in San Francisco.* She narrows her eyes. *So why is an Italian associated with a Mexican American gang? And how did Gambino or Fiore lure him onto their payroll?*

Rachel taps a finger on her chin. *But what if the right hand doesn't know what the left hand is doing, and Lucca's double-dipping? That's a dangerous game. Then again, maybe he doesn't care.*

She revisits his rap sheet. *He's notched eleven felony arrests in four years, ranging from gun possession and robbery with a knife to a slashing arrest, four for criminal possession of a controlled substance, and one for driving while intoxicated.*

Short of a brief stint when I sat a few yards behind him outside the dining hall, he's been on the move. That is, until he entered Fronden Library, scoped it out, and transformed into a female. Clever. I have to hand him that.

Rachel remembers his panic-stricken look a minute ago as he patted his clothes, dumped the purse, and bolted toward the library. *I bet he left the keycard behind.*

What seems like only moments later, Lucca reappears on the sidewalk. The distance closes as he runs full-tilt toward the dorm. *And I have to give him points for speed.*

Angling the periscope almost straight down, she watches Lucca enter the building. Her heart accelerates as she uses her keycard, then slips unseen and unheard into Brittany's dorm room. Faint ambient light reveals that the young woman is under the covers in her bed. She's wearing a hot-pink eye pillow and a pair of over-the-ear headphones.

Rachel takes her position against the wall, where the door will conceal her when it opens. *Watch yourself. This guy is fast on his feet and has a history with guns and knives and a don't-care attitude. It adds up to a person with nothing to lose—the most dangerous kind.*

Using a fireman's carry, Joe hoists Brent from his wheelchair at the base of the cliff overlooking Bellingham Bay. He relocates him onto the sandy ground between a myriad of driftwood and water-smoothed stones, a safe ten yards from where Emma's old wheelchair is supposed to land once Mick heaves it over the cliff.

"Sorry about the cold, wet ground, Buddy," Joe says. "The good news is that you're upright—at least for now. The bad news is that just like we discussed, before Rafferty and I leave, we'll position you as if you face-planted after being tossed over the cliff." He holds up a reassuring hand. "But we'll scoop out a large enough space for you to breathe."

Brent shakes his head. "I'm not worried about that. I've been through a lot worse. What I'm concerned about is how we're doing on time. It took us a fair amount of it to get down here."

Rafferty, right behind them, says, "It's nine fifty-three."

"We're only ten minutes later than I expected," Joe says. "I didn't factor in the mud slowing us down."

"In race-car driving, timing's everything," Brent says. "So it's a good thing that Jennifer and Marci already 'crashed' my clothes." He gestures at the shredded and dirt-smeared outfit he's wearing. "And you two still have to set the incriminating evidence in place. Then after you position me and the wheelchair, you have to cover your tracks as you leave. That's going to eat more time. It's a good thing we have until midnight."

The pelting rain does nothing to cover the maritime air. It still smells briny.

Brent scratches his left arm where his prosthetic is usually attached. "I sure hope Adam's careful with my bionic arm when he goes over the side."

The three men look up to the cliff's edge when they hear Adam screaming at Mick. "Stop and think about it. Please, McPherson. Killing me won't solve anything." From a seated position in the wheelchair, Adam raises both arms, pleading. The left one, glinting metal, is Brent's prosthetic.

Brent gasps when Mick raises the back of the wheelchair, dumps Adam over the cliff, and then hurls the chair after him.

Adam lands on the rock shelf with a thud that knocks the wind out of him. *Oh, shit! It's barely wide enough to hold my frame.*

In the distance, he hears the crash of waves in the bay.

He turns with care to peek over the edge, then immediately turns back.

Squeezing his eyes shut, he hugs Brent's prosthetic arm to his chest and lies statue-still as rain lashes his face.

God, please let Brittany be okay.

———

Lucca checks his cell phone one last time. The display indicates that it's eleven fifty-five. *No calls or messages from Fiore. It's time.*

When he engages the keycard on Brittany's door, it emits a soft click. Freezing, he waits for a beat before pushing it open a small distance. Through the dim light, he sees a blanket-covered figure in bed—*Brittany. She's wearing large headphones and has something pink over her eyes.*

His heartbeat accelerates as he slips the knife from its sheath.

Two steps past the edge of the door, he raises the knife in a vice-like grip.

Before he can take another step, an arm reaches around his neck, placing him in a chokehold. Then a hand grabs the wrist of his knife hand and wrenches it behind his back.

The blade drops from his grasp.

His attacker kicks it under the bed.

With his windpipe blocked, Lucca can't make a sound.

The person behind him pulls his body tight against theirs. Other than breathing, they don't make a sound.

The hand behind his back gropes for purchase. Fighting for air, he tries to dig his fingers into his attacker's belly, but all he can get is fabric. *Damn it. They're solid muscle.*

The attacker squeezes harder.

Riptides of fear pull at Lucca's chest. His vision fades in and out as he struggles for oxygen, but he refuses to give up. *I'm not going down like this.*

Ramming his hips back, he rocks his attacker's balance, but their hold remains tight. A wave of hollow desperation overtakes him when his attacker disables his free hand. The dorm room diminishes to a murky blue-gray as his sight grows dim.

A leg sweep takes him down, his face smacking the floor, bones crunching. A moment later, his breath bubbles the pool of blood under his face.

Zip cuffs growl as they cinch his wrists so tight they cut into his flesh.

A pair of black tactical boots enter Lucca's line of vision. He lifts his head and cranes his neck. His eyes follow a pair of black-clad legs to a female's chest, then her face.

She pulls a cell phone out of a pocket and makes a call. "Rafferty, it's Tanner. It's over. Brittany's safe, and her would-be killer's trussed up like a Christmas goose."

Lucca drops his head to the floor in defeat. *A fucking woman did this to me?*

Bonetti cuts her shoulder mic, pulls a burner from a pocket, and speed-dials Fiore. The call goes straight to voicemail.

"Hey, Boss," she whispers. "You were right and wrong. Right that Adam's too chickenshit not to obey your orders. But wrong about who's doing the murder. I just watched McPherson push Brent Gooding over the cliff on the bluff."

She looks at the time again. *Nine fifty-seven.* "I wonder why the rush. It's still two hours before midnight." She shrugs her shoulders. "It doesn't matter now. It's done. I'll call it in on my way to the main house."

Taking long strides through the wind and rain, she disconnects the call and replaces the burner in her pocket. Then

she switches her mic back on and calls in the homicide she
just witnessed.

Rafferty's cell phone vibrates as he focuses on Adam lying
beneath the cliff's edge on a shelf-like projection. It's just wide
enough to hold his frame. *Don't move, Buddy.*

He removes the cell phone from his pocket. The display indicates the time is nine fifty-seven. The caller is Special
Agent Tanner.

"Rafferty." Relief floods his system as Tanner, with
rapid-fire concision, relays the gist of events.

"Good work, Tanner. I'll get the takedown details at the
debriefing." He disconnects the call.

Mick is faking the aftermath of rage, standing with his
hands on his hips overlooking the cliff.

Rafferty motions to him that he's going to call. Then he
moves to where Joe and Brent can hear him.

Mick picks up immediately.

"It's over," Rafferty says. "Tell Adam that Brittany's okay."

"It's two hours before midnight. Why'd he jump the
gun?" Mick asks.

"I don't know why Fiore's guy accelerated the timeline.
But it doesn't matter now. Tanner got him."

Mick gets on his knees and then leans over the cliff's edge.

Rafferty's too far away to hear what he says, but when
Adam fist-pumps the air and shouts, it's an unmistakable,
"Yesss!"

"It'll take us a while to get back up there," Rafferty says.
"Then we'll help you get Adam. It's good that you remembered that ledge from when Hemingway backed Jason Hughes
over the cliff when he saved Cynthia Winters."

"We wouldn't have been able to pull it off otherwise,"
Mick says.

"Keep Adam company until we arrive," Rafferty says. "That's a skinny ledge. And in this rain, it's probably scary as hell. We'll be up there soon as we can." He disconnects.

He turns to Joe and Brent. "Okay, you guys. We'll leave Emma's old wheelchair down here for now."

———

When they reach the bluff about twenty minutes later, Joe is stunned to see Mick's wrists in handcuffs behind his back.

A few of the uniforms stationed at Pines & Quill stand at a distance like they don't want any part of what's happening. But two of them, Chris Lang and Herb Johnson, hold their ground—feet wide apart and arms akimbo—between Mick and Bonetti.

"I don't know what crawled up your ass," Chris says to Bonetti, moving to remove the cuffs from Mick's wrists, "but he didn't kill anyone."

Bonetti lurches forward.

Joe bolts toward the group. "Stand down, Bonetti," he yells. "What the *hell* do you think you're doing?"

Spinning around, she hisses, "When I was patrolling the grounds, I saw Sean McPherson"—she jabs a finger toward his face—"push a man in a wheelchair over the cliff. *I'm* the one who called it in." She redirects her finger toward her puffed-out chest.

Just then, Chief Simms strides onto the scene. "And we thank you for your diligence, Officer Bonetti. But in this case, it's misdirected. Sean McPherson is part of a joint task force. His actions this evening are part of a sanctioned sting operation, an *illusion*, if you will."

As Bonetti deflates, she mumbles under her breath.

Joe is not positive what he heard, but he'd swear part of it sounded like, "Fiore's gonna have your head." *Damn, Bonetti? The dirty cop? Is she planning something?*

Adam shouts from over the cliffside. "Hey, what about me?"

Joe feels the heavy weight of dread press him into the earth as he heads to the cliffside with the others to help Adam.

CHAPTER 26

"Never, ever use repetitive redundancies. Don't use no double negatives. Proofread carefully to see if you any words out."
—William Safire

With a dish towel over his shoulder and his blue-and-white striped bistro apron secured at the back, Niall is in his element—the spacious open-plan kitchen of the main house. Since he was a young boy learning from his grandmother, cooking and baking have always been how he expresses his feelings, whether he's happy, sad, upset, angry, or—like tonight—sick with fear about what's happening out on the bluff and the myriad ways it can go wrong.

So though it's almost eleven o'clock on a stormy night, the scent of ethereally light shortbread with finely ground espresso beans wafts through the air and mingles with the piquant aroma of freshly brewed coffee. He hopes to soothe not only his nerves but those of the people gathered around his table: his wife, Libby, his mother-in-law, Maeve, his

sister-in-law, Emma, and two of the writers in residence—
Jennifer and Lucy.

Hemingway nuzzles Niall's waist.

"I know exactly what you want, Big Fella." Niall leads
his four-legged companion over to the sink. Then, looking
over his shoulder before pulling out a mixing bowl with a bit
of batter, he sets it on the floor.

Hemingway's tail swishes lickety-split back and forth,
back and forth.

"Don't you tell Libby," he says, setting it on the floor.
"Or I'll get in trouble."

"You sure will," Emma says.

Niall nearly jumps out of his skin.

Emma stifles a giggle. "Your secret's safe with me. Do
I smell what I think I smell? I came to see what I could help
with, but if those"—she points toward the oven door Niall
pulls open—are butterscotch-glazed coffee shortbread bars,
then I've already got my work cut out for me." Then, grinning,
she pats her baby bump. "You know, I'm eating for *two* now."

"I always eat for two," Niall says, rubbing his stomach.
"The problem is, there's only *one* of me. I don't know whether
we should dig in now or wait. Mick says the best part is the
golden, gooey butterscotch glaze, which becomes deliciously
fudgy as the bars sit in the cookie jar."

Emma places her palms on the gray-veined marble
counter. "In the interest of science," she says, winking, "I say
we test some *now* and then more *later*. That way, we can
compare and contrast."

"I second the motion," Lucy says, joining them. "I know
I've said it before, but it bears repeating. I'm a foodie. And a
shameless one at that. What smells so darned good?"

Niall laughs. "They're butterscotch-glazed coffee shortbread bars. Give me just a minute, and I'll have them on
the table."

"Okay then," Lucy teases, tapping her watch. "I know a thing or two about being timed."

Niall nods. "I can't even begin to imagine that kind of pressure."

Emma shakes her head. "Me either."

Lucy twists her lips to the side and thinks for a moment. "It's fun," she explains. "But it's also terrifying because I compete against the clock and other riders. I know it sounds crazy," she adds before heading back to the table, "but I wouldn't have it any other way."

"Niall," Emma says, "Mick texted a few minutes ago and said they're on their way, they're soaking wet, and they have good news. Libby's getting towels for them to dry off with. I want a job too." She wrings her hands. "I'm loaded with residual adrenaline from all the worrying I did while Mick was out there 'killing'"—she makes air quotes—"Adam. Now I'm antsy and need something to do while we wait. What can I help you with?"

Movement over Emma's shoulder catches Niall's attention.

Approaching from the foyer, Mick walks behind Brent's wheelchair. Adam is between Joe and Rafferty. Shivering from cold and the aftermath of fear, Adam shoves his hands into his armpits. Chief Simms brings up the rear. Their clothes are dripping with rainwater.

Mick texted that they have "good news" to share. I wonder if it means we're no longer in danger of closing Pines & Quill's doors because of the deaths. Nobody wants to stay where they fear getting caught in the mafia or gangland cross-hairs. Can we finally relax the "red alert" status we've been on since May? My goal with Libby has always been to offer a safe harbor for writers to enjoy protected writing time.

Libby rushes toward them from the mudroom with thick bath towels she warmed in the dryer. But Hemingway and Maggie reach the men first.

Hemingway's tail makes rapid figure eights as he sniffs the prosthesis across Brent's thighs.

Brent rumples his ears. "That's a good boy."

Maggie greets Rafferty by leaning into his thigh. He squats down and scratches under her curly chin. "Good girl," he coos.

Amid a chorus of "How did it go?" "Is anyone hurt?" and "Tell us what happened," the guys dry themselves, slip out of their shoes, and head to the dining area—Mick to Emma, Joe to Marci, and Rafferty to Ivy.

Chief Simms heads straight for the coffee mug Niall proffers. "Oh, man, can I ever use this." He shivers. "Thank you."

Niall places two platters of shortbread bars on the massive dining room table—one at each end. The individual bars are topped with a chocolate-covered espresso bean. *Comfort food. We all need that. But especially the guys who were out on the bluff.*

Maeve and Libby make their way around the table with stainless coffee carafes, filling each mug.

Niall brings a hot mug of spearmint and lavender tea to Emma. "I know it's one of your favorites."

"It's my *absolute* favorite." Emma beams. "Thank you."

In bullet-point fashion, the guys tell the others what happened. The listeners get to hear it from three perspectives: Mick from his viewpoint on the bluff, Adam from the ledge beneath the precipice, and Joe, Rafferty, and Brent from the base of the cliff.

"Mick dumped Adam over the edge like he was trash in a wheelbarrow," Brent says, widening his eyes. "And then he hurled the wheelchair like Thor throwing Mjölnir, his hammer."

Niall grips the back of Joe's chair. *Holy Toledo! If I'd been Adam, I'd have been scared to within an inch of my life.*

"Say the hammer's name again," Lucy prompts. "I can never pronounce it correctly."

"Mee-ol-neer," Brent says slowly, rolling the "r" at the end. "The "o" is pronounced like the "ough" part of the word 'thought.'"

Lucy repeats it after him—"Mee-ol-neer."

Brent nods. "Good job."

Niall takes in the warm camaraderie of the gathering, and his earlier worries begin to dissipate. *Now that Gambino and Fiore are dead, there's no one left to settle any scores with Mick.* He wipes his hands on his apron and smiles. *That means Pines & Quill will be safe again.*

The mention of Thor and his hammer have the people at the far end of the table talking about their favorite Marvel movies. But the conversation where Niall's standing at this end—right behind Joe and Chief Simms—is entirely different.

Joe tells the chief what Officer Sophia Bonetti muttered under her breath. "'Fiore's gonna have your head.'"

Stunned, Niall absorbs this new information. *The guys said there's still at least one dirty cop in the precinct. It sounds like Bonetti may have been on Fiore's payroll.*

The chief furrows his brows. His hands tighten around his coffee mug. He shifts his gaze from Joe to Mick, then Rafferty. "I want the three of you to find out everything about Bonetti from the moment she was born. Who is her family? Who are her friends? Where did she grow up? Where did she go to school? Who are her past and present partners? I want to know *everything.*"

Emma places a hand on her belly. "Couldn't you just arrest her?"

The chief shakes his head. "I'm afraid not, Emma. Muttering something under one's breath isn't grounds. And so far, her work has been exemplary." He sets his now-empty mug on the table. "Are you familiar with the saying, 'Keep your friends close and your enemies closer'?"

Emma nods.

"Knowing that Bonetti might be a dirty cop puts us at an advantage." Simms leans forward and then makes his point using empty coffee mugs. "Gambino," he says, setting the first mug on the table, "was *the Boss*—the irrefutable head of the crime family."

Niall lifts a stainless coffee carafe from the sideboard. His hand trembles as he refills the chief's mug.

Simms sets another cup next to the first one. "Fiore was *the Street Boss*—the second in command. He was trying to push Gambino off the proverbial throne and take it for himself." The chief raises an index finger. "But now, they're both dead. So, if Bonetti's in somebody's pocket, and we give her plenty of space, she might lead us to *the Underboss*—the third in command." He places the third mug on the table. "*That's* who I'm interested in because once word's out on the street that Gambino and Fiore are dead, *they're* the new leader of the crime family."

After refilling the other two mugs, Niall replaces the carafe on the sideboard. *I always knew that crime families have a hierarchy, but I didn't know how they work. Now I know there'll always be someone next in line.*

He pulls the dishtowel from his shoulder and wrings it as worry rushes back like a stampede.

CHAPTER 27

"No tears in the writer,
no tears in the reader."
—ROBERT FROST

The next ten days at Pines & Quill are business as usual. The deciduous trees on the property—the big-leaf maple copse around Dickens and the blue-elderberry glade surrounding Austen cottage—are busy sprinkling leaves on the ground. Their autumn colors—orange, yellow, and red— are clear, sharp, and beautiful.

The writers wake early and meet Libby for brisk sessions of tai chi in the pavilion. Then they invest what's left of the mornings and long afternoons in their cottages, working on their manuscripts.

In the evening, they meet in the main house and discuss their day's work around the massive dining table while enjoying Niall's gourmet cuisine and wine pairings. Afterward, over dessert in the Ink Well, they draw cards from the

Observation Deck and employ their learnings during the next day's writing session.

Brent Gooding has made tremendous progress in his latest suspense thriller, *Checkered Flag*. Even though his publisher bumped up its due date, he's confident he'll hit their target. And though time away from home has been exhilarating—he's even gathered fodder for his next novel—he's looking forward to returning to his family in Daytona Beach, Florida.

Jennifer Pruett is working on more than her mystery novel, *Now You See It*. She's actively wrapping her head and heart around the fact that she will be a grandmother. During her most recent phone conversation with Elaine, her daughter informed her that she's decided to go full term and keep the baby. Further, she's relocating to Las Vegas to be closer to her mother.

Adam Richmond is pleased with the storyline in his current crime fiction novel, *Good Bones*. While writing it, he realizes that his relationship with his family and business is in "fixer-upper status," and he's committed to strengthening and renovating everything he holds dear when he returns to Houston, Texas.

Lucy Fleming hasn't given her manuscript, *All that Glitters*, another look. She's been studying maps, ridden into town to donate items she'll replace later, and made an appointment with, and then visited, an attorney to initiate divorce proceedings and update her will.

Her last ride off the Pines & Quill property was three days ago after researching the speed mail travels between Bellingham and Chicago. She doesn't want anything to get there too early or too late. *I want it to arrive on Goldilocks time—just right.* After mailing three letters—one to her soon-to-be ex-husband and one to each of her sons—she went to the local branch of a national bank where she has a secret savings account. She opened it years ago with funds she received from a product endorsement. She has never touched it, so it's a fairly substantial sum.

Finally, she figured out how to sneak the Pines & Quill journal from the Ink Well without getting caught and how to have its absence remain unnoticed while she had it. She'd snuck it back in this evening, October twentieth—the final evening at the main house before the writers in residence are taken to the airport tomorrow for their return flights home.

Lucy checks her watch. *Three o'clock. It's dead, dark, and quiet at this time of the morning.* Bundled in winter cycling gear, she slips out of Dickens cottage and tapes an envelope on the door handle. Then after easing into her backpack, she hefts her bicycle onto her left shoulder and starts walking. Located at the north end of the property, she doesn't have far to portage her bike before she catches a smooth path, hops on, and starts pedaling through the fog toward Chuckanut Drive.

"I'll be just fine." Colin's words slur just a bit as he assures his friend he's fine to drive. "I've made the drive from Bow to Bellingham hundreds of times after a few beers."

"It was more than a few beers," his friend says, bringing his fingers to his lips as if he were smoking a joint.

With a click of his key fob, Colin unlocks the car door, slides onto his seat, and starts the engine. He lowers the driver's window and pulls the shoulder strap across his chest. "See," he says to his friend, who's standing next to the car, "I'm even putting my seatbelt on."

His friend nods. "Well, at least if you're in an accident, you'll be okay." He raps the top of the car twice. "See ya later, Buddy."

Colin gives his friend a two-finger salute and exits the condo parking lot. A few minutes later, he heads north on Chuckanut Drive—a twenty-four-mile curvy route that hugs sheer sandstone cliffs.

From the throaty purr of his car's engine to the clicking of the wiper blades, every sound is muffled as though the blanket of fog he's driving through is made of the white wool it resembles.

He catches a movement in his peripheral vision and turns his head to look out the window.

A deer clears fog-soaked hedges into soft, quiescent shadows.

Colin places a calming hand on his chest and feels his accelerated heartbeat. "That could have been bad," he says to the empty car.

He's tired. To keep from nodding off, Colin lowers the driver's side window and lets the cold fresh air wash over his face and keep him awake for the remaining distance.

Wide-eyed, he passes Oyster Dome, Larrabee State Park, and Woodstock Farm without incident. On the outskirts of Fairhaven, he jerks his head upright when his chin hits his chest. Realizing he's on the wrong side of the road, he overcorrects.

A thump is followed by a scream of twisting metal. *The car's dragging something underneath it.* With a few jerks of the steering wheel left then right, it finally lets loose.

He looks in the rearview mirror to see what it was, but the fog has already swallowed whatever he'd hit. *It was probably a deer.*

Outside the main house's mudroom door, Niall inhales a deep breath of fresh air. Other than the petrichor emanating from the rapidly drying grass, there's no evidence that it had rained. He checks his watch. *Eight o'clock. The sun rose half an hour ago and burned off the overnight fog.*

He rests his hands on his hips and looks into the far distance. *The twenty-first of each month is always bittersweet for me. It's the last day of the three-week residency for the current batch of writers. After lunch, Mick will drive them to the airport.*

Off to his left, Hemingway lies in a patch of sunshine where apricity—the warmth of the sun—covers him like a wool sweater. *He misses Maggie.*

Niall whistles. "Come on, Boy. Our guests will be at the table any minute for their last breakfast at Pines & Quill."

The two of them head back into the house. Niall is a little heavy of heart. *Just as I get to know the writers in residence, it's time for them to leave.* And then October evokes an additional layer of poignancy as it's the last month in the year to host writers. Instead, they host family and friends over the holidays, which is joyful in a completely different way.

This morning is a much smaller group without Maeve, who returned to her condo in town. Joe and his family live in Bellingham, too, and returned home with the girls' school schedule. Rafferty, Ivy, and Maggie returned to Seattle, where Ivy—a special education teacher—is also governed by a school schedule.

But Niall's buoyed that he'll see them again in November and December. They, along with Maeve, Ian and Fiona, Emma's family, and a host of others, will converge on Pines & Quill for Rafferty's and Ivy's wedding. *Oh, how I'm looking forward to that. Then, when they head to Paris for their honeymoon, Cynthia Winters will join us. I can hardly wait to hear all about the silent retreat at the Amritapuri Ashram she stayed in in a remote fishing village on a small island off the southern tip of India.*

Libby puts her arms around Niall's waist. "You look far away," she says into his neck. *What would I do without the love of my life beside me? Please, God, take me first. I don't ever want to find out.*

"I'm just pondering the holidays. I'm excited to see Ian and Fiona. It's been a while since we've seen our son and daughter-in-law. And I'm thinking about the menu Ivy, Rafferty, and I discussed for their wedding." He pulls Libby into his side. "You know I love to cook for a crowd."

"I do. Speaking of which," Libby says, nodding toward the entrance, "here comes one now."

"Here comes one what?" Brent asks, leading the way.

"A crowd that I love to feed," Niall says.

"It smells *so* good," Jennifer says. "I'm going to miss your cooking. There's no magic in the world I know of that can help me conjure it."

"What are we having?" Adam asks.

"I bet I can answer that," Mick says.

Emma laughs as Mick makes a show of sniffing the air.

"Based on the scent of butter, yeast, sausage, and sage, I'm willing to bet Hemingway's tail," he says, tweaking the tip of his four-legged companion's tail, "that you made buttery breakfast casserole."

Niall smiles. "Ding, ding, ding. You win the prize." He nods at Mick. "*You* get to pour coffee." Then he looks at Emma. "And *you* get to pour juice."

As the writers take seats around the table, Brent says, "Hey, where's Lucy?"

"She's probably running a bit late, last day and all," Adam says.

"That's not like her," Jennifer says. "She's a self-proclaimed 'foodie' and is always on time, if not early."

"While we wait," Niall says, "I'll tell you about the casserole. The word 'buttery' in the title refers to my homemade croissants, which make a rich foundation for the golden-topped baked dish." He holds a finger to his lips, then whispers the rest. "The *secret* is toasting the croissants before building the casserole. It adds caramelized notes that can stand up to the bits of browned sausage, sage, and melted Gruyère I blend throughout."

Adam rubs his hands together. "Well, I for one can hardly wait."

"I'll call Lucy's cottage," Libby says, excusing herself.

A moment later, she returns with a perplexed look on her face. "That's odd. She didn't answer."

Mick stands up. "I'll run over and check on her. Be right back." He taps his thigh. "Come on Hemingway. I'll race you." The two of them head toward the front door—the shortest route to Dickens cottage.

A few minutes later, Mick and Hemingway return. Mick's holding an envelope in one of his hands. "This," he holds it up, "was taped to her door handle." He hands it to Niall, who opens it and reads, "Look in the Pines & Quill journal."

Niall walks into the Ink Well and returns a moment later with the open journal. He reads the newest entry out loud. "I'm sorry to have left this way, but I *hate* goodbyes. By the time you read this, I'll be well over the Canadian border. And though I wasn't the one who got to die in the illusion, I had a great time helping to plan it and a wonderful time at Pines & Quill. While here, I made some life-changing decisions. I've initiated a divorce, and I'm relocating to Canada, where there are many athletic opportunities. I wish the best for each of you."

Niall sets the journal on the sideboard. "Well, I wish Lucy the best too." He heads to the main part of the kitchen, slips on hot mitts, opens the oven door, and pulls out two covered dishes. He returns to the dining area and sets a casserole at each end of the table. Still standing, he raises his coffee mug and offers a traditional Scottish toast: "*Slàinte Mhath*, Lucy—to Lucy's good health."

The others follow his lead phonetically—"SLAN-chuh Vah, Lucy"—then drink from their mugs along with him.

Niall smiles as he lets his gaze drift around the table. Then he lifts his mug again. "It's been a distinct pleasure to have you as our guests at Pines & Quill. Godspeed—may the wind be at your back."

On the return trip from Bellingham International Airport, where Mick and Emma dropped off Jennifer, Brent, and Adam to catch their afternoon flights, they stop at Dr. Freeman's—Emma's OB/GYN—for Emma's eighteen-week prenatal care appointment.

After checking in at registration, they take a seat. Mick looks around the room at the women in various stages of pregnancy. *There's only one other man. He's young and has the "deer in the headlights" look of fear. I wonder if I look that scared?*

Mick turns to Emma. "Are you *sure* you want me to come in with you?"

Emma squeezes his hand. "I'm positive. I don't want you to miss a thing."

Before long, Regina, Dr. Freeman's assistant, calls them. On the way to the exam room, Regina has Emma step on a scale. "You're right on target," she says.

Mick's heart swells with pride.

In the exam room, Regina notes Emma's weight on a computer, then checks both her heartbeat and the baby's, Emma's blood pressure, and her hands and feet for swelling, logging the details on the computer as she works. "Everything looks great. Dr. Freeman will be with you in just a few minutes. Before she arrives, please change into this," she says, pointing to a folded gown on the countertop. "Because you're almost halfway through your pregnancy, today you're having a pregnancy ultrasound scan."

Mick leans forward in the molded-plastic chair. "What's the scan looking for?"

"The scan helps us to understand how your baby's growing, check fetal movement, see the growth of the baby's internal organs, and detect any anomalies."

Mick sits bolt upright. "Anomalies?"

"The scan helps us to detect if there are any problems."

Mick laces his fingers together to keep them from shaking. "Is that common?"

"The scan or the occurrence of problems?" Regina asks.

Mick swallows. "Both."

"Yes and no," Regina says. "Yes, the scan is a normal part of the checkup process between eighteen and twenty weeks. And no. While problems do sometimes occur, they aren't common." Regina washes her hands, then continues. "The pregnancy ultrasound scan checks many aspects of the baby's internal organs, including the shape and structure of the head, face, length and cross-section of the spine, abdominal wall, heart, stomach, kidneys, arms, hands, legs, and feet. In addition to this detailed look at how your baby's growing, Dr. Freeman will check the placenta, the umbilical cord, and the amniotic fluid."

"Are you *sure* it's okay for me to stay with Emma for the entire process?"

"Absolutely," Regina says, taking hold of the door handle. "Now, if you'll excuse me, I'll give you a chance to change." And with that, she slips out the door and pulls it closed behind her.

Emma turns to her husband. "Mick, are you scared?"

"No," he says. "I'm terrified."

———

What seems like an eternity later, Mick opens the Pines & Quill van front passenger door for Emma, then hops into the driver's seat.

Turning to Emma, he grins. "Well, Mrs. McPherson. Connie's due date hasn't changed. At least not yet. She's still scheduled to arrive on March twenty-sixth."

Emma pats Mick's hand. "You know we can't count on that date. It'll probably change a dozen times between now and her arri—"

Mick's heart leaps into his throat. "*What?*" he croaks. "What's the matter?"

Emma takes Mick's right hand and places it on her belly.

His eyebrows fly reflexively into his hairline. "It feels like she's playing soccer in there."

Emma laughs. "And we've still got twenty-two weeks to go. Dr. Freeman said that right now, Connie's the size of a cucumber and she's only going to get bigger."

They drive toward Pines & Quill in silence, each lost in their thoughts.

The late-autumn days are shorter. And though the sun doesn't set for another hour, the light is waning. The sun hangs low in the sky, changing from baby blue to pink, purple, and orange.

"This time next year," Mick says, "we'll be picking out a Halloween costume for Connie."

"I hadn't thought about that," Emma says, laughing. "But you're right. What do you think she should be?"

"A cucumber," Mick grins. "Definitely a cucumber."

Turn the page to read an excerpt from
Innocuous: A Sean McPherson Novel, Book Six

PROLOGUE

*"The way to write a thriller is to ask a question
at the beginning, and answer it at the end."*
—Lee Child

Jane Allen narrows her brown eyes as she gingerly inserts the tip of a hypodermic needle into the dropper end of an empty eyedrops bottle. Then she presses the plunger with her thumb, refilling the container with clear liquid. Her heartbeat accelerates.

I can't believe it's already the end of January. Tomorrow, February first, I fly to Bellingham, Washington. And this— she examines the small, innocent-looking green bottle—*won't even get a glance from TSA.*

After refilling the syringe to repeat the process, Jane looks at her reflection in the mirror over the sink in her cozy New York City apartment. When her husband divorced her and she relocated from the Midwest, she quickly learned that "cozy"—at least in the Big Apple—is code for small, even cramped. And that one month's rent in this bustling melting pot of cultures is equivalent to three mortgage payments in Nebraska.

Turning her head from side to side, Jane smiles at her fifty-eight-year-old, makeup-free face. It's framed by shoulder-length brown hair threaded with gray. With undiluted confidence wrought from previous experience, a smile burgeons at the thought of what she's about to pull off.

She turns to take in her entirety—all sixty-four unassuming inches—in a full-length mirror. Not dictated by fashion, Jane's dressed in an understated outfit in her preferred style—effortless and breezy. A look in her closet reveals an earth-tone color palette: brown, sienna, taupe, gray, white, and black, with a few pieces in a pale rose shade. *If Mom were alive, she'd dub this outfit "frumpy" and exclaim, "Jane, do something with your appearance."*

She thinks back to her youth. *I hated being called "Plain Jane." Who knew I'd leverage it to my advantage?*

Turning to the sink to continue the painstaking task, she shakes her head and clucks her tongue. *Society tends to underestimate unassuming people. They tend to regard us as innocuous.*

———

On January thirty-first, Father William Keeling walks through the entrance of the formidable-looking Maine State Prison. At the security checkpoint, all visitors—including correctional institution priests who serve the inmate population—sign in and empty their pockets. Next comes a full-body manual pat down. Then a full-body wand, followed by a full-body scanner. After that, an armed guard escorts him to the infirmary to perform the last rights for "Preacher," as everyone at the prison knows him.

The clank of the steel door slamming shut behind him no longer scares the shit out of him. Nor do the calls, whistles, and tattooed arms that reach through bars trying to grab him as he walks by.

Entering the hospital unit, Father Keeling glances around the sterile space before sitting beside Preacher's bed on a hard, molded-plastic chair.

Outside light enters through a double row of glass bricks where the ceiling meets the exterior wall—a reinforced concrete slab.

A tired-looking physician stands on the opposite side of the bed. His lab coat hangs open, revealing a coffee-stained shirt.

The grim-faced guard stations himself, cross-armed, in front of the door.

Preacher, the seventy-something-year-old prisoner, suffers the final stages of pneumonia. He presents cyanosis—a blue color around his mouth from lack of oxygen. He angles his heavy-lidded eyes toward the priest. "You expect me to shrive myself? I've already confessed. I'm just not sorry for what I did."

"I can't grant you absolution," Father Keeling says, "unless you're sorry for the sins you've committed."

Preacher tries to turn his head toward the priest, but the effort is too much. "I'm *not* sorry," he gasps. "I did God's work. I'll be rewarded for that."

Father Keeling leans forward and rests a blue-veined hand pocked with sunspots on the bedside. "You *killed* two people. That isn't God's work."

Preacher squeezes his eyes shut as he wheezes. "What my fifteen-year-old daughter and that boy did was an abomination. Her giving birth to a blind baby is proof of God's punishment for their wickedness."

"What about your wife?" Father Keeling asks. "She didn't have anything to do with it."

"She tried to stop me from killing that evil boy." Preacher's body curls against a coughing spasm. This time, blood spatters the thin pale green blanket pulled up to his chest. He wipes his mouth with the back of a limp hand. "It's not my fault she stepped in front of the gun when I pulled the trigger."

Preacher suffers another paroxysm of coughs and sucks in air through intermittent wheezing.

When the doctor moves to put an oxygen mask over his face, Preacher tries to knock it away. "No," he says in a hoarse whisper. "No, noooo."

Fifteen minutes later, the guard escorts Father Keeling back the way he came. But this time, they stop outside the warden's office.

When the priest raps on the reinforced glass window, the warden glances over his laptop and then motions him to enter.

Father Keeling steps into the office and shuts the door behind him. "Gunnar Olsen—Preacher—just passed away. Does he have a next-of-kin on file?"

Book reviews from awesome readers like you help others feel confident about deciding if a book is for them.

So if you enjoyed *Illusionist,* please consider leaving a review on Amazon, Goodreads, or BookBub.

To be among the first to hear about *Innocuous,* book six in the Sean McPherson series, please subscribe to my newsletter at www.lauriebuchanan.com, where you're always welcome to stop by and say hello.

ACKNOWLEDGMENTS

A deep bow of gratitude to:

You—the reader. Thank you for choosing *Illusionist*, book five in the Sean McPherson series. I hope you enjoyed it. If you did, please tell everyone, especially in the form of a review. They make a world of positive difference.

The Sean McPherson Street Team—advance readers who shout their support and encouragement from the social media rooftops to their friends, families, and followers. And who additionally ask their local acquisitions librarian to acquire the Sean McPherson series and their local bookstores to carry the series.

SparkPress—my publishing house. A formidable team of experts who safeguard each of my manuscripts from vision to publication: Brooke Warner, Lauren Wise, Mimi Bark, and Tabitha Lahr, to name but a few.

Professional sources—Thank you to *Vickie Gooch*, detective in the Major Crimes Unit of the Idaho State Police; *Rylene Nowlin*, DNA specialist at the Idaho State Police Crime Lab; Dr. Glen Groben, forensic pathologist; Danny

R. Smith, private investigator and author of the Dickie Floyd Detective novels; Camille LaCroix, forensic psychiatrist; Chuck Ambrose, psychologist; *Anthony Geddes*, chief public defender and lead counsel in death penalty cases in Idaho; *Brent Bunn*, US Marshal; and *Raul Garcia*, member of the Ada County SWAT team. Your individual and collective insight is invaluable to the storylines in the Sean McPherson novels. Any procedural inaccuracies are entirely mine.

Blackbird Writers, a collective of mystery and thriller writers. I'm grateful to be part of a flock that fosters and supports each other's work. Thank you.

Christine DeSmet—my writing mentor and coach for over a decade. You discover where my stories are initially left wanting, then pilot them into safe harbor with feedback that always proves invaluable.

Andrea Kerr—my eagle-eyed beta reader. You ensure continuity and note repetition, wooden dialogue, and poor pacing or description. Your insight lends depth.

Candace Johnson—my copyeditor. You triage my manuscripts from spelling to structure and everything in between, ensuring they live to tell the tale.

Len—my husband and the real-life inspiration for Niall MacCullough. Oh, the delicious meals you make for me to test-drive and then weave into the storylines.

It truly does take a village.

ABOUT THE AUTHOR

photo © Len Buchanan

Laurie Buchanan writes the critically acclaimed Sean McPherson novels—pulse-pounding crime thrillers with heart-stopping twists that plunge readers into the depths of malice, the unwavering quest for justice, and high-stakes consequences.

A cross between Dr. Dolittle, Nanny McPhee, and a type-A Buddhist, Buchanan is an active listener, observer of details, payer of attention, reader and writer of books, kindness enthusiast, and red licorice aficionado.

Her books have won multiple awards, including Foreword INDIES Book of the Year Gold Winner, International Book Award Gold Winner, National Indie Excellence Awards Winner, Crime Fiction/Suspense Eric Hoffer Awards Finalist, PenCraft Award for Literary Excellence, and CLUE Book Awards finalist Suspense/Thriller Mysteries.

Laurie's writing studio is in the hayloft of a historic carriage house in the Pacific Northwest. Her husband, Len, a private pilot, and Henry, their not-so-standard Standard Poodle, join her on daily walks. She always carries a camera because sometimes the best word choice is a picture.

To learn more, please visit Laurie's website at
www.lauriebuchanan.com.

Looking for your next great read?

We can help!

Visit www.gosparkpress.com/next-read
or scan the QR code below for a list
of our recommended titles.

SparkPress is an independent boutique publisher
delivering high-quality, entertaining, and engaging
content that enhances readers' lives, with a special
focus on commercial and genre fiction.